SWEET, SOFT SURRENDER . . .

"Come, lady. Julian. Fair one." He drew her to him and kissed her so gently that little chills began to slide up and down her arms. One hand rubbed her neck slowly and played with the curls at her ears. "Do you yield the day?" He bent his head and kissed the long curve of her throat where the pulse hammered, then continued the soft, slow kisses until her skin ached and she leaned toward him.

"Aye, I yield." The words came in a soft moan as she put both hands on the broad shoulders that were so invitingly near. They looked into each other's eyes before his mouth claimed hers again in a long drugging kiss that seemed to meld them into one fiery unit of passion. . . .

Books by Anne Carsley

THE WINGED LION
DEFIANT DESIRE

DEFIANT DESIRE

Anne Carsley

A DELL BOOK

Published by
Dell Publishing Co., Inc.
1 Dag Hammarskjold Plaza
New York, New York 10017

Dell ® TM 681510, Dell Publishing Co., Inc.

ISBN: 0-440-12019-5

Printed in the United States of America

First printing—December 1982

To Kay and Don
who knew the reasons
long ago

And to Sam
in fondness and pragmatism

AUTHOR'S NOTE

The interpretation of the character and motives of Queen Mary Tudor is generally the one of history except that often too little cognizance is taken of the sufferings she, Tudor princess and queen though she was, endured in her life. The writings of Carolly Erickson, *Bloody Mary* and *Great Harry,* along with Prescott's book, *Mary Tudor,* and *Elizabeth the Great* by Jenkins have been most helpful in this regard.

Some liberties have been taken with the medical knowledge and superstition of the period, this supported in part by interpretations of Paracelsus and theories prevalent in Arabian medicine at a slightly later time.

A secret passage and exit were added to the Tower of London in a section which was later demolished. It might have existed.

HISTORICAL NOTE

When Mary Tudor became queen of England in 1553, she was welcomed by the majority of her people. She had been made prisoner, ostracized, tormented for her faith, forced to practice it in secret, denied the rights of her birth, made to repudiate Katherine of Aragon's marriage to Henry VIII and bastardized, used as a state pawn by father and brother alike. Her accession was regarded as a triumph of justice. But her marriage to Philip of Spain, the likelihood of the Spanish Inquisition being introduced in England, her fierce dedication to Catholicism in a country separated from that faith for twenty and more years, and the policy of fire and sword used to restore it, made her hated and despised by 1557, the year in which *Defiant Desire* begins.

England was a country of turmoil in that year. It was a time of factions, intrigue, and plots; a time of danger for noble and commoner alike. The queen was aging and ill, Spain was powerful, and France loomed large. The next Catholic heir after the childless Mary was Mary Stuart, soon to wed the dauphin of France. English Catholics would welcome her rule. Spain would try to keep England by whatever means. The majority of people looked to Princess Elizabeth, twenty-four, Protestant reared, often a prisoner, as England's hope. Many intrigued for her death, however, and Queen Mary at one time consigned her to the Tower of London. She maintained a policy of complete silence, for her danger was great. The queen did not consider her heiress to the throne and believed her truly a bastard as Henry VIII had proclaimed.

Queen Mary's supporters hoped until the end that she would bear an heir to the English throne. She fancied herself pregnant many times and thought she was in the very year of her death. Many people thought that Philip would try to take England in the event of civil war and rule by fait accompli. Mary Stuart, queen of Scotland, had a legitimate claim as Catholic heir through Henry VIII's sister, Margaret of Scotland. Princess Elizabeth would be expected, if she came to the throne, to marry quickly, and her husband would rule through her. No woman could rule alone or even contemplate it; everyone adhered to this belief.

In the year 1557 great changes were in the air. Policies and beliefs changed daily. and life often hung in the balance. Civil war was considered a real danger. It is a matter of historical fact that Philip of Spain, called king of England by Mary Tudor alone and not by Parliament, contemplated possible marriage to Elizabeth after his wife's death and did propose such later.

When Elizabeth did come to the throne, she was given less than six months to rule by speculators on the Continent.

CHAPTER ONE

"Mistress! You must come quickly! There's a man to speak to you. He says it is urgent. Mistress!" The heavy door slammed back as Elspeth nearly tumbled into the room, carried forward by her own weight.

Julian pulled herself up on the window seat from which she had been watching the pouring rain while her book lay forgotten in her lap. Now cold air streamed in, and she shivered in spite of the old cloak she had wrapped around her shoulders earlier.

"Another beggar? Turn him away as gently as you can. We have little enough for ourselves." She sighed, knowing how true the words really were.

"He's a gentleman, mistress, and there are others outside waiting. They might be from London same as those others. You know, king's men!" Her brown eyes goggled at the memory, and she twisted her stubby fingers in the worsted of her skirt.

Julian felt the familiar lick of fear but kept her voice calm. "Now, that is nonsense, Elspeth, and you know it. Queen Mary rules now in England, and no one has come to question us in over three years."

"Then why are those men here?" Elspeth grumbled and tried to smile, but her features kept their look of dread.

Julian shook out the folds of her old gray gown and pushed her hair back into a demure knot at the back of her neck. "Very well, I will see to this matter, and then we must start the mending if there is to be anything to wear this spring. Doubtless they have taken the wrong road and only want directions."

"Let me get a headdress for you. And your good shawl, where can it be?" Elspeth began to rummage through a chest in the corner.

"I go as I am." Julian jumped up and ran into the icy hall. She could not face more fussing and fright; it was better to deal boldly with what she must.

She fancied that she could hear the scuttle of rats in the closed-off rooms, and the musty smell of disuse was all around her as she went down the curving stairs and into what had once been the library. Now it held only several books, a battered chair with a canopy, and several stools. A tall, soberly dressed man in his late thirties was examining the French romance she had left there the day before. He lifted a thin, serious face to her as she entered.

"May I be of assistance to you? I am Julian Redenter."

"Lady Julian Redenter, daughter to the late Gwendolyn and Lionel Redenter of Redeswan Manor? You are she?" He tried to keep the incredulity out of his voice and covered it with a cough as he drew a small case from his pouch and opened it, looking first at her and then down.

She tried not to shiver in the chill as she held her head high. "That is my name and my house." The pride of her family rang in the words.

He had inscrutable brown eyes, the same color as his hair, and he watched her carefully as he extended the case for her to see. Julian knew that he expected refreshment, candles, a fire, the very rudiments of courtesy, but the days were long past when guests came to Redeswan Manor.

"Do you recognize this?"

Julian looked down into the pictured face of her mother as Lady Gwendolyn had been in her youth, as she herself might one day look. Gleaming chestnut hair curled around the piquant face with its high cheekbones. The eyes were a deep aquamarine below winged dark brows. The lashes seemed dusted gold, and the small head sat proudly on a long neck. Slightly parted soft lips shone pink and expectant as if of a kiss. An emerald necklace cascaded to the molded bodice of a green gown. The likeness was set in the Tudor rose of red and white, enhanced by pearls and emeralds. The woman overshadowed the jewels, for she seemed to live and draw breath.

"Not Holbein, but one of his better imitators." She could hear the husky voice of her mother in those early years. Julian had loved the rose and cried when it vanished. Of course it had been sold so that they might live, but the child she had been could not know that. "Your father gave it to me on our marriage day," Lady Gwendolyn had often said, eyes alight with remembered happiness. It was fortunate that she had not known of the shaking sickness that was to destroy the remnants of her beauty, rend her mind, and finally, fourteen months later, take her life.

"Where did you get this?" Julian heard her voice grate harshly. "Who are you?"

He folded the lovely thing away. "I see that you do. Lady Redenter, I am Sir Guy Edmont, and I bear the queen's command regarding you. Here is my authority." He put a square of parchment embossed with the Tudor seal into her suddenly nerveless fingers and stepped back.

The writing marched, small and square, across the page: *Fetch the woman, Julian Redenter, to London with all possible speed. Let nothing delay you.* It was signed, *Mary, the Queen, given at Greenwich this twenty-fifth day of March, 1557.*

Julian fought back the fear that threatened to overcome her. Had they not always dreaded something of this sort during the years of the boy king's reign? Why now, however? She kept her face impassive as she lifted her eyes to Guy Edmont. "I will need time to prepare."

"There is no time. We must leave within the hour." He spoke brusquely, then hesitated. "Do not fear, lady."

She inclined her head. "I hasten to obey. I trust that I may inform my household?"

Red touched his sallow cheeks as the beginning warmth in his eyes died. "Of course, but none of them go with you. You go alone."

"But surely my maidservant who has been with me all

my life . . . ?" She heard the tremble in her voice and
stopped abruptly.

He shook his head, his eyes never leaving her face.
Julian went to the door, her back stiff and straight as she
had been taught.

Minutes later she sat in her room, the old cloak around
her shoulders, a horn cup of sour wine in her shaking
hand. Elspeth sat on the stool before her mistress, tears
and words mingling.

"Promised your sainted mother on her deathbed, I did,
that I'd take care of you always. Swore by the Virgin and
all the saints. Her the wife of a great lord and living this
way, raising you like a peasant, and all those men coming
every few months with questions about religion and rights,
making people say things they don't understand! Shame-
ful! Now taking you off to London to face God knows
what! Look at you, nineteen and unwed, no chances even.
A husband could have protected you!"

She rose to clutch Julian to her shaking bosom. The
girl's own panic subsided a little as she yielded to the
warmth of feeling. She patted Elspeth on the back and
drew back to look into the round red face still puckered
with anguish.

"Well, this may all be a mistake and best settled at the
source. I'm sure I will be back before long. You will be in
charge here, Elspeth, so listen carefully. And calm down, I
would not leave to the sound of weeping." Julian forced
herself to be brisk about household duties and their small
store of coins while she gathered up her only other presentable gown and shoes, then wrapped the cloak closer
around her shoulders. "I am as ready as I will ever be.
Remember, Elspeth, to say nothing to anyone in the village about this; no need to frighten anyone." She was
suddenly anxious to face her fate, to be away from this
despair.

Elspeth fumbled in the folds of her black gown and
held out what appeared to be two small branches twisted
together and fastened with a bit of green ribbon. "Take
this with you, dear child, and keep it with you."

The girl held it on her palm gingerly as she asked, "Is this not a treasure to you? Should you not keep it?"

The dark gaze flickered, and for a moment something strange and alien looked out of the familiar eyes. "It is the hawthorn that I plucked long ago and carried as a blessing. It brought me here, and that was all I ever needed. Now it is yours."

Julian stowed the talisman in her pouch, suddenly remembering that Elspeth was known to have uttered incantations over kitchen stews and the various plantings. Now she seemed to have invoked the protection of the old gods on her mistress, for the hawthorn was sometimes considered the symbol of the witch.

"Pray for me as I for us all." The ritual words sprang to her lips, and she used them as a farewell. She shut the door and heard Elspeth give way to a fresh burst of tears that mingled with pleas in a dialect Julian did not know.

Guy Edmont stood at the foot of the stairs, cloak and hood in place, a purse in his hand. "For the household." When she merely stared at him, he put it down on a convenient table. "It is time to go, Lady Redenter."

Perhaps he meant well, perhaps he was really only following orders, but Julian felt walled away, so much so that she could not respond to the civility with which he helped her to mount the waiting horse and gave her gloves so that the reins might not bruise her fingers. His men, some ten strong, rode before and behind while he remained at her side. Rain sluiced down, and there was the rumble of thunder in the distance as they moved into what had once been parkland and was now simply ill-cleared woods.

Julian turned her head for one last look at Redeswan Manor as it lifted in a mass of stone, pinnacles and turrets etched against the dark sky. Would she ever see it again, this once proud home of her ancestors, now fallen even as they? The old ballad moved in her mind: "Spins now Fortune's wheel from me, down, down, away." Droplets and tears mingled at the corners of her mouth as the cavalcade began to move.

It was still raining a week later when they entered the

capital city in the late evening. Julian was conscious of
evil smells, flaring torches, a rush of people, buildings that
seemed to lean over on each other, and more noise than
she had ever heard in her life. They had been wet since
early morning on leaving the inn where they had briefly
rested, and now she could only think in terms of food and
rest from the jolting; she had forced herself not to think of
what probably waited at the journey's end.

They were forced to slow their pace now because of the
massed crowd that flowed in the narrow streets. The soldiers pressed close around Julian, but she saw beyond
them to the open area directly in front. A tall pole stood
off in the distance with what appeared to be the remains
of a fire around it. A sickening charred odor drifted with
the wind, and she felt her stomach churn. She turned her
head sharply to try to escape the smell that was all around
her, and the wet hood fell back to let her hair stream free.

At that moment Sir Guy lost all patience and called in a
deep voice, "Let us pass! We travel on official business!
Make way!"

A woman standing a little back in the crowd cried,
"Another one to be burned, is it? Will that be the wench's
fate? Her today, the lot of us tomorrow, I say!"

The others began to mutter and push as the soldiers increased their pace. Their anger spat on the wet, chill air.
"Spawn of the Spaniards!" "England wants none of you!"
"Devil's get!" A fat bearded man yelled, "Let the pretty
one come over here!" Several men near him took up the
cry.

Julian felt her cheeks flush with excitement and a different kind of fear from that she had known when the
queen's men confronted her. This was woman-fear of vio-
lation. She jerked at the wet hood and urged her mare
back into the safety of the soldiers.

"I'm robbed! Thief! Thief!" The angry cry came from a
tall man in black who stood apart from the throng around
them. He was fumbling in his robes and cursing. Someone
scurried from the fringes, and another started in pursuit as
the man called again, "My purse, my papers, all gone! Ho,
a reward to whoever catches the thief!"

Many in the crowd started for the nearest street. Others began to slap their clothes as if to reassure themselves that they still had their belongings. Some bunched nervously together and looked about with caution. Sir Guy took this opportunity to urge his men forward into a wider avenue that led away from the grisly scene of the burning.

Julian turned back almost involuntarily and caught the eye of the tall man who now stood easily, head thrown back, teeth flashing as he laughed at what might have been a private joke. His profile was etched clear and sharp in the torch flames; so might one of the old sardonic gods of Greece have looked. The thought ran in her mind, their glances locked, and her heart began to hammer as he sketched a half-mocking bow. Her lips parted, and she smiled gaily, freely, as one hand lifted in salute. Then they swept around the corner and rode into the darkness.

The bold face of the stranger was still with Julian as she dismounted an hour and more later in a dimly lit court-yard at the back of a huge sprawling building. Guards in dark clothes rushed forward to confer with Sir Guy, who spoke briefly with them before turning to Julian. She saw the frown on his face and the worry in his brown eyes before he assumed the proper impersonal tone.

"Madam, you will follow these men at once. It is commanded."

She gasped in surprise. Was she to be thus hurried to her fate without food or rest and with the stains of travel still upon her? It was not to be borne. "Where do I go? I asked for an explanation. I am still a free citizen of this country." She stood in the drizzle, head high, chestnut hair shining. It was a relief to speak boldly, and she was intoxicated by it. "Answer me, sirs. I was summoned to the queen's presence. Am I thus expected to be led to prison?" She waved disdainfully at their surroundings.

"This is Whitehall Palace, Lady Redenter, and these men will lead you directly to Queen Mary's own chambers. You were expected yesterday." The speaker was a short, burly man who stood next to Sir Guy. His air of command was evident, his tone one of barely suppressed anger.

Julian felt the world whirl around her. It had been necessary for her pride and the new courage that the exchange with the handsome stranger had given her that she question those commands that had disrupted her life. She had been certain that she was to be carried away to a dark prison and left there to languish. Her voice did not tremble; she was proud of that as she said, "I obey gladly."

They stared at her, and Sir Guy gave her the flicker of a smile before he bent to listen to the angry mutters of his companion. Julian knew that he wished her well and was sustained as she followed the two guards along the endless corridors, out into a small garden, along a hedged walk, and up to a small door that was opened as they approached. She walked hesitantly into a bare entrance where another guard pointed to a curtained area.

"Enter. You are awaited." The harsh voice of the man seemed to thrust her past the purple and black velvet hangings. She heard him resume his place as she entered.

The room was small, lit by one pale candle that burned steadily in the stillness. A fire glimmered in one corner, and the walls were muffled in darkness. It seemed incredible that the woman who sat at the simple desk in the corner could see to write, and yet she drove the pen swiftly across the paper in front of her, oblivious to the girl who stood at her back.

Julian hesitated, then cleared her throat sharply. She was cold and wet and frightened. If she was to be conducted to her fate, let it be swiftly done. In the space before the woman turned, Julian saw that she was small and slender, her back erect under the enveloping gown that was banded with rich fur. Rings gleamed on her fingers, as did pearls on her hood. Shadows caught the set of the determined jaw, and then Julian knew what she should have known from the first.

From her knees she whispered, "Forgive me, Madam the Queen. I am your most obedient servant." It was the litany of safety. Her blood chilled as she thought of the demand she had been about to give the person she considered to be the waiting woman of the queen. Had not

Elspeth ever said that her tongue was too sharp and ready for her own safety?

The low deep voice spoke flatly, "Say you so? What if I say that you lie, Julian Redenter? That you lie as others have done to their great sorrow. Look at me, girl!"

Julian obeyed. The queen was short but held herself erectly. Her face was thin, the chin stubborn, the lips folded over themselves. The sandy, graying hair was partially visible, but her brows faded into the softly wrinkled forehead. Flesh drooped over the lids, yet her eyes, dark and penetrating, held Julian. She could not look away from that gaze that seemed to know and accuse and demand.

"Be careful how you speak lest your tongue betray you." Something curled under the harshness and waited to break out.

Julian shivered inwardly, for that same note had been in her mother's voice there toward the last, pain and anger held inward with no bearable release except in nightmares. But this woman was the queen of England. The silence lengthened and drew out as their eyes held. Then Julian bent her head and prayed for sincerity.

"Your Majesty was ever the loyal servant of your royal father and brother, yet your loyalty was doubted in their reigns and still proved true. Must not the quality of compassion ever be exemplified in the sovereign? I appeal to your justice."

"You have a smooth tongue, girl. I despise such." The queen swung round and sank back into her chair. She glanced at some documents spread out on the table before her, then up at Julian. "Sit on yonder stool near the fire."

Her tone did not alter, but something told Julian that she was no longer in as great a peril as she had been at the end of her speech. What did one say to such a woman? The very act of breathing might be dangerous!

The queen tapped the first paper with one finger, and the shimmering jewels caught the fire of the candle so that they flamed anew. "Ah, yes, treason is everywhere. Your father, Lionel Redenter, fought against mine in the Pilgrimage of Grace in 1536. He had goodly holdings in the

North Country, but they were stripped from him while he yet lived and hid in the crags of that fastness. He was caught and slain when he visited your mother in the next year. He died before her eyes. You were the child of that last coupling, I believe." She might have been reciting a list to a waiting tirewoman.

"Aye, Your Majesty." Julian remembered how her mother's stories had made Lionel come alive for her in the days before Lady Gwendolyn's illness descended completely and life became one fierce struggle.

Her own struggle had just begun.

CHAPTER TWO

The queen continued to speak in her expressionless tone. "Yet my father, King Henry, was merciful, for he gave the widow a tiny pension and allowed her to live in the old manor close to the Welsh border, Redeswan. Commissioners were sent regularly to investigate the household. Your father, I note, was the last heir of his line; his own father fought for the Plantagenets at Bosworth Field. Yours has been a warring house."

Julian kept her head respectfully bent, but she was remembering those days of watching and waiting, the endless questions and speculations. All had to swear an oath declaring King Henry to be supreme head of the Church and their loyalty was constantly tested. Even the child she had been was not immune from demands. Later King Edward's men had asked theological questions and more protestations of loyalty. She shuddered, remembering how they had been harried.

The queen's voice caught her up. "Aye, you remember as I do. I, too, was besieged and I a princess of the blood royal. How could I say that my sainted mother had not been true wife to my father? How could I deny the Lord Pope and destroy my soul?" Her eyes glittered with past agony, and one hand went up to wipe away the tears. "And yet I feared for my life and so I signed that paper!"

Julian knew that it was dangerous to speak unless bidden, but she could not restrain herself. "Yet you were spared to take the crown, madam." Just so had she introduced another train of thought to her mother when the malady was upon her.

Queen Mary stared down at her with that penetrating look as one side of her mouth twisted downward. "You are bold, Julian Redenter. Are you crafty? Would you plot against your queen? They do, you know."

Was she truly mad? Julian shivered even as she said, "Forgive my presumption, Your Majesty, but who has better cause than I to be loyal? My father died in the company of those who held you to be trueborn daughter in the authority of the Church. My mother served yours in her imprisonment and did arrange to wed my father under the good graces of that sainted lady. My family was closely watched in the years before your accession and was often rated by the commissioners of the king. Only with the coming of Your Majesty to the throne did we begin to breathe more freely. My family has ever served the throne, and I am no exception. I am the servant of Madam the Queen now and forever." She lifted herself from the stool and knelt at the queen's feet. What would be the consequences of her boldness? There had been nothing else to do; she had seen too clearly the beginnings of hysteria.

Queen Mary's low voice rang on a different note. "Aye, child, you have reaped the bitterness, I know right well."

Julian was very still as footsteps rang on the floor, and her whole body tensed with expectation and a rush of warmth for this beleaguered woman. Then a new voice spoke over her bent head in soft, sibilant tones that held a slight amusement.

"Rise, Lady Redenter. You are believed true to us. In such times it is necessary to test everyone. Welcome to our court."

Julian rose and looked at the man who stood beside the queen. One slender hand was on her arm as if to restrain her from any sudden movement. He was slight in build, but his manner was one of great authority. His hair and beard were golden, his pale eyes steady and cold as the sea. He wore black velvet slashed with gold and one great ruby winked on his thumb. Julian knew him, as who in England did not? He was Philip of Spain, ruler of many lands, powerful beyond the telling, titular king of England and young husband to the rapidly aging queen.

"Majesty." Julian breathed the word as if in awe, but the cynical side of her nature warned her to be doubly cautious now. She shook with tiredness and hoped that both took it for fear before greatness.

Queen Mary said, "I sent for your mother when I came to the throne, but she pleaded indisposition, though nothing serious. I sent gifts in token of my gratitude for her service to my mother. Then, occupied with matters of state, I forgot my duty. The commissioners who checked reported no disloyalty, and the matter faded. Now that my husband has returned from abroad, I hope to conceive again. England must have an heir, and I will have only those loyal ones around me. You were tested by the manner of the summons and by our treatment of you here this night." Her voice was soft and gentle now, the gruffness muted.

"As others shall be. It is my idea." Philip of Spain touched his chin as his eyes glittered at Julian. "You will join the ladies-in-waiting here, and monies shall be dispensed to your household at Redeswan. Does that please you, madam?"

Deep emotion rang in his voice, and it was not solicitude for his wife. Julian sank down again in a curtsy and heard herself murmuring her gratitude in meaningless phrases that went on and on. She thought of herself as she must look, wet and bedraggled, hair tumbling down her back, and called it foolish to think that she might have stirred the interest of the king, who was noted for his not always discreet admiration of the ladies. *Doubtless I have read too many French romances,* she thought as she rose again from her curtsy to see that Philip had retreated as silently as he had come and the queen had turned to ring a little bell at her elbow.

The woman who entered in response to it was tall and blond. She wore spangled purple velvet, and despite the shadows under her dark eyes, her manner was self-possessed and cool. She surveyed Julian with a questioning glance even as she knelt to the queen.

"This is Lady Isabella Acton. Her husband was slain fighting for me in Wyatt's rebellion several years ago. Her dear loyalty illumes my days. She will guide you. See that you are worthy of the opportunity given you." The queen waved them out with an exhausted gesture.

In the passageway outside, Isabella turned to Julian. "You will share my rooms for now. Some of my gowns will fit you until we can get you others. I vow, you are not fit to be seen as you are."

Julian had not held her tongue before the queen and saw no reason why she should hold it before this woman. "It is far from London to the Welsh border, lady, and the roads are not of the best. Your gracious hospitality is appreciated. I would not willingly discommode you."

The brilliant eyes flashed. "Be warned, country girl. This court is a dangerous place, and you had best conduct yourself accordingly. Now come."

"I am grateful for your warning," Julian answered, her head erect with pride.

The next few days were spent in the preparation of gowns, instruction in court dances and proper topics of conversation, lessons on the lute and virginals, some coaching of her soft voice in the songs the queen preferred, and a pointed interview as to her religious views. Isabella was present at all of these, both distant and correct; the flash of fire she had shown earlier did not come again. Julian followed her example, for she knew the warning had not been lightly given. Thus she gave the circumspect answers to the priest and fought to hide her resentment at his questions.

One morning Julian was sent to walk four of the queen's spaniels in the garden by the river. It was a misty, chilly day, and the branches of the trees overhead, newly leafed out, rattled in the wind. The opposite bank of the Thames was shrouded in fog, and the water ran dark below. The path where she walked was muddy and her clogs heavy; already the dark brown of her gown was stained and damp. The golden dogs foamed around her feet and yapped at each other in their delight to be free. All the freshness of spring was in the air as Julian felt her spirits rise to greet it.

A bird screeched suddenly and rose from a bush directly in front of her. She jumped and dropped the leashes. The spaniels separated and ran toward the copse which bordered on the bank, yapping as they went. Her foot caught in one of the roots, and she tumbled sideways onto some rocks that formed part of a grotto. Her hair fell loose over her shoulders and blew in the gusting breeze. Julian began to laugh as she tried to rise and caught her foot in the hem of the gown; it was all too much at once.

"These beasts nearly tripped me. What are you doing with them if you cannot control them?" The annoyed voice spoke just behind her. "Here, I will help you up unless you prefer to sit there."

"It is not the most comfortable seat in the garden, I assure you," Julian said tartly. She took the long-fingered brown hand that was stretched down to her and untangled her hem quickly as she rose. The two little dogs barked eagerly for attention. "Thank you, I . . ." Her voice trailed away as she looked into the face of the man who had averted trouble with the crowd the night of her entry into London.

He was very tall, in his early thirties, with crisply curling black hair above a high forehead. His brows were dark slashes above gray-green eyes, and his mouth was sharply modeled with an arrogant set to it. She saw again the chis-

eled profile, the ears set close to his head, the lean lines of
his long body that the stark black of his doublet and hose
showed to advantage. His shoulders were wide and supported the weight of a gray cloak almost the same shade as
the river mist. A silver chain hung around his neck and
emeralds glittered on one hand.

Now he stared at her in a puzzled fashion, his hand still
on hers. A flicker of movement caught her eye just then,
and the other dogs rushed toward them, barking as they
came. She looked beyond them and saw Isabella Acton
making her cautious way along one of the lower paths in
the same general direction from which the man had come.
His glance followed hers and grew cold. Had they kept a
tryst in the drizzle? No matter, Julian thought. What
concern could it be of hers?

He released her fingers and said, "Of course—I saw you
in the streets the other night. That is why you seem familiar. You are one of the servants in the palace, I see. I am
glad that things have turned out well for you and that you
were not being led away to prison." He smiled and the
dark face, brown from the sun, was transformed into brilliance. He had a tiny cleft beside his mouth that lent
warmth to his chill exterior.

Julian felt that warmth touch and envelop her. Her
heart began to hammer, and she felt herself tremble as fire
mounted in her cheeks. She tried to take her eyes from his
and could not; the world seemed to fade away so that only
the two remained. Neither moved, but she saw the pulse
throbbing in his neck and the faintest touch of perspiration appear on his brow.

She heard herself say, "Sir, I do thank you for your
concern. It was most gentlemanly of you."

He gave a short laugh that held no mirth, then reached
out and pulled her to him, crushing the whole length of
her body to him so that she felt the pounding of his heart
and the rising of his manhood through her full skirts.

"Let me go!" She struggled against the firm hands, suddenly afraid of what had been set in motion.

"In due time." The words were almost whispered as he
set his mouth to hers so fiercely that his teeth ground into

her lips. One strong hand held her head still, and the other secured her body against his. His tongue forced itself into her mouth, and he bent her backward as she yielded to his power.

He overwhelmed her, burned her, set the sweet juices running hotly in her flesh. She felt herself beginning to dissolve and meld with him. She wanted to be closer to him, to feel those long fingers on her naked warmth. Their tongues drew heat and wound together. Her breasts began to ache as she lost all will except his.

Then he set her back from him, and they looked full at each other. His face was cold now, but Julian's breath came in gasps, and she could feel her lips ache from the force of his kiss. The little dogs whimpered at their feet, and the distant call of a boatman on the river mingled with the low roll of thunder in the distance.

"You have set a spell, mistress. Did you mean it so?" The words were light, intimate as a finger touch. "Might you be . . . kind . . . at another time?" The look in his eyes told her what he meant most clearly.

Anger flickered through Julian. Did he think her a casual tumble simply because she had been caught up in an unknown emotion? Would it be different if he knew her to be under the protection of the queen? The simple precepts of her proud house spoke for her as she lifted her chin and looked him squarely in the face. Desire roiled in her, the first she had ever known. She no longer wondered at the romances and what they could inspire.

"You take me lightly, sir. I was not taught so nor would I practice it now." She drew back slightly and shook out her skirts.

Little points came into his darkening eyes, and his mouth quirked upward. "Do you know who I am?" There was almost an air of sadness about him as he watched her. "You are not afraid of me?"

"You are doubtless a great lord. Should I fear you?" She tipped her face up toward his.

He touched her chin gently. "Better for you that you should, little one. I will leave you to your Ned or Thomas as is meet."

Just then a shrill whistle sounded from the bank, and they saw a small barge approaching. A man stood in the back of it, looking up toward the garden where they stood. The dark man beside Julian gave an answering call which might have been a bird at twilight. He walked a few steps away, then turned once more and cupped her face in his warm fingers.

She felt her pulses throb as her arms lifted to his shoulders. His lips were soft and cherishing now, tender as rose petals in the spring sun. Passion was leashed down so that gentleness might flower. The force of her own response shook her as she tried to hold back so that he might not see the longing written upon her face.

He moved back, and once again that wry, self-depre-cating smile crossed his mouth. His bow was as to a great lady rather than the servant wench she knew he thought her to be. She curtsied gravely before him, aquamarine eyes brilliant with the beginning of strange tears that she did not understand. They looked at each other for another moment before he turned and stalked away into the mist and drizzle down toward the waiting barge.

Julian felt a mixture of joy and sadness. How she wished that she had someone to confide in or at least to tell her who he was! A man so handsome must surely be wed, she thought, or certainly troth-plighted. She gathered the leashes and started up the muddy path, murmuring endearments to the little dogs which had, after all, brought him to her. She could not resist a swift look at the river, but the barge had vanished. There was a wildness, a hunger in her blood that had responded to the same in him; her instincts told her that there was that between them which must come again. "Let me see him again! Bring him back." She whispered the words to the Virgin, to Isis, to Aphrodite, then smiled at her fancies.

The deep earth smells mingled with those of water and rain. The thunder rattled overhead, the wind struck icily at her, but Julian did not hear or feel. She was thinking of the gray days at Redeswan and their struggles for bare existence when Elspeth would remark, "Ah, Lady Julian, if you but had a good manageable husband!"

Julian had tossed her head boldly. "If ever I wed, it will
be for true love. I will guide my own fate." Then they
laughed together at such outlandish notions, but Julian had
always known that she spoke the truth.

Now she smiled in memory. Life and excitement were
opening up before her, and love wore a face whose name
she did not know.

CHAPTER THREE

The great palace of Whitehall gleamed with a thousand
candles. The lavishly decorated walls and ceilings glowed
with color, not only with paintings and carvings, but with
gold and silver and priceless jewels. Tapestries of exquisite
silks also adorned the walls, moving in the little winds that
were always present so that the figures and animals depicted on them seemed almost lifelike. Sweet scents flooded
up, and the Tudor rose, that mingling of red rose and
white, was shown everywhere in carvings and embroidery.
The hart of the English stood with the eagle of the
Hapsburgs, red and yellow twined with black and white in
the united symbols of the sovereigns on the banners that
fluttered everywhere. Music and talk rang out, servants
scurried back and forth, the assembled court and various
guests along with Queen Mary and King Philip waited for
the first lavish revel of his return to begin.

Julian waited with the others who were to take part in
this section of the revel. The anteroom was impossibly
small, but they took no notice of each other as they
awaited the signal to appear. The watchers had banquetted

heartily, but this troupe had barely touched bread, cheese, and watered wine. Now they stood numbly, muttering lines and rehearsing gestures, or gazing earnestly into space.

Julian had a very small part, but she had been coached in it over and over by the frantic Master of the Revels, who could not be satisfied with any of the performances, either of the great or the lesser mortals. She was terrified, but her heart thrilled to the sounds of the trumpets, the salutations to the rulers, the roars of those gathered, and to the deep voice of Mary as she praised each portion of the pageant. Julian had seen the queen several times since the night of her arrival; she had been distant and gracious with no sign of the emotion of that first encounter. Now the girl let her thoughts drift. What if the queen were delighted by them this night? From such moments court fortunes were made; a pleased ruler would grant much and who more so than a queen besotted? A foolish dream perhaps, but it helped to quell the fright. She would ask for Redeswan to be truly hers.

The music from the hall died, and the applause began. In a few minutes lackeys would begin to roll the huge painted machines that constituted the undersea kingdom of their own masque into place. The curtain would roll down, and their enchantment would begin. The music of England and Spain wound together over the patter of the court fool while the jugglers and tumblers entertained the throng in this pause. Julian's throat grew tight; she would not be able to speak or move. Her legs were frozen and trembling.

The torches flickered and dimmed. They would be relit in a matter of minutes, but this was their signal. "Move! Move!" The Master of the Revels gave a hiss of pure anguish. Instantly they began to move and obey without thinking as they had done in the last few days. Julian followed the swaying skirts of the girl in front of her and did not pause to wonder that her body responded.

Quick hands lifted her to the "rock" that she would occupy, and others spread her gown so that she could rise swiftly when the time came. Once settled, she twisted her suddenly damp fingers, then put them down on the wool-covered structure that represented the dwelling of the sea creature. She must not spot her pale skirts. She was almost at the top of the painted scene and could look through the carved waves. The thrones and jeweled figures, the rapt courtiers, the whole gay scene, faded before the sight of the dark man she had met again only a fortnight ago. Her eyes saw only his tall silver-clad figure standing to the left of the king as he whispered in his ear.

The massed candles flamed again into brilliance, the music rose to a crescendo, and the curtain was moved away. The company gave a collective sigh as the high pure voices of the minstrels rose in florid description of the sea kingdom. Light blazed in Julian's face as she lifted her arms and swayed with the others in the movements she had learned. Awareness of him coursed in her blood and heightened her excitement. Now she would meet him on his own ground as an equal. Now he would see her as fair woman, not as a serving wench with whom to dally.

The sea beat upon the rocks, their kingdom rose to light and air, the eagle came to be made thrice welcome by water maidens who, in turn, were welcomed by his feathered followers as they sang of the mountains and plains of their own land. Then the beast rose in the distance, somber and evil. The music lowered to a single ominous note. The dancer-soldiers of both kingdoms marched forward to do battle and bring justice.

The heavy body sagged and fell. A wild song of jubilation began as those victorious mingled their banners, and the torches were lifted high. Then the four sea princesses rose proudly to speak as one, the eagle and his followers joining in. "So, gentles all, our lands united do choose the right and conquer evil as is our bounden duty." Then there was silence as the six girls poised at the top of the scene, goddesses all, spoke clearly, each in her turn and rising as she did so, "Deus veult," that cry of the crusaders of old.

Julian heard her own voice, low and carrying, filled with the fervency of the moment. She knew that all eyes watched, including those of the dark man, and was glad that the iridescent blue-green gown she wore was the very color of her eyes and gave a glow to her pale skin. The skirt was made in the manner of a bell and stood out to emphasize her small waist. The sleeves were long and puffed up over lacings of dark blue which came to white lace at her fingertips. The wide collar stood away to show the beginnings of her bosom. Her chestnut hair was wound with ropes of tiny pearls and fell to her hips. She had known herself lovelier than she had ever been when the maids helped her dress, and now the warming flush lifted to her cheeks. In moments, now, he would seek her out.

The players sank low before the king and queen while the last notes of the music died away and they waited for the accolade. The accented English held only the faintest hint of a lisp as the king said, "We are pleased, well pleased. You will come forward before us, one by one, and receive our thanks."

Julian heard the gasps. This was honor, indeed. She lifted her eyes to see that both rulers were smiling, but the dark man now stood back from the dais and gazed off into the distance with an expression of boredom. Her heart slammed in her chest, and she whispered softly, "Let him find me fair." A vision of the hawthorn in bloom rose up in her mind just then, and she remembered Elspeth, who had given so generously of her charm. Then all faded as the players went to receive the accolade.

When her turn came she was conscious only of eyes seeming to bore into her, not only those of the courtiers but the seeking ones of Philip, the watchful ones of the queen, who was suddenly stiff in her golden chair.

"Ah, Lady Redenter. Most charming. An enchanting pageant." The king's voice coiled around her and held for a second.

Julian kept her head bent as the gruff voice of the queen echoed his final words. Then the Master of the Revels touched her arm, and she smiled blankly into his bearded face as he moved away to make room for the next player. Her knees shook from nerves and the depth of her curtsy, but she was able to tell that the dark man was no longer at the dais. Annoyed with herself, she walked over to one wall and began to study the painting

of a forest that hung there. Dimly she heard the music begin for dancing.

"Welcome to court, Lady Redenter." His voice was
deep and warm, the syllables slightly clipped, the sound of
the sea in them.

Julian swung round, the flush rising in her face. The
gray and silver that he wore accented the browned skin
and black hair; the brilliant eyes were a deeper gray and
expressionless. He wore no jewels except the silver chain.
His own person was adornment enough, she thought.

"You have the advantage of me, sir." Her pulses were
hammering wildly and the hall was suddenly very hot.
Devil take the man that he could affect her so! She recalled Lady Gwendolyn's passionate memories of her
husband, thoughts recollected in sickness and not meant
for a girl's ears, which had stamped themselves on her
whole life. Love was partial enslavement just as the romances said.

"I am Charles Jonathan Varland. Will you dance with
me?"

Wordlessly she took the arm he held out, and they
paced into the open area where others moved in the
stately tread of the pavane. Their fingers touched, melted
together as the flames rose between them. Charles Varland's face was impassive, but awareness emanated from
him. They drifted in the patterns of the dance, but they
might have been alone for all the notice they took of their
surroundings. His eyes went over her, and it was as intimate as the caress they had shared in the garden.

"Did you find the masquerade amusing, my lady? Are
there other parts you plan to play?" The tone was silken,
polite. "I vow, you quite fooled me with your talents."

Julian said, "I did not notice that you offered your
name, Lord Varland. I assume that is your correct title?"

"It is. Am I to assume that you did not know me?" He
bore heavily down on the same word she had used.

"How could I? Isabella did not say . . ." She stopped at
the angry look on his face.

"Isabella Acton? Have you been prattling to her of
me?" He leaned closer to her as the rhythm of the dance

slowed and faded. "Hold your tongue, madam, in matters that do not concern you!"

Julian was thankful for the anger that blazed through her; it was more understandable than the longing for his touch. "I will say that you are far too certain of yourself, my lord. Pray let me leave you to commune with that self!" She turned and walked away from him so rapidly that she almost collided with a young man talking to a dark-haired girl several feet away. Their surprised laughter rose as she went on.

She only wanted to be away from the disturbing emotions that Lord Varland aroused, yet she did not forget that moments before only he had existed for her. A great emptiness permeated Julian then; never had she felt so alone or deserted. Those of her household at Redeswan, few though they were, had shared fear, poverty, and pleasure together. Elspeth had been confidante and friend more than servant. Life had been simple then. Still, she would not change.

"Julian." It was Isabella, first faint lines furrowing her white brow, the smile unreal on her face, who put one slender hand under the girl's elbow. To the casual observer it might have been a friendly gesture, but the grip was so strong that Julian would have had to wrench herself free. The informal address was strange in this formal court. "I must speak with you. Walk with me."

They moved to the fringes of the hall with just a few steps, then Isabella said, "I say this as one who wishes you well. Lord Varland is not to be trifled with; leave him alone. Your entire future could be placed in jeopardy."

Julian believed her to be jealous and could not resist such a priceless opportunity to learn something of the dark lord. "I did but dance with him in courtesy, Lady Acton, as with any court gentleman. What have I done amiss?"

The dark eyes glittered at her, but the outward demeanor was unruffled. "You are a maiden and ward of the queen, who will find you a good husband, for she is kindness itself in such matters. You will not understand grave matters of the court, of course, but Varland was high in the favor of Protestant King Edward and went on a mis-

sion for King Henry, his father. He wed in Italy, and the
girl died in strange circumstances. Tales circulated and
were silenced. He met King Philip in the days before he
became our queen's husband and thus is in favor now. He
is said to be betrothed to a great heiress of the Rothsoon
family, but she has never been to court. His reputation is
one of despoiler of women and worse. It will not go well
that you accepted his attention this night."

Julian remembered the tenderness of the garden, the
way he had bidden her go to her rustic love and had almost warned her against himself. Was that the way of a
lecher, a man of no beliefs save that of lust? But she must
not anger this woman, the powerful friend of the queen.

She said innocently, "Is he a pariah, then? Would such
a lady as yourself be seen in his company?"

Isabella's grip had relaxed, but now it tightened again.
"You must guard your reputation. It and the queen's favor
are all you have in this world and all you can bring to a
husband. Be polite but no more, even as I am."

Julian almost told her that she had seen her in the
garden, certainly coming from seeing Lord Varland, but
caution held her tongue. "I have often thought, Lady Acton, that I would wish to remain unwed rather than give
my life and self over into the keeping of a man for whom
I did not care." This was no more than truth, but it deflected Isabella's suspicions.

She laughed avidly. "So did I once think. It is the way
of maidens. You will heed my words?"

"Naturally, my lady."

They walked on toward a little anteroom where several
girls were playing on the virginals while another strummed
a lute. A servant moved among the several gentlemen with
goblets of wine. He came up to Julian and she took one,
for she was suddenly very thirsty. The heady concoction
lifted her spirits, and she was able to smile at Isabella easily. The blond woman watched her for a moment and
seemed satisfied.

"I must attend briefly on the queen, then I will return
for you. I think it likely that you will soon be in full at-

tendance on her if you comport yourself properly." The tiny lash was in the words again.

Julian said nothing and continued to smile. Isabella rustled away without a backward glance. It was a relief to see her go, and now Julian could sink down on a stool and listen to the music that drifted around her. Bits of conversation eddied also, much of it meaningless, more background than clarity: ". . . an eye on the girl, best be careful," "not likely for war . . ." "whose wife?" Laughter, covert glances at Julian, and then whispering. She wondered idly what they were talking about. Would she ever belong here or stand laughing with friends?

One of the girls was singing now. It was a tender ballad of love and spring in the greenwood, a fair maiden who sought her knight and found him after many trials and vicissitudes. The words made Julian think of her own proud declaration and the very real possibility that the queen would choose a husband for her who would not be to her liking. Few women wed whom they chose and then only in a second marriage. They sang of love, that was well enough, but reality dominated marriage.

She shook off the bitter thoughts and listened to the melody that was just beginning. It was one familiar to the courtiers; they paused in their conversations to listen, and one of them joined his voice with that of the young dark-haired girl who was singing. Julian took another sip of wine and felt it mingle with tiredness and excitement as the words of passion and love unrequited rang in her mind and rose softly to her lips: "Alas, my love, you do me wrong to treat me so discourteously. . . ."

People were moving by the door now. An older woman, stiff in purple brocade and diamonds, paused to listen. The queen's own dwarf, Jane the Fool, unwound herself from a cushion near the virginals and looked up, yearning evident on her perfectly formed face. It was a strange moment of sharing; Julian felt the warmth pervade her.

Her eyes prickled slightly as the song rose in greater intensity, and at first Julian thought that it was the guttering candles that seemed to make the pool of shadow just inside the door. Then she saw that it was Lord Varland, obviously looking for someone, his eyes sweeping back and forth, the dark face haughty and unreadable. He saw her, heard the words she sang, and their glances locked. With a strange prescience she sensed the interlocking of their fates and knew that he fought against it.

He turned away and then back while the others watched. Julian could not help herself; it was as if cords bound them. The faint lute notes fell into the hush, the women's voices and her own twined around the yearning words of King Henry's own song made in death and love: "Greensleeves was all my joy . . . Greensleeves was my heart of flame. . . ."

CHAPTER FOUR

Julian stood in the richly appointed room that housed the royal library and looked about with delight. Spring sun washed through the stained-glass windows which were set high and wide in the thick wall. Here were the true treasures of the kingdom, she thought in awe; with time she might partake of them all. Several precious volumes lay out on a table set against one corner. They were bound in leather and shimmered with gold. She touched one; a Latin work on some abstruse religious doctrines. Another was bound in green velvet, ornamented in silver, written in both Latin and French. Curious, she opened it and saw that the tale was one of the hunting of various beasts and the proper manner to capture them. One of the illuminated drawings showed the elusive unicorn fleeing to the shelter of the pure maiden. On the next page a basilisk lifted its deadly head. The colors and lines were so clearly delineated that the creatures seemed real.

"They are beautiful, are they not?" The slow voice spoke at her side, and a slender finger traced the outline of the basilisk. "And deadly, if the old tales are to be believed."

Julian froze for a second, then looked up into the enigmatic eyes of Philip of Spain. "Your Majesty!" She dropped to her knees with one fluid movement, the golden dress shimmering around her.

He snapped impatient fingers. "Rise. Rise. In solitude we may be less formal. Have you come, even as I, to escape the crush of the court? You English are so exuberant! In Spain we know the value of silence."

Julian backed away a little as she said, "Her Majesty sent me to fetch the works of St. Thomas Aquinas, saying that I must read to her from them later." She did not add that the queen had remarked on the soothing qualities of her voice, thereby causing several of the other ladies to give each other sharp looks.

"Most edifying. However, the day is fair and fresh. It seems that a walk in the gardens would be good for those headaches she complains of so much." He sounded the very disgruntled husband, but the movement he made toward Julian was practiced and smooth. "I have a few moments from the affairs of state, Lady Redenter, and would speak of other things. Will you sit here and tell me of that barbarous land you live so near? Wales, I believe it is called?"

It was a command for all the light tone of the words. He did not wait for an answer as he took her arm and guided her toward a velvet-lined bench near the window. The swift running Thames could be glimpsed just beyond the tossing branches now newly green in the erratic weather. Philip turned her to face him and kept his hand on hers. She forced herself to remain still, and the look on her face was politely agreeable.

"Your Majesty, the queen will be awaiting my return."

"It is not yet noon. She will be praying and will not thank anyone daring to disturb her. Now, tell me as I have

bidden you. I must know more of this land that our son
will one day rule." His voice sharpened, and the strange
eyes bored into hers.

"Your Majesty surely has many able informants who
are far wiser than I and certainly more clever." She heard
her voice as if from afar.

"But none more fair." His fingers stroked hers briefly.

Gods, the man thought that her attempt to escape was
merely flirtation! She said swiftly, "Your Majesty has commanded and I obey. What is it that you would like to
know? The crops, the weather, the boundaries? I do not
actually live in Wales, you know, but on the border."

He laughed, seeing her flee before him. "The pleasant
homely matters of daily life, madam."

Julian was reminded of the basilisk and the stare that
could destroy. She spoke of the hills and the clouds, the
little villages and winding roads, of the unexpected dwellings of another day that one sometimes found, heather
and blooming flowers, warmth and spiraling birds, the tac-
iturn people and their need to live out their lives in peace
as they had done in long years despite the many upheavals
caused by the Tudors and Plantagenets, of the children
with whom she had played in her youth and the
knowledge they had shared. Then she wondered suddenly
if Philip really believed he could father an heir from the
queen, who was now in her middle forties, older than
Julian's mother had been when she died. There had been a
false pregnancy, she remembered, soon after their marriage, and the queen had been devastated. Philip had only
just returned after an absence of nineteen months.

"You love that country and your manor, Redeswan, do
you not?" He spoke still more softly, and his hands slipped
up to her wrist. His breath came warm on her cheek. His
eyes were hot and hungry.

Julian tried to move away and found herself trapped by
his soldier's body. She did not dare repulse him; guile was
her only weapon. "Majesty, I did promise to return
quickly to your wife, the queen. You have honored me
with your attention."

He put one finger on her lips to silence her. In another

second he would pull her into his arms. Queen Mary would not blame her husband; a man with a man's needs was one thing, a lightsome lady-in-waiting another. She turned her head sharply and heard his intake of annoyance. She could faint, see a ghost, grow nauseated. How did one reject a king?

A soft footfall sounded in the doorway just then, and a familiar voice said, "Shall I return at a more fitting time for our conference, Your Majesty?" It was Charles Varland already turning discreetly away.

Philip moved back from Julian and hooked both hands in his elegant sleeves. He said casually, "Come in, Charles. I arrived early and was listening to this young woman tell me of her part of England. Enchanting. Almost the same as your talk about that seacoast of yours, that Cornwall. No, I am ready. Come in, man."

Charles Varland gave a quick bow, but his eyes raked Julian and she knew that he thought they had been at dalliance. She rose and made her curtsy, knowing that she must leave as quickly as possible even without the book. The king smiled intimately at her and waved her away. Varland's lips tightened, but his face remained impassive.

As Julian edged back she heard the king say, "Now, Charles, what is this nonsense about the campaign?"

She tried to compose herself as she walked back to the queen's rooms. It was certainly no shock that the king had interested himself in her; rumor had it that he had even brought a mistress back to England under the name of kinswoman, and his escapades in Brussels in the past months had caused the queen much grief. It was the casualness of it that set her blood ablaze. Did he consider a woman a thing to be used and tossed aside? Varland, too, had spoken of bedding her within minutes of their first speaking to each other. Was she to see her life in terms of a man only? Yet honesty told her that Lord Varland could easily hold her heart.

The queen was speaking to several of her assembled ladies when Julian entered the bedchamber, which was hung with the colors of Spain and England. She seemed to have forgotten her headaches and interest in abstruse theology, for she wore a shimmering pink gown, and her small face was alight beneath her coif.

Her deep voice was tremulous as she said, "I know that my womb will soon quicken. The Virgin has heard me now just as she did when I prayed for my lord husband's return. I shall offer thanks to her in a special way. Ladies, two days from now in the very early morning you will dress in your oldest clothes even as I, and we will go forth to give largesse to the poor. This is both meet and worthy, a thing blessed by Our Lord." She waved slender hands in dismissal. "Go now, I would be alone."

They scattered quickly, and Julian found herself beside a brown-haired girl with very pale skin who looked familiar. As they walked out she recognized her as the girl over whom she had stumbled running away from Charles in the hall. Julian hoped that she would not remember; there had been enough confrontations for one day. She said in a low voice, "What sort of expedition are we bidden on? I am fairly new to court and unfamiliar with such."

The girl fell into step with Julian and spoke breathlessly. "It is all marvelously exciting, don't you think? All those handsome Spaniards who came with the king, some of them may go with us. Oh, but you don't know! In the days before she came to power she used to go out into the country with her attendants, all dressed poorly, for they had little else, and give what she could to the people. She was often in poorer straits than they, and many did not know that she was heiress to the throne."

She paused for breath, and Julian smiled into the guileless brown eyes. How open and friendly she was! The caution that Lady Gwendolyn had bred into her daughter did not lead to easy words, but Julian was conscious of her need for a friend at this court. She said, "I am Julian Redenter, newly come and very uncertain much of the time."

"I am Blanche Parker of Kent. Don't worry, you'll soon be at ease. Now is such a good time to be here. The king back, new gentlemen at court, mummings, hunts, the queen happy and spending less time on her knees. Everybody will know it's the queen when we go out to give largesse but will pretend they don't; I have heard my mother say that old King Henry loved such disguisings."

Several courtiers passed just then and looked long at Blanche, who was flushed a pale rose with her excitement. Julian felt her own heart lift as she vowed to remain as far from the king as possible and hope that he would forget his drifting interest. Blanche took her arm and began to chatter in a low confiding voice about Spanish gentlemen, her concern that at twenty she was not yet betrothed, and the coming venture into the streets.

"And you need to be careful, Lady Julian—that dark lord Varland can hurt your reputation. Naturally, he says he is of the true faith now, but he went to all those German places in the last reign, and there was talk about his wife—maybe murder, you know. Why, I've heard it said that if he were not in such favor with the king, the queen would have him investigated by the commissioners."

Lord Varland did not need her defense, but Julian heard herself say, "He was most courteous to me when first we met. Perhaps it is court gossip only."

Blanche looked at her wide-eyed and continued to chatter. Julian knew that the girl saw more than she gave away and hoped that her own passion was not evident.

Julian did not have to worry about finding old clothes; she had the gown she had worn from Redeswan. Therefore, she spent much of her time before the expedition in Isabella's apartments reading, practicing on the virginals, or walking in the Long Gallery of the palace. She felt as though she were poised over a yawning abyss in danger of falling no matter what precautions were taken. Ward and lady-in-waiting to the queen of England, the whole brilliant court before her, unlimited opportunity ahead—all this should be enough, Julian tried to tell herself. But in this suspended time, she knew that she wanted to shape her own world and move freely in it, that she must matter in her own right as a person.

The next afternoon Julian walked swiftly along the passageway that led to the chapel. She wanted to relax in the beauty and peace there as well as seek respite from the emotions that divided her. The queen had sequestered herself, and there had been no call for the younger ladies, so this was the perfect time. She put one hand on the ornate door to push it back and was pulled forward as someone jerked it from inside. She struggled to catch herself from falling, and then the familiar shiver of excitement began as she looked up at Charles Varland.

"What are you doing here? I did not know you were of the faith!" The inadvertent words rose to her lips before she could shut them away.

"Is God of one persuasion, then?" He wore deep gray velvet now, and the gray of his eyes was that of ice in January. "But you, now—have you come to seek one whose name may not be spoken? Best to be very careful. I do not recommend the chapel for assignations."

"Is this taken from your own experience, my lord?" The words flared from her, and sparks flickered in her own eyes.

Charles Varland caught her satin-covered shoulder and held it. "You are suddenly everywhere I look. Are you other than you seem? Surely you have been warned?"

She tried to jerk free. "Everyone warns me in nebulous fashion, and many of those admonitions are against you! Let me pass!"

He pulled her to him, and his mouth was hard on hers. She felt herself growing weak, beginning to tremble as the sweet melting fire rose. His hand was already reaching for her breast when she twisted away and leaned against the wall to compose herself. Varland's face flamed with real anger; it must be seldom that he found himself repulsed.

Julian said again, "Let me pass, Lord Varland. I did not come here to snuggle in corners with the court rake." She wanted to hurt him, to rebuke herself for that momentary yielding. His face did not alter, nor did he move.

His voice flayed her as he said, "Ah, of course not, you look far higher. Kings, after all, can give more jewels, estates, titles. Another bit of caution, my dear: Get what you can before you yield to him, for he is easily bored." He moved aside for her to pass and began to adjust the lace on his cuff.

Julian's temper rose hotter than in many a day. The

print of her palm was emblazoned the length of his lean brown face before she was aware that she had lifted her hand at all. She glared at him, her eyes brilliant and hard in the shifting lights of the chapel, where the compassionate Virgin looked down.

"Look to yourself before you sully my name!" The growl of all her fierce pride was in the words.

Of all the reactions she had expected from him, the last was laughter. It boomed against the carved ceiling and halted abruptly as he leaned close to her. "That was a very predictable reaction, Lady Redenter. Really, you must look to your bag of tricks if you expect to come out with more than you had before you went in. King Philip will not remain in England for long. He wants the queen to declare war against France and is busy seeking the support of the lords of the realm in this. He will stay only until war is declared. After you have learned to be less violent, I may renew my own search for amusement. By then, of course, you will be wiser." He held the door open so that she might pass through.

Nothing touched the man! Julian felt the tears burn in her eyes and blinked them away so that he might not see and be gratified that he had hurt her. "I will pray for the benighted state of your mind, Lord Varland. From all I hear, you stand in great need of prayer, and your behavior to me has truly confirmed it." Her small chin lifted, and the chestnut hair rippled back from her white forehead in shimmering waves. She would not quail before this man, however bold he seemed. Still, her body longed for his touch even as her mind rebelled.

His bow was perfect, his voice cool and correct, as he said, "Prayer is always an excellent thing, Lady Redenter. I wish you success in your endeavors. Good day."

Then he was walking arrogantly down the passageway, his long lean body erect, dark head high. A man as no other, the man who would haunt her dreams and her days. Julian did not know if this savage longing she felt was the delight of the romances. Clearly he thought her less than a lady, but he wanted her, too; every inch of her hungry flesh knew that. Was this how the queen felt toward her young husband? The way that Lady Gwendolyn had been seared by Lionel Redenter? Julian wanted Charles Varland's eyes to go warm with longing and gentle with cherishing, but more even than that, she wanted to know and understand him, to be his and he hers.

Her palm still tingled where she had slapped him; she could not be sorry for that. Though her body hungered, Julian Redenter still held by the pride of her generations and felt that must be her solace in the time ahead. She did not think he would seek her out again, nor would she go about alone. The laughing face of Blanche Parker rose up before her, a friendship worth the having. She would walk with Blanche or even Isabella until the king left. She would be no pawn!

Her course set, Julian walked toward the safety of her rooms, feeling all the desolation of one bereft.

CHAPTER FIVE

The fresh damp wind smelled of fish and earth, gray clouds hung low in the sky, but even at this early hour people rushed by intent on business and paying no attention to the group that had just alighted from the plain barge and now made its way up from the waterfront. Some were ladies-in-waiting, servants from the palace, and guards in old clothes set to watch. The queen had come even earlier, rested at the house of one of her nobles, and would soon join them in one of the smaller lanes of the city proper.

Julian had acquired this knowledge from listening to the

sleepy comments around her and had exchanged half-smiling yawns with the others. The strangeness was beginning to wear off, she felt, and soon she would feel a part of the court. She had seen neither Blanche nor Isabella this morning, but a sleepy maid had been sent to tend to her needs.

They picked their way through narrow streets filled with refuse, horsemen, shopkeepers crying their wares, peddlers, countrymen come to the city for the day, sightseers, and wanderers. They headed away from Thames Street into the heart of the city in an excitement that made the blood run faster. Julian listened to the raucous cries, laughter, and curses on every side, and wondered that the company was not known for what it was. To her, they seemed to stand out by manner and bearing, rough clothes not withstanding. The air was cold and there was little talk, but her sharp eyes had caught the glances some of the watchers on the street gave them. The bitter anger was very apparent. She wondered that the others did not see; her own senses were sharpened by years of caution.

Her own old shoes were scuffed and clompy and she wore a gown of dark wool that was rubbed and shabby, with a cloak of black cloth which was too short. Her hair was concealed under a coif and veil such as a housewife might wear. She moved easily in such clothes, for she had worn them most of her life. Some of the other ladies stumbled in their shoes or moved awkwardly in the shorter gowns.

A hoarse voice muttered just behind Julian, "Gentry by the look of 'em, out for a lark so early in the day so they can tell about it over loaded tables tonight."

"Aye, spies for the Spaniard." Another mutter, this time louder, more dangerous.

She could not help turning to look. Three men and a woman suddenly became very busy over a load of fish. Several young boys who had been walking close to them now moved to the other side of the street. Julian wondered if this whim of the queen's was as selfless as she must have thought; it seemed the height of foolishness, for anyone knew that Mary was no longer loved or admired by the subjects who had once welcomed her so eagerly.

Several of the guards dropped back, hands placed well in view on their knives. The whole party began to walk faster as the streets widened once more, and prosperous shops, wood-framed and tall, rose on both sides. The passers-by moved more slowly and their clothes were richer. Shoppers mingled with merchants who cried their wares while others sauntered by to watch. The whole scene pulsed with a vivid life; everyone seemed vitally intent on his own business, yet there was time to savor. To Julian, fresh from the quiet of country life, it was as if a thousand things beckoned her attention.

One of the ladies, a few years older than Julian, said petulantly, "We have walked so far, I vow, that I have a blister. Would that we could have sent the wretched poor jewels; I would have done so gladly."

Another near her shushed softly, her finger to her lips as both pairs of eyes raked Julian. This time she knew that they thought her a danger, perhaps a tattler to the queen, who had so favored her that she brought her from obscurity. Her pride made her hold their gaze as she tilted her chin. The daughter of the Redenters might have little else, but she had that. It was a faint triumph when they turned away and began to walk faster.

They turned another corner, paused before a hill which lifted onto an even busier area, and looked toward the cathedral of St. Paul's, which dominated this section of the city with its great buttresses and the thin spire that seemed to reach through the clouds themselves. Here, thought Julian, was the faith triumphant and yet benignant; there was no thought of the fear that the human servants of that faith inspired.

Her stomach lurched; the cup of broth the maid brought had been long ago while it was still dark. The cookshop just yonder was producing pasties, and the smell made her mouth water. She would just dash across and spend one of her precious few coins while the party was moving slowly toward the cathedral. They would never miss her.

A cry rang across the street and caused all eyes to stare in horror at the boy who shouted and ran. "No Spaniards! Send Mary with Philip! No more fires!" He was ragged and dirty, but his young face blazed with passion as he dared the watchers to check him. Several of the guards from the palace started toward him, but one of the ladies seemed about to faint and they hesitated.

Julian knew he referred to the burning of heretics, which had increased greatly in the past year. "Elizabeth for England! The true queen!" he cried. This was dangerous talk indeed, and the people looked fearfully at each other. Mary's sister, aged twenty-four, daughter of Anne Boleyn and Henry VIII, was the nominal heiress to the throne if the present queen had no children, but she walked in danger of her life should Mary's uncertain temper turn.

A ragged cheer began, for which royal personage could only be guessed. One of the guards could take no more, and he ran for the boy, sword out as he cried, "Treason!" Others from the street joined him in pursuit of the lad, who now ran fleetly between two fat merchants who did nothing to block him, and he vanished from view.

The party from court began to reassemble. Some of the ladies had very pale faces under the blithe manner they tried to assume. It would be a foolish Londoner indeed who did not recognize them for what they were. Evidently the guards thought so, too, for they began to urge them along. Julian's hunger was even sharper for the brief excitement, and she darted across to the cookshop, where several other people were waiting as they made low-voiced comments to each other.

The shop was poised at the end of one lane and on the corner of another so that it caught customers from both as well as the main avenue. One lane was very small and dark, the tall leaning houses seeming to reach for each other. Julian ventured around the edge and looked into the length of it as she wondered how the inhabitants could stand the noisome air of the place. She started to retreat, thinking that surely all of the city could not congregate at the shop, but was stopped by a hand on her shoulder.

The man's face was partially muffled by a dark hood, but she saw that part of his nose and one eye were gone. His lips were full and red above a straggly beard that appeared to grow out of one side of his face, for he held his head at an angle. Another man stood grinning at his elbow; with a shudder Julian recognized the slack stare of the idiot.

The first man flicked her coif aside and touched the bright strands of her tumbled hair. She jerked back, one hand raised to claw at him. His laughter was low and heavy. The other man began to rub his hands together in a washing gesture.

"Pretty lady come to admire St. Paul's. Pretty lady has money for starving beggars. Pretty lady will kiss us both. How do you like that, Bart?" He rolled up the remaining malevolent eye at his companion, who giggled.

"Let me go this instant." Julian spat the words out as she tried to jerk free.

He twisted one arm up behind her back and pulled her back into the shadows. "Don't try to get away. We can both take you right here and no one would pay the slightest attention, but you wouldn't want it in public, now would you, little flower?"

They both laughed, and Julian aimed a kick at her captor with one of the rough shoes she wore. He dodged and she saw, even in the dimness, that his eye went flat and dead. The one called Bart balled up his fist and came for her as he cried, "Hurt! All time want to hurt m'fren. Hurt!" His hand connected with her ear, and the world spun.

Then strong arms pulled her free and sent her sprawling into the muck as a sword flashed bright over the attackers and made rivulets of blood on the one-eyed man's face. He howled and backed away, then threw himself on Julian's rescuer. The sword lifted, and this time both men ran as it wove a net of steel on the cold air.

"Are you all right?" Charles Varland sheathed his sword and lifted her to her feet. His eyes were so warm with concern, angry words might never have passed between them.

Julian felt the curious pull between them as the realization of the danger she had just passed burst over her. She swayed, her voice coming out thinly as she said, "I just wanted one of the pies. I meant to run and catch up with the others. My lord, I thank you. You truly saved me."

There was the clatter of running feet just then, and Charles dropped his hand to his sword. A small rotund man with glistening red cheeks ran up and doffed his cap to Julian. "They lost themselves in the crowd—no way of catching them now."

"Thank you." Charles was bareheaded, little dark tendrils of hair curling at his ears. The glance he gave Julian was one of concern mingled with some emotion she could not identify. "This is Matthew Horton of my service."

Julian acknowledged the little man with a smile. "How did you come so handily here?" The closeness of Charles Varland made her nervous yet expectant. Horton flushed and moved away several paces.

"May I offer you food and refreshment, Lady Redenter? There is a most respectable inn close by here. Matthew shall inform your party of the circumstances and that you will soon join them. A maidservant shall attend you; you will not lack for chaperonage. As to your question, I had business here in this section of the city and will join the court party later. After you, of course." He remembered her fear for her reputation. The gray eyes seemed to ignite, and one corner of his mouth curved up in a half smile to expose shining white teeth and the slight cleft of his cheek. "Will you come, Julian? There is nothing to fear and none shall know. Please?"

She hesitated, knowing well the risk she took. The queen's ladies must be above reproach, since many a good marriage was made through her favor; Julian dared not think what would happen to her if the queen withdrew from her. But the temptation was too great. Varland was totally different now, and this was an adventure. Besides, he had saved her from attack. Was his invitation a way of apology?

"I will come, but I dare not linger." She smiled at him,

a quick vagrant smile that brought an answering one to his own lips.

"I am honored, Lady Redenter." He lifted her hand to his mouth and held it there. All her senses opened up as she looked at him. They might have been new met with none of the acrimony of their previous clashes. He let her go reluctantly and spoke to Matthew. "Go find the party and speak as you have heard me here. Be discreet."

He caught Julian's hand and drew her close to him as they made their way through the crowded streets, taking several sharp turns and coming finally to a doorway set in a wall that would be shrouded in greenery if this were summer. He knocked twice, and the door swung open to reveal a tall manservant.

"Food and wine in the small chamber. And send Dame Ross to me immediately. Arrangements must be made for a chaperon for the lady."

He departed with a bow. Charles and Julian went along a narrow hall and into a richly appointed room hung with cloth of silver and blue. Quantities of plate were displayed to advantage, and several pictures hung in a pattern of color on another wall. Julian crossed to the blazing fire and put out her hands.

"An opulent inn, sir. And you are well known here that they obey you so readily?" She could not wholly trust him even yet for all that he stood smiling and debonair, that strange smile transforming his stern face.

"I bring much custom here." He waved her to a seat and removed the crimson cloak from his shoulders. "Your given name is odd, is it not?"

She knew that he made idle conversation to put her at her ease. "As a child I thought so. The firstborn son of our family was always so named. My father never saw me, and as he was the last of the direct line, my mother named me Julian."

"I know of your family. A brave house and one which suffered for it. Ah, here are refreshments."

The servant spread the array before her and departed, deftly catching the coin that Charles tossed. There was loin of beef, oysters, fish, bread new made, cheese, dried apples, mince pie, marchpane, malmsey, and claret wine. She reached out hungrily and drew back.

"Surely all this is not for one person. Are you not joining me, sir?"

He smiled briefly. "I broke my fast most heartily earlier. I did not know what you liked. Eat heartily lest mine host be offended."

There was enough food to feed those at Redeswan for a week. Julian felt her appetite dwindle as he watched her. She drank some of the rich wine he poured into a silver cup and felt it ring in her head. The cheese was dry in her mouth, and she found it hard to swallow. The feeling of unease that she had felt ever since entering this place was even more pronounced now. She rose abruptly.

"I thank you for the rescue and the hospitality, Lord Varland. I must go. They may be looking for me. I must not anger the queen; she has been good to me and has burdens enough these days." She saw where that line of thought might lead and stopped abruptly. She was babbling, she thought despairingly, possibly because he was a man of silences, mysterious as the mists. "I mean, I really must go. Would you fetch the servant?"

Charles Varland stretched lithely and waved one hand. "You will never last the day if you do not eat. The queen will make sure that all the poor have been tended. She can survive a riot, feed with one hand and burn with the other, all in the name of God. She deceives herself and destroys this land, all in the name of God." His words were slow cadenced and bitter, but he checked himself as if by force. "Have I not told you all will be well?"

"She is the queen. You speak near treason!" Disquiet rose even more strongly in Julian, and she looked around for the old cloak she had worn earlier. "Moreover, she has been both kind and gracious to me."

"You would not betray an idle word given among friends." His tone was soft; his smile did not falter.

"Of course not. I but warn you as you did me." She could not help the thrust. "Now, call the servant. Please, Lord Varland."

"Are you afraid of me?" He rose and crossed to where she stood.

"Of course not!"

"You should be."

The words were spoken so softly that she could not grasp their meaning at first and merely stared at him.

"Enough of this byplay!" He fairly spat the words as he towered over her. "This thing between us shall be settled so that I can put my thoughts where they must be. You thought to dally with the king and with me while being the pure virgin well worthy of a rich lord, did you not? Ah, no, little maid, you shall pay the price of your wandering eyes." His eyes were cruel now, but she saw the passion in them. "Come here."

"You promised to take me back immediately! Will you break your word?" She stood proudly, her breasts heaving under the thin wool of the dark gown, her back very straight.

"What is one's word to a wench?" He pulled her to him as he laughed hauntingly. The chiseled face was devil-handsome in the glowing light.

"Let me go or I will scream and rouse the inn!" She jerked back and slammed at him with her closed fist.

"Pray do. This is my house, and my servants obey me implicitly as you saw. My plan worked perfectly, did it not?" He laughed again and set his mouth to hers, despite her struggles.

CHAPTER SIX

Julian felt him loosening her clothes as he held her easily
with one hand while his mouth ravished hers. She tried to
pull away and twist free, but he held her strongly. Her
dress ripped and the sound added fury to her struggles,
but she was powerless against his desire. He put both arms
around her body and locked her to him even as his mouth
possessed hers. She could not breathe; she knew that she
would faint if he continued to hold her so.

His tongue reached for hers and wound about it, then
teased and thrust as she turned her head the little that she
could. His lips crushed and softened her own. One hand
moved smoothly across her now bare breasts and twined
fingers over her thrusting nipples as Julian, responding
fiercely against her will, heard the pulses of her blood
hammer in her ears.

Charles pushed her slowly to the floor before the fire
and lay down on the length of her so that she was doubly
crushed. Now she felt the hardness of his manhood and
knew the hunger of his body. She was helpless before his
determined demand on her flesh, and she knew that she
wanted him, though not in such an assault. He lifted his
mouth from hers and looked down at her face while his
hands scooped her breasts together.

"Ah, you are fair!" He breathed the words softly, but
his eyes were gray pellets in the dark face.

She struggled all the more but could not move. The red
flush came into her face, and her mouth began to tremble

as control left her. Now the tears welled into her eyes as she blinked them away. "Surely you can find a woman who will have you without rape! Or is it that they call you murderer truly?" She was beyond caution, or she would not have dared the anger that she knew lay just behind his imperturbable surface.

His answer was to strip the skirts and shift from her in one movement. Then as she lay naked before him, caught in the shock of the moment, he tossed his own clothes aside and reached for her. He reckoned without the agility of one who was country bred. Before the hard arms could grasp her, Julian rolled free and, in one lithe pull, caught up a brand from the fire and held it before her as the flame flickered precariously close to his eyes.

Charles sat very still, his mouth quirked in that smile that was no smile, the light of the fire and the candles glowing on his long, hard-muscled body, which was brown even low on his flat stomach. He was lean and firmly built, his back, stomach, and thighs flowing together in a dark statue the Greeks might have envied, they who so loved male beauty. His shaft was still hard and long, faintly shining on the tip, well erect. His face might have been carved also, so clear and pure did it seem.

Julian said, half to herself, "You do well to hold yourself so high, my lord, for you are ravishingly handsome, as you know."

He stared at her, at the slender body that seemed a mixture of light and shadow, the body that Julian had often examined in the quiet of her chamber at Redeswan, sighing that her breasts were not fuller, her hips more rounded. Now she saw the vindication of that in a man's eyes and knew her beauty.

He said, "Put that brand down before you set the house afire. You cannot escape, and I will have you. Resign yourself to it." He started to rise but drew back abruptly when she thrust the brand directly at his face.

"I doubt that you will be interested in anything but your own disfigured face, and do not think that I will hesitate to burn it either." She reached for the torn gown and pulled it about her, thankful that he had at least torn it straight down so that she could get into it quickly. "Did those men really attack me so that you might fake a rescue and so turn my heart to you?"

"They did it well, don't you think? The queen's plans were the talk of the court; more fool she to go out with the temper of the city the way it is. I thought it a good time to settle the vexing thing between us, and you will have to admit that it worked." He stretched lazily, but the wary eyes never left hers.

"Did you expect me to be so grateful that I would tumble into your arms?" She observed with dismay that the blackened end of the brand was falling off, the fire dying from the rest.

"It did not matter so long as you came with a minimum of fuss and maidenly cries." He came up to his knees and crouched there so that he was partly between Julian and the fire.

She edged back and groped for another brand, but he moved so quickly that she was forced to retreat. She stabbed at his shoulder, and the still hot end came down on the flesh with a little hiss. He ignored it and stalked her intently as she moved toward the door.

"My man stands guard out there, and he will not let you by."

"You are indeed the foul fiend!" She swung the brand before her in an effort to fan the flame, and in that instant he caught her. Her weapon clattered to the floor and rolled free to smother out in the residual dampness there. Charles swung her up in his arms and carried her back to the cloak. He held her for a moment, then lowered her to it.

"Now, madam, I can bind you and take my pleasure. You will surely admit the hunger that I have felt in you. Satisfy it and we can both lead our separate lives with no more ado. I have no time for foolishness such as this. I should have tumbled you in one of the empty rooms of Whitehall and had done." He spoke harshly, but there was a puzzled look in the depths of his eyes.

Julian stared at the straight, lithe body, at the leashed power of it, saw the determination in his face, and knew

that he meant every word he said. He would have his
pleasure of her before she left this room. Her flesh tingled
at the thought.

"I am virgin." She hated herself for saying it, for
bending her womanhood before the attacker as she remembered the fervor with which she had sung "Greensleeves" to him, but her only future lay in marriage, and
no man would have a despoiled woman.

"You can lie about it. All women do. I will not wed
you." His eyes went black and dark for an instant as he
gazed beyond her. "I am betrothed; she is meek and amiable as you are not." Charles smiled suddenly, and the
young man he had once been was very evident.

Julian wanted to weep more for what she wished she
could have with him than for the rape she faced. "I did
not ask it, did I? Take what you will and set me free. I do
not suppose it will do any good to say that I did not lure
you, although I cannot deny the feeling that came unbidden." .

He sat down beside her and touched her shoulder
gently. "Aye, Julian. I know. How well I know. It is with
us still. Yield to me and I swear you shall be free."

The tears sprang to her eyes and trickled onto her
cheeks. "I am not weeping from fear of you. I am angry."
She dashed her hand across her face and glared at him.
"You have proven yourself a liar."

"Come, lady. Julian. Fair one." He drew her to him and
kissed her so gently on the lips that little chills began to
slide up and down her arms. One hand rubbed her neck
slowly and played with the curls at her ears. "Do you
yield the day?" He bent his head and kissed the long curve
of her throat where the pulse hammered, then continued
the soft, slow kisses until her skin ached with it and she
leaned toward him.

"Aye, I yield." The words came in a soft moan as she
put both hands on the broad shoulders that were so invitingly near. They looked long into each other's eyes before
his mouth claimed hers again in a long drugging kiss that
seemed to meld them into one fiery unit of passion.

They nestled deeply into the cloak that lay on the rich

rug in front of the fire. Julian remembered the virginals she had played, the lute the woman at court had caressed, and knew that Charles did the same to her body now. His mouth left hers, went to the hollow of her throat, down to her rosy nipples, lingered there, then went to the curve of her stomach and down her slender legs, then up to her nipples again. His hands were feathers drifting over her warmth, they were brands to burn and heal, they were igniters that did not quench.

She felt the tightness in her loins ease as the sweet juices began to loosen. Her breasts ached and throbbed, the feeling repeated in her maiden softness. It seemed that her blood ran very near to the surface and that she had been empty all her life. Her flesh burned and her hands reached out to touch and fondle him, rejoicing in the hardness that sought to make her his in a union that seemed foretold by the stars.

His mouth took hers again, and this time she yielded eagerly to the probing thrust of his tongue, knowing it to be the precursor of another thrusting that soon would not be denied. His hands moved along her naked sides with almost maddening gentleness that set up quivers under the skin. She felt her breasts crushed against his chest and moaned softly that their hunger grew apace.

She lay beside him now, in the crook of his arm, her legs spread wide against the new throbbing that made her writhe as his fingers touched her softness there, withdrew, then thrust a little more deeply, returning to touch and linger. Her lips reached up for his, the kiss slow and deep as they drank of each other's banked passion. Soon his hand was spread across her woman's mound, moving and inciting, as her hips shifted slowly and the fires grew higher. He touched and lured her with an exquisite tenderness.

Beyond the hands that stirred and excited her, beyond her own shy touching of his rampant manhood, beyond the eagerness and fear that seemed to grow with equal parts, Julian remembered how she had crouched on the edge of a cliff in her childhood and wondered how it would be to jump, to fly through the mist. Now the gray eyes were of that mist, and all life had come down to a dark man who was teaching her glory undreamed; a man both harsh and gentle, a man of contradictions.

Charles had held back as long as he could, the strain showing in the curve of his mouth, the long erectness of his flesh, and the luminous quality of those gray eyes. His gentleness never wavered, however, as he drew her to him for one long kiss before sliding down with her into the rug itself, his hands firm on her hips.

The first long thrust seemed to Julian that it would split her apart, and she struggled a little under the impaling body that moved only slightly. It was not pain so much as a fullness, an invasion that was not altogether welcome. Charles held her tightly so that she could not move, and his mouth was hard on hers so that she could not twist away. Gentleness was done; this was a commanding man who would take as he had given. The twist of anger translated itself into sudden stiffness, and the next deep thrust brought the beginnings of pain. Her head moved back and forth as his mouth left hers and went to the rosy, turgid nipples.

The drawing, nibbling sensation brought a soft sound to her lips, and Charles looked up to smile at her, a look of possession and hunger touched with a sadness that rendered him oddly vulnerable. He began to move in her then, and Julian forgot all thought, all dreams, all half-rendered pain. Time compressed itself; she was burning, aching, hungry flesh, woman pierced by her lover's power yet made anew by it. She mounted, soared, teetered at the moment of last endurance. Another thrust and she would die of it, she knew that. Yet they moved together in one fusion, drifted down the river, and came to the rapids. They lifted one long moment, and then Julian was flung upward by the very force of the explosion that seemed to shatter her. Her breath came shallowly and her hands clutched Charles hard.

"It's all right. Lie quietly." The gentle arms enfolded her, and his mouth touched her wet forehead where the curls clustered. She could hear his heart as it hammered, and the warm hands shook a little at the very power of what they had caused and experienced.

His voice came again from very far away as she felt him relax against her and flip a corner of the rich cloak over them both. Then there was no sound but the crackling of the fire as the delicious lassitude filled her veins and drew her down into sleep.

It might have been hours or minutes later that Julian woke to the sound of a door opening and of words being whispered in a soft voice. Some strange caution held her still. She opened her eyes slowly and saw that she lay alone before the now dying fire. Charles was standing at the door, clad only in a thin lawn shirt, a glass of wine in his hand.

". . . for the lady. She will be spending some little time here. You know the things to get."

The person on the other side of the door must have ventured some comment not to Charles's liking, for his voice rose a little, and she heard the next words clearly.

"Say that I retired to ponder the state of my soul. They will understand. I will be in touch when she palls." He laughed a short laugh and shut the door quietly.

Julian lay very still as the impact of all that she had heard washed over her. Did he deliberately plan to keep her here? Did she want to leave now that she knew the glories of the flesh? How could she judge?

He settled down beside her and kissed her eyelids as his hands went to her breasts, which already hungered again for his touch. Julian opened her eyes and stretched, smiling at him as she did so.

"It must be late, Charles. I must go back to court. No excuse will suffice for a long absence." She watched him from under long eyelashes that dipped as if in maidenly modesty.

"You do not wish to stay here? Have you not found pleasure in our joining?" The words were light, almost teasing, but he could not conceal the secretiveness in it.

Pleasure? Ah, God, such delight in the garden of the forbidden. Julian knew now why the priests railed so against the blandishments of the flesh. She hesitated, and Charles took her in his arms, his mouth drinking of hers, evoking her willing and eager response. The sweet fire between them had not been put out; indeed it but burned brighter.

He looked down at her with satisfaction. "You will linger here, then." It was not a question.

Until she palls. Julian heard the words again. Pride flamed high as she heard him a lifetime ago speaking of his betrothed even while admitting the power of the attraction that drew him and Julian together. She, daughter of the Redenters, mistress of Redeswan, would be no man's leman.

He cupped her face in one hand and laid the other on her pale breast where his lips had so lately tasted. She shivered as the warmth began to suffuse her. The pulse hammered in his own throat, and the chiseled face was brightened by that quirking half smile of his. She wavered, longing again to feel his hardness in her, to know the delight they could give each other. Together they could make up enough tales to make the court believe them; she had no doubt that gold would buy much silence, and who could prove later that Lady Redenter, faithful lady to the Queen's Majesty, was no virgin? Why could she not take this joy and be grateful for it?

Half persuaded, she put her arms around his shoulders, feeling the chill that shot over his skin at the barest touch from her. The firm muscles contracted as she, in her turn, pulled him closer. Surely this was a gift from the capricious gods of the Greeks, she thought, for who else could sing of such delights? Aye, she, the virgin, had been shown how passion could be by the man she might have loved had things been different. If their paths diverged as they must in the practical world, would she not have this to remember as she lay beside the suitable husband who would be chosen for her? Her flesh was her own; how could she bear another's touch after this?

"Julian, lady, I will show you such delights." His mouth took hers possessively as her fingers sought the curling hair at his nape.

She yielded for a moment, and then a small, stern face rose in front of her. Julian saw the glory that lit Mary Tudor from within as she laid herself bare for love of the deceiving king of Spain. She remembered Lady Gwendolyn, dying in savage pain, crying out to the husband that only she could see, whose memorial she had been, "None but you, Lionel, so did I swear it!" And now Charles, scheming and entrapping her, taking her though she herself had gloried in the taking. To this pass could love and passion bring you. Julian Redenter would be herself, inviolable. So her decision was taken.

CHAPTER SEVEN

Julian drifted her fingers around the side of his cheek and moved her head so that his lips touched her cheek. She shivered a little, and as she had hoped, Charles leaned away to look at her.

"You are cold, lady mine?" The deep voice held an undertone of a passion beginning to build all the more strongly for delay. The fire crackled and threw long shadows on the rich walls.

Julian said, "You will surely think me peasant, Charles, but I vow I am most terribly hungry. For something hot, that is. And I feel sticky. Would it be possible to fetch water for me?" A poor excuse, she thought, in view of all the pleasures they had had, that she could even think of anything so mundane as food. *He will think me addled.* She almost said the words out loud and caught herself just in time. "Humor me, I beg you." Her lashes drooped down again in what seemed a parody of modesty to her.

"For you, my dear, anything that you wish." He smiled

down at her with a look so intimate that her heart actually hurt. "We will take time for ourselves, will we not?"

Julian thought that she could not carry through with her scheme. How could they have shared that passion and not . . . ? She fought the thoughts back; her path was chosen. Here was no chivalrous lord of romance but rather a man of the world, accustomed to taking what he wanted and tossing the rest aside. She knew nothing of him but that bit of gossip and the way he had connived to have her. Did she use him ill? Even now she could turn back.

He was saying, "I'd best go myself and rouse the servants. I will not be gone long, Julian. Take wine and refresh yourself." He rose and began to dress sufficiently so that the rest of the household might not be shocked.

She had counted on this, for his tone had been so dismissing of the servant earlier that no one would be expecting any other instructions. If this were like other great houses, and there was no reason to suppose that it was not, he would be a good ten or fifteen minutes simply reaching the servants' quarters. They had not come that far from the street, and the passageway was emblazoned in her mind.

"Charles?" Her cry was suddenly frightened as she held out both hands to him.

He turned back to her, and behind the casual manner, the half smile, she saw the cynicism in his eyes. Just so had many women called to him, she knew. The expertise that had given her pleasure beyond the telling was well earned. He caught her up and kissed her lightly on the lips.

"Do not fret, sweeting, I will hasten. Pleasure delayed is pleasure doubled, or so they do say." The door banged behind him, and she heard his retreating footsteps.

Now there was no time for thought or regret. She tossed on shift and skirts, wrapped the torn gown around her and secured it with the cloth from her coif, which had been brought along after the skirmish in the streets. She thrust stockingless feet into the old shoes and pulled her cloak over her shoulders, then slipped into the quiet hall.

Every step that she took seemed to echo back as if a

giant clumped behind her. Even if she were discovered, he would do nothing but rebuke her, perhaps hold her prisoner for a time until, shaming words, she began "to pall." Still, Julian went cautiously along the narrow passage, took the turn she remembered, and saw the door at the end that led to the doubtful safety of the streets.

Suddenly she heard a muffled clatter and a bang as if someone had dropped something heavy, but there was no sign of a panel or any visible doorway along the wall here. She assumed that a room must be somewhere just beyond, possibly even the kitchens. That thought drove her to fright, and she rushed at the bolted door that had given way so easily to Charles's knocks.

Her small hands were strong, but the bolts did not give way easily although they had been freshly oiled. She heard the clattering sound again, and this time some ripe curses came clearly to her. She slammed again at the bolts and saw that they were beginning to move. With a strength she did not know she had, Julian threw them back just as a light began to shine at the far end of the passage.

She almost tumbled into the street and pushed the door shut. Moments later she was around the corner and scuttling rapidly down the lane, her heart hammering as though she had been battling for her life. The air was cool and bracing, the time something like midafternoon. Was it possible that she had been with Charles only a few hours? More like eternity, she sighed.

The passers-by paid no attention to her, but Julian pulled the cloak up and over her bright head and held it under her chin with one hand. She bent her legs and began to walk with a slump that might have come from years of carrying the burdens of the poor. Julian had learned much from her games with the village children and from listening to Elspeth's tales; the commissioners who came to investigate the family each year had more than a few times thought the daughter of the house to be "strange in the head" for the staring looks that she put on. She had been scolded for it, but the pretense had turned more than one inquiry.

The Thames was not far away, the smell of fish and

mud mingling with the freshness of impending rain. Charles's house would have fronted on the river, and now she must find some way to get out of the neighborhood in which he was likely to send pursuit, if he inclined to so lower his pride. She sped on, taking relief in the simple act of motion as she went toward St. Paul's.

Ordinarily she would have taken excited interest in the rushing life of the streets with processions, gawkers, beggars, merchants, booths, and shops of all descriptions, but now she was conscious only of the plan that had come to her in those moments of decision in Charles's arms. Once again the streets were wider, and she saw now that bands of soldiers walked along, their faces grim and set. One such band surrounded several prisoners whose hands were bound behind their backs; they looked so young that Julian was driven to pity for wondering what their crime might be.

It was with a towering sense of relief that Julian came at last to the hill and looked up at the cathedral, which seemed poised over the rest of the city in both warning and blessing. This was the landmark of London, a meeting and business place, gilded in beauty and crowned with worship. So Lady Gwendolyn had told her, and now her daughter would claim sanctuary there.

Julian was conscious of glowing tapers, a brilliance of colored glass, images of the saints, and drifting incense inside the great vault of the old cathedral. All the accouterments of what the last reign had called "Popery" had returned in full force with Mary Tudor, and Julian's eyes were assaulted and lured by the beauty before her. Tapestries, jeweled statues, rich vessels, velvet cushions, the lifted cry of the psalmist to his fierce God as worked in silks, a shining Book of Hours lying open on the seat into which she slipped; all these bemused Julian so that she let the cloak slip from her head as she looked about in awe.

The chapel at Redeswan had been partially restored after it became permissible to hear mass again, but much of it had been destroyed in the first savagery of revenge on the "traitor Redenter," as he had been styled by the furious Henry VIII. Julian heard the lilt of plainsong and understood the peace it could give. She sank to her knees, folded her hands, and looked up at the altar as she wondered how best to gain the attention of a priest without going to confession.

There was a murmur to the side of her just then, and she saw a cowled monk motioning to someone beyond her. She turned to look but saw no one. Her head swung back, and she saw that he was gesturing toward her head, that it should be covered in the gesture of respect. Quickly she rose and made her way toward him as she pushed the tumbled hair back from her suddenly flushed face.

"Father, I am in trouble and need of help."

"Cover yourself, daughter, and go on your knees not only for yourself but for us all. This has been a bitter day, and what are the troubles of one compared to the sufferings of Holy Mother Church?"

She could not see his face, but the set of his shoulders suggested age, and his voice was tremulous. "Good Father, I have come from pursuit in the city, even from attack by those angered against the queen. . . ."

"What is this? Surely there is respect in God's own house?" The newcomer was tall and spare, white hair crowning a vigorous face that was now showing anger in the light of the tapers. "I am Father Stephen. Woman, what need have you?" He looked into the strained face of the girl and waved the other priest aside as he drew her discreetly into a corner. Faded blue eyes questioned her.

"I serve the queen, Father, and when she went to perform an act of charity this morning, there were outcries against a group of us. We were dressed in old clothes, but they knew us for the court, nonetheless. I was in the end of our procession." She caught a quick breath and launched into the dangerous part of her tale. "Words were bandied about. I was frightened and became separated from everyone. I was chased by several men and my gown was torn, but I escaped safely and have been sitting in a cookshop whose mistress thought she was being kind to a waif. My few coins were lost, and I have just been in a haze of fear. . . ." She let her voice trail away. This man

was no secluded priest of the unworldly type. He seemed
to see through to her soul.

"And you are trying to get back to the queen's household, then?" He wasted no sympathy on her, nor did he
question her. There was a tenseness about him that went
beyond such small matters. "How do I know that you
speak the truth? Perhaps this is another scheme to torment
that most faithful daughter of the Church."

Here at least Julian could speak freely. "I was lately
summoned from the country to serve Her Majesty, and
she has my most faithful duty. I swear it."

He said, "They shouted against her in the streets and
maligned the king, her husband, crying out against the
fires that purge the heretics, shouting against the Queen's
Majesty herself. There was a pitched battle, a small one
that was quickly put down, but eloquent of the times. She
performed her errand of kindness but has retreated in pain
and grief. I think she will venture no more among her
people." His eyes flamed with a holy zeal. "This is an evil
age."

Julian breathed out in exasperation. Heaven deliver her
from all fanatics, be they Protestant or Catholic. "My
name is Julian Redenter, lady-in-waiting to Her Majesty. I
would not cause her further grief by vanishing or seeming
hurt. Will you help me?" This time her voice had the ring
of the aristocrat, and Father Stephen peered more closely
at her.

"There are those at Whitehall who will know you?"

There was a commotion at the back of the church just
then as several men strode in, not bothering to give rever-
ence due. Julian saw that one of them was Matthew, the
servant of Charles Varland. Another figure, taller and well
cloaked, with a hat pulled down to conceal his features,
stood apart. Julian would have known him in sackcloth or
shroud, so strongly did her blood leap. It was Charles himself.

Matthew walked purposefully toward her; the aureole of
bright hair and proud stance had easily marked her. Two
men followed him closely. Father Stephen moved back a
little and left her to face them. They came up fully to her,

and Matthew, the picture of concern and determination, put a hand on her arm.

"You must come back with us, lady. Your husband is most anxious about you when you have these spells. Come now, all is well at home. There is no need to run away, you know." He nodded to the men who advanced to her side.

Julian felt the blood rise to fever heat in her. She had not thought Charles would go to such lengths to have her back. Surely that meant that he regarded her as more than a casual plaything? She had only to go with them now, and in the space of half an hour they would be sitting over wine, savoring the growing hunger between them. It might be the only passion she would ever know. Julian struggled briefly with herself and knew that she could not yield herself in such a manner; she was as she was, her pride equal to that of any man and more than most.

She lifted both hands and crossed them on her breast, then shook the chestnut hair back so that her profile gleamed pure in the light of the tapers. Her voice rose deep and throbbing in the undertone of the chants to God that still moved through the air of the cathedral.

"Get you from me, evil one! You lie and I call on the power of the Virgin and all the saints to bear witness that I am none of yours. I swear it upon Her and the Queen's Majesty!"

Her eyes flicked back to see if Father Stephen was watching. He was, but his face was impassive, not a lash moving. Matthew was fully equal to Julian, for he dropped his hand from her and looked sorrowfully at her, his earnest face quivering.

"Now, now, the Virgin will tend you and the babe. Come with us quietly, for we disrupt this worthy place. You can come back tomorrow and pray here if you will just come with us now." He was all sweet reason and kindness to a demented woman.

Julian looked at the dark figure in the back. Charles had not moved, but she could believe that he was indeed the Dark Lord that he was called. Memory of his tenderness shook her, and she put it resolutely by. Father Stephen stirred at her back, but she dared not turn to look at him. In the far door she saw that a knot of people was gathering, and some of the religious of the cathedral had drifted nearer.

She spun around and knelt before the priest in the position of supplication, and her voice rose up again in the plaint of the lost and driven to whom the Church had ever offered succor. "I claim sanctuary, lord priest. I claim the right and mercy of the fugitive. I claim sanctuary." Her voice that had once held the lilt of "Greensleeves" now spoke the ancient litany of safety.

The thin hand fell softly on her bowed head as Father Stephen said, "It is your right, daughter, and not mine to grant. But you have claimed it and here we stand."

Julian let her breath go with a hiss of relief. The hand pressed firmly on her head so that she could not rise without being off balance. He said, "These are none of yours?"

"They are none of mine nor ever will be." It was as if she wrote the epitaph to passion's glory. "None of mine."

"Go, sirs, from this place. This matter will be sorted out, and you may explain yourselves on the morrow."

Another voice spoke into the stillness, a voice with the sound of the sea in it, a voice now gone hard and emotionless. "Have done. Have done." Charles, too, could speak the epitaph.

There was the tramp of feet, a brief silence, and then the surprisingly strong hand was lifted from her head and placed on her shoulder as Julian rose to face the clear eyes of the priest. She wanted to cry or run after Charles and say that it had all been a joke, a bit of teasing. Pain reached out for her, and she had a glimpse of what life would be like from now on.

"Thank you, Father." She hoped that she sounded sincere.

The blue eyes were scornful on hers. "You will do well in the court mumming, lady. Who am I to sit in judgment on you? You serve Her Majesty, and that must be sufficient; I can tell your sincerity there, and your eagerness to return does you credit. I have helped you for her blessed sake. Arrangements will be made to convey you to White-hall."

Julian bent her head, knowing that the course of her life was shaped by her actions this day and that she would never again be the same. She had chosen the path from the garden of the rose, and so it must be.

CHAPTER EIGHT

Julian lay back in the bed which seemed to get harder with each passing hour and twitched the coverlet toward her chin. The book of Roman exploits in Britain had not served to bore her into slumber, and she could no longer bear to glance at the chivalric romances she had once loved. Now she knew their bitter fruit.

"How terrified you must have been! How fortunate that the good priests brought you straight here in their own barge! Are you really better, Julian?" Blanche put aside the book of religious verse that she had been reading to Julian and regarded her with anxious eyes. "It is a pity that you have had to remain abed these past days, but just think—you have had the attentions of the queen's own physician."

"A great honor," Julian agreed. A great safety, too, for that gentleman had believed her tale of chills, a ringing in the ears, and a fever that came and went. It was not the season for plague, but one never knew. He had ordered rest and isolation. Blanche was the only friendly visitor. The queen's friend, old Lady Clarence, had viewed her from the door, remarked on the efficacy of prayer, then had gone away to make her report. "What news is there?"

"The king still presses for war against the French, but the queen and her advisors have not yet agreed. There are balls and masques every night, and the Spaniards are so courtly! One of them told me about war; he said the king only came back to get our support. Oh, it's so boring to talk about that when we ought to be out celebrating the May!"

Julian laughed, and the other girl joined in. Under their chatter of gowns and gentlemen, Julian wondered if she dared broach the subject of Charles Varland. She was passionately eager to know everything about him, yet she knew the gossip of the court. Her pretense of illness had shut her away, and though it had been her safety, she was weary of it now. Blanche's easy friendliness made her wonder at the caution she had learned from her youth.

There was a clatter at the door as the little maid, Nan, burst through it. Her face was so white, the freckles stood out in splotches. She tried to speak and could not, her hands twisted in the skirts of her gown, and her eyes were platters. Julian and Blanche stared at each other, then stiffened as a small figure came through the door and stood watching them.

"Your Majesty!" Blanche was a tumble of rose silk on the floor.

"Madam the Queen!" Julian tried to struggle out of bed, became tangled in the sheets, and could not move without making herself ludicrous.

Mary Tudor wore a simple green gown and coif. The morning light was not kind to her furrowed face and veined hands, but anyone would have known her for the queen. Two ladies were behind her, but she waved them away and fixed Julian with a penetrating eye.

"I trust you are recovering, Lady Redenter."

Julian whispered, "Aye, madam, I shall soon be able to resume my duties." Her mind raced as she tried to conceive of what enormity could have brought the queen of England to her bedside. "Indeed, I have much improved these past days."

Mary said, "My conscience has troubled me concerning you, Lady Redenter. I feel that I have not done my duty properly toward the daughter of one who gave my dear mother solace in her trials. You are a young, untutored girl, and my court is not the model I would wish it to be." The sandy brows drew together, and she regarded Julian so steadily that the girl felt she knew her secret. "I have addressed myself to the matter, however, and have determined that you shall wed."

Julian felt as if dealt a hammer blow. The queen seemed to take her surprise as her due and forged rapidly on. Blanche had risen from her curtsy and backed away respectfully.

"True happiness is found in marriage, for it is a reflection of God's relationship with his Church. Lady Julian Redenter, the husband I have chosen for you is of the North Country, one of those who, like your own family, held with me and mine in dangerous days. His grandmother was partly Spanish, and he still maintains ties with that dear land of my husband, with whom I have consulted. He will give you a steadying hand, and you will give him heirs."

Julian found her voice as she pushed back the bedclothes and swung herself to the side of the bed. She was thankful that she had earlier pulled on the blue bedgown to cover her nakedness. "The Queen does me great honor, far more than I deserve, yet I had not thought to wed so early."

"You are nineteen, girl, and ripe for it." The comment might have been made by Elspeth. "Lord George Attenwood is not yet fifty, his only daughter is a nun, he has no sons, and his lands are wide. He has been a widower these eight years. I have sent a message to him informing him of my decision and bidding him come to London." She smiled rustily at Julian, and the girl saw her delight in the matchmaking.

"Begging the Queen's pardon, I am grateful, but I do not wish to marry." Julian heard herself speak the words and could not believe that she had done so. Blanche paled, a red flush mounted in the queen's face, and even the little maid shuddered. Julian could not stop; the experience with Lord Varland had taught her to fear enslavement of the senses. Who could say that this Attenwood might not rule her flesh in the same way? She wanted tenderness and caring if ever she were to wed. "Ah, madam, I would not willingly give my body and myself into the keeping of another to use as he . . ."

Queen Mary bent toward her, and the sudden warmth of her smile made Julian's heart shake. "You are virgin and fearful. That is natural. I will caution Lord Attenwood well, for you are near and dear to me by virtue of your own sake as well as for your mother's." Her face clouded abruptly. "Many times I was told I would wed this one and that. Told that I would be given for policy's sake. I was willing—as a princess must be—but only in my later years did I come into my happiness. I want my ladies to be happy. Do not fear marriage, my dear."

She was oddly childlike, this woman who held all their lives in her hands and who could speak so yet order persecution and death. Julian said, "It is not that, madam. I do not want to wed—ever."

"You would be a holy nun?" The sandy eyebrows flew together. "Once I, too, thought that. You must search your heart. One or the other, certainly."

"But, madam . . ." Julian stared into the queen's eyes and read the dawn of anger there. She had to do something and quickly. She let her body go limp and slid in a heap at the queen's feet. Ignoble, perhaps, but she dared not provoke the Tudor rage that she knew from court stories lurked just beneath the surface. Now she began to breathe in shallow gasps as someone slipped a pillow under her head and began to fan her. The queen ordered that the physician be called; and moments later, she felt him touch her forehead and neck.

"She is still weak and must rest. There is no danger or cause for concern." Then she was lifted and placed in the bed. A pungent odor assailed her nostrils and she began to move cautiously.

Queen Mary spoke in measured tones. "Mistress Parker, you have been wanting to visit your family in Kent. Take

Julian with you, talk to her, speak to her of duty, of the need for one's life to be settled. Need I speak of your own interest in this matter?"

"No, madam. I understand." Blanche was subdued, her tone low.

"We will visit there on the royal hunt that His Majesty loves within the next fortnight. Her betrothed-to-be will be with us." She sighed heavily, then turned to Julian before leaving the bedchamber. "You are ungrateful, just as this country is ungrateful!"

After the door had been closed, Julian opened her eyes and looked at Blanche, who had been given a cup of wine for her. The girl's hand was shaking so that the liquid splashed on her gown.

"Julian, how dared you do that?"

"How dare she order my life?" She reached for the wine and drank deeply. "It is not fair. A fat old lord, coming to court once a year, demanding heirs, and forcing one's unwilling flesh! Why should I submit to being given as if I were a lap dog?" Julian realized how deeply she felt and wondered if Charles Varland had only been the culminating factor.

"You are exhausted. Soon you will regain your strength and, with it, wisdom. Julian, for all our sakes, walk carefully." Lighthearted Blanche looked at her friend as though she stood in the shadow of the block.

Julian put a hand to her head. She must walk alone and wait for some opportunity to present itself. Had she not ever done so? "The fever, it is returning, I fear."

"Kent will cure you; it is the loveliest part of England." Homesickness rang in her words, and Julian felt a sudden pang of longing for Redeswan.

Blanche had not exaggerated; spring and the May, together with warm red brick and rolling fields, pleached gardens, and eager welcome, made Wynoton a haven for Julian's spirit. Blanche's father, Sir Edward, seldom went to court, preferring to remain on the lands that had been his for generations. Her mother, Lady Sarah, was as gay and flighty as her daughter, but her young sister, Jane, was, at ten, as sober as if she were three times that. Thomas, the six-year-old heir, also had a stately manner.

"I wonder that you can bear to leave here." Julian and Blanche were sitting in the garden late one afternoon, watching the early roses blow against the low stone walls and laughing at the hound puppy's attempts to catch his tail. Julian's hair blew long and free over her shoulders, and her yellow silk gown was the color of the daffodils at her feet.

Blanche looked up at her friend. "The court is excitement, the very hub of the kingdom. I can always return here." Her glance went beyond Julian and the brown eyes flamed into brilliance as she recognized the approaching figure on the walk. "The neighbors know we are here."

The tall blond young man in his early twenties, Willian Parton, acknowledged the introduction to Julian almost absently, his eager gaze not leaving Blanche's vivid face. He offered his arm to both young women as they strolled, but Julian excused herself, knowing that they no longer saw her. Suddenly she passionately envied Blanche for this life and the love that was hers. Charles Varland's mocking gaze danced in front of her eyes, and she felt a stab of pain.

Restlessly she left the garden proper and drifted into the trees at the edge of the woods. The air was sweet and fresh, the shadows long at this time of day. At first she did not see the embracing couple standing under the spreading elm. When she did her embarrassment was acute.

"Your pardon, my lord, my lady. I was dreaming and did not look where I wandered."

The Parkers drew apart. Lady Sarah laughed, seeming as young as her daughter in the twilight. "My dear, we have not shocked you! It is the spring, I vow, that and my lord's bold words!" She shook out her skirts and touched a slender finger to Julian's cheek. "You are too serious, child. Stay with us and we will make you gay. I must hasten to view the dinner; the new cook is a terror!"

After she vanished down the path, Sir Edward sank down on a conveniently placed bench, stretching out one stiff leg before him. "Will you sit with me, Julian?" As she slipped into the space beside him, his smiling face grew grave. "Do you wonder at us, my dear?"

Julian answered with all her heart, "I am charmed, sir. Am I amiss in thinking that Blanche may soon be betrothed?" Might it not have been this way for her, too, in an English garden with her love nearby, if the fortunes of her family had been different?

"So we hope. Our lands march together, and it would be a good match. But tell me—would you say that my lady and I are happy, that we have a good life here?" The brown eyes, so like his daughter's but without their laughter, fixed themselves on her face.

Julian said, "Surely that is not to be commented upon by a stranger, sir." She saw small Thomas elude his nursemaid and dash behind a flowering bush to hide at the far end of the lane. A bird cried softly from the wood and was answered by another. Smoke curled up beyond the gracious house and drifted on the freshening breeze that was still cool for May.

"But I ask it, Lady Julian." There was the faintest hint of a command in his words.

"A good life, as you have said, Sir Edward. Rich in love and contentment and promise for the future." Julian felt the trickle of suspicion but tried to allay it with her truly felt words.

"Sarah was eighteen when I wed her. I was already in my forties, my wife and two sons died in the plague, and I went to foreign wars. I saw her first at the wedding, and she had fancied herself in love with another. Archbishop Cranmer kindly interested himself in my affairs, and so the match was made. Her father commanded and she obeyed. She wept often that first year, and I absented myself for very pain. Yet of it all came what you see now." He did not look his age as he gazed gravely at her. "The world is so arranged, the order of things set. From adherence to the rules comes happiness."

"That established order you admire burned your benefactor at the stake for heresy only last year, Sir Edward. Better to say that your happiness was a fluke of the capricious gods. I do not accept such credulous thoughts."

Julian started to rise and was halted by his firm hand on hers.

"You have had to fight for life and safety, I know that. Do not turn from the queen's will for you. What will you do if she turns you out?"

"Beg in the streets of London, my lord, rather than go supine to a fate of convenience!" She drew back and swept him a court curtsy. "If my lord will excuse me?"

Sir Edward sighed. "Bold words, my dear. Prepare yourself, for the royal party comes on the morrow and your betrothed with it."

Julian left him, walking swiftly down the smooth paths and past the flowering shrubs around the slender goddess with her perpetual horn, to nearly upset Thomas as he dug busily in a hole at the root of a tree.

"My lady! There is treasure here. You can find it if you dig by the light of the moon. It will be up soon, you know. Would you like to help me find it?" The round face set in straight brown hair regarded her earnestly.

Julian wanted to laugh and cry. All was illusion in this mad world. "Thank you, Thomas, but I must seek treasure of my own. Will you forgive me this once?"

His bow was his father's, grave and polite. "Aye, fair lady."

The child's accolade walked with her as she went to her room to scheme and try to blot Charles Varland from her dreams.

Wynoton had originally been built to house a large family; consequently each member of this one had privacy and to spare. Julian was now greatly thankful for this and that her own chamber overlooked the entrance to the park where the court party would come. She told the hovering maid that the fresh air had wearied her and that she would sleep long. Then she sat at the window and watched the moon rise over the moist green land. The little talisman of hawthorn, a tangible reminder of Elspeth and home, was clutched in one hand.

Suddenly, savagely, Julian was whispering, "What am I to do? I cannot have Charles, nor do I really want so cruel a lover." She forced herself to forget the tenderness in his touch, the melting warmth of the gray-green eyes, and to remember only the casualness with which he had spoken of her. "I will run away before my body is made a pawn. I will work in a cookshop, an inn. Gods, what am I to do?"

The impasse closed around her and boxed her in. Appeal to the queen would be useless; Julian herself had closed that door by her defiance. Philip had wanted her for a moment's dalliance, no more. The Parkers, however kind they had been, could not see the dilemma she faced. A woman alone in London would quickly suffer far greater indignity than an older husband. The moonlight shone pale in the garden and stretched long fingers over Julian's arms and face. The rose scents lifted to her nostrils, and far in the woods an owl hooted.

She lifted the hawthorn and invoked the image of the tree in full white bloom, shimmering in the moonlight. There was no conscious thought or plea in her mind, only a great longing to be free from this coil that pressed down upon her. Time seemed to bend forward as she saw herself, the young child wondering at Lady Gwendolyn's frenzy, later the girl explaining her education to the king's questioners, then recalling Elspeth's mutters in the kitchen as they rode away, herself before the possessed queen and then in Varland's arms. Was it fancy or dream that she saw herself on the crags of a seacoast, a ship riding to sea, flames behind her?

Sleepiness then hammered her down. She was so weary that she could barely walk to the bed that was spread out for her in the moonlight from another window. She fell across it as though bludgeoned, clothed as she was, unable to remove even her slippers. The rose scent deepened in the cool room as Julian turned on her back, already asleep, so that the white face was fully outlined in the light. The owl called again and was answered by another.

So vision and dream and desperation were welded into one.

CHAPTER NINE

The mare's hooves beat steadily on the woodland path only faintly illumed by the rising sun. Trees and vines stretched overhead in a green canopy as the birds in them shrilled a morning chorus. Julian held the reins lightly, feeling herself at one with her surroundings. The despondency of the past days was gone; she was light and free. She gave the mare her head and let her run; it was a relief to be active, for she had been so at Redeswan.

How easy it had been, after all, to slip into the old riding habit given her by Isabella while one was being made up for her and go out of that peaceful house to the stables where one of the few coins she had left assured the eager help and silence of the groom there. "A short ride only. I could not sleep and do not wish to rouse the family." The first slow walk and then the full gallop over the meadow and into the woods—the intoxication of it was delicious. She had no plan beyond simple escape for the day. Surely the queen's health would not permit her to take part in the lively hunt, not even to be with her adored husband would she risk losing an heir. Julian knew that she could face the risk of rudeness to her hosts; a sudden fever she would say. Who could disprove it?

She went on into the wood for the next hour, her mind drifting free, feeling strangely removed from her difficulties and from the ache of Charles. Her stomach began to growl with a hunger she had not felt for days despite the rich foods Lady Sarah had had prepared. It was far too early for berries, and she had brought no other money with her. Perhaps she could find a farmer and beg a bowl of milk if she went toward the road that must eventually lead into a village.

The sound of a far-off horn came to her ears just then, followed by the cries of hunters and dogs yelping in pursuit. She had come too close to the hunt and must reverse her path lest her way be blocked by the very thing she had come to avoid. She pushed her heels into the mare's flanks and turned off into an even narrower trail which forced them to a walk. The sounds faded behind her as she rode, and she mopped her wet brow with the sleeve of the brown habit.

The path curved upward, then down abruptly in an incline that was too steep for the mare. At the side of a ledge of rock was a shimmering pool, fed by a spring back in the cleft. There was a tiny edging of sand on one side; a few inches above it butterflies whirled in gold and purple madness. Julian dismounted in one movement and twisted the reins around a branch. Water might still the pangs for lack of food.

She drank swiftly and then lay back on the sand to let the warm sun beat down on her unprotected face. Once again she felt at one with her surroundings and remembered the exhaustion of the past night. Time drifted by as she thought that this was likely the peace before devastation. Something in her held back and waited. She dozed briefly.

"And what am I to do, wait until you deign to call? Let me come." The voice, soft and breathless, was oddly hard. "You know that I hunger . . ."

"No, there is discretion to be observed. You are foolish to think otherwise."

The second voice was hard in its turn but matter-of-fact. It pierced Julian's senses and almost made her sit up; only her innate caution bred of a hard school held her quiet. The sun burned on her lids, and she lifted them slightly without moving the rest of her body.

"You don't have to go yet. Why can't we stop here?" A gasp and a pause.

"That is why." The second voice now held leashed anger.

Julian could see them only hazily against the sun. Two men—one burly and tall, with sandy-colored hair, and lines grooving a long face, the other slender and blond with the quick movements of youth—stood on the bank above. Her senses were heightened from her encounter with Charles; she knew what she might not have otherwise known, that these two held intimacy beyond the ordinary.

The whisper again. "Has she seen? Gods, they are everywhere! I would like to . . ."

It faded before the older man's quick response. "Only a country wench asleep. No harm done. Come."

She strained her ears as she heard them move faintly into the bushes. The sense of being watched stayed with her, and she did not shift her position as she longed to do when she risked another quick look under her lashes. It was well that she did not, for the blond man had retreated only a few steps and was still watching, his face malevolent in the sun.

Julian thought herself a rational individual, all the more so for the emotional excesses of Lady Gwendolyn's latter days, but now she knew that evil was in this fair place, walking in the full sunlight. The hawthorn tree glimmered in her mind, behind it the altar of St. Paul's. Was she going mad? She fought for balance and somehow found it in her memory of Charles Varland's quirking mouth and brilliant eyes. She lay quietly.

The older man's voice was warm and caressing as he called, "Come now, the lodge is not far. Hurry."

The sense of evil retreated with their footsteps, but Julian forced herself to count slowly to one hundred before she stretched, yawned, and sat up, the picture of country laziness if anyone still watched. The mare still stood placidly, cropping the new grass. The slant of the sun showed that it must be well past noon. The scents of water and lush earth came to her as a bird burst into a stream of notes close by.

She jumped to her feet and ran up the incline, not even pausing to brush her gown when she tripped and fell to her knees. She knew only that she must leave this place as quickly as possible. She pushed the mare to speed when they burst out of the edges of the wood. They fled over the long golden meadows, around the crests of hills, through one copse after another, across a smooth road, and down almost to the curve of the river.

The high note of a horn brought her up short as she looked to her left. At the same moment a hunting party, brilliant in russet and gold, topped the nearest rise at her right. She swung her head and saw that there was no reasonable escape. The two groups were advancing on each other, and she could not doubt that this was the royal party itself. Several figures detached themselves and rode toward her, waving as they came. She had no choice but to remain where she was. This would be private parkland, and she could not risk flight; for that there would be no explanation.

"Who are you, madam, to ride alone within the bounds of the royal preserve?" The three men were middle-aged, bearded, a trifle weary. The one woman was much younger, blond and lively, with sparkling eyes and a sensual mouth. Julian recognized her instantly as Jane Dormer, favorite lady of the queen and betrothed of the Spaniard, De Feria. It was too much to hope that she herself would not be known to the lady.

Jane Dormer said in a dulcet voice, "Why, it is Lady Redenter, sent to the country to rest. I vow, you look quite . . . brisk." The white teeth shimmered in the light, and the men watched her covertly. "Well, ride along to the royal lodge with us. A lackey can be sent for your clothes."

Julian said, "The lodge?" She felt as blank as her words. "I rode out early and became lost. It is better that I return to Wynoton."

They were riding together now; the other parties had merged behind them, and she heard the laughter combined with snatches of song and cries of hunting exploits. The river glinted in the distance, and the massed trees rose up behind a long low building with four turrets. Barges were drawn up at the bank while figures moved back and forth from them.

"Well," Lady Dormer answered, "the Parkers and their household as well as other notables from the surrounding estates were summoned earlier to the feast in honor of the day's hunt at their Majesties' own lodge of Tevo. We will be glad to have you earlier."

Julian started to protest and, looking at the lady, knew herself fairly caught. Jane was the queen's own confidante, cautious and careful of her mistress, a dangerous enemy, friend to a select few. It would be useless to appeal to her, and Julian would not stoop to what was so clearly expected. The random thought brushed her mind that Jane was said to truly love the Spaniard. England and Spain seemed to have merged, she thought resentfully.

Now she said, "Then perhaps my gowns may be fetched. I cannot appear in this garb, and my face is burnished by the sun."

"We came by barge from London and are well equipped. You shall be prepared for the occasion in my own gowns. We are, I think, of a size."

Julian inclined her head. "You are too kind, madam."

The other girl began to laugh, the sound lifting on the wind as the others surged around them.

Venison and other delicacies were being prepared, tumblers and jugglers were everywhere, gallants bawled out war songs for their ladies, stories were exchanged, and dogs ran madly about. The sun was just setting when Julian made her way out into the courtyard and stood looking around her. The queen, it seemed, had come only to be with Philip and was resting long in her chambers. The members of the court who had come were mostly young and ready for the gaiety promised.

The rollicking music stirred Julian's blood, and her foot began to tap. Her moss green skirts billowed, the long lacy sleeves swaying in the freshening wind. Jane had gone to attend her mistress, but Julian had not been left unwatched; even now the tall maidservant stood near her. Petty it might be, but Julian had derived a goodly deal of satisfaction from the fact that Jane's dress had required special lacings before it fit her.

Wine was flowing now as she looked around for Blanche or Lady Sarah. Some of the men wore elegant little masks of black as they postured before a small group of ladies who fanned and laughed. Suddenly one of the gentlemen spun away in a quick movement and held out a gloved hand to Julian as he gestured toward some of the musicians. He did not remove the dark cap that covered his hair, and the mask slanted over his nose. She took time to think it strange, but by then he was whirling her in the rapid paces of the dance.

The others stood back to give them room at first, but as the music skirled more wildly, they joined in so that the entire courtyard was a mass of light and color. Julian was moved along so rapidly that she was hard put to keep her balance, and her partner put supple fingers on her waist. The touch was knowing and sure; even as she recoiled from it she knew that she could not escape. The light eyes of the king of Spain glittered into hers.

She could not have spoken even if the noise had permitted it; her tongue was frozen in her mouth. His lips under the jutting mask were curved in a set smile of amusement, but his eyes waited for her reaction. Julian forced her own lips into a polite court smile as she inclined her head in a gesture of obeisance. If the queen wanted her bound by honorable marriage, might not King Philip use that facade to pursue her all the more? Unwed girls were closely guarded; wives were another thing entirely, though all knew that the queen was naïve in such matters.

The dance required swift running steps which slowed and then quickened as the gentleman whirled his partner into one finale as the music drummed to a stop. Julian's feet and body kept perfect time. If she showed fear she would demean herself; this catlike man played with her as she had seen the barn cats deal with tiny mice. Her palms were damp and cool, but the night was warm. Her face felt as if it would crack with the smile that did not alter. Around them the courtiers spun and laughed, apparently oblivious to anything but the pleasure of the dance, yet she knew that tongues would wag later, and that this latest venture of the king's would be reported to the exhausted woman who even now lay in her room. Pity touched Julian, and her eyes softened so that her face seemed to bloom.

"Madam." Philip of Spain whirled her expertly, his eyes saying what his words did not as he swung her close, his mouth closing on hers in the ritual kiss that was in so many English dances. It should have been a light, glancing thing, a salute; instead it was a drawing, grasping hunger with a touch of mockery and laughter. Julian felt her mouth respond even as she went stiff.

"Madam," he repeated as he bowed before her in the final movement of the dance, "you are the spring's very self this night. I do not flatter myself that I have brought such brilliance to your face. Can it be that you already know the whereabouts of that one to whom you shall belong? That fortunate gentleman, but shall I say his name?"

She did not doubt that everyone knew who he was and that tongues were even now whispering their poison in the queen's ear. He led her circumspectly around the courtyard in the full blaze of the torches and the pale light of the rising moon.

Julian knew she must not provoke him.

"Your Majesty is pleased to compliment me. I thank you." She set her chin and let her eyes say what her mouth dared not.

"You English are so difficult, so hardy. In Spain these things are arranged with a flick of the hand." He was only a hairbreadth from voicing his demand, and Julian knew it.

She must save herself as best she could. Her eyelids drooped as if in modesty. By all the beloved saints, what was this that she seemed to stir desire in all the wrong people? Another woman might have been flattered, but she was coming to know that Charles Varland had laid his brand upon her and no other would suffice in this life.

Her voice rose slightly as she asked, "And is Your Majesty long for these shores? How goes the progress of the wars abroad? It is ever so exciting, and you honor me so greatly this night. All those years in the country and I never thought to dance with a king!" She gave a little laugh and swung her skirts as they walked. Several people close by pretended to ignore them, but she heard the muted laughter and saw the sly looks. She let her giggle lift again.

Philip glanced coldly around them, and his shoulders grew stiff. His gaze shifted to her, and she felt the anger behind the eye slits. She had been right, she thought with relief. Proud Spain could not endure the slightest touch of ridicule, could not stoop to a foolish country maid with her head turned. They were standing too long. The musicians were moving uneasily, and some of the courtiers were removing the masks that had been so amusing. Someone laughed uneasily and a dog began to bark.

The king of Spain lifted one gloved hand in a quick gesture. Immediately the rollicking music began again. Under the cover of it he said with easy malice, "Checkmate, Lady Redenter."

Since he was incognito in the manner of the court, she could not sweep the elaborate curtsy that she had been taught. The facade must be maintained. She answered, "May I bid you good evening, Your Majesty? I must pay your wife my respects." She certainly had no intention of going to the queen, who would likely only excoriate her, but it would free her from his baneful presence.

"Sir." The steady voice came from behind them, but she had heard no one approach.

"Ah, yes. You are both prompt and obedient. It is a virtue that must be encouraged in such times as these." Philip of Spain took Julian's elbow in his hard grasp and turned her to face the man directly in the light. "You may find her willful, but court beauties are often that if I remember my bachelor days. Lady Redenter, I present to you your betrothed, Lord George Attenwood, staunch supporter of our throne in the north country. Lord George, Lady Julian Redenter, one of the treasures of this court."

Julian caught her breath and felt the world slip awry. It did not take Philip of Spain's laughter to tell her how neatly she had been trapped. Truly, one did not refuse a king, even indirectly, with impunity. The queen believed all women should be wed, so she had consulted Philip, who had mentioned Lord Attenwood. Philip knew that many of the English nobility hated him, and he sought to ingratiate himself with them. That much was common gossip. But what did Julian Redenter have to do with affairs of state?

"My lord, Your Majesty." Her voice did not falter as she bent in the proper respect to her future husband, the man who had been with the younger blond one that afternoon and whose voice had throbbed with passion for him. Then she lifted her eyes to the knowing ones of Philip of Spain.

CHAPTER TEN

George Attenwood had eyes the color of slate set in a weatherbeaten face that showed few marks of the fifty years she knew him to be. His body was well set and firm, his forehead high and intelligent. He looked Julian up and down, not missing the sun flush on nose and brow. His straight mouth thinned a trifle, and his long fingers twisted together in a convulsive gesture instantly stilled.

He said, "With your permission, Majesty, may I walk with my lady?" The possessive word was not lost on either Julian or Philip.

The Spaniard smiled. "With our blessings." His glance flickered to Julian, and she saw the cruelty there. Then he pulled aside the mask, and they knelt as etiquette demanded. A tall man who had been hovering close by now came pushing his way through the courtiers who had moved nearer.

Attenwood took Julian's arm, his hand squeezing so tightly that, short of jerking free and causing a scene, she could only follow his rapid pace into the shadow of the wall where the torchlight cast a red glow on them both. The pulse in her throat began to throb at the glitter in his eyes, but she held her head high. He said, "I will be brief, madam. I trust that you have not become enchanted with court life, because when we are very shortly wed, we go to my estates in the North Country, where you will remain. The women of my house are secluded as is proper. In the meantime, remember that you will bear a noble name."

Julian said, "Is Your Lordship always so much to the point?" Antipathy clawed at her, but she forced her lips into a polite smile. "You overwhelm me, I vow."

"I think it is better that we understand each other from the outset, madam. Their Majesties have approved this match, our names are old, and your family has borne sons in the past. I need an heir, you protection. You will hold yourself in readiness for my commands."

Insufferable! Julian's pride flamed out, and she cried, "I do not wish this marriage and have not given my consent! Do not treat me as if I were your brood mare! When I wed, if I ever do, it will be to a man, not a . . ." She stopped in horror, both hands flying to her mouth.

Attenwood's face twisted into jagged fragments, and the red-tipped torch burned in his eyes as one hand lifted, almost casually, to the side of her face as if to catch at an errant curl. The pressure of those fingers and the burning sensation of his touch made her flesh crawl. Anyone looking at them now would see only a lover bending eagerly over his lady who, properly, was withdrawing a little.

"You understood what you saw this afternoon." His voice was perfectly level, conversational. "I knew I recognized you. My sight is very keen."

Julian had read with horror old chronicles from the Redenter library filled with the tales of those who loved the same sex. She had few illusions about the life she would lead with Attenwood. What of the boy who had looked at her with hatred? Would he not hate his master's wife? She could not marry this man!

"I understood, my lord. As you must understand now. Your life is your own; I will say nothing. But this marriage cannot be."

"On the contrary." Attenwood smiled in real amusement. "Nothing has changed. You stand there so boldly, a veritable Amazon or perhaps a guardian goddess, a picture straight from a tapestry, I warrant. Perhaps the getting of an heir will not be the task I dreaded. Prepare yourself to be Lady Attenwood, madam! And if you think to babble of my predilections, remember that your mother died raving. Mad women can easily be confined." He swung around, bowed, and strode away.

Julian cursed her foolish lapse into anger. Something told her that Attenwood was yet more perverse than his liking for young men. The latent cruelty that sometimes emerged in Philip of Spain was a light thing compared to what she felt festering in Attenwood. To whom could she turn? The queen would not believe her, she knew that; Julian had known the very real innocence of this woman she served.

Where was Blanche? There was no sign of the other girl, and the feast was waxing yet more merry. She supposed she need fear nothing more right now from either Attenwood or Philip, who had departed in the wake of the messenger. Suddenly she was so exhausted that she did not care about any of them. Not even the thought of Charles Varland could stir her just now. Among all the rooms in this lodge there must be someplace where she might rest and yet be safe. She began to make her way inside, hoping that she could find the rooms where she had changed clothes what seemed a full century ago. Jane Dormer would be with the queen, thus there would be a modicum of privacy. Merciful stupor was already clouding her mind; she welcomed it, for the rending experiences of the day were being shut away, granting surcease from what must be faced later and endured not only on the morrow but all the days of her life.

CHAPTER ELEVEN

"Wake up! Wake up! What is the matter with you, girl?"
The high voice penetrated the peaceful fog around Julian
and pulled at her, the urgency of the cry communicating
itself through layers of sleep. The hands on her shoulders
were hard and demanding.

"What is it?" The words lay heavy on her tongue as she
twisted around in the truckle bed and finally managed to
sit up. The face above her was vaguely familiar, one of
those she had seen around the queen in the first days at
court.

"Get up! We leave for London immediately. The queen
has been gone these several hours with those closest to her
and the king. Messages have come and the council is
meeting! Hurry!"

"What has happened?" Julian tried to regain her senses.

"Who knows? We but obey. Come as you are, there is
no time." She pulled at Julian again, and this time the girl
rose quickly, heart slamming against her ribs.

She was no wiser when they reached Greenwich Palace
hours later. Jane Dormer's green gown was all in disarray
from the journey by horse and barge. The other people
with whom she had come, lesser ladies, one or two somber
gentlemen, a gaggle of servants, none known to her, had
whispered among themselves a little and then remained
silent. She had made a comment or two and retreated, not
into the contemplation of her own difficulties—which
seemed too numerous for sanity—but into pleasure in the

warmth of the day and the flowering countryside, the
broad sweep of the Thames and the crowned sight of London. Just so had she had taken Redeswan to her heart
when life seemed unbearable in the long days of her
mother's dying.

Once inside the lovely, ornate palace that had seen so
many of the great happenings of this and previous reigns,
people clustered together in little groups to talk and speculate. Julian wondered again where Blanche was and what
her family would think. Tension balled high in her stomach as she found herself unable to do more than sip at the
ale which was passed by glum servants. The whole gay,
gossiping, intriguing court was paralyzed by this sudden
shift. Julian thought of the way the people had eyed them
sullenly from barge and high road, and she shivered. What
did all this mean?

"My lords and ladies, hear me." The chamberlain, clad
all in Tudor green and white, rapped for attention as he
stood, tall and spare, in the center of the winding stair-
case. The courtiers ceased their buzzing and eyed him
raptly. "Her Majesty the Queen bids me convey to you
that a message has been sent to the king of France advis-
ing him that a condition of war exists between our
countries. She bids you pray for the success of our arms
and those of imperial Spain."

There was thunderstruck silence for a long moment.
Julian felt her blood thrill in excitement that the expected
embroilment of England in the flaring wars of the Continent had come at last. Suddenly several young men near
her cried out, "God and Queen Mary for the right! Glory
to our arms!" The call rang out and was raised to the raf-
ters as the mercurial court gave release to the fear that
had plagued it. The older men whispered in the shadows
of a tapestry, and Julian caught sight of their faces; both
were anguished and hard. Tears ran down the cheeks of
one of the maids who clasped the hands of her young
mistress in similar distress. "God and Queen Mary! For
King Philip!" It rose over all, and Julian was suddenly agonized at the thought of death on far battlefields and of all

those who must die. England had stood inviolate for years. What would this mean?

She had to escape. This was her first time in the palace that was one of the favorites of the queen, and she had no idea where the ladies-in-waiting were housed or if she had clothes there. It did not matter; she slipped away and walked blindly down the long corridors, away from the noise and rejoicing. Whatever war meant, it could not affect the plans that George Attenwood had for making her his wife. He was certainly too old to fight.

She put one foot in front of the other aimlessly, observing that the walls grew richer in hangings, the occasional furnishings more valuable. This must be the way to the more important lodgings of the queen. She reached the end of a passage and saw that a small garden glimmered in the sunlight beyond the door. Perhaps a maidservant or lady would be there, and she could ask directions. A tall chair stood just inside the little room that gave onto the garden proper, and a silk-covered volume rested on the seat. Ever curious about the printed word, Julian bent to take it up.

Her fingers brushed against what appeared to be a loosened page, and she felt her stomach contract that the beautiful thing might be inadvertently damaged. It was, she saw, a Spanish work having to do with religion and the punishment of the various degrees of heresy. Carefully she turned to the page and saw it for what it was, a crude drawing done by a master hand.

The old woman wore a crown tipped with flames, and she laughed horribly as she held a man marked with the pomegranate of Spain to her bosom. One hand beckoned others decked with the Hapsburg eagle. Jewels were piled to one side of her, apparently to be given as largesse. Wide bare feet trampled on the Englishmen who lay bound at them. Flaming stakes bordered the edges of the paper. "The unrighteous whore who suckles Spain and destroys England must be dealt with." The searing words were set out in faultless Latin and English by a clerkly hand that knew how to shape the vileness of them.

Julian sent the thing from her in one quick motion. The

virulent hatred it represented frightened her just as much as the streets had done when they were filled with silent, staring people or with shouting, angry ones. This was the very heart of the court, close to the queen's own chambers. She, Julian, had sworn her loyalty, but what of all those who could not agree or obey the changes in religious persuasion and yet were loyal subjects of the Tudor queen?

There was a cautious movement from behind one of the hangings just then, and Julian drew back instinctively. The woman who stepped into view held several innocent appearing pages in one hand, but Julian saw that they bore a resemblance to the sheet she had just thrown down. She stared at the newcomer for a long second, then Isabella Acton's face turned a delicate pink as she recovered her aplomb.

"Lady Redenter, what do you here? I assume that you are looking for the apartments of the ladies-in-waiting. Come, I will show you where they are." She kept her eyes from the page that now lay on the floor.

"Where am I now?" Julian edged closer to her. "What is it you have there?"

Isabella snapped, "You are rude, insufferably so. Your manners want teaching."

Julian snatched at the pages then, and Isabella, unprepared, was too slow to pull them free. They tumbled to the floor, and the likenesses of the queen stared foully up at the women. Isabella's face changed as her lips drew back over white teeth and one hand went swiftly to the pouch at her waist.

Julian caught her wrist and held it in the grip that she had learned from the village boys at Redeswan. "And your loyalty wants evaluating, Lady Acton! Will you tell me why you spread these revolting things about? Are you not the queen's dear friend?"

Isabella lifted a sharp gaze to Julian's honestly puzzled face. "What do you intend to do about your discovery? Let me tell you—before you rush away to summon the guards—that other lives besides my own are in peril, English lives. Are you so enamored of the king's advances that you will place us all in peril?"

"I find his glance and touch loathsome, madam!" Julian spoke the words so fervently that some of the color returned to Isabella's face. "I care nothing for the struggles and policies of the court nor, indeed, who rules so long as I and those close to me are left in peace. It has been so under Queen Mary, and for that I am grateful. She has restored dignity to me and mine."

"And plunges us into war! Dotes on her Spanish husband to the ruination of this land! Destroys and maims her people. Returns to a religion which is no religion!" Isabella's voice was shrill, her manner no longer cool but urgent.

Julian took her chance boldly. "I take it that you value this cause of yours, Isabella. And your own life. There can certainly be no illusion about the fate of traitors, and I think that you are that. What are you trying to do?"

"The queen will not be harmed, only brought to see the will of her people!"

"She still values your opinion highly. What will you give me to maintain my silence?" Julian hoped that she sounded greedy. "Keep your plots, Isabella Acton; I care not. But I think that you greatly care about this scheme of yours."

Contempt flared in Isabella's beautiful eyes, but her hands were steady as she clasped them in front of her. "Money, jewels, a younger husband than the one chosen for you? What will insure your silence?"

There was a burst of conversation in the corridor and a man's laughter as footsteps came toward the anteroom. Isabella went white all over again, for the incriminating papers were spread all over the floor, and one glance would suffice to tell what they were. Julian did not doubt that there were others who placed these things all over the palace.

"I do not wish to wed Lord Attenwood. He revolts me. Truth to tell, I want no man as yet. The idea of the marriage must have come from the king, but surely war will occupy his mind now. He may even leave England. Speak to the queen, turn her mind from this for any reason that will suffice insofar that I remain at court, and I will say nothing of this."

"You think to lure Lord Varland!" It was a hiss of pure rage.

"I care nothing for your popinjay lover, Isabella. Take your choice now." Julian grated the words out, not knowing that her cheeks were flags of color in the dead white of her face and her eyes blue flames.

"I will do as you demand." The agreement was reluctant but there.

"Swear it. Swear it by your Protestant faith." Julian knew she had the mark there. Heresy meant the flames if proven.

"I swear by the true faith." Isabella's face lit up with fervency.

Julian swooped to the floor and began to gather the papers, and Isabella joined her in the quick action. As the little knot of men went by, one pausing to look longingly at the garden where the flowers were fully in bloom, they saw only two girls engaged in gathering up some blown materials and patting their gowns into place.

He called, "Best to take yourselves into the air, ladies. 'Tis no day to be indoors as we must be."

"Aye, sir. We do just that." Julian let her voice lag as if duty held her. They passed on, followed by several guards of the queen's household who seemed to attest to their importance.

Julian said, "Another thing. Lord Attenwood spoke of almost immediate marriage. That course must be deflected soon. Within the next several days. You see, Isabella, my silence is cheaply bought. I want only my freedom."

Isabella Acton stowed the offending papers in the billowing sleeve of her gown and started toward the garden, Julian at her heels. "I have given my promise, and it will be done. The queen heeds me in much, that is true."

The sky was cloudless overhead as they emerged into the summer day. Pink and white flowers danced in one corner of the small garden, and a trill of birdsong lifted up. Julian breathed deeply and felt the heaviness lift from her spirit for the first time in many days. She asked, "What has turned you against Queen Mary? She plainly loves you, did she not say so?"

Isabella's look held contempt again. "My husband supported her for the throne and died for her in Wyatt's rebellion. I lost our child in the agony of it. She is obdurate and will yield nothing. There is no tolerance in her. It does not matter that many of her subjects grew up away from the Catholic faith as she knows it. They will still die unless her will prevails. My husband, my Thomas, believed in her right to rule and died for it; he did not believe she should order the souls of her people. Sooner or later he would have died a traitor's death. It was then that I vowed to fight this tyranny. There are others, and we fight in whatever way we can."

Julian sighed, remembering her childhood and youth, the promise she had given to the queen. "For all their sakes, keep your word. I shall expect to hear that Lord Attenwood's attentions are elsewhere."

"You shall be free. Do not belabor it. Do you care for nothing except yourself, Lady Redenter?"

"Nothing, as you shall find to your cost if you betray me." Julian made her face hard and cold. She wanted to add wildly that she was pushed into corners and had to fight as best she could with whatever weapons that came to her, that the queen had rescued her and given her hope, that she had sworn an oath to the woman who had led so bitter a life, that Isabella did not fight alone as she, Julian, must do. But she could not; she could only stare at her enemy and hope that this opportunity would free her. The future must take care of itself, for now Julian could see only one day at a time.

"My first assessment of your character was not amiss, I see." Isabella had recovered her nerve now, and her nostrils twitched with distaste. "See that you, too, hold your silence."

"As the grave, lady, as the grave." Julian spoke briskly, as if the matter were receding from the forefront of her mind.

"Aye, even so." Isabella walked swiftly across the grass and vanished in the doorway.

Julian had won her victory, and strangely, she wanted to weep for the loss of honor.

CHAPTER TWELVE

The king and queen were much in evidence in the next few days as they moved about the court. He had eyes only for his wife, and she shone in brilliance for him, the years fading before the joy of a pleased husband. The ladies-in-waiting were sent away though he occupied her time as much with battle plans as with love, said the court wits in safety of their respective circles. Time passed agreeably with mummings, small hunts and hawking parties, flirtations, discussions of battle strategy among the men and gasps of admiration from the women.

Julian spent much of her time in Blanche's company, for the other girl had returned the morning after the incident with Isabella. William Parton was pressing his suit and she was hesitating, excited by the renewed liveliness of court life and not yet ready to retire to the quiet country. The story that Julian told of being lost was accepted without question, especially in the light of the declaration of war and the fact that on the very night of the hunt party, news had come to the queen that an uprising, backed with French support, had occurred in the North Country. Philip was waging war on the Continent, and England's support was desperately needed.

"Father explained all that over and over. All I did was

ask if William might have to go." Blanche sighed as they looked at gowns in her rooms. "How dull it will be here if the men go. What of your own betrothed, Julian? I saw him that night. He seems very well set up. Older, of course, but then you act much older than you really are."

Julian turned off the query with a laugh and went to walk in the Long Gallery. Blanche was dear and uncomplicated, but she longed for someone to whom she could talk freely. She dreamed of Charles Varland often now, not in the passionate fury that had been between them but in the brief aching tenderness they had shared. What would it be to love truly and without fear?

"Madam!" The hard voice sent chills along her spine, and she whirled around to see George Attenwood, clad in brown velvet and fur, a great sword at his waist, walking toward her. A priest and several men waited a short distance away.

"What is it, Lord Attenwood? I thought I had made myself quite plain when we last met." She had nothing to gain by rudeness, but the man must be discouraged.

He faced her now, and she saw the leashed anger in him. "Our personal business must wait, Lady Redenter. The queen is sending me back into the north as her personal representative to investigate and deal with this uprising; pockets of it may still exist, and I am given full power to harry with fire and sword."

He would enjoy that, Julian thought. "You leave now?"

The thin lips moved in semblance of a smile. "Aye. I have expressed myself most pleased with you in the presence of Their Majesties. The wedding is being planned, and you will remain in attendance on the queen until I return. Try not to weep at this necessary postponement."

"Why me? Surely you can get an heir from one who is willing?" Julian asked the question in honest bewilderment as she tried to fight back the distaste for him that must show in her face.

"You will be willing, my dear. It is the process of bringing you to that willingness that renders the spice." He lifted her hand to his lips, and his tongue traced a pattern on her open palm. The slate eyes met her aquamarine ones, and Julian saw anticipation there.

"My lord, we must hasten." The priest was walking forward, apparently he was to travel with them.

Julian pulled away and lifted her white face to him. "Holy Church protect us all from evil." The shaking voice caused them to look at her, and she caught the brief suspicion in Attenwood's glance before he bowed punctiliously.

"Hold that in your mind until we meet again, lady mine." Only she could hear the derision in his voice.

The priest said, "Pray for us all, dear child. Our cause is just."

"I shall go to the chapel now." She turned as if she could not bear to watch them go, then walked on shaking legs in that general direction while they went from her. *Curse him. Curse him.* The words rang in her mind as she moved, and a thought began to take shape. There was but one path of safety now, and right gladly would she take it.

She felt the need for action. It would be a blessing to ride out in the park, but that would entail a change of clothes, grooms, servants, and explanations. A long brisk walk by the river on the far side of the grounds would clear her head and give vent to the emotions that she did not dare release openly.

Her brown velvet gown was too warm for the pace she took, but it did not matter. The path where she walked had not been fully cleared as yet by those who kept the palace grounds, and new growth rioted everywhere in tangled blossoms and dropping feathery branches. Ferns swayed in the warm wind that dimpled the water of the Thames. She paused to pick a flower from one of the bushes and held the golden blossom to her nostrils for a heady breath. As she did so, she caught a glimpse of the figure standing under the concealing branches of a tree close to the path and only a few yards from her. Something about the stillness of it held her back.

"Julian Redenter?" The question was low-pitched, and instinctively she moved a little closer. He moved out then, a short square man with a nondescript face and powerful body. "Lady Julian?"

A messenger? But she had not known that she would walk here. "Yes, what is it? I am Julian Redenter."

He seemed to slide over the space between them. She caught her skirts in both hands so that she might run, for fear had begun to swell in her mind. Rape—and by a peasant! Then he had her in both hands and was pulling her back under the tree, one hand over her mouth. She bit down with all her strength, but it did no good; the skin was hard as horn. He was chortling happily to himself, and she realized with panic that her struggles amused him.

It was not to be rape, it seemed, for he was squeezing her throat, ignoring her twistings and thrashings. Thought was blurring for Julian when he lifted the fingers from her neck long enough for her to get a gulp of air and spoke to her in a hard guttural voice.

"Drowned because your lover couldn't marry you, that's it. I waited—they said you'd come out soon enough, and here you are. Can't touch, just drown you—what a waste! They said you'd know why this was being done. By the time your body comes up none of it will matter."

The inexorable fingers closed on her throat, but the brief respite had enabled her to raise her hand to his face. She brought the fingernails down the length of it with all the power that fear for her life could bring. He cursed savagely but held on to her. The world tilted, and he released her mouth to wipe the blood that she felt on her fingers. There was no power in her to scream; all she could do was flail with her body and arms. Death was very close and she knew it.

The thought drove her to a final act that did not take conscious thought. With the last of her strength she drove her fingers into the hollow of his throat in a trick she had seen fighters in the village do. He gagged but held on and began to pull her along as he moved toward the river. Darkness enveloped her as sounds faded away. Then she was thrown back onto her side, gasping and gagging in the river mud while growls and cries forced themselves into her consciousness. There was a final curse, a rattle of metal, something sharp digging at her, then a great splash. Hands were on her face now, and she opened her eyes.

The dark face of Charles Varland stared down at her, and directly behind him was a huge gray dog, its mouth bloody. Heaven or hell, how did he come to be there? But what did it matter so long as he was there? She opened her mouth to tell him, but nothing would come out except a tiny mewling sound.

His face twisted and he drew her to him, cradling her as the tears began. Her arms went around him, and they held each other close, her name a litany in his voice, a tenderness she had never thought to hear from the arrogant lord.

They stayed that way for a time until Julian's shivers began to slow and the reality of his warm body, smelling of sun and leather, the strength of his powerful arms, the dark curls fanning against her cheek, overcame the nightmare of the past minutes. She stirred tentatively, and he rose to carry her back in the depths of the greenwood where a shield of greenery hid them completely. He lowered her into a small cleft in the ground where ferns made a nest and then stood away to look at her.

"You are all right, Julian? What madness is it to walk alone this way with times as they are? You could have been killed."

She tried to speak and found that she could only muster a hoarse whisper. Her throat felt on fire. "Where is he?"

"In the river with his throat torn out. He jumped at the last minute trying to get away from Osiris here." The dog whined at the mention of its name, and Charles dropped a caressing hand to the smooth head. "Probably some lout thinking he could get away with several robberies or worse around the grounds here. You are fortunate that I happened to be giving Osiris exercise; few people come along here." He bent to look at the bruises on her throat, touching them with an exploratory finger. "You will need to wear jewels or scarves for a while. You are not otherwise injured? He did not . . ."

"No. He meant to kill me. It was deliberate. He was waiting for me and said I would know why." She had begun to shake again, the wet skirts and bodice of her gown making her chilled even in the warmth.

Charles shook his head. "I don't wonder that you are

upset. Most women would still be shrieking with terror. But who would want to kill you? Julian, lady, this is a terrible thing, but it is all over."

"It was deliberate." Julian knew that she would walk in fear through the days and lie awake in the nights waiting for the terror to come again. She could expose Isabella and her friends—she was both dangerous and expendable.

Charles saw her face go even whiter as the pupils of her eyes dilated and the hollows under her high cheekbones grew deeper. Her hands clutched convulsively, and her whole body went stiff. He sank down beside her and began to kiss her face, her fingers, her bruised neck, while his hands rubbed warmth into her chilled flesh. "You must get out of that gown." He picked up a small flask from the ground where it lay with his cloak and held it to her lips. She turned her head away but he forced it on her, lifting her hands so that they closed around the sides. Then he began to work on the laces of her gown.

Julian drank deeply and saw the shapes around her grow more distinct. She felt the sun penetrate the fearful cold that engulfed her, the warmth of the dog as he settled at her side. The weight of the velvet gown was removed from her unresisting body and spread in the sun to dry. Then Charles rubbed her partially wet hair with one corner of his cloak, paying no heed to the great stains left on the soft fabric.

"It is so cold, Charles. Cold as the grave. Is it punishment, do you think? What else could I do? She meant to have me killed." Over and over the words repeated themselves as the aquamarine eyes stared beyond him.

"Julian. It is all right. I am here." When she made no response, Charles set his mouth on hers, kissing her long and deeply, moving his long fingers over the swell of her breasts and onto the smooth bare arms. He trailed kisses over her face and murmured endearments. Then he drew the slender body to his own and held it the length of his so that every part of them touched while his mouth drew tenderly on hers.

Julian was wrapped and laved in warmth as she opened her eyes and looked into the green-gray ones so close to hers. They held only answering warmth and caring, his mouth and hands spoke of the same, and her own mouth softened under his. Her breasts felt as if they would burst free from the thin shift and bodice. Her blood, so nearly frozen, began to move freely, hotly, in her veins once more. She lifted her arms and touched the powerful shoulders, the pulsing muscles of his brown neck. He kissed the corner of her mouth and made as if to hold her while they rested.

"Charles. Charles. Dear Charles." Her voice was clearer now, devoid of nightmare.

"You are sure? I do not want to hurt you." His touch was a drifting feather, a cloud, a rose petal on her skin.

"I am sure." Her eyes shone into his.

Then the greenwood faded for Julian as he gathered her to him, and their bodies met in the very restoration of life itself. This was gentleness and cherishing, flame running liquid under her skin, a yearning that built and grew until it encompassed all things. His fingers played in the soft curls of her hair, went along her chin, cupped her face for a moment, and went to the tumescence of her nipples as she murmured in the transport of pleasure.

Then they lay naked together in the ferns while the soft winds blew over them, the dog Osiris standing watch. Julian sought his mouth in her turn, letting the urgency of her lips and hands speak of her hunger. His back and thighs were muscular, very firm as her hands slipped over them and rose again to touch his manhood, which was ready for her. Charles watched her intently as she touched him and withdrew, the chestnut hair falling over her face in the light.

"Lady mine, come." The words might have been blown on the breeze that brought the scent of flowering trees to them.

"Aye, my dear lord."

The long sweetness began once more, stretching to infinity as he moved gently into her, thrusting and moving with the rhythm of her. His mouth drank of hers, and her arms held him closer still. He grew in her so that it seemed she would split with the force of him. She expanded and drew him deeper in a mingling of rich juices. Their tongues thrust and played, then locked together. She was flaming, rising, tearing, and convulsing, that strange yearning melting into light. They soared, swung on the winds of heaven, rose and fell into the shattering glory that was all the richer for agony shared and postponed. She felt him move in her and remain as he positioned her so that they still locked together. The force of the release drew her down into the whirlpool of sleep, her last sight that of the carved face tender above her own.

When Julian awoke she saw that he was fully dressed in sober green wool, the kind any merchant might wear, and sitting a little apart from her as he rubbed Osiris's big head, seemingly deep in somber thought. His cloak was over her, and the brown dress hung on a branch so that the wind might more easily reach it. He turned his head and saw her watching him. Instantly his expression grew completely impassive.

"Have I slept long?" She had to say something to break the stretching silence.

"An hour or so. You were exhausted. Your gown will soon be dry, and I will see that you reach the palace without being noticed. A word in the ears of the guards who patrol these grounds will make sure that women can walk safely here once more; they have been too lax of late. It would start gossip if you speak of this, I think."

"You are right. My maid is discreet and will say nothing when she tends me." Julian looked at him, remote and strange, not the man who had lifted her to the heights and shown her the tenderness of which he was capable. She certainly had reason for discretion and should be grateful that he wished for it also. Had he not saved her life? "Charles, I owe you gratitude beyond the telling. What can I say?"

Charles Varland stood up and began to pace, the dog at his heels. His voice was curiously muffled. "Julian, I did not mean for this to happen. I wanted to comfort you and bring you back to the world of the living. The passion that is between us helped your anguish; that is my only excuse. I would not willingly involve you in the maze and the contradictions that my life has been. You will be safe from me in the future, I promise you that. I have some self-control, after all."

Julian had been in pain often enough to recognize it even in the mask of courteous remoteness that he strove to show now. "I wanted it, too, Charles. Please believe that. You have no cause to reproach yourself on my account." Her heart lifted. At least the mockery of their previous meetings was no longer between them.

He whirled around and she saw that he fought for control. "No cause! If you but knew!" Then the cool mask fell and he was himself again. "I have been laggard. There are responsibilities that I must attend to." He spoke as if to himself, his gaze far-seeing.

"Do you go to war?" She began to fumble for her clothes.

"War?" His glance focused on her, but she would have sworn that he did not see her. "That is one way to put it. There are many kinds of war, are there not?" Osiris whined and the sound seemed to return him from his contemplation. "Julian, you are no longer thinking that this was a plan to kill you? You were taken with the fright of the moment. I should not like to think of you in fear of shadows."

She stood up, the cloak concealing her slender ripeness. Julian Redenter, too, had her pride. He must not see that she longed to throw herself into his arms. As always, she must walk her own pathway. "I do not fear the shadows, Lord Varland, for I have been among them all my life and am not yet overcome."

He gave her a faint smile. "I will walk by the river while you dress. Osiris shall remain with you. Call when you are ready."

Julian looked at the dark face, the bold nose and arching brows, the faint lines under his eyes, and knew that he, no less than she, bore the marks and scars of passion's consuming flame.

CHAPTER THIRTEEN

The step was stealthy and gliding in the warm dark as the shadow seemed to detach itself from the wall and move toward the bed. Julian flung herself upright, her hands grasping for the little dagger that she always carried now. Her body was tense but shivering with expectation. She had been so near sleep that she could not distinguish dream and reality.

"What do you want?" She heard her own voice rise harsh and dangerous even as she drew her legs under her in preparation for defense. "Who are you?"

"Mistress! Mistress! It's Nan. You've been riding the nightmare again. I heard you groaning and came to see if I could help you; I was sleeping right where you told me to, just there at the door." The little maid's face was twisted with the nightly concern for her mistress, her eyes wide with apprehension. "Are you all right, Lady Julian? The guard is not far away, you need not fear."

Julian wanted to laugh but knew that if she did it would bring on the tears that had pressed upon her since the attempt on her life almost a week ago. A week filled with daily watchfulness, covert contemplation of Isabella's smooth, pale face, mingling with ladies and courtiers, never in the solitude she had come to crave. A week of fitful slumber, night horrors, and waking shrieks; a bane of some sort, she had told Nan when asking her to sleep in the chamber with her, and not worth disturbing others at this tense time. "It will pass soon," she had said, knowing that her fear looked out of her eyes and communicated itself to the impressionable maid.

"I am sorry, Nan. The same thing, you know. Let's try to rest again." Julian knew that she would not sleep, but she must go through the motions.

"Aye, madam." Nan continued to stare at her mistress even after returning to her pallet across the floor. She lit a candle and the guttering light made the shadows even more evident in the chamber, showing the stoutly bolted door and tiny, high window.

What tales would she spread among the other servants for all that Julian had cautioned her to silence? Julian sighed and tried to dismiss the matter that hammered at her vitals. She knew that her life was sought and that only by constant guard could she save it, but she had walked that path before as had all at Redeswan. No, the true pain was that Lord Varland had not come near her in the past days, nor had she seen him about the court as she did her duties by rote. They had shared so much together, and yet he had escorted her back to the edge of the palace grounds, in circumspect silence, careful that none should see them and further smirch her reputation, bowed politely, and left her, adjuring her once more not to venture out as she had done. Surely he could have inquired after her, spoken to her, been in the same world with her.

Julian fought back the fantasies that came unbidden even as she knew them to be the only antidote to the sick fear that plagued her. She, supple in his arms, drinking of his mouth, delighting in the thrust of his spear that impaled her again and again. He, bold and impatient, bending before the passion that took them both. They, together in the dear aftermath of love, held in the bonds so willingly taken, bodies one flesh. "Never, never. It will never be so for us." Tears trickled out her tightly closed lids even as she called herself fool, weeping for a man who must hold her so light once she had yielded to his first touch. She looked for anger to strengthen her and found only pain.

At midmorning of the next day Julian sat under a flowering bush with the obligatory needlework and savored the peace of the bright day. The river sparkled in the sun that gleamed off the surfaces of the green leaves and was reflected on the climbing roses of the bower. Lady Clarence frankly dozed in her seat, and the other two older ladies-in-waiting compared stitches and yawned. Gay groups of courtiers strolled up and down the garden paths, and snatches of laughter and song came to Julian's ears and rose with the birdsong just above her head. She was not sorry that Lady Clarence had instructed her to remain with them, though some of the younger ladies regarded it as a penance. Here her turbulent spirit could find surcease, she thought, knowing that her eyes still looked for Charles Varland though her head was decorously bent.

She heard the murmurs of respect, the assured steps, and the low commanding voices in one breath, and then they were before her little group, the sovereigns of England, arm-in-arm as any man and maid might walk. Philip was smooth and sleek, the little lines of discontent gone from his eyes, his heavy mouth curving up. A man satisfied, Julian's mind whispered coldly, as she started to kneel with the others only to be caught up by the queen's husky voice.

"No ceremony, ladies. We but walk in our gardens as other folk do. Parting is so soon, too soon. Sit you back now." Her eyes drifted over them, unseeing. Julian knew that she saw only Philip, who would soon leave her bereft. The sun etched the lines in the worn face and neck, brought into relief the harsh veins on her hands. The deep rose gown could not hide the ravages of age and tears. Once again Julian saw the face of Lady Gwendolyn, and she ached for this woman, queen or no, who loved as her mother had.

Quickly Julian lowered her own gaze but not before the amused laughter came into Philip's face. She had been caught pitying the queen! Pray God others had not seen. She began to fuss with her skirts and reach for her needlework, but the smooth words pierced her so that she stood irresolute.

"Look, madam, who comes yonder but Lord Varland!" Philip spoke to his queen, but the light gaze flickered from her to Julian and back again.

Julian felt the upswing of emotion that seemed to blot out the rest of the world as she looked at the tall, lithe figure in green and silver coming slowly toward them. Her ears rang, the blood ran hot in her veins, she felt set apart and yet more alive than she had ever been. She could not think, she could only feel.

"Ho, Charles, I had begun to think that you would not return before my sailing date! To refuse my commission and then not bid me farewell—that would have been gross insult to your king and pain to your friend." Philip stepped forward a little as if to meet Charles. This was honor indeed, for proud Spain did not relax any demands; others obeyed.

Then Charles was coming more fully around the flowering borders, making his bow, and saying, "Your Gracious Majesties, allow me to present Geraldine Rothsoon, my betrothed, who has promised to wed me in the spring."

Spring! thought Julian wildly. *But it is scarce full summer now. He will be free for months yet. Surely I but dream, soon I will wake.* She stood with the others, very still and proper, her body frozen, staring at the girl who must hold Charles Varland's heart.

Geraldine Rothsoon could not be seventeen and looked less. She was very small, her head well below Charles's shoulder, but she was perfectly formed with a pure oval face, curling black hair, and black eyes. Her gown was palest pink with billowing overskirts and sleeves of a deeper shade. A veil of pink lace seeded with tiny pearls drifted over her shoulders, and a huge pink pearl shone on one slender hand. The pale face was flushed with color as she made some response that the roaring in Julian's head did not allow her to hear.

Philip smiled as he lifted the girl from her curtsy. A liveried messenger stood poised just beyond Charles, and the queen's anxious face looked toward him as she waited for the moment to beckon. Charles wore his usual look of disdain; not once did he glance toward Julian or give any sign that he knew she was there. Julian felt the powerful pull of him and thought that he must know.

"For one so fair I must forgive your determination to

remain in England." The king relinquished the girl with a half sigh as she blushed and moved toward Charles. "I wonder that you have waited so long to wed, my lord."

He put one hand under her elbow, and Julian could see the tenderness in the gesture. "And I, in my turn, wonder that my fair Geraldine will have me." Charles turned the small palm upward and kissed it in a courtly gesture that might have been a love motion.

The queen said, "Marriage is a good and commendable estate, Lord Varland, and we well recommend it to you. I see that so young and fair a bride, with rich estates to be maintained, will keep you in Cornwall. Is it not true?"

"Even so, madam." Charles's face set in hard lines as the small girl swayed against him. "My lady tires in the early heat, Your Majesties. May we have your leave to retire?"

Philip of Spain looked warningly at his wife. "With such men as this in England, traitors are less to be feared until we come again." He touched her arm and her frown faded. "Go, Charles, and our blessings upon you."

Queen Mary was not one to dissemble; she had ever been honest and blunt, but now her distrust of Charles Varland was as plain as the adoration for Philip on her face. She smiled, a bare creaking of the facial muscles. "God and Our Lady bless you and may your marriage be fruitful." Then she turned away toward the messenger.

Julian knew herself to be fair that morning despite the past racking days. Geraldine's beauty was that of a heavenly queen, her own was that of earth, of the very fullness of the spring. Her gown was golden and simple with flowing sleeves and a wide trailing skirt. The chestnut hair, unbound, tumbled down her back and clustered in curls at her temples. It was not the way a proper lady in attendance on the queen should dress, but much was excused in these days of leave-taking. Now the very simplicity of her attire made her stand out, and she knew it.

She stepped forward, smiling, knowing her eyes to be as cold as Charles Varland's face. There was no way to know if the manner of his announcement was deliberate; she remembered his changed manner after he saved her life and wondered what had so altered him. She said, "And I, Lord Varland, must offer you my felicitations on your coming nuptials. Lady Geraldine, I know your lord only slightly, but he is indeed a man of honor."

The eyes that looked at Julian might have been a thousand years old, but the pretty lips smiled and the fair face blushed again in shyness. Charles did not show any emotion—he might have been carved from stone—but the lash about honor did not escape him. He drew Geraldine back toward the shade and motioned to a maid who had been hovering close by.

"As the queen has said, marriage is a holy estate, Lady Redenter. You will enter upon it soon, I trust?" He turned without waiting for an answer and supported his betrothed away, his own back stiff and unyielding.

Julian tried to find anger and could not. She was beyond tears or hurt, and could only be thankful for her outward calm. The other ladies had settled themselves at another low request from the king, who waited for his wife to finish her business. Even the day was the same, brilliant and warm. Did it matter that the light was gone from one young girl? In that time of bitterness, under the amused eyes of the man who had wanted to dally with her himself, in the sight of the gossiping, curious court, Julian Redenter knew what she had only partially admitted to herself behind the iron barriers of what she called her pride. She loved a man pledged to another. She, too, was victim to the all-devouring, immolating passion that had enveloped her mother, that she saw in the queen. She loved Lord Charles Varland, not only with her hungry, seeking flesh, but with her mind and soul, foolish though it might be.

"You will naturally pray for the swift return of your betrothed from the north, Lady Redenter? I fear the court will be far less gay than formerly, now that we embark upon our necessary war. When you are wed, I shall command Lord and Lady Attenwood to visit Spain. He has relatives there, you know, and lands as well. Our country can be harsh; you might wish to remain in Madrid while he travels." Philip's voice was as soft as the bee flight toward the flowers, but his eyes were in her bodice. "It is good that Lord Attenwood has Spanish connections. That is one of the reasons that I considered him a good choice for your husband and so I told the queen when she consulted me. Would it please you to come to Spain, Lady Redenter?"

He played the double game with her and Julian knew it. At the court of Spain for the best of reasons, safely wed, well chaperoned except when he wished it, her husband acquiescent and rewarded—she could have no illusions about what Philip intended now. She made her voice uncomprehending, dull, but raised it just enough so that her words carried. "No, sire. I wish to remain in England always, even though I am sure that Spain is most fair. England is my home."

"You forget. England is ours, too." He spoke the words just as Mary turned toward him, her small face twisted.

Julian bobbed a curtsy, knowing that she must be alone, knowing that she must divert suspicion or walk in more danger than she had ever imagined. She said, "I believe that the world is other than I have supposed it to be, sir. Greatly do I yearn toward the peace of God and his Church. After I have searched my soul further and counseled with the priests, I will seek the cloister if it is willed."

Philip of Spain gave a short bark of laughter as his eyes raked her once again. His wife lifted one hand in a benediction of simple faith that shamed both the girl who sought only escape and the man who called himself the head of God's armies.

"If that is your wish, child, none will pray for you more than I. But be most careful; God is not mocked, either by the high or the low." The fervent voice of the queen rang harshly over the garden, bringing a gay tinkle of song nearby to an abrupt halt. "Go now and we will speak of this when the sad days are come upon us." She put her fingers possessively on Philip's sleeve, and color rose to her sallow cheeks. "Husband, there are grave matters to discuss."

Julian curtsied again and backed away as the royal couple walked on. Matters of bed, she thought coarsely, for had she not worn that look herself? Did all life come down to that? Why not act truly on her improvisation of the moment? Why not seek the cloister and be free of earthly entanglements? Or at least make a retreat there? She would surely be safe and no one would look askance. One of the older ladies bent to Susan Clarence, and Julian heard the whisper as perhaps she was meant to. "Convent, indeed! That one has greedy eyes for our pious king and other gentlemen as well."

She heard her laughter rise high and shrill as she swung back to face them. "I leave you to the shredding of reputations, ladies! Is there so mortal a sin as youth?" Their shocked gasps followed her as she spread her skirts and ran over the grass toward the palace.

Julian walked up and down in the Long Gallery, careful always to remain where there were plenty of other people. She felt as though she were being hacked to pieces inside as her mind filled with pictures of Charles with his bride as they slept, loved, and lived together. What was she to do now? It was not as though she had ever thought they would marry; did she intend to be a victim of passion, helpless before it all her days? Never! She would live with the wound of love, for there was little choice, but her destiny would be her own.

That night the court was very gay with songs and mummings and the more lively dances of the English countryside. Queen Mary normally did not approve of such things, but now she cared for nothing but the smiling man at her side. Julian, brilliant in cream-colored satin, danced and sported, drinking deeply of the cool wine that was always being offered the dancers, and laughed at the sallies of English and Spanish alike. Her normal reserve left her, despite her announced yearning for the cloister and peace, so that many eyes followed the queen's lovely lady, wondering how they had missed her before.

She danced with a mincing young man who kept addressing her in bad verse as they whirled close together and spun apart in the measures of the dance. Her eyes, it seemed, were the very lights of heaven and her skin like the new-fallen snow. His cold, damp hands clutched her hot ones, and suddenly the whole dance seened very funny as the room revolved around her. Odd, his lank golden hair and sprouting beard were upside down. And how shrill the music was! What were the musicians doing?

He said, "Is my admiration of your beauty so very funny? I vow, lady, your amusement is unseemly!"

Now she was upside down with him and they were both spinning into darkness where there was no sound. But wait! Someone was laughing, an angry laughter that went on and on. She, Julian, was being pulled down into a wet hole by eager hands. They were trying to kill her!

Reality caught briefly at her, and she saw that she was lying across a couch at the end of the hall. A ring of faces, curious and amused, was above her. She heard someone say "too much wine," "flown with it," "silly chit." Or were several people speaking? Nausea roiled up in her, and she fought it back as the darkness floated nearer.

"Take her to her rooms." The cool, authoritative voice of Isabella Acton silenced the others. "I will tend her." Julian saw her shadowed against the candlelight and fancied that she smiled at her victim.

"No. I will have none of her. No." Her voice grew weaker as she realized that she had not drunk too much wine. One or more of the cups must have held a poison! Her death would be accomplished one way or another. She tried to sit up and could not. Already servants were approaching to obey Isabella. "No!" The cry faded as she began to shake.

"Not so. She goes into the private sickroom of the queen, there to be tended by her servants. Lady Redenter wrestles with her soul and must be near the priests in this travail." The tall woman who spoke appeared as another blur to Julian, but power rang in her words.

Isabella snapped, "She has had too much wine. I can deal with it."

Before the whirling mist took her utterly, Julian heard the woman say, "Those are the orders of Her Majesty, Lady Acton." A cold hand touched her sweat-beaded forehead as if in salvation, and Julian wondered who should be thanked for both life and death. Then she fell into oblivion.

CHAPTER FOURTEEN

Julian awoke to a white world; covers, walls, bedgown, even the ivory image of Our Lady in the side niche and the flowers climbing in the far window appeared all the same shade. She sat up so suddenly that her head reeled and her whisper seemed to hang on the air. "Is this the very anteroom of eternity?"

The earthy laugh that rang out reminded her of Elspeth, but the tall, spare woman who rose from the stool a few feet away was at least in her sixties, and her face was severe though her snapping brown eyes held merriment. Her gown was of black cloth and might have been thrown upon her in the dark. She leaned over Julian to touch her forehead, and the girl caught the scent of roses.

"You are better. I knew you would be. I am Mistress Wheeler, a caretaker of this retreat for those who fall ill and need privacy; it was established by the queen's own mercy."

"How long have I been here?" She was amazed at the fact that she still lived and felt reasonably well, though very weak. "I thought Lady Acton asked to care for me."

Mistress Wheeler said, "You cried out in your pain as you were purged of the black bile. That delicate lady would not lift a hand in such circumstances, I can tell you." She gave a large sniff and surveyed Julian appraisingly. "You're far too thin. Men don't like it. Well, you were brought here late the night before last, and it is now early morning. Can you drink some broth, take a little wine?"

Julian felt her stomach contract. "I did not drink too much wine. There was something in it." She met the woman's eyes unwaveringly.

Mistress Wheeler laughed again, the warmth surging into her face. "It is not for me to say, surely, but you are young and your marriage delayed. What more natural than faintings and imaginings?"

"What more natural than the will of God seeking to express itself over frail flesh? Have a care, woman." The priest who entered soundlessly was black-browed and swarthy, his flesh seamed by harsh suns, his eyes dark lances as he watched them. He waved a thin hand and Mistress Wheeler, shaken, scuttled away.

Julian pulled the sheet up around her neck, conscious of her weakness as well as the first pangs of hunger. Only she could know how close to death she had come. That realization made her shiver, and she dropped her eyes before the stare of the priest.

He said, "Madam the Queen is ever concerned for souls. She has bidded me speak with you daily and help prove you fit—if indeed you are—for the cloister, since you have shown yourself doubtful over marriage. If you are chosen, then the troth will be broken. Our God can be a harsh master, Lady Redenter. There has been gossip about you. Her Majesty feels seclusion will be beneficial."

Julian felt the chills rise even more. Obviously the man was chosen because he was a fanatic, probably one of the more serious in the train of Philip of Spain, even one of those who encouraged the queen in her policy of burning heretics. This would be a dangerous road, she knew, but the only one to take. Caught between evil marriage and the cloister, a man she did not want and a man betrothed to another! Trapped by her own device between a dangerous bargain and a killer with only her wits to save her! Play for time and take each day as it came; she had heard that advice often enough from Elspeth in her youth. Now it was to help her again. She composed her face into an expression of dutifulness and looked at the priest.

"Truly, sir, I am drawn and repelled by this world, yet lured by another. Counsel me, I pray you, in this that I may not sin."

The hard stare did not alter nor did he move from his rigid stance beside the bed. "First, pride must be removed and the soul . . ."

Julian heard his voice rise and fade as he spoke on and on, dwelling always on the difficulties of faith and the terrible penalties waiting for those who sinned in thought or deed. What had the gentle Nazarene to do with this? The thought cried in her brain, but she dared not show the slightest glimmer of doubt. All her senses warned that danger was near.

"I will come again on the morrow. I can see that you will need much instruction." He gave her another sharp look, then strode from the room as she fell limply back against the pillows.

Mistress Wheeler was beside her as soon as the door clanged shut. There was no laughter about her now, and the odor of fear was in the air. She put her mouth close to Julian's ear. "That one is Father Sebastino, very close to the king, very watchful for heresy. Why, it is said that on his counsel one of the maidservants from the palace was recently found in deepest sin and burned for it!"

Julian drew her breath in with horror but knew that she must not give it credence; that way lay madness. She said, "I could eat, I know, if I might sit in yonder garden and ponder all that has been told me." She was proud of the fact that her voice did not tremble. More than ever, she must keep her outward demeanor calm. She saw that Mistress Wheeler was as afraid as she and this, strangely, gave her courage.

For the next three days Julian partook of the peace of this retreat as she walked in the little hedged garden where white flowers of alyssum, climbing roses, edging plants, and pale lavender blew in scented masses. She was left alone by the now cautious Mistress Wheeler, but the priest reminded her of a great bird of prey as he exhorted by the hour, his baleful eyes unblinking even in the summer sun. She saw no one else and was thankful for it; here she was at least safe.

The strain of the past weeks left her in this time; her strength came back and with it her resolve to win this game of balance. There was a spring to her step, a new sheen to her hair, and the slenderness of her face rounded enough so that she could tell it even in the still waters of the tiny pool in the garden. She was sitting beside it on the morning of the fourth day, dreading the appearance of the priest and fearing he would know it, when Mistress Wheeler entered.

"Lady! Lady Redenter! You are quite revived, I know!" Flags of color stood in her sallow face as she peered anxiously at Julian, who had risen to her feet at the excitement shown. "I thought you ought to know ahead of time so that you could be properly grateful to the good Father. It might be helpful for you."

Julian knew that her face was white. "What is it, Mistress Wheeler? What news do you bring?" She would have sworn the woman held little liking for such people as Father Sebastino or Isabella Acton. Was she, too, a dissembler?

"I have servants to mind, you understand, this is not my only task. Well, what with the king and queen off to Dover day after tomorrow, and there being less work to do then, it seems that the Lady Abbess of St. Marguerite's will take you for a retreat. Father Sebastino's request. The queen will be so pleased!"

Julian felt as if heavy gates were shutting out all light and air. Was it to this that her impetuosity had brought her? The convent of which Mistress Wheeler spoke was a small one, a severely cloistered order in a poor section of London, famed for its rigidity; few who entered ever left it on any pretext. Life there was said to be harsh yet a blessing to the truly dedicated. The queen might be told that Julian had chosen that life and believe it. Doubtless Father Sebastino had an interest there, ascetics all, and believed that to place a court lady would bring benefits on earth and heaven.

She spoke carefully. "I believe I have heard of this convent." So she had, words given in casual jest for comparison of a lady's virtue. An odd remark at this court, and she had chanced to ask Nan. The girl's recoil had told her enough. But for that she might have thought this a blessing, a quiet time in a comfortable atmosphere, talks with a worldly Abbess grateful for Mary's return to the ways of old. Did fate hang on a chance word?

"Aye, lady. The holy man is most interested in your soul." Again, Mistress Wheeler spoke as by rote.

Julian suddenly caught the meaning of her earlier words. "Why does the court go to Dover? Does it have to do with the war?"

"The Spanish fleet was sighted in the Channel a few days ago. The king leaves with it. The younger ones of the court will go; it is said the queen will need all comfort when her husband leaves. We who remain will order things."

"Strange that I was not summoned." Here was Isabella's hand again; she felt the bite of that lash.

The woman came close to Julian and took her hand. "You are known to be ill but recovering. The Father has explained all. Come and rest now and ponder your good fortune." She pulled slightly, and the girl did not resist but allowed herself to be led inside.

Julian knew that if she had once nearly had a friend in this woman, she had one no longer. Gold, security, or simple fear had touched her, and like Julian herself, she was forced to yield as best she might.

"Mistress, would you summon the girl, Nan, to me this afternoon? I need another gown, and there are books that I would request which she can fetch for me." Julian had only the thin white robes provided for the sick, and now she felt that this would be regarded as a reasonable wish.

"You are supposed to be sequestered here, but I see no reason why you may not see the servant." Mistress Wheeler hesitated between being the taskmistress and the watcher. One look at the girl's quiet resignation sufficed. "She shall not stay long, however."

Julian walked back out into the garden, but she dared

not give vent to the fright and rage that rose in her, crowding out the yearning for Charles that rose unsuspecting in her stress. The bold anger of the Redenters that had driven Lionel against his king and taken another ancestor on Bosworth Field now came to their daughter in her need. She would not allow herself to be pummeled by fate or traitors or even kings who wished dalliance. So much depended on Nan and how loyal the girl was to her. Indeed, why should the servant care? What argument could Julian use? She did not know if Blanche were back at court and, if she were, what a court lady could do in such circumstances as these. A small, savage grin curved Julian's lips. She herself was of the court, but she also had survived much and was yet unscarred.

"Except by the wound of love." She spoke the words absently into the scented wind. "And I can endure."

The afternoon sun was low in the west when Nan came to her, the freckled face pale and fearful. She had the closed manner of the servant before the master, dull but willing. Perhaps a year or so younger than Julian, she bore the marks of hard work and caution. It was to that caution, so familiar to herself, that Julian spoke.

"Tell me what you have heard of the happenings the other night. What do they say about me?" Much depended on the answer, and she watched Nan closely as they walked up and down the paths of the white garden.

"Oh, lady, I know it is not true that you drank and flirted and are to be kept in seclusion for unbecoming conduct. Lady Acton talks much of how shocked she is, and the older ladies agree. Others think you most daring. Some say that you have chosen religion. But now the talk is all of the trip to Dover." Artless eyes looked up at Julian.

The last emphasis on the word religion caught Julian up, and she stared at the girl. "I have not chosen religion; it is being chosen for me." Quickly she outlined the events of the past few days and saw Nan draw herself further back into caution. "Will you do something for me and be silent about it? I cannot do this thing. It is my own fault; I wanted only to think, and now I am being forced. If I am there when the queen returns, she will never argue with an accomplished fact. I can offer you nothing, Nan, for I have nothing except by largesse of the queen. You may be punished if you help me. I mean to run away, you see."

Nan said, "I would help anyone to escape the bonds of the old faith. You have been kinder than some in this place. What do you want me to do?" She slumped a little, and the light of intelligence blurred in her eyes. "I will be safe, lady. Can you think they would question me long?"

"Are you Protestant?" As soon as the words left her mouth Julian was sorry that she voiced them. What if the girl were in league with Isabella and that party? Had she inadvertently walked into the camp of the enemy? "Forgive me, I did not mean to pry. I am overwrought."

The mask of the servant lifted and fire transformed the girl's pallid manner. "I and those like me must live, Lady Redenter. How can we afford such luxuries as thoughts? I do as I am told. I will do as you tell me. Is that enough for you?"

"It will have to be." Julian looked her straight in the eye and decided to give herself away completely. "Is Lord Varland still at court? You must know him, he . . ."

"I know him. He is kind to those who serve him and generous as well. A worthy gentleman." Nan tossed a strand of hair out of her eyes and averted her face. "He has ridden on ahead with others of the king's party to see that all is in readiness. His betrothed remains at his house here, suffering, it is said, from exhaustion."

Julian thought quickly. Charles was powerful and in favor with Philip of Spain; any request he made would surely be granted, and Mary would uphold his promise. Charles could not refuse her his protection, not after all that had been between them. There was no other to whom she could turn, and this coil was not to be resolved by herself alone. She remembered Nan's silence on the subject of her bruised neck and the incurious way she had produced coverings for it. Did she think Julian sought Charles Varland in passion for an illicit relationship?

She said, "There is no more time, Nan. Will you bring me these things?" Her instructions were swift and to the point as the servant nodded in instant comprehension. "Again, I must thank you for the risk you run."

Nan's eyes darted back and forth as her face assumed the dull look once more. "Aye, lady. I have it. Yes, yes." She counted on her fingers with a maddening slowness. Julian looked past her and saw that Mistress Wheeler was approaching. How had Nan known? She herself had heard nothing.

"You are done with the servant?" She barely waited for Julian's nod before waving dismissal at Nan, who backed away so rapidly that she almost tumbled over her skirts. "Go and obey your lady." Her voice was not lowered as she added, "The quality of service is worse every day." Then she watched Julian closely and her words were almost sweet. "Lady, I bring a message for you from one who is greatly concerned for your well-being."

Charles had heard of her difficulties! Eagerly she grasped the parchment that the woman held out and broke the seal. The world spun around her as she read, "Father Sebastino has my approval in all that he does. We knew each other in Spain. When next I see you after your sojourn in the convent of his choice, I shall be interested in your choices." The initial "A" was slashed across the rest of the page. How neatly she had been trapped by the pervert and the fanatic and the kindness of the queen, who sought to help her ward in a hard decision.

Mistress Wheeler's eyes were avid on her. "Lady, are you well? Is there anything in the message to distress you?"

Julian knew that she had probably read it and might even be in the pay of Attenwood. She revolved to face the woman, taking a lesson from Nan and adapting it to her own need. Her eyes went a little blank, and she smiled vaguely. "No, no. I was just thinking the world seems so far away these days. Where is the good Father?"

"He cannot come to you until after the royal party has left, for he attends the queen and offers her ghostly counsel. The king himself urged it. But he is most eager to teach you; he himself said it before Her Majesty." Mistress

Wheeler was growing nervous, and her fingers began to pick at her skirt.

Julian sank to her knees in the middle of the path and spread her arms wide. "I know that the blessing of the spirit will come upon me, and I have the holy man to thank for it. I must have solitude in which to pray. Ah, the blandishments of the world are as nothing . . ."

"Aye, truly. Truly." Mistress Wheeler gave Julian a horrified glance and moved away as rapidly as decency would allow. "Of course you need quiet."

Julian watched her go and heard a muttered "Touched?" as she rounded the nearest corner. She did not think she would come back unless compelled, but Julian knew she must keep all her senses alert. The waiting was to be the hardest part of her hastily formed plan, and well she knew it. George Attenwood played with her for his own pleasure, and Father Sebastino was dangerous; she would need all the luck in the world in order to circumvent them.

The smell of fresh grass and lavender floated on the warm air, and the sun rested gentle on her shoulders as she continued to kneel in the white garden. A delicately veined leaf blew inches from her face. The birdcall came round and soft at her side. She was conscious of the sweetness of life and freedom even while the words of Elspeth rang in her ears as they had done in all the years of her growing up. *Praying is fine, but sometimes you have to use the wits the Good Lord gave you.*

The corners of her mouth turned up, and her courage was renewed.

CHAPTER FIFTEEN

The cloud-covered moon gave only a dim light in the silent night, and the wind rustled faintly as the small figure lay on top of the garden wall for a second to listen before sliding down the heavy vines that grew there. A dog barked, hesitantly at first, then loudly as it was joined by others. The sound held and faded as suddenly as it had begun.

Julian expelled a long breath and moved away from the protecting greenery, over the palace grounds, and into the shadows of the trees, every instinct urging her to run just as caution kept her pace slow. She had wound the skirt of the woven brown gown that Nan had brought up above her ankles and tied it in places with strips of cloth. Her feet were bare, her face smudged with garden dirt. A brown hood covered her hair, and slippers of brown leather were thrust in the band at her waist. A shawl covered her shoulders and hid the small bag around her neck that held the several coins she had unashamedly kept when given them by Lady Clarence to distribute at the time of the queen's ill-fated venture into the streets to give largesse.

She let her mind turn back to the agony of the slow hours when she waited for Nan to send her materials, the ever present danger that someone might inspect the packet or decide to exhort Julian herself once more, the wait for the palace to quiet and the moon to go behind the clouds, and the self-questioning that she continued to do, and the

final realization that she must find Charles Varland and
force him to protect her if he would not do so willingly.
How gladly she would return to Redeswan now, she
thought, and how heavenly the peace would seem! But the
royal anger would follow unless it could be blunted, and
for that she must have a friend who was powerful.

She was in the woodland proper now and could run as
she had been cautioned was unbecoming a lady. It was a
relief to move freely after the days of inaction and fear;
her blood ran headily in her veins, and she had cause to
be thankful once again that she was no pampered girl such
as Charles's betrothed. Her own body was strong and her
spirit unhampered thanks to the comparative freedom of
her rearing. There was advantage to being out of favor, it
appeared.

Julian lost count of the times she ran, paused, ran
again, and finally walked with intervals of rest during the
remainder of the night as the moon dwindled and the
birds began to give off sleepy chirps when the darkness
lifted. She passed some dwellings and open fields, then
little copses, went along short paths that gave way to open
roads, still rutted from the spring rains, now lined with
flowers and dusty vines. She could have gone on forever,
she felt, but when she heard the distant gurgle of a spring,
knew that it was time to rest and reconnoiter.

She settled in the considerable space behind the
branches of an overgrown bush whose thick growth would
be hard to penetrate even if one stood only a few feet
from it. Then she spread the shawl and lay down, thinking
that sleep was impossible. The road near at hand seemed
well traveled, but how could she know if it were the one
she sought? It might be that she moved in a circle; people
did when they were lost, and she was not yet that familiar
with the territory of this new life. A bird cried once and
then again, a rabbit moved in the undergrowth, and the
water rattled briskly along. Time blurred and Julian
drifted, warm in the arms of Charles Varland.

Light was in her face, dazzling her eyes and burning
them. There was a sharp sound and a clatter; it seemed to
her that she ran before a pursuing mob straight toward a

cliff. The snorting sound came again, and then she woke, both hands clutching the grass at her sides, her heart hammering madly. Memory returned instantly and with it the knowledge that her face was itching under the caked dirt, that the sun was squarely in her face, and that it was the sun of midmorning. An old horse was poking along on the road beyond in response to urgent mutters from its master and was whinnying displeasure.

She turned over on her side and drew into the shade. Hopefully she would be able to tell if this road were well traveled enough for her purpose. If so, there would be time enough to put her plan into operation. The sun inched higher, and she saw only a peasant couple ambling slowly along, their backs bent under heavy bundles. Her mouth was dry and hot, the dress prickled on her back, but she waited for perhaps another half hour without seeing anyone else. Something must be decided before night. She scrambled to her feet and went closer to the road where it curved around a bend. The voice that spoke almost at her feet made her jump and shriek.

"You stepped on me! I'm trying to shoot the Spaniards! Get down!" The heavy voice broke on the last words but not before Julian threw herself flat on the ground in anticipation of attack. The snickers that began burst into open laughter then.

She balanced herself on hands and knees and glared into the freckled face of a boy about eleven years old. Dark blond hair stood up in tufts all over his head, and two teeth were missing on the left side of his face. Eyes as green as the branches above them shone into hers. An expression of wariness crossed his face as he surveyed her. He had been crouching behind a bush, his makeshift bow and arrow at the ready; now he rose slightly.

"Well, the Spaniards might have been coming. Uncle John thinks they will sometime. I was just practicing."

Julian sat back on her heels and burst into laughter that rose and mingled with the boy's relief. Tears formed in her eyes, and her throat ached as the blessed healing swept over her that she could laugh in freedom on a summer morning. When she could speak she said, "But we are at war with France. You have the wrong enemy."

He stiffened. "All the same. England for the English!" A young bantam of a lad, bold and brave as he stood there, his weapons folded under his crossed arms.

Julian rose in her turn and smiled down at him. "Our land is well defended by such as you, Master . . ."

"Ned. Edward, really, for the late king, you know." His grin was bright.

"I am Bess." She put out a grimy hand to his equally grimy one. "Can you tell me the way to the Canterbury road? I am lost and must get there as quickly as possible."

"Why? Are you running away? I tried it once, only I wanted to go to London. They found me."

Julian swallowed hard, her mind swinging back to when she was this age, romantic and full of dreams, ready to brave the world for a cause. "Edward, can you keep a secret? A truly important one?" At his eager nod, she continued, "My betrothed is going to fight the French and sailing with the king when he goes, except that he thinks, as you do, that there's enough fighting to do here in England. Scots and the like. So I am running away from my mistress in London and will join him when the party reaches Canterbury. Then we'll go north. Will you show me to the road and keep silence?"

"Come home with me, Bess. None's there but Mum, and she never goes out. We'll do better than show you the road; we'll help you down it." He was suddenly older than his years, his eyes anxious on hers. "Please say you'll come." She protested in vain; the green gaze did not yield. "Please."

"I should not, but I am grateful." Julian could not greatly fear anything this brilliant morning with the wind in her hair and her body strong and lithe under the hot gown. Was it to take this experience to show her that she was not truly of the royal court? Her feet were sure on the paths as she followed Ned through the woods and around a maze of paths that might have been trodden by deer but never humans.

The house was a thatched hut in a clearing. One side of

it was covered with roses, and a thick vine twisted over the door. Ned called out and then pulled her in after him before she could resist. As her eyes adjusted Julian saw the woman lying on a wooden bed. She was heavily pregnant, and one foot seemed to be deformed, for it twisted back on itself. Two clumsy crutches were close at hand. The girl felt pity well up in her as Ned launched himself at the woman, spilling out the story and embellishing it so that she had to laugh and tell him to cease his chatter.

Her name was Mary, her husband a woodcutter often gone days at a time, visitors were almost nonexistent, and Ned did what work he could where he could. The thin, soft voice said, "He will walk with you; a woman alone is always in danger. You shall wash and take my shawl; it is more the garment a servant would have. Yours and the talk we exchange will be payment enough."

Julian hoped that she could remember the tissue of lies she spun that morning to Mary and her son as she spoke of her dictatorial mistress who wished to keep her unwed and of her love for her handsome Andrew. She told of London, the sights and sounds, the processions and the public gatherings, as much of the court as a servant might be expected to see, adding the tale she had told Ned, and ending, "We, too, seek only peace to live our lives as we may."

"That will never happen while hell's daughter sits on the throne! We lived by the river once and had a good living. My neighbor informed against me for a chance remark, and I was put to the rack, which made me as you see. We had to flee for our safety and our lives, such as they are! What sort of life will my son have in such circumstances?" She tossed fretfully on the bed, and Ned came near to murmur soothing words.

Julian felt the heat of anger once again. "It is truly bitter. How can I thank you for your help?" She had availed herself of water and comb. Now she was clean again, and her face shone in the dimness; her hair, coiled demurely beneath the hood, still gave off glimmers of light. The brown gown was shaken out, and the new shawl, dark and ragged in places, gave the appearance of the country.

Mary reared up on the bed, and her face was transformed by the fury that Julian did not dare show. She spat, "What good is prayer? Who is there to hear? Get your man to join with those who would set the Princess Elizabeth on the throne and free us of this yoke to Spain. Let him fight here where the battle is! Will you do it? Will you?"

"Aye." Julian wanted only to escape this flood of understandable emotion and go into the hot noon, but something stronger held her. "Are there many who feel as you do? Who have suffered as you?"

"Many. As many as the sands of the sea." Mary slumped back in weariness and closed her eyes.

Ned pulled her skirt, and Julian followed him outside. "She gets so lonely, Bess. Did you mind?" She shook her head, and he grinned with relief. "Then come, the road is long."

The road was indeed long, and they hastened along it, a peasant girl and her young brother, bound for who cared where. It was the road of the pilgrims, travelers to the coastal cities, royalty and tradesmen, the road of history. Julian was conscious of ruts, dust thrown up by carts and animals, the chaffering of one laborer to another, the burning heat of the sun. She forgot safety and adventure and the discomfort that Mary had aroused in her concerning the queen; she thought only of food and drink, of rest for her burning feet.

The sun had lost something of its power when she saw, at a crossroads and in the shelter of three large oak trees set well off to the side, a small inn which had long ago lost the one coat of whitewash it had been given. The carving of an ill-favored bird straddled the roof, and a lettered sign below proclaimed this inn to be the White Pheasant. Ned glanced uneasily at the sun, and Julian read his mind. Soon he must hasten back to his mother, then she would be alone. Not for the first time, she doubted the scheme that had come to her when she learned from Nan that Charles had gone ahead to the coast to make sure, with others, that all was in readiness for the royal departure. If she followed and confronted him there, made her demands known or her plea given, whichever seemed most expedient, then she would have the best chance for success. He was by no means indifferent to her, betrothed or no. She shrugged back the pain that thought gave her; one must do the best one could, and she was not one to blindly submit.

They entered the taproom of the inn only to find it filled with drinkers, most of whom seemed to know one another, for they bawled insults back and forth in amiable fashion. Another group, perhaps laborers on the way back to their village, sat over tankards in a corner and muttered to themselves. A huge woman, dark hair straggling down her back, rushed in and out among them, her high voice raised in answer to complaints and comments alike.

"Hurry, Madge, got to be on the road before dark." "Satisfy a man's thirst!" "Ale, over here!" "That good-for-nothing Henry still drunk?" "I asked for wine! Do you have it or not?" "Getting it fast as I can!" "Coming!" "Wait your turn!"

Julian and Ned stood just inside the door and listened. The cries, though basically good-natured, might turn angry at any moment. She had spent stolen time in the inn at the village below Redeswan in the days before a horrified Lady Gwendolyn had been informed and was now surprised at how much she had absorbed. There was a sudden push at her back that sent her to the dirt floor. A large, evil-smelling man stamped past and paused a foot from her.

"Wine! The wine of Bordeaux! I will have it now!" His angry voice lifted over the hubbub.

"Sir, this is a poor inn. I have none such." Madge's words were softer than the other comments had been.

"Poor comfort for the traveler to Canterbury!" The man snatched at the end of a table, and so great was his size, several drinkers tumbled from their low stools to the floor. Others retreated before the start of drunken anger.

Julian threw all her strength against the widespread legs just below the knees and Ned joined her. The drunken man, caught off guard and unbalanced, toppled as if he were a felled tree. His head cracked on the side of another table and he lay still.

The inn was silent for a second, then cries of delight arose along with clapping. Madge hurried toward Julian and Ned, who stood laughing in surprise at their own feat.

"Take him outside and throw him across on the other side of the road. Lazy louts to let him try to tear up the place! I ought to close down for sheer exasperation!" Madge laughed as some of her chastened customers rushed to do her bidding. "Girl, that was quick thinking. It saved us a fight. Will you drink good wine, you and the boy?"

Julian remembered Nan's face before Mistress Wheeler, her own dullness before the commissioners of the king, and she assumed that look now. "I would ask another thing, good mistress. It grows late and my small brother must return to his master. I am for my village, but a night's lodging would be a blessing, and I could help you here in the taproom for my food."

Madge examined her curiously, the small eyes intent. Julian repeated her request in almost the same vein. Ned pulled at her hand, and she looked down at him with the same expression. The woman blew her breath out. "That's the way it is, then? Can you handle this work with direction?"

Julian said, "Aye, mistress." Then she said her piece again and saw the woman look around at the waiting men whose eyes had taken it all in. The unconscious man had been taken outside and those men returned. "He pushed me. I pushed back." She put both hands on her hips and looked around.

Madge grinned. "You shall help me this night and welcome, girl." She raised her voice to the men. "And no fooling with her, either. She pushes back."

The room exploded with good-natured laughter, and under the cover of it Ned whispered, "I must go back, Bess. Will you be all right?"

"Of course. Go with God, my friend." Her voice shook a little at the loss of this good friendship.

Ned lifted his head. "I'll tell Mum you're fine, Bess." Then the small figure was darting out into the light and toward the road.

"Ale to celebrate!" A beefy farmer called out the order,

and others took up the cry. Madge waved her hands in mock horror and spoke softly to Julian, "Your village? Where is it?"

"Beyond Sittingbourne and off the road. My husband is a farmer there. Shall I fetch ale, mum?" She kept her voice flat and steady, the dull look unwavering. Could she hope to fool this shrewd woman who must match wits with others constantly?

The clamor behind them rose again, and Madge yielded to it. She pointed out tankards and supplies, and they began to work. There was no time to talk or even think, for the inn continued to fill and empty, the tale of the drunkard repeated with variations all evening. Julian was thankful for her hood and the set expression of her face as well as for the bundling shawl that hid the contours of her figure. Once again safety had been bought, and she was still whole.

The thought rang clear in her mind and almost made her smile as she set down yet another tankard before a gesticulating man. *Hermes, god of wayfarers and thieves, watch over me, for soon I shall be both!*

CHAPTER SIXTEEN

Julian slipped noiselessly from the communal back room where Madge had tossed in earlier abandon with a lover and now slept snoring heavily. She knew it was very late; the air had that feel about it that conjured up visions of demons and ghosts while good folk remained safely abed. The inn had calmed down by the time Madge sent her to sleep, but she did not doubt that several drunks must still be sleeping on the floor. The noise of Madge with her lover had roused her, but weariness had been too great for concern. Now she only hoped the woman was truly exhausted.

Nothing stirred as she made her way to the small stable just off one side of the inn. Her eyes this past afternoon had not deceived her; two horses stood chewing placidly inside, and the door, a ramshackle thing at best, swung ajar. She moved toward the nearest and touched it with gentle fingers, murmuring as she did so. The moonlight slanted, showing the reddish coat and wide back of the mare. A working horse but surely well enough to travel rapidly on. She threw the shawl over its back and attached the makeshift bridle with trembling fingers as the soft mouth drew back over great teeth. Any sign of fear and she would be lost; one whicker would be enough. The penalty for horse stealing was death, and anyone would uphold such a sentence.

She put her bare feet into a crevice in the wooden wall and gave silent thanks that the mare stood close by it. Then she was on and urging forward. There was no other sound except the soft clop on the dirt as they went out of the stable and around the edge of the inn.

A maniacal howl split the air, and the mare quivered as Julian went stiff. Discovery might come at any second; the gold piece she had left for the horse might adequately cover its value, but she did not think Madge would quibble at keeping both. The cry came again and dwindled to a low sob. It was almost female in nature, and she hoped that the person making it was only having a fearful dream. She did not wait to find out. She dug her heels into the mare's sides, and moments later they were moving down the Canterbury road.

Speed was the essential thing now. Julian leaned over the animal, urging it to greater effort as they went along. Her murmurs were soft and compelling, an attempt to keep herself from thinking as much as to encourage horse and rider. The road was wider here since it was much traveled, and the dimming moon gave enough light for free movement. She rode until it was full day but too early for many to be about. A grove near the road gave protection, and she was able to go deeper into the wood where it was moderately safe to rest. Still, she jerked awake often in that hot day and felt the strain of the journey and the masquerade telling on her. But she lived and was free; that was enough.

She started out again in the midafternoon, a dangerous time, but this was the day that the procession would be setting out from London. It was not all that far from the capital to Dover, even moving slowly overland. Time was still the important factor. Once again she rode and watched, pausing only to water the mare at a convenient stream, wash her face, and press on. She feared that her description might have been circulated, so she let her hair down in two plaits on her shoulders, unfastened the belt of the brown dress and turned it on the wrong side, let her dirty bare feet hang, and rode with an intent expression on her face. Many called to her but none ventured near, and when she dismounted she held her little dagger at the ready. She had taken bread and cheese from Madge's store of supplies, but her stomach contracted and she was able to eat little. All that mattered was reaching Dover and Charles as soon as possible.

With all the urgency that pressed upon her, Julian was still able to look upon the beauty of cultivated land, orchards, woodlands, and drifts of flowers under the summer sun and find all fair. Blanche had not jested when she called Kent the fairest part of England. But she could not help but see the marching soldiers and hear the sharp comments of some of the travelers or miss the palpable tension as the columns went by. Canterbury town she bypassed along with some other people who wished to hasten on to the coast. The shimmering cathedral, holiest of those in the land, rose above the walls and seemed to shed beneficence into the pure air.

Soon Julian could smell the sea breezes and taste the tang of salt on her lips. The downs were softly contoured, the horizon blue and misty, even the green here seemed muted. She had been riding once again since early cock crow and had tried to make herself as presentable as possible, since today, for good or ill, would mark the end of her journey: the brown dress was rearranged and brushed with a stiff green branch; her hair was bound demurely behind her head and she wore no coif to cover it; her face was clean and shining; her mouth curved up with excitement.

She patted the mare's neck as she breasted the last hill before the seaport and paused briefly to look out toward France and the shimmering Channel, where gulls rose and dipped. "You shall have corn and hay in plenty, my beautiful one, if all goes well; if not, we starve together." She could not imagine that matters would not resolve themselves favorably. Had they not gone well thus far? Surely the hand of Hermes was over her. She crossed herself hurriedly and murmured to the Blessed Virgin at her own whimsy, then turned the mare toward the great chalk cliffs and the castle set high on them. Here her fate would be decided, but by her own hand and none other.

"I seek Lord Charles Varland. My business with him is urgent." Julian faced the stern guard at the entrance to the grim castle that guarded the harbor. Her chin was lifted, and she gave him stare for stare. His companion eyed her with relish and smoothed his gloves.

"Aiming a bit high, aren't you, sweeting? Won't I do?"

Her gaze was cold. "Lord Varland. Is he here?" A pang touched her. What if the journey had been in vain and Nan wrong? He might have gone to Cornwall or just out into London.

The elder guard was saying, "He is here and so are some other gentlemen of the court, but I'd not disturb them for a draggly wench in search of a thrill. . . ."

She rounded on him and the aquamarine eyes spat fire. "I serve the Queen's Majesty, and we are at war. News does not always travel by coach and is announced by trumpets. Get him this instant!"

The command in her voice nearly convinced him, but he was cautious. "Jeremy, fetch Lord Varland here. Warn him, however, and the lady stays here while we wait."

Julian stifled a smile at her change from wench to lady

in the breath of an order. Her legs shook with relief, but she could not yield as yet. Her expression did not change as the other guard went rushing to do the other's bidding. She folded her arms and stood very straight in the pouring light.

It seemed hours and years yet only seconds before the tall figure behind the guard resolved into that of Charles. He seemed taller, more somber still, and the lines from nose to mouth were more pronounced. He wore dark gray today, adorned with no jewels, and she knew that his eyes would reflect that same darkness. The blood thundered in her temples at the sight of him, and her mouth was dry as she struggled for speech.

There was no need. He paused before her and executed a perfect court bow. Then, looking gravely at her, he said, "Madam, you bring news of our sovereigns? Come, let us speak privately." He extended his arm, she took it, and they swept into Dover Castle, leaving the staring guards behind them.

The room into which he steered her was the first available, very dank and cold, a type of storage place. He slammed the heavy door and turned to her, rage palpable in the lines of the dark face. Julian faced him determinedly; after all she had endured, this was just one more hurdle.

"Madam, have you quite taken leave of your senses? Has the madness come upon you that you appear in this manner? Do you think you will have any reputation left that you pursue me in such a fashion?" He drove one fist into another and glared at her. "How did you come? Where is your escort?"

"You think that I pursued you for your manly attributes!" She almost choked on her own rising anger. "Truly, your vanity has taken over your own senses. Nay, I have come to you for protection, fled to you as the only resource in a world that seeks to twist and mold me . . . gods, you are laughing at me!"

Charles leaned against the wall and roared with laughter. Julian stamped her foot and advanced on him but thought the better of it and scowled instead. When he could catch his breath, he gasped out, "Forgive me, but your words are right out of the old romances! The gentle, clinging woman and the noble knight! Except your face is shiny and your hair tangled and you give me murderous looks that quite belie a soft request. It makes me think you want to stab me!" He collapsed into laughter again.

Julian's dignity fell from her, and she took the opportunity offered. She could not quite laugh at herself, but she said, "Well, Charles, this reception is not out of any tale of chivalry, but my tale is long and well worth the hearing, and my request to you will be an honorable one. Will you hear it?"

He sobered instantly and the dark look came over him again, quite erasing the youthful appearance amusement had given him. "Aye, lady, but it shall be in more salubrious surroundings and when you have refreshed yourself."

He himself conducted her to a small inner chamber which was hung with tapestries and blazed with candles. Water was fetched, and she washed hurriedly while he spoke with the servant outside. Then she smoothed her hair, bound it back, sipped the tangy wine he had poured out for her, and settled herself on a comfortable chair. Her awareness of him grew by the second; did he feel it as well?

He sat across from her in a carved, high-backed chair, the very figure of a remote lord. His long fingers played with the figures of gargoyles that made up the arms, and the gray eyes glittered in the light as she talked. Julian felt herself before a judge, but her voice rang musician sweet as she summoned all the lure in her power. She told him everything, holding back nothing, speaking of Attenwood, the subterfuges she had used, the trickery employed, trusting him at the end with her hopes and her very life.

"Believe that I would not interfere in any relationship between you and Isabella, but she did try to gain my death twice, and I suspect that that attempt to force me into a nunnery was well known to her. Charles, I ask you to use your influence for me and my safety."

He turned his goblet around and around, then held it up to the light. "You are eloquent in your own cause, Lady

Julian, and have shown yourself as brave as any woman I have known. Still, there is much to consider. I am not so powerful as you think." He stood up abruptly. "These matters must rest for a time. I have been at council for the past day and find myself in need of fresh air. You will come with me."

"Charles, do not toy with me. You are a man of decision and know what you will do." She stood up, too, and lifted her gaze to his.

"Do not order me here, Julian. I do not take well to that from women." The banked fire in his eyes began to glow. "I shall order as I like. Is that quite clear?"

She nodded. What choice had she? Did he believe her story? He was her last resource and she knew it. One last weapon was left to her, and she would not quibble before use of it. The timing must be chosen, the opportunity taken when it was presented.

An hour later they walked on the beach that seemed to stretch to infinity below the great cliffs and the port city. Gulls cried in the brilliant sky, and the salt tang was in their nostrils. The fresh wind drove out the heat of the day and whipped color into their faces. They were alone in a secluded world, and yet their own ghosts walked with them. Julian wore the white and green clothes of an archer in the royal service, old but still good and far too small for the young man who had once worn them. The fit was baggy, but the coat covered much of that, and the cap hid her chestnut hair. The shoes were large and uncomfortable, but cloth had been stuffed into their toes and they would do. Charles had not changed clothes, but he had added a long dark cloak and cap that disguised him to some degree. Nothing could alter his air of nobility, but he did not seem a peer of the realm in those muffling folds.

Julian stopped suddenly and jerked at the toe of one of the offending shoes that had threatened to trip her. She hopped on one leg, swayed, and sat down in the shelter of a rock. Charles came back and stood watching, an amused grin on his face. She took off the footgear and handed it to him. "Can you fix the thing so I can walk?"

"Of course. How can you be so helpless in small things

and so bold in others?" He laughed once, and then their eyes locked so that neither could look away. His tongue moistened the carved lips, and the pulse in his throat began to beat.

Julian knew that her opportunity had come. Here on this stretch of deserted beach, in the golden noon, she could offer the only thing she had left. Instinctively she arched her body forward just a trifle so that her breasts strained against the cloth of her coat, and the shirt underneath parted to show the creamy skin. The curls at her temples had strained loose from the plaits and now blew gently against her face. The aquamarine eyes were the color of the sea in early morning, and the flush on her cheeks was that of a climbing rose. She began to tremble, and the world faded down to the man in front of her.

She moved very slowly to put both hands on his as she leaned inward so that he could feel the rasp of breath in her throat. "Charles." His name was a caress as her mouth parted so that he saw the tip of the small pink tongue. The gray eyes ignited then, and they tumbled backward on the sand, mouths locked, tongues probing savagely, his hands hard on her breasts. Desire licked at Julian and burned aside all else. They pulled at each other's clothes, twisting and jerking at each knot or tie. The world swam in front of Julian as she saw the lift of Charles's manhood, the strong shaft that alone could assuage this hunger that threatened to split her apart.

He caught her roughly to him, and they lay in the shadow of the rock where their clothes had fallen. His mouth was caressing her neck, her breasts, her stomach, while her small teeth clenched on the cries she wanted to utter. Her hands went down him and caught the long shaft, touching the pearled tip and moving on it so that he cried out with the pleasure of it. Then he pinned her hands down and rose above to thrust deeply into her and hammer through her warmth. His face was avid, almost greedy, and she knew that hers must be the same. She felt the spreading heat, the lifting rhythm, the feeling that she would melt and fall if he did not sheathe himself more powerfully yet in her wet loins. She caught his bare buttocks and raised her own to them, but he twisted a little and pulled her down beside him. His mouth found hers and their tongues joined.

She pulled back in her turn but kept her mouth on his, her hands running up and down the smooth expanse of his skin. The hard shaking had started again in her body, and his answered it. She could not hold on much longer, yet she could not yield. Charles moaned as she took her mouth away. Then she was astride him, fitting him into her flesh, her hands on his shoulders and his startled eyes gazing into hers. The feeling was different; it was one of power and strength and thrusting as his body gave and answered. He lifted her so that they sat joined with her legs behind him as they writhed for a long moment that went into eternity. Then she threw her arms around him and heard his groan as the holding ceased and they fell into timelessness.

Joined still they floated in the mist of the netherworld, a place of liquid and peace. Julian felt the first stirrings of his captured member and tensed her own responsive flesh. Her skin grew warmer, and she felt her nipples lift as the return of passion was heralded. She opened her arms and sought to pull him to her the more closely. A gull cried above them as his thumb and forefinger circled her wrist and pulled her hand down. The gray eyes shone expressionlessly into hers as he extricated himself from the embrace that was suddenly so different.

"Charles, what is it?" She pulled the shirt across her lower body and wondered strangely if this were the way Eve had felt after the sin in the garden. Sin? How could love be a sin?

"Clothe yourself, Julian." He was dressing hurriedly now and glancing about at the empty stretch of land and sea to make sure that none had seen.

"Charles, what is it? Tell me." She was on her knees, scrambling for her clothes as best she could while watching him.

He looked down at her, at the white body, the spilling hair, and the oval face. The lines around his mouth twisted, and his teeth glittered in the sun. "You have obtained what you wanted, Julian Redenter. What do such as you know of holy vows or good intentions? You have bought my obedience with your flesh. Would you have tried some other method if that had not worked? Serpent!"

All Julian's honesty rose to do battle. "Blame me not completely, Charles! You, too, wanted this. I did not wholly lure you! And, Charles, I do most truly care. You must know that. Did I not come virgin to you?"

"Virgin your mind has never been. Let be. I will protect you because of what you have purchased this day. But from this day forward there is nothing between us. Do you understand me?" He draped the cloak around his shoulders, and it blew in the freshening wind.

"Aye, Lord Varland." The formal title did not sound ridiculous as rendered by the half-naked girl. To Julian it was the mark of what she had gained and all she had lost.

CHAPTER SEVENTEEN

Trumpets rang out in the still air, faded and rose again in the triumphant salute to the sovereigns of England. The watching crowd exploded in a fervor of enthusiasm that was contagious. Julian clutched her cap with one hand and shouted as loudly as the rest. She, too, was drunk with excitement and freedom. It was her first outing in three days, and she was sick of cold walls, dark chambers, and hiding.

An old man in front of Julian swung round, his mouth gaping toothless in the bright sun, gnarled hands lifting as he waved to a young woman who was holding a baby aloft. "Let him see this glorious day that the Spaniard departs this land! Let him see!" Those around him muttered uneasily and drew a little apart, but their eyes belied their action. He caught Julian's shoulder. "Eh, boy, you don't want to waste your life in foreign wars, do you?"

The onlookers grinned as she drew back, shaking her head. The archer's costume did not resemble the trim ones now in the service of the queen, but a discerning eye might make the connection. More jostling might jerk the cap awry also. She put an eager look on her face and waved as if to someone over in the densely packed section closest to the royal entourage. Then she melted back into the people, laughing in spite of herself at the old one's remarks about young men today.

The trumpets rang again in a proud voluntary. She scrambled up on a pile of rocks recently vacated by two small boys and looked toward the harbor. The sight was a magnificent one, for the sky was pure blue and the water almost the same shade. The chalk cliffs seemed to tower into infinity and throw their reflection between earth and heaven. The massed ships hung poised on the quiet water as if waiting for a signal. Farther out she could see the tall sails and gathered power of the Spanish fleet, which boasted the colors of that country. Dominating the harbor, however, was the great flagship waiting with wings spread, pennants of red, yellow, and black hoisted, the banners of Spain triumphant. She could see the massed soldiers on her decks and see the honor escort below on the sands of Dover. A boat waited just beyond them, the oarsmen standing at attention.

Julian took a deep breath of the tangy air and craned her neck to see if the royal pair were yet in sight. They must be, for the sound of cheering had begun again; the English ever loved a brave show. In this moment of waiting she paused to wonder again if Charles had kept his word and spoken to Philip when he and the queen lodged last night at the castle. He had escorted her curtly to the small room in the depths of the castle and bidden her remain there so that none might see her and wonder. His gaze had looked past her face as he commanded obedience, and then he had not returned. She was risking much for this breath of freedom, but surely she could be safely back in the castle before she was missed; there could be no harm in watching such an occasion. Fortunately, she thought, everyone had had the same idea, and even the guard at the gate waved her on that afternoon. What was one more late archer?

Now the massed ladies and gentlemen were bending before the approaching couple, and the common folk were silent in awe. Philip of Spain was all in white and flashing diamonds that caught the sunlight and gave it back in the myriad colors of the rainbow. His bare golden head and small beard shone in brilliance. Mary wore cloth of gold sparkling with gems, and her slender figure moved with pride in what must be one of the most anguished moments of her life, the departure of her beloved husband from English shores.

Julian strained her eyes but could not see Charles anywhere in the banked rows of the nobility. She had had ample time to think of him in the past few days when she was alone with nothing to read or amuse herself. Whatever their episode had made him feel toward her, she must hope that he would keep his word. She could not believe that he hated her; his hands had spoken only of passion.

"Move over. We were here first." The boy who confronted her might have been twelve or so; his face was smeared with the dirt of the docks, and there was wine on his breath. The one with him was younger but just as dirty, and his hands were clenched into fists.

She pitched her voice low. "There is room for all."

The first boy said, "No. You leave." His mocking eyes were too wise for his age, and she saw the dawning comprehension in them as he reached for her cap.

She pulled away, thinking to call out, but those around them were immersed in the pageantry and music far in front. Suddenly three other boys, slightly older than the ones with her, converged on her perch. All were laughing, but their faces were hungry.

She felt rather than saw the tall presence beside her and felt the others shrink away. The low voice was accented and half amused. "What is this? Five against one on such a day? Is there no respect in this benighted port?"

Julian looked into black eyes below black brows in a swarthy face. The newcomer might have been thirty, surely little more, and his rich dress marked him as one of the Spanish party. The boys scattered before him, and she stared, unable to flee lest they return to taunt her.

"Boy, you can see better from the beach. Walk along with me. Those urchins can be dangerous." He smiled with one corner of his mouth only; the effect was somehow deadly.

"No. No. I thank you." She spoke slurringly, knowing that she could not hope to fool him. As it was, his eyes began to glitter in altogether too familiar a look for her bruised spirit.

The lively Spanish air of salute ceased suddenly, and the trumpets rang in a lower key. The crowd had parted enough so that she could see ahead to the royal couple, who stood a little apart while a priest spoke solemn Latin over them. Then in the same breath, young voices lifted in English song. The man beside her took a step forward, muttered under his breath, and remained where he was. Julian dared not move, but all thought of her predicament left her as the sense of the music caught and held.

"The land fair as the blooming hawthorn and the country of eagles united but now to part, yet to come again shall be my right good will." The simple words were for the king and queen, yet they might have been for the parting of lovers anywhere. "For one alone I am returning." Julian felt the chills on her back and thought of Charles Varland as he had been when he comforted her beside the Thames.

The man beside her was shifting impatiently; sentiment seemed to be no part of him. She glanced at him out of the side of her eye and wondered at the strange fear he aroused in her. Then the final phrases of King Henry's song of farewell came gliding on the warm air, and a woman beside Julian began to weep unashamedly. "I depart but pray right well to come again. . . ." A tall

country man in front of her cleared his throat, and a child
was shushed.

The music died away, and the people surged forward
again. The Spaniard brushed by Julian as his hand
touched her breasts in an intimate gesture. His eyes shone
into hers for a moment, and then he was gone toward the
gathered nobility. She told herself that she was not so easily shown to be a maid, that she was but a keener observer
than most.

Now all was silence as Philip bent the knee gravely before his wife and spoke words of formal farewell, which
were tossed aside by the wind. Then the combined music
of England and Spain rose once more as he stepped into
the boat and was rowed slowly out to where the great ship
waited. The guns roared in salute and farewell. The people
were silent now, and the little figure of the queen stood
ramrod straight as the stretch of water between England
and Spain grew wider.

Several hours later Julian sat demurely on a stool beside
one of the faded tapestries and tried to look as if she had
been there all day. She wore the brown gown again, and
her hair tumbled loosely over her shoulders to contrast
with the sun flush on her cheeks. How fortunate she had
been! Thoughts of all that could have happened ran
through her mind, and the face of the dark Spaniard with
his insinuating glance rose up. No one had paid the
slightest attention to her as she joined the milling throngs
in the streets of Dover after the formal ceremonies were
concluded. The precisely arranged function now fell into
disarray, and people wandered where they would, even
into the lower areas of the castle proper. Likely it would
be a different matter when the queen returned, but now
she experienced no difficulty, was just another young lad
in the royal livery, and found the secluded room.

Tension stretched her nerves taut as she pictured all the
possible things, favorable and unfavorable, that might happen. She had wanted so desperately to order her own
destiny and was now at the mercy of another. Father Sebastino's lecture rang in the chamber as if he stood before
her. "Woman is naturally subservient before man. This is

God's law and to flout it is a sin. Did He not make woman of man and later? Meekness is to be cherished. For woman to be other is to invoke the fires of punishment."

"No! No! I will never accept that!" She was the victim of her own memory as she cried defiance to the empty room.

Suddenly the heavy oak door banged against the wall and bounced back. Charles, resplendent in green velvet and cloth of gold with diamond-patterned white hose, stood there, long fingers hooked into his swordbelt. His face was even more that of the falcon as he watched her from under hooded eyes.

"Charles, what news? What did the king say?" Julian could not contain her eagerness.

"I trust that you will not mind assuming the archer's garb just once more, Lady Redenter? You ride with two of my men to London within the hour." His tone was casual, but there was a tiny ripple of scorn in it that brought a flare to her forehead.

"Tell me what happened!"

"Did you think I would not know that you ventured forth today despite all the danger of discovery? All the danger to me and mine as well? You thought only of yourself, madam, as always. My trusted men followed you just as they have watched during your stay here. When they lost you in the crowd, one waited by the gate here, and the other sought you." Charles spoke so carefully and slowly that Julian realized he controlled himself only with an effort.

"I am sorry." She spoke contritely. "It was just that there was no news, and I could not bear it any longer."

"Could not?" He gave the words an air of mimicry that made her shudder.

"Aye, my lord, could not. Do you find that so strange?" She knew that she should try to conciliate him, but the words seemed to come unbidden. Her breasts began to tingle, and she felt the warm pulses between her thighs. It would be impossible if he read the longing in her eyes.

He folded both arms across his chest, the candlelight

glittering off the carved planes of his face and reflecting on the tapestry beyond. "You have used me for your purposes, madam. That which you sought is yours and may you take pleasure in it! You are to be returned to the retreat at Greenwich that, ostensibly, you have never left. No coercion is to be placed upon you either to take the veil or to wed for the period of a year. You shall serve the queen actively, and after the twelvemonth is done, may ask for return to your manor if that is your wish. It will, of course, be granted. Bribes are to be given to those directly concerned, and the queen agreed to this—as she did to more important things—because King Philip asked it directly. She wanted to give you choices that she never had, she said."

Charles paused and ran one hand through his dark hair in a gesture of weariness. Julian wondered when he had last slept. She had had nothing else to do and was quite restored from her journey, although emotion had taken its own toll of her.

She said, "Did the king ask why?"

Charles laughed harshly. "Of course he did. He is no fool. I told him that I wanted you for my mistress, that I had taken your virginity, and that you found the ways of love most delightful. I could scarcely contain my repugnance at such lies."

Julian knew that he wielded the whiplash to satisfy his own anger and could not take offense. She came very close to him, her aquamarine eyes lambent under arching brows. The very passion of gratitude that she felt shone in her face, and her voice shook as she said, "Charles, I know what you must think and I regret what I had to do, but I thank you with all my heart for the help you have given me. You who are a man cannot know how bitter it is for a woman to be bartered and ordered about as though she were a thing for pleasure or a receptacle of pleasure!"

He moved back from her, and she saw that nothing she said or did would change his feelings. She lifted both hands in a gesture of resignation. As she did so, the gown gaped loose from its hasty lacings, and her bosom shone milky white and soft in the pale light.

It was then that the storm broke in Charles Varland, and he shoved her away so violently that she almost tumbled over the stool. His shadow seemed to lengthen and grow menacing in the chill room as he loomed over her. It was then that she realized he was very drunk and at war with some demon inside himself, the demon of fury that now looked out of his eyes.

"What do you seek to get now with that body of yours? A sinecure? A child you will say is mine? I invited you to be my mistress once and you fled to sanctuary, did you not? Ah, no, wench! My duty and pleasure are elsewhere!" He lifted one hand as if to strike her, then jerked it back as he fought to calm himself. "Give it out that the king of Spain took special interest in you. Say that in your country fastnesses and see if you do not see a rich and powerful lover in your future!" He threw the taunt at her and waited, a cruel grin showing the tips of his white teeth.

Julian faced him, head up, as she swept the graceful curtsy of the English court. "In my country fastnesses, as you call them, we know the meaning of honor. It is only at the court that one must learn the devious ways of dishonor; I will say that I have had good teachers. Will you do me the courtesy to withdraw, my lord, that I may prepare for the journey to London?"

He gave her an incredulous look that stripped her bare. "Aye, I will withdraw. At least one man has your measure." He laughed unpleasantly and strode from the room, swaying only slightly as he went.

"I still live and shall be free. Blessed Virgin, let that be enough!" Julian whispered the words in the still room, hating her traitor flesh that wanted the touch of his hands.

She knew herself foolish to listen for a returning step in the hall but could not restrain the leap in her heart at each small sound. It was an actual physical relief when the two men of her escort came to fetch her. By that time she wore the garb of the archer and had rolled her brown gown in a pack to carry with her.

The elder man, tall and blunt of feature, with hard, knowing eyes, spoke before she could give greeting. "By command of Lord Varland we ride fast and hard this night. There must be no delays. He has ordered it." His companion, so like him that they might have been brothers, grunted in agreement.

"I am ready, sirs. Let us ride." She strode out ahead of them, her glance challenging. There would be no faltering before others. In time she might come to believe that she could live with the wound she bore.

The horse given her was young and fresh, the pace hard. She welcomed it as they pounded away from the port and toward Canterbury. There was no speech between the men and herself; she expected none. They had their lord's orders and would carry them out unquestioningly. The straight road curved slightly in the distance as the torches of pilgrims who marched by night came closer to the holy shrine. She wondered if they had come from abroad and landed only that afternoon. Would God that she could find solace in prayer!

As the night hours faded into dawn and dawn gave way to morning, Julian found herself recalling every word and gesture that she and Charles Varland ever exchanged. She put different speeches in their mouths and other actions to their bodies but the result was ever the same: given the people they were, they could have done no other. She recalled what she had been told of his dead wife. Likely pain had made him as he was. Not for a second did she believe, as gossip had it, that he had been instrumental in her death.

We are as we are. The words rang in her mind, oddly comforting and yet bitter. Within that framework she might try to order her life. She was not such who could love again or in a lesser fashion, for Charles Varland had imprinted himself in her heart and mind as long as she lived. Very well, accept that. Accept the fact that she could not have him. She clenched her teeth against the rising sob and thought of Redeswan. Home. If she could but return there with enough money to hire labor, breed animals, grow food, and have a garden, perhaps take a yearly journey to one of the smaller cities of the realm to buy books! That would be enough in time. It must be.

So Julian came to her own measure of peace as they rode toward London town and all that awaited her there.

CHAPTER EIGHTEEN

Julian stretched her neck forward to ease the strain, then let her eyes lift to the glory of the stained-glass windows on her left. Abraham walked with the boy Isaac, angels hymned to Sarah of the blessing her womb would bring forth; here was Jacob's testing, yonder the long journey into the land of Egypt. Mystic blue, pale rose flaming to heraldic red, shimmering green and ivory white, all colors mingled and faded into hot patches on her gown. The prayers and entreaties for those far away and those joined in battle became one long litany to the Christian God. Candles of the finest make available burned steadily, for there was no breath of air in the chapel. Purple and gold tapestries adorned walls not covered with religious scenes and served to make the entire room hotter. Julian felt a trickle down her back and hoped that the new golden gown with the folded and draped overskirt of yellow satin would not be stained.

Her knees felt as if they were cracking. Well they might be, she thought, for the queen and her ladies had knelt here for more than two hours, and the ordeal showed no signs of abating. Surely Philip of Spain could have been prayed out of Purgatory twenty times over with all the pleas that had gone up for him in the month since his departure! He was well, victories had been won, yet still the queen could not rest easily.

She shifted one of the pained knees and heard an indignant sniff as Lady Clarence was jostled a little. Julian bent her head again, but now the crick in her neck was worse. Her eyes went once again to the window depicting the suffering of the saints: Sebastian and his everlasting impalement, Anthony and the flames, Teresa of the sorrows repeated. Did broken knees count for anything? Her lips twitched at the whimsy, but her nervous mind darted back at the idea of heresy.

Sternly she lowered her glance and felt eyes on her. She could not help but look up, and then the dark gaze locked with hers in complete recognition. The man kneeling diagonally with several others of the court just across from the bevy of the queen's ladies was the one who had stood with her in Dover and who had known her for a woman. He seemed quite at home at court. Now, as then, one corner of his mouth lifted, and the full red lips shone in the flickering beam of sunlight.

She held her face steady and forced her glance downward. Her whole body was chilled, no need to fear for the new gown now. Life at court had been dull and predictable since her return, and she had even begun to feel bored. She had returned to the private room of the ladies with the quick help of a serving girl on the day following their departure from Dover. There had been no sign of Mistress Wheeler or Father Sebastino, although she learned later that the latter had gone to stay and instruct at one of the monasteries near the outer portion of the city. Orders had come from the queen that Julian was to attend her the very next afternoon. She remembered the soft words of Her Majesty: "You shall be instructed and taught as is best for a young girl. This is best done at my side." Nothing more had been said, but now Julian prayed, walked, stitched, read, and waited with the older ladies. She even slept in the room of one of them, Lady Dalton, sixty if a day, and given to snoring. Nothing was said about marriage or the cloister—it was as if they had never been. Only Isabella Acton remained at the periphery of her vision, eyes shuttered and watchful. She was safe, Julian told herself, and that was enough for now.

". . . and the Father, forever." The chant rose, drifted, and fell as the company surged to its feet. Julian pulled back from the past and moved on stiff legs behind Lady Clarence, who tottered and seemed about to fall. She put one hand to the lady's elbow in the same instant as a strong, warm hand closed over hand and elbow alike.

"Allow me, madam." The soft accented Spanish voice belied the glittering eyes as he deftly maneuvered them toward the door and out into the comparative coolness of the hall. He said, "You can only be Her Majesty's most redoubtable lady, Lady Clarence. Your servant, Alphonso Diego Ortega, late of the suite of His Majesty, King Philip."

Lady Clarence performed the introduction of Julian with the slight distaste that she always exhibited toward the girl; she had not forgiven the insult of the garden on the day Charles told Julian of his betrothal. Julian curtsied now, but her legs were shaking.

"A pleasure, estimable sir." Could he sense the strange repulsion she had for him?

"The pleasure is mine, ladies. I must hasten, for I have been honored by private audience with the queen."

Lady Clarence could be deaf when she chose. "Are you new come to England, sir?"

"Aye, madam, only within the past several days." He bowed and walked rapidly away.

"Come, girl." Lady Clarence stalked along, and for once Julian did not bother to resent the abrupt command. What game did Ortega play, knowing as he did that Julian had seen him in Dover in July and this was now August? Where had he been in that time? All Spaniards came to court; they were not loved elsewhere. She could only hope he would not mention their earlier meeting. Her blood iced, for she knew that danger was once again near her, and this time there was no one to turn to. Charles had not returned to court, nor would she seek him out; it was done between them, and acrimony sat where love might have been. Her body did not know the way of her mind, however, and the nights were long, filled with heated dreams and shattering thoughts.

The court had been quiet due to the war and the king's departure, but some of the younger courtiers would have danced, as an old prelate had been heard to remark, "until the very Satan gathered his own." That night was no exception, but the queen had looked in briefly and gone away to papers, granting her ladies permission to linger for a time. Julian wondered if she had gone to weep instead, so ill and frail did she seem. Yet her prayers were for a child.

The Spaniard's reappearance had roused Julian from the lethargy into which she had dropped, and the bloom shone on her that night. Her new maid, Joan—Nan had vanished, and Julian did not dare make inquiries—had dressed the chestnut hair high in front and on the sides but let the maiden curls fall free down her back. It was intertwined with white ribbons, and a band of pearls laced the curls at her temples. Her gown was white with a wide, trailing skirt of blue, the patterns picked out in pearls. The bodice was modest, but the scooping showed the full lift of her bosom. The long puffed sleeves ended with delicate blue lace that fell over her slim hands. When she entered upon her new state, several new gowns had been made for her inasmuch as she could not serve the queen in her old ones. Lady Dalton had volunteered this information quite cheerily; the queen always looked through Julian, for all that she was unfailingly civil to the girl. Julian knew the queen was familiar with all that had happened and had done, however reluctantly, as her husband wished.

"Madam, would you honor me?" It was the tall Spaniard, elegant in violet silk and golden hose, his fingers glowing with the wealth of a dukedom, bending above her. "I will promise to return you right swiftly to the company of these illustrious ladies." He gestured and bowed at the older group, who hemmed Julian in.

She hesitated, then lifted her chin and met his amused gaze. One hand went out to him, and she did not falter as

he led her in the graceful whirl of the English dance that
allowed no time for conversation. What did he want of
her? Of habit, her eyes swept the room, the small gallery
with the musicians at the far end, and the side doors, for
the dark figure of Charles Varland. She would cease to
watch for him in time, she told herself, not really believing
it.

The music slowed and ceased. Ortega bent the knee to
her and rose. Julian made as if to retreat to the company
of the others, but he held her fast with the apparent light
pressure on her wrist. "We will dance again, lady, this
time in the music of my country, the zarabanda." The
slow clicking of castanets and tambourines began as
Ortega's feet began to weave with the motion of his hands.
Julian had little choice but to follow him as best she
could. Her teaching in this newly imported dance had
been sketchy, the steps slow and seemly. This was an assault on the senses that teased even as it tantalized. They
alone occupied the polished floor; they alone were the tar-
get of all eyes. The branched candles whirled before
Julian's eyes, and the tapestries seemed to grow into one
swirl of scene and color. The Spaniard's red mouth and
black eyes might have been those of a demon from the
plains of his hot land. She felt her blood rise and bloom in
her cheeks.

Ortega whirled closer to her now, and the smile was on
his lips only. "Madam, I bear the compliments of the king
of Spain to you. He has protected you and made possible
your freedom in which you take such pleasure. There is,
however, a reckoning to be made."

Julian hissed, "I have no idea what you are talking
about, sir."

"Then I shall enlighten you."

"I am weary. Let me go." Julian pulled back and put a
hand to her head, the curls tumbling forward as she did
so.

Ortega caught the other hand and swirled her effort-
lessly toward one of the windows that stood open to the
night air. She saw the moon glowing silver in the sky and
caught the heady scent of flowers from the knot garden

just below. There was no time to dissemble, for he stood
in front of her, blocking all view of the others.

"You are devious, Lady Redenter, and I admire that.
You are in close attendance on the queen and are thus
privy to the state of her health. His Majesty of England and
Spain is naturally concerned as to the possibility of a child
and the overall well-being of his dear wife. We shall dance
together often and speak of these matters."

"Who are you to command me?" She forgot her pose as
she flared out at him.

"I thought you were stronger than you looked to be.
You were a fine boy in Dover town." He leaned so close
that she saw the fine sheen of his skin in the close warmth
of the nook. "There are ambassadors and emissaries
aplenty in this land, all with pomp and state to be
maintained. I am a gentleman, newly arrived from Spain,
eager to see the sights of this country that belongs to us
now. I am also a friend of His Majesty. I leave you to
consider these matters." He bowed elegantly, his long slender legs showing to perfection in the tight hose.

Julian blew a sigh of relief. If occasional reports on the
queen's health were all he wanted, she would be glad to
oblige, after suitable reluctance, naturally. It appeared that
Philip had left spies in England; this was only one of
them. She smiled inwardly; a handsome spy he was, and
certainly no one could object to speech and dancing with
one so obviously of Spain. Even the queen might approve!
Her glance shifted toward the ladies who were whispering
and looking, not at her, but at Ortega as he danced with
Isabella Acton, regal tonight in green satin that became
her pale skin. They were chatting amiably as they moved
through the figures of the dance, but Ortega's face was
composed, his smile slightly fixed. Julian felt the warning
chill, the frisson on her backbone, and wondered if it foretold the future.

In the next few days Ortega was much in evidence from
the several daily masses to the various strolls in the
gardens and on into the evening dancing. He had seen the
queen, it was said, and had been much impressed by her
wisdom and devotion to duty. He spoke no more to Julian,

but sometimes she felt the flickering heat of his gaze on her. This was a time of waiting and she knew it.

One hot morning Julian was walking with Lady Dalton in the shelter of one of the arbors near this palace of Whitehall, where the queen had chosen to linger for a time. It was the grease season, the time of the hunt, and many of the remaining courtiers wished to go forth, but the queen disliked this activity and had all but forbidden it. The inactivity grated on everyone, and Lady Dalton was explaining her view of this to the uncaring Julian.

Suddenly there was a burst of quick movement on the patterned path near them, heavy steps, and a shrill voice cried, "Hasten, I must lay my knowledge before Her Majesty! There is no time to waste, I tell you! Hurry, my head spins in this awful heat!"

"Lady, please, not so quickly!" The heavy, pounding steps came again along with deep breathing and two figures, one very small and slender, the other large and rounded, came into view beyond the sheltering vines of the arbor. The smaller one stumbled and fell, gave a whimpering cry, and tried to rise as the other bent over her.

Julian saw the fascination on Lady Dalton's face and thought that perhaps it was repeated on her own. Any break in the dull routine that did not directly involve oneself would be welcome. Already the heat pressed down, and there were no breezes from the river that lay turgid in the sun. They had this little drama to themselves, for no one else was in sight.

The large, plainly clad woman was helping the other to her feet as they emerged. Julian could not help the gasp of recognition as the small pointed face and tumbling curls came into view. The agitated girl was Charles Varland's betrothed, Geraldine Rothsoon. No longer the poised beauty on the arm of her handsome intended, the girl showed the effects of strain and possible illness. The blazing sun showed tiny lines at her eyes and the lids were swollen from weeping; even the delicate skin was yellowish, though her cheeks still carried that bloom of red which seemed to show health.

Her rolling eyes focused on Julian in the cool morning gown of white silk, her hair lifted high off her neck. The shrill voice cried out, "Lady, lady, I must see Her Majesty at once. He kept me there, you see, and I could not get out. I have to tell, have to . . ." The words trailed away, and she looked at Julian in dismay.

The servant behind her said, "There, now, pretty one, come and sit down. You must rest, and we'll think what to do."

Geraldine Rothsoon threw back her head and screamed twice, the high anguished sound bouncing off the far walls of the palace itself and so piercing and penetrating to those nearest that Lady Dalton put her hands over her ears. Then the girl, her face composed, said, "Prisoner, he kept me. You can't do that, traitors can't do that. Can they? Tell me, lady, can they?"

Julian saw the stern face of Charles before her inner eye, the carved profile etched in her heart, the man she would always love regardless of his own feelings for her. What ailed the Rothsoon girl she could not imagine, but there was only one "he" that she could be speaking of, and Charles was not here to defend himself. Her decision was quickly made.

She crossed to the girl and put both hands on the shaking shoulders as she made her voice very steady. "Of course not. You shall surely see Her Majesty, but will you not come into the cool with this lady and myself for a few minutes and refresh yourself? We will help you."

"Who is she? What are you saying?" Lady Dalton was dithering in the background, her hands raised nervously, gray head slanted to one side.

Julian wanted to stamp her foot. Charles was menaced; she had to find out what this was all about before the girl spread gossip all over the court. Already the screams were bringing people closer. She could see two palace guards running toward them and several girls, their dresses bright shimmers in the heat, were hurrying along. She lifted her gaze to the servant and saw the urgent concern there.

She said, "Lady Geraldine, I met you in the garden one

day. The king and queen were there. You wore pink. Do you not remember?" Pray God the girl would not think of Charles and cry out again.

The limpid gaze hardened and Geraldine said, "I must see Her Majesty. I want to talk to her about Charles Varland, my betrothed. The matter is urgent." Her voice was rational, her face very still. "If you will help me, I will come with you. If not . . ." Her eyes rolled back again in a frenzied look.

Julian leaned very close. "I will help you, but you must be silent and come. There are those who would prevent Her Majesty from receiving her people, you know." She made her face conspiratorial.

Geraldine nodded and held out her hand to the servant who took it. Just then the guard arrived along with two older courtiers and the young girls who had heard the cries. "What is it? What has happened? Who screamed?" The guard's sword was out, and his fellow was just dashing up, his pike at the ready. Geraldine moaned softly, and Julian clamped an arm around her waist, feeling the sharp bones of her rib cage through the thin gray gown. Lady Dalton opened her mouth to speak, the sharp old eyes riveted on Julian, for whom she had little love. The group poised as antagonisms made ready to spill out.

"Faith, ladies. Such cries frightened the beast so badly that my dagger made swift work of him. There is nothing more to fear, Alphonso Diego Ortega has slain the enemy."

The company swung as one to the elegant Spaniard, who was fastidiously wiping the slender blade in his hand with several leaves and smiling gaily at them all. "The ladies were walking together when this rat crossed their path. Naturally they were terribly frightened and screamed, as what lady of delicate breeding would not? I was taking the air and rushed to the rescue. All is well now." He spoke the last words so firmly that the guards began to grin, but one of the other ladies caught her skirts close around her ankles.

Geraldine's weight bore softly against Julian, who had

eyes only for Ortega; his dark gaze was riveted on her in a kind of triumph. In her own head there whirled again the movements of the zarabanda of doom.

CHAPTER NINETEEN

It took the combined efforts of Julian and the servant, along with Ortega's soft-voiced comments, to get Geraldine to the room that Julian and Lady Dalton shared. The older lady yielded to his flattery about needing her and was now quite willing to help. Geraldine, however, was beginning to have second thoughts and resisted. In the end, it was Ortega who swept her up in his arms, murmuring about "the vapors," and deposited her in the comparative solitude of the room. He then left the servant ministering to her with Lady Dalton's almost useless help and drew Julian apart in the anteroom.

"That girl is very ill. How did you come upon her?" His dark gaze was very serious and he seemed genuinely concerned.

Julian spun a short tale dealing with Geraldine's sudden appearance and obvious illness and her own wish to help. She kept her face serious as she talked. Surely the man would leave soon and she could find out what this was all about and how it concerned Charles. Charles was all that she had considered. She had spared no thought for the young girl and her desperation. What kind of person was Julian Redenter that she could not sympathize with one of her own kind?

She ended, "Your help was most gracious, Señor Ortega. We do not need gossip rushing around the court at times such as these. Shall I walk back with you to the gardens?" He would have to take that hint!

"Ah, no, you do not rush me away so quickly! I still send messages to His Majesty that do not go by official channels, you know. I will be brief. Is there cause to think that the queen may be carrying a child? The slightest chance?" A muscle jumped in his cheek and the red lips thinned a trifle as he watched her face.

Thoughts ran wildly through Julian's head. King Philip had many sources of information; Julian Redenter was certainly not one of them. Did Ortega play his own game? Everyone knew of the queen's bitter longing for a child and the false pregnancies she had had in the past. A child would bind Philip to her, and England to Catholicism and the Inquisition. If the queen died bearing one, he would seek to rule through it in her name. He might return with fire and sword if she did not. Julian's mind warned her to be cautious and confusing.

"I think not, sir. She is beyond the age. Your questions lack taste. I will bid you good morrow." Ortega would not know from Julian that the queen's flux had not come and that she thought herself with child even now. The country called her "barren and good fortune for it," but Julian saw only the hopeless love she bore for Philip of Spain.

She watched as the red anger spread over his face and fire shone in the hell-dark eyes. The red costume edged with brown fur seemed vastly appropriate, and he bulked taller as he drew himself up. One palm smote the other as he spoke very slowly so that she should not misunderstand a single word. She listened and felt as if the powers of all darkness were arraigned against her.

"That girl in there is the betrothed of Charles Varland. She is an heiress in her own right; she will recoup his greatly diminished fortunes and restore his name, which was tarnished by association with the Protestants and that other marriage. She wishes to give the queen information that will only make her more suspicious of Varland than she already is."

"Nonsense, the girl is distraught, high-strung!" To

Julian's own amazement her voice was rock steady. "Why did you act as if you did not know who she was?"

The anger smoothed out of his face and one side of his mouth curved up in a smile. "Julian, I am the friend of King Philip and, as you may have guessed, more than a casual visitor to this land. My king is the friend of Charles Varland and has protected you both. I ask little of you in return for all that has been done. I know that you love Varland, and he is a lucky man. You cannot wed, of course, but you would not wish him to be in danger, would you?"

Julian's aplomb left her, and she caught at his arm with both hands. "Is he?"

"Not yet. Calm her down, find out what the difficulty is, and meet me here in the morning. I take it that you will be agreeable? Queen Mary can be most determined, and Philip is far away." Ortega smiled in a most friendly manner. "I think that her betrothed must be notified to come as quickly as possible. It is time for a wedding."

Julian caught her skirts around her and gave him a perfunctory curtsy. "Even so, I must leave you now, my lord." She was proud of the fact that she met his momentarily baffled dark gaze and did not flinch before she turned her back and almost ran back to her bedroom. She must find out what this coil was all about.

Lady Dalton had declared herself exhausted and in need of rest, so Julian was left to talk to the maidservant, Alice, who continued to mutter prayers and bathe her charge's forehead while she whispered out the tale of their adventure. Geraldine was quiet now, and the flush still burned in her cheeks so that she seemed brilliantly beautiful despite the yellow tinge of her skin.

It seemed that Geraldine's father, old Lord Rothsoon, had lived to be a great age; all the others of his family had long since died. She was the doted-upon child of his third wife and had lived all her life in the family estate in Cornwall, where Charles Varland's own castle was. The marriage had been agreed upon after Varland's wife had died—Lord Rothsoon saw nothing strange in wives doing that—and then he himself had perished while riding a newly bought horse. The Church had been designated protector of the girl until the betrothal could be brought to a wedding. There were no other relatives, and Charles had apparently not been eager to do his duty. Then his summons had come. Geraldine and her chaperons and servants must come to London immediately, there to lodge at his home on the Thames. He himself would welcome them, and when his court business was done, they would marry. But the young girl had sickened and grown pale. Varland's own physician had tended her, and she seemed better.

Alice sank down on a stool and fanned herself wearily, the brown eyes bulging with importance. "Then Lord Varland came back and they talked long together. She wouldn't have anybody near her, said she had to be alone. Of course, I watched her, my nursling from two years on up! She went back looking for him and stopped at a door, listened for a while, and came on back. Then she made me get up early and have a waterman at the door that gives onto the river. She was coughing a lot but seemed better. Then she started a great deal of laughing and said she didn't want to marry, ever. I came with her—what could I do? Then she started this about the queen. My poor little lady." She lowered her hands into her lap, and Julian saw that they shook.

Geraldine Rothsoon sat up in the bed, supporting herself on slender white hands, the glossy black hair falling over her shoulders and framing the enchanting oval face. "They were talking about deposing the queen and making the country Protestant. How could I marry a traitor? Anyway, he is all dark and huge. I don't want to marry, and I don't want to marry Charles. I heard them and I saw them. Important men talking treason."

Julian approached her. "Lady, you must rest more. You must not tax yourself."

Geraldine looked at her and the small knowing mouth turned down. "You are Julian. He spoke of you. It is true, all that I have said. Do you still want him? The ax shall have him instead. What do you think of that?"

"I think that God must give you grace, for you stand in

sore need of it." Julian resisted the urge to slap the triumphant face even as she went cold for the peril that Charles stood in, whether or not the words were true. If a man's betrothed—his wife in God even though the vows had not yet been uttered—denounced him, who could say that the accusation was not true? Charles would not be believed.

Geraldine began to laugh, rocking back and forth with the force of her merriment. It was ugly, bold laughter that went on and on, twisting the beautiful face into a travesty of the purity that had been there. She was curiously like Ortega, and Julian felt the same thrusting fear of a girl younger than herself.

Alice cried, "Lady, please stop it! You will wound yourself again. Please, Lady Geraldine!"

Julian watched in horror as the slender hands began to beat up and down as Geraldine's face grew pinched and she fought for air. The girl gasped, and then blood spilled from her throat and nose, cascading over the front of her gown and onto the bed. It seemed to go on and on before Alice snatched up one of the wet cloths and pressed it to her mistress's face. Even then the red mass continued to ooze.

"Put her flat while I fetch more cloths!" Julian gave the command sharply, just as she had once helped to calm Lady Gwendolyn. How could a person lose so much blood and still live? Yet the laughter still continued, and now Geraldine was coughing, a hideous tearing sound that rent her small body.

"Blessed Jesu! Pray that we are in time!" The shriek came from Lady Dalton, who had just entered the room, her face bold in spite of the genuine horror on it.

"Murder! Look at the blood!" Another lady-in-waiting whom Julian vaguely recognized swayed against the door and seemed ready to faint.

The tall figure of the court physician, followed by his younger helper, appeared in the frame. "Stand away, all of you. I must examine the lady. Quiet, now. I must think." He gestured imperiously to the helper; his own hands must not be soiled by contact with so gross a thing. "Get out, all of you." He whirled on them and they retreated, even Alice, whose face was blotched with tears.

Julian saw that Geraldine was being lifted up by the helper and that the blood was flowing harder, then the door was shut in her face and she could see no more. She felt her face harden into a mask that must face the others Lady Dalton had brought with her. If she and Alice could have been left alone, it might have been possible to staunch the bleeding, but the physician might even consider it a good thing and allow it to continue. If that happened . . . she dreaded to finish the thought.

"Why did you bring him?" She snapped the words out at the older woman and saw the eyes of the several servants and ladies who had gathered. They were hot with curiosity and suspicion.

"The poor girl had to have someone." Lady Dalton was all injured innocence. "Poor child, crying out that way. Poor lost thing."

Julian said, "I must have air. Let me pass." The cluster of bodies had grown in just that short a time, and she felt the urge to pound at them and scream. As she pushed through to the fringes she heard one comment that stopped her in her very tracks.

"Another girl ill in strange circumstances! Varland should be put where he can do no more damage!"

The courtier leaned toward his friend and said so that Julian could hear, "Watch out. That one is said to be eager for him."

She heard the subdued sound of their laughter as she ran for the blessed quiet of the garden. There in a quiet niche she knelt before the image of the Virgin and prayed passionately for the health and soul of Geraldine Rothsoon before she dared utter her true prayer for the safety of the man she so desperately loved and longed for, Charles Varland, who stood in deadly danger. The delicately carved face above her was only ivory, however, and there was no comfort. The air was warm against her face, down which the tears slipped, and the image of the hawthorn tree rose full in her mind, the symbol of life beyond life.

When Julian went back to her room after minutes or

hours—she had no idea which—the crush of the curious was standing well back, and the small crumpled figure of Geraldine was lying on a litter supported by four servants. The physician was speaking importantly to Lady Dalton, his tones round and ringing.

"You likely saved her life by coming to fetch me, madam. She has cause to be grateful to you."

Julian saw that the blood still ran from Geraldine's nose and bubbled frothily from her lips. She wondered if the queen's own physician would tend Geraldine and what would happen if he did. In her youth she had often helped Elspeth tend wounds, and the stopping of the blood flow had been the first thing. Why should this be any different?

"The purging will benefit my lady. Evil humors beset her." Loftily, the physician signaled to the carriers who bore Lady Geraldine away, the maidservant following after. The courtiers looked at Julian, and she felt the weight of their suspicion as a palpable thing. There was little enough to amuse them these days, and this tale had all the earmarks of a true scandal.

She said clearly, "Lady Dalton, will you go with me to the chapel to pray for the poor lady?"

The older woman gasped but nodded. It was a shame to leave the fascinating gossip, but on the other hand it might be useful to observe the demeanor of the girl. Julian easily read the conflicting emotions that crossed her face and, in a moment of sheer malice, extended her hand. Lady Dalton took it after a second of hesitation, and they walked from the hall together.

Julian did not meet Ortega the next morning, for she kept Lady Dalton beside her and made sure that the woman had little opportunity for gossip. The drama of Geraldine's appearance and sudden illness overshadowed even the discovery that one of the kitchen maids had been caught in the attempt to poison a dish set aside particularly for the queen. It was clumsily done, and the girl was hauled away for questioning within minutes. The great, it was remarked, must expect such things. The queen had sequestered herself on matters of state, and the court had little to do but speculate.

Very early on the second morning after Geraldine was stricken, Julian was summoned, along with several other ladies-in-waiting, to attend the queen. There was still no news of the girl's condition; even the most avid knew nothing. Julian felt the stares but carried herself calmly even though she knew that her face bore the marks of the sleepless nights. The copper morning gown was now looser than it had been, and her hair refused to be coaxed into a semblance of order, so she bound it back in a huge knot on her neck, then pinched her pale cheeks to give them some faint color. It seemed to her that she had always been suspended in this eternity of waiting, that there was to be no relief from its torment.

When they entered the private chamber of the queen and made their obeisances, Julian saw again that she had lost that brief bloom happiness had given. Now she looked her forty years and more as her hands shook slightly from weariness, the lines on her drooping face pronounced and sharp. Whether by intent or purpose she waved the others away and beckoned to Lady Clarence, then to Julian, who was nearest her. The purple-and-gold-hung chamber was muffled and dark despite the blazing candles. It was very hot; the sweat stood out on Julian's face, and she found it hard to breathe. Heaps of jewels, papers, shoes, and gowns were tossed together in piles, but two portraits of Philip of Spain stood beside the ornate bed.

Mary Tudor spoke as if to herself, her eyes on the portraits. "No rest in all the long nights. I do truly think that I bear England's heir, Spain's heir, within me. Too early to know, they say, but I know."

The tired voice trailed away as she submitted to the gentle hands of Lady Clarence, who divested her of the robes and handed them to Julian. The clinging underrobe shone opaque in the candle glow, and Julian glimpsed the rounding of her stomach though she stood straight. One hand went downward and rose again. She had thought herself with child before and the country had rung with merriment, for by then she was hated.

"Aye, when the news came that my dear lord had taken San Quentin, that great victory, then I knew." She sank into a chair, and Lady Clarence, eyes alight with love, began to brush the sandy hair with soothing strokes.

Julian began to fold away the robes and place the jewels in their leather containers and silken bags; the flashing emeralds, milky ropes of pearls, delicate opals, golden chains, slipped smoothly over her hands. She picked up a necklace of delicately wrought gold links, each set with huge blazing rubies. It reminded her of Geraldine's blood pouring over the white face and soaking the bed. She fought her revulsion lest she fling the thing from her.

"Madam." The whispered word from the door caught them all by surprise, and their eyes swung toward it. A middle-aged servant stood there, black dress melding in the darkness, white face shining with the traces of tears. She fell to her knees before the queen, who waved impatiently and waited.

"Your Majesty, the girl is dead. The bleeding began again, and she could not speak."

The queen crossed herself, and all followed her example. Then she said, "I will order masses sung for her young soul. What of Varland?" Her voice grew hard on the name.

"He arrived only an hour ago, and the physician would permit him only the briefest moment. He waits beyond the door as bidden."

Mary the Queen turned to look at Julian with the considering eye that her father's courtiers had learned to dread and wisely so. "Lady Redenter, come here that I may see you more clearly."

The shortsighted eyes watched closely as Julian, heart hammering, moved to obey. The girl knew that propriety demanded she lower her own eyes in modesty and awe, but an instinct older than any court's told her that she stood in the presence of an affronted lioness, and boldness was her only safety.

"How may I serve Your Majesty?"

CHAPTER TWENTY

The queen's first words took Julian by surprise and belied the light in her eyes as the stubby lashes swept down. "Go to Lord Varland and remain with him until my priest, my comforter, can arrive. You have suffered losses and will know what to say. Say that I, too, will condole with him upon his great loss."

Julian bent in the prescribed curtsy, wondering if this were the real reason she had been summoned. Surely the queen was not being devious; that was not in her forthright nature. Was a plot still afoot? She could think of nothing else at this moment except Charles; the longing that swept through her body shook her to the marrow. "As Madam the Queen commands."

Queen Mary spoke fretfully. "I wanted to help you, the daughter of my mother's lady. Honorable marriage, the peace of the cloister, but no . . . and yet my lord husband has pointed out the precariousness of your youthful upbringing . . . who can know the right?"

Julian felt the chills go down her back. She did not doubt the goodwill of the queen, but this sounded as if someone had been speaking to her in an attempt to put aside the bargain that Charles told her had been struck. She lifted her eyes to the queen and said with all the power of her faith, "God knows the right, and he has raised you high. I rest in your wisdom." Not in her wisdom, thought the girl, but in the simple honesty that had always marked Mary Tudor as girl, woman, and queen.

"You are dutiful in your words. See that your actions are such." She shut her eyes wearily, waved Julian back, and motioned for Lady Clarence to continue with the brushing.

Julian rose on shaky legs and followed the servant to the side room, which was richly appointed with tapestries and velvets. A carved screen depicted the agony of the Christ and the glory of the Resurrection. Shimmering rugs in several shades of purple lay on the floor. Charles stood looking out the window at the expanse of parkland beyond the grounds proper. She watched him for a second, noting the way the warm wind blew back the dark hair and lifted the sleeves of his white shirt.

"My lord, I am sent by Her Majesty . . ." She spoke the words the queen had ordered, her voice low and gentle, her mind busy. Here was no grief-stricken lover, no shocked betrothed. His face was stern, the nose-to-mouth lines very visible, the gray eyes watchful. He wore breeches and boots of black and a black cloak lay close by with his sword on a stool.

"Julian, tell me what happened and do not fear to speak the truth to me." He stood well away from her; she might have been another man rather than the woman he had once held in his arms and lifted to the heights.

Julian felt sudden disgust for herself that she could think of such things when Geraldine lay dead. What manner of person was she? One lewd and gross, it appeared. "It was in this manner, my lord." She progressed with the tale in a low voice and had reached the account of Geraldine's frantic desire to see the queen, when Charles took several steps toward her, one hand held out.

"Don't, lady. What could you have done, after all? She was always frail." His dark eyes, almost black in the light, glittered at Julian in direct contrast to the soothing voice. He hissed under his breath, "Weep, wail. Hurry!"

She stared at him, wondering if he had taken leave of his senses and what she should do. The fingers on his reaching hand waved toward one wall that was covered by a tapestry depicting the Last Supper. He let it fall as though she had stepped out of reach and whispered again, "Wail!"

Julian obeyed instantly. What more natural than that they should be thrown together and an eavesdropper placed close by? How had Charles known? She began to sob, gasping out a little of the tale, speaking of the fever and all that had been done for Geraldine. Her voice rose higher and dropped as though she fought to control herself. She let it rise with an intensity of emotion that was not entirely feigned as Charles murmured soothingly.

"Geraldine saw you with others at your house—heard something—convinced of treachery—came to inform." The disjointed phrases came between her sobs, and she saw the dark face above her go white. In an impulse of tenderness she added, "The queen looks with child—that is her main concern. Be careful."

Charles moved well away and said, "I will summon your maid to you. I thank you, madam, for all that you tried to do for my betrothed." His eyes bade Julian weep more strongly, and she did so even as she looked out from behind her sheltering hands.

One of the tapestries was in her line of vision. At first it was a shimmer of blue and gold, then it resolved into the faces of the disciples, and one of them had human eyes. She swung away, then lifted her face to Charles. His lids dropped in agreement, and she began to appear that her feelings were controlled.

"My lord, forgive me. I was overcome."

"Aye, lady. I, too."

A step glanced off stone, and they looked up to see a slender priest whose fringe of white hair gave a halo effect. He hurried toward them, his hands outstretched and his eyes warm. "My son, I have heard the most grievous news. Let us go to the chapel and seek God's comfort."

Julian said, "I must return to the queen very soon. I wait on her now." She bent her head respectfully to the priest and went into the hall. As she walked she felt the eyes of the disciple figure boring into her back and wondered who it might be. If Charles were truly suspected of wishing to destroy Geraldine Rothsoon, then both she and he stood in the greatest danger from the several court factions. She almost wished for Philip of Spain, who at least knew how to control those he ruled. The queen of England swayed in several directions and could be trusted in none. Indeed, she was the wounded lioness made vulnerable by love.

In the next weeks, which saw August grind deeply into September, Julian was kept more closely in attendance upon the queen, who seldom spoke directly to her but watched when the girl least expected it. Isabella was often present with the older ladies, her manner restrained and deferential. Julian still feared her, but there were no more attempts either to discredit her or to take her life. The courtiers were cool and few spoke to her except when necessary, but Julian was always conscious of the danger that waited to pounce and yet toyed with her.

She learned, as all knew from the gossip and talk, that the body of Geraldine Rothsoon was interred in the church of her fathers on the Cornish coast and that masses would be sung for her soul in perpetuity. Charles had gone with the cortege as was seemly and would return to the palace soon to confer again with the queen, who would either give him the estates by virtue of the fact that he had stood almost as husband to the dead girl or claim much of it, as was also feasible, by right of the crown.

"He ought to be banished at the very least! If you had seen that poor child gasping for breath there at the end . . ." Lady Dalton always had the power to gather a group around her, and these days were no exception. "A man like that is dangerous!"

Julian was passing at the time and felt her stomach knot in anger. She knew that they wanted her to flare in response, and once she would have done so. Now she went close and spoke as if to Lady Dalton alone, "Dear madam, do forgive this intrusion, but I vow I did hear Her Majesty asking for you. Quite sharply, as a matter of fact."

Among her ladies the queen continued openly to say that she would bear a child, and her temper was short these days. Julian knew that she was even now closeted with papers from Philip; it was a safe gamble she took, and the white face Lady Dalton raised was sufficient for her own ease. If she could not defend Charles openly, she would do what she could in other ways.

Lady Dalton was forbiddingly silent that night as they lay in their beds, but she did not speak again of Charles that Julian could hear. Perhaps the queen had rated her; at least that was a normal relationship. In these days Julian sometimes longed for the days of Blanche's careless friendship or Elspeth's caring. She saw Ortega at times, but his eyes were hooded, his manner remote. He, too, was waiting. All her instincts told her that.

Ortega sought her out one night as she sat idly at the virginals remembering the night she had sung of Greensleeves to Charles and felt the fire between them. He wore brown velvet slashed with fur in spite of the heat, and his smile showed the tips of his white teeth, giving him a feral appearance. His smooth-tipped fingers brushed across her hand as it lay on the instrument.

"You are much alone these days, Lady Redenter. How can that be with so fair a lady?" He smiled down at her. "What of Her Majesty? Does she continue in health? Will His Majesty truly have cause to rejoice at the birth of a child? One hears much of that possibility these days."

Perhaps it was the loneliness and the ostracism she had undergone, the days that passed without a civil word or glance, but Julian found herself forgetting caution and thinking only that the man before her knew of her passion for Charles and might someday help them. She said, "Aloneness is good for the soul, sir. I do sometimes think that Her Majesty needs more of it, however. She labors long for one who may be with child. And yet . . ." She paused and her words went ahead of her wisdom as the doubts took shape. "Yet, I do doubt it. She is too gaunt, too jutting in shape, and the fever besets her, for I have seen her wet with it in the mornings."

She stopped as Ortega bent to her, his face serious as she had never seen it, earnestness in every line. "Is this idle speculation? Verify it for me and you shall not regret it. If anything happens there will be civil war at the worst, and Philip can intervene to hold the country stable. If there is a child, what could be more natural than that the father, a prince of the true faith, should rule rather than the heretic, Elizabeth? If she tries for power there are ways . . ." His words trailed off, and he gave Julian a calculating glance. "The king's friends will be remembered, Lady Julian. If you want Lord Varland it is possible for you to have him."

In later days Julian was to be proud of her reaction to the bait. It made up in some small manner for the way she had felt about Geraldine. She answered, "I do not deal in human lives. I am a maiden and know little of these mannerisms of breeding women. Seek elsewhere for your informer, sir."

Ortega stood up and smiled quietly. "I spoke honestly to you and see that instead I should have hedged my words round with sentiment and protestations of propriety. The loss is yours, Lady Redenter." He bowed elegantly and left her looking after him.

When Julian was summoned to wait on the queen the next afternoon, she was conscious of the heavy atmosphere that pervaded the private chamber when she entered. Several ladies-in-waiting sat sewing near the open window that looked out onto a garden; their spread gowns drooped in the heat that pressed down, and the altar cloths on which they worked trailed on the floor. Lady Clarence had given the queen a fresh coif and now sat beside her mistress as she wrote a lengthy letter. Thunder mumbled in the distance, and the tree by the window swayed in the hot wind.

"Play softly on the lute. Nothing jangling." The command was sharp, and the queen did not turn, but all knew that Lady Clarence spoke with her voice.

Julian touched the instrument, sank to the stool, and drew forth the notes of an old ballad that ran water soft into the ears of her listeners. It helped her to forget how hot she was in the green satin gown with the puffed sleeves and the lace over the bodice. Her hair was partially hidden under one of the plain coifs the queen liked her ladies to wear and it, too, was hot.

" 'The prince of Spain, he came over the sea. The

prince of Spain he will come no more to me. Never, never, to me.' " The gruff voice spoke into the silence and hung there. Mary the Queen turned to face them and spoke the words as though to a close friend. Lady Clarence, greatly daring, reached for her hand and held it as the small face twisted. "They chant it in the streets, I am told. 'Mary, Mary, quite contrary.' All the rhymes. Ungrateful! And I have tried to do so much!"

"Madam the Queen has done much! Is not our country returned to the true faith? Do not the holy priests and nuns rejoice in their restoration to honor? Are the souls of the faithful not at peace?"

The ladies swung as one to the slender figure standing in the doorway that led from the queen's chamber. Isabella Acton, her pale beauty enhanced by a flowing white gown, her hair a coronet about her head, advanced toward the queen.

"Forgive me that I am bold, but surely the Queen forgets that she endured much adversity and was preserved by God to rule? I have loved you long—I cannot bear that you hurt so, my dear lady."

The queen stood up, her very human pain gone, the ruler of England standing taller than her wont in the golden gown. Isabella sank to the floor in a billow of skirts, head bent in case the Tudor rage should break forth. Mary's harsh laughter rang out, and Julian shivered at the sound of it. Then one hand went out to raise Isabella.

"Dear friend, you have spoken truly. I will forgive the fact that you were also impertinent. Come, sit with me for a little while as Lady Clarence rests. These are not easy days."

Lady Clarence moved away at the queen's wave, and the ladies resumed their chatter as Isabella sank on the stool at the edge of the table. The small drama was done. Julian watched, aching for her mistress and trailing one finger across the lute strings. The other woman was opening up a small packet of silk, saying as she did so, "Ah, Majesty, I should not distract you, I know, but will you

see what I have found in the goldsmith's row? The instant
I saw it I knew you would be enchanted even as I."

Her voice was soft so that it did not carry to the others
at the end of the room, but Julian heard a strange note in
it and wondered as she tilted her head over the lute. So
long as Isabella Acton was in her presence, the woman
chilled her blood. She heard the queen's pleased exclamation and the little laugh of discomfort she always gave
when someone offered a present; she was poor in her
youth.

"'I thought it would remind you of pleasant days." Isabella held up a small rounded object, perhaps half as big
as her own fist. It sparkled in the light, first faintly orange
and then pale rose. A golden stem shone from one end
and a jeweled leaf hung from that.

"Ah, the pomegranate! My mother's own device and the
very symbol of Spain. I remember she had a necklace
hung with these." The queen was openly laughing now, the
harsh lines of her face smoothed away.

"And, do see, the little seeds are here on one side.
Worked most cunningly, are they not? You need only to
pull the stem and it will open up." Isabella put the pretty
thing into Mary's palm where the light caught it and reflected off the polished sides. "Take it, madam, for it is my
gift."

"Isabella, how can I? It must have cost you greatly. But
how very thoughtful." She held up the jewel and called to
the others. "Ladies, come and see!"

"Open it, madam." Isabella rose when the queen did,
and that queer note was in her voice again.

Mary's fingers touched the stem and drifted over the
little leaf. She could take a child's joy in a present and
liked to prolong the moment of revelation. Julian rose to
go nearer, smiling at the queen's pleasure. The others were
coming closer, murmuring as they did so. Isabella leaned
closer, one fingernail pointing at the stem as the queen's
hand rose to it. Julian saw her face and the fleeting look
of triumph that passed over it. Then she saw again the
little garden and the lampoon of the queen, heard again
the sick, angry voice speaking of the death of her husband

and the Catholic queen who was the cause. Laughter had been on Isabella Acton's lips then, and it was the same laughter of a few minutes ago.

Julian Redenter wasted no time in thought. She cried, "Madam, no! Do not open it!" Her own strong hands that had scrubbed and worked at Redeswan had twice the power of either woman's, and she slapped the jeweled fruit away from them so hard that it rang on the floor and bounced toward the oncoming women.

Mary Tudor turned on Julian and her royal rage blazed out. "You are demented! I banish you from my sight, from this court! Count yourself lucky that you are not in the Tower! To raise your hand to the sovereign is death! Get out!" She put both hands on her hips and advanced toward Julian.

The girl stood very still. Had it been an innocent gift after all? "Your Majesty, I feared for you. . . ."

Isabella's face was white to her hairline, and she was shaking as she cried, "The girl is mad to touch you, Majesty! I will fetch the jewel!" She turned a fierce face to Julian, then ran to fetch the golden thing.

Julian ran for it as well, but both were too late. Lady Dalton, her curiosity always uppermost, had abandoned the horrified group and picked up the pomegranate. Now she pulled at the stem, and the globe fell in sections into her palm. In that very instant, her scream of mortal agony tore the air. She fell heavily, her face contorted and her heels drumming on the floor. Her breath rattled in her throat and then it stopped.

Mary Tudor turned to face Isabella Acton, who stared at her, her face expressionless. "You meant to kill me. Why?"

"You are Antichrist." The words fell into the room as if they were huge stones. Isabella was carved ivory, beautiful in adversity though the dark eyes glittered with hate at last unveiled. "I serve God."

"Guard! Guard! To me!" She beckoned to Julian. "You shall tell me later how you knew. I am grateful, and you shall know the measure of that gratitude."

The guards burst in then and surrounded Isabella at a wave of the queen's hand. The small woman whom some had disdained showed no emotion or fear; none had ever questioned her personal courage. The other ladies stood well away from Lady Dalton's body and several were crying.

The queen said, "I loved you well, Isabella. Now you pay the penalty of heresy and treason. Take her away!"

Julian knew that Isabella could implicate her by association, but that was a danger that could be borne. What was harder to endure was the pure courage of the other girl as she said, "If you had died, I know that I would not have lived. I die for the true faith. May God destroy you for the murderer you are, Madam the Queen of England!"

Julian thought then that if ever her time came to face death she could not do it with such bravery; she was the lover of life and would always place that first. She could not feel sorry for Isabella; the girl had tried several times to kill her, but she could honor her stance for her beliefs.

CHAPTER TWENTY-ONE

The people were tightly massed together in the place known as Smithfield. Children stood hushed beside their parents, and the usual collection of mangy dogs were silent and skulking. The early morning air was hot and sultry. Banked clouds seemed to hang close to the ground. The slow tapping of a drum was the only sound in the stillness that seemed a palpable thing.

The queen of England, dressed completely in black and flanked by her guards, her ladies following in double file, crossed to the wooden seats that had been erected for them. They all sat, Julian slightly behind the queen and next to the watchful soldiers.

"Let justice be done!" The gruff voice rang out, and the royal hand came down sharply.

Julian forced herself to look at the tall stake and the piled wood, some green and the rest seasoned. Several hooded men stood by with blazing torches, and off to the left, two priests conferred. She saw without surprise that one of them was Father Sebastino. It was so still now that she could hear her own heart hammering and the sound of the crackling torches as they were lifted high against the clouds.

Soldiers covered the area, their weapons at the ready. Priests walked about in the crowd, and none dared draw away. Julian clenched her teeth; she could not pray to the God who allowed all this to happen. She could not bear it. How could Isabella endure such torment? All the stories she had ever heard about the death heretics suffered came back to her, and vomit roiled in her throat.

Now the drum tapped more ominously, and a file of black-clad priests came toward the stake. In their center marched a tall muscular man with a black hood over his head. It was the small thing in his arms that drew the attention of the crowd. Julian's keen eyesight brought every detail vividly into focus. The long spill of pale hair tumbled over his large hand and was the only touch of color in the procession. The bare feet were stumps that curved back on each other, and the dangling fingers were nubs of themselves. The small head turned back and forth, the mouth open in a scream that did not come.

Julian put her hands over her face, but they were instantly jerked down by Lady Clarence, whose fierce, vengeful eyes glittered into hers. The old woman's strength was surprising but the passion was not, for dearly did she love the queen. Mary gave Julian a sidelong glance then, and the same fierceness was there. The girl was forced to watch; there was no other recourse.

Now Isabella was being chained to the stake, and those with torches drew nearer. She threw back her head, and this time Julian saw that her mouth was bare and bloody.

Her teeth had been knocked out. They piled the faggots around her so that she stood on a tall mound, and then the priest was called forward. His murmur bore plainly on the hot air as he spoke of mercy and the true faith. The gurgling cries rose as Isabella fought the chains that held her in place.

"I commend your soul to God." The priest lifted his hands and stepped back.

"Light the fires!" The queen was impassive, convinced that she was totally in the right, her face set in righteous lines.

In vain Julian tried to remember summer days at Redeswan, Charles's face over hers in passion, the tenderness of her mother in the early days, the beauty of a Kentish garden. It was no use. There was nothing but blood-murder in front of her, and the drama must be played out. She had inadvertently brought Isabella to this, and now she must suffer as well. Her head rose and she did not turn away.

The torches dipped down. The flames caught at the dried wood first so that the crackle sounded hungry. The travesty that had once been a fair woman flailed and tried to scream now but could not. Smoke now hung greasily on the motionless air, but it was not enough to suffocate the victim. The crowds were still; they knew their own danger after four years of this rule.

Julian saw the flames reach Isabella's tattered skirt and flare up onto her arm. The white face contorted even more and then was seen through the sheen of fire and tears. It went on and on, for the fire burned sporadically, now savage, now fading away. The body tossed, twisted, burned, and burned. The smell of roasting meat and vomit rose acrid to the nostrils.

It seemed to Julian that she felt each flame lick at her own flesh. Three days ago she had feared that Isabella Acton held her own life in jeopardy. Now she was ashes and raw flesh in the cruelest of deaths. Nothing was worth that, she vowed, not any belief, person, or thing accounted holy. All that mattered was life and the quality of it. Fury burned in her until it seemed that she must cry out with it;

in this time she hated everything and herself most of all. She felt bruised and torn; it seemed that she could not hold herself in check much longer.

The crowd was now murmuring the prayers for the soul of the dead, followed by those for the safety of the king and queen. Julian made her lips move with the others, for she knew that eyes watched. Then Father Sebastino lifted his arms for silence and began a long diatribe on traitors, heresy, and the necessity for the Church to root out all such. Under the darkening sky, the scent of burned flesh in her nostrils, the smoke causing eyes to water and smart, Julian thought once again of the pagan rituals described in the old books. Was this so different?

Time blurred mercifully after that as thunder rolled in the distance and lightning began to flicker. When the hot wind rose and rain fell in little drops, the litter was brought for the queen, and her ladies followed after. Julian's last memory of Smithfield was the hideous stake with the smoking charred remains and the cries of the priest before his god of flame. She was so exhausted that one foot would scarcely move in front of the other, and when the woman brushed against her in the street, she almost lost her balance. Hard fingers caught hers for a second, and when she was released there was the rough feel of parchment in her hand. The woman, well cloaked, had vanished into the crowd that lined the streets to see the queen pass. There was no jeering, but Julian felt the dull weight of their hatred.

Once back at the palace, she went to the rooms she had shared with Lady Dalton, and there in the blessed release of privacy she read the Latin scribble in a hand she well knew. "The river bend at noon for your life. Osiris." Her hand shook as she put it down. This could be no trap, for who would know of the incident when Charles had saved her life? She felt a little of her anguish recede in the knowledge that he was here and wanted to see her. The reason did not matter.

It was raining steadily as she approached the meeting place, but the oppressive heat still remained. She wore a black cloak and hood; her dagger was long and unsheathed in her hand and a shorter one, legacy of the ever careful Elspeth, was in her sleeve where it could be easily reached. She heard the warning growl and the soft command before the brown-clad figure rose up out of the wet underbrush and called to her.

"Charles! Oh, Charles!" Nothing else would come, but that was enough. His arms caught her to him as her own went around him, and they clung together, swaying slightly while the huge dog whined at their feet.

Julian felt her hard-won control slipping from her as everything faded except the warmth of his body and the gentleness of his touch. She burrowed her face down in the soaked cloth of his collar and gave herself up to the moment. Charles held her for another instant, then pulled back slightly so that her wet face lifted to his.

"Julian, I have learned that Isabella broke when she was put to the torment. She gave several names, yours among them." He nodded at her gasp of horror. "She was a true servant of her faith and knew that she would die for what she attempted. Yet who can blame her for trying to lessen the agony? She said that you knew all along, that you were being paid to kill the queen in your turn, and that you serve those who would set the young queen of Scotland on the English throne."

"That is madness!" Julian stared into the set dark face, where a new harshness shone. He was dressed as a common man, but his pride was that of a lord of the realm.

"This kingdom is mad. But, look you, there is no time to stand here exploring motives. Come with me to the coast. We have friends there who can keep you until a safe ship can be found for France, which shelters some of our exiles for reasons of her own. You can come as you are."

"What of you?" He did not ask her to come with him out of charity, surely?

"Julian, for God's sake! Can you not understand? Even now soldiers have been sent to arrest me for treason. You know the penalty for that! You will suffer it also!"

"Treason?" Her mind had gone blank and fuzzy. She heard the steady drip of water from the trees behind them and the snuffles of Osiris as he dug busily at a hole. "You and Isabella worked together, then? Geraldine was right about you? The gossip was right?" She was not really surprised, but the deeper implications shook her to the depths.

"I am one of many who work for the accession of the Princess Elizabeth to the throne. Mary is sick and mad. Philip of Spain is foolish enough to think that he may be able to rule in her name if she dies; he would set all England afire with the Inquisition if he could. He has been my friend, but I knew long ago that this cause to which I have pledged myself would demand sacrifices. Love, honor, friendship—there is no room for them. Can you understand that, Julian? All those who try to save England from foreign intervention and internal battles over religion know the risks we run and are prepared for them. France is dangerous, too, and her agents are here among us. The little Scots queen, Mary Stuart, will wed the king of France, and you know her claim to the English throne through old King Henry's Catholic sister, Margaret. We must be ready for anything!" Charles's voice rang with a passion that Julian had not seen behind the mask he always wore with her. All mockery and sarcasm were gone. This was a man devoted to one thing only.

"Thrones, queens, religion! I do not want a political lesson! Charles, you and those like you make scenes such as the one today, do you realize that? Why was Isabella not rescued or at least given something to make the agony bearable? Queen Mary has been kind to me; she has suffered so much and I thought only to save her life, not kill Isabella. You knew all the time that she tried to have me killed, did you not? What do I care for Philip of Spain or Geraldine or the makers of plots? One ruler is like another; your precious Elizabeth can be no different! It is human relationships that count." She was crying now, but she did not want to stop the tears or the words. She was one of the betrayed ones.

"I owe you no explanations, Julian, but I have fought long with myself." His voice went low for a minute, then rose and steadied. "You are an innocent, and I would try to save you if you could bring yourself to let me." The very fierceness of his words made her look at him and see the tight cords in his neck, the throbbing veins in his temples. "Geraldine had a disease of the lungs that affects her family and killed many of them. Philip, my friend, could destroy this land. Do you think I came easily to plot against the ruler, I whose ancestors were at Hastings, or to forsake my word to a young girl and forget the hand of friendship given me when I wanted only to die? Why am I explaining all this? You will not listen!"

Julian saw the depths of his pain and wanted only to assuage it. "Charles, I am listening—do not tear yourself so."

He plunged on. "My wife, my Beth, died in a religious brawl between Catholic and Protestant. There was a street fight, and she was caught in it with only a servant to protect her. They raped her; that knows no religion! Seventeen years old and big with our child!" He controlled himself and spoke firmly. "The princess is the true heir; she is both devious and intelligent. She has borne herself well under the reigns of her brother and sister. She is the hope of England. Under her rule it would be possible to live sanely."

Julian shook her head. "You are just as fanatical as those who burn in the name of the faith. No one tried to help Isabella, and yet she was as much a zealot as you."

"She wanted to die for the Protestant cause." Charles gave a low whistle and Osiris came running to him. "We must go. Enough of this."

"I am not going." She drew the hood up over her head and faced him. "The queen promised that, in return for saving her life, I might have the ordering of my own. She said that this had been promised by intervention of the king but that she would now give me dowry and land in my own right. I was to think on the matter, she ordered, and speak to her again after . . . after Isabella . . ."

"And you count yourself better than I in this?" Charles caught her arms and shook her. "By what reason?"

"I will have Redeswan, my home, my people, in security." As she said the words Julian saw the house lifting up before her, the dwelling of her fathers, and it seemed to symbolize the endurance of the Redenters. "She will give it to me. The queen has given her word. They will know that Isabella lied."

"You sign your death warrant, Julian. Why are you so stubborn?" The gray eyes were mystified. "Is it because I have not lured your body or promised you a passion that is no longer within me?"

His words seemed to strike Julian, but she saw the torment in his face. He fought his own feelings and she knew it. "There is no difference in people like you and those who follow the queen. Let all of you destroy yourselves. I am sick to death of politics and cruelty, Charles!"

"Then there is no more to say." He drew the wet brown cloak around his shoulders, and the raindrops dripped on his dark head to slant down the high bones of his face. "Go with God, Julian, the God in whom I no longer believe. I hope that you live long enough to know that the battle, as you say, is every Englishman's and every Englishwoman's battle, and until it is won no person in this land is safe or deserves to be!"

"With God, Charles Varland!" Her voice trembled in spite of all her efforts.

He pulled her to him then and their lips met in a fusing kiss that ignited the fires between them once more. His mouth shaped itself to hers as their bodies crushed against each other so closely that they might have been one flesh. Their tongues probed and locked. His hands wrapped themselves in her tumbling hair and her breasts began to burn. Julian felt her senses swirl as the honey began to trail languidly in her veins.

The stiffening began in his arms and gradually transferred itself to Julian's own so that she remained within the circle of his embrace, an individual apart and made of ice. His mouth shifted from hers and his head turned very slowly toward the river. Now that she could think again, she saw that Osiris was poised and looking in the same direction. There was the slap of oars and an indistinct murmur of voices, a loud curse, and then more sounds of rowing. She turned her glance to Charles's shuttered face, and he nodded grimly.

"We may have been seen but then, too, we may have seemed any man and maid."

Julian hesitated, wondering if she should not go with him even now. But he would send her to France and exhaust himself in the wars that always came of religion. There was passion between them, but his cause would come first. She might never see him again. Then, too, she acknowledged that she was afraid of the immolating love that could destroy. Love him she always would, but her life was her own. Julian Redenter was alone as she had always been. But Redeswan still stood, and she could have it if she were careful.

"Julian?" The question was in his voice again.

"I cannot be other than I am. No, Charles." Her flesh yearned toward him as she spoke, but her common sense won out.

He shrugged, their eyes met for the last time, and then he was gone, Osiris with him, and only the waving branches marked their passage.

Julian wrapped both arms around her bosom and looked after him, the pain tearing at her. She regretted her choice even as she knew that there was nothing else she could have done. He did not care for her; had he not said as much? Any man might try to help a woman with whom he had had pleasure such as they had shared. She put the agonizing thoughts from her, knowing that she must live with her choice from now on.

She retraced her steps in the rain which had now begun to come down even more steadily. The bitterness of this day would remain with her always, she thought. In the agony of Isabella Acton's death a new hardness had come to Julian. Now she would fight for her safety as she had always done, but the future lay bleak before her and she knew it. It was devoid of illusion and love, but life remained, and that was the dearest thing of all.

Her chestnut hair streamed down her back, the black gown clung to her supple body, but her face was a mask. She would have welcomed tears, but they would not come; there was to be no release for her that way. She was so intent on her thoughts that she almost slammed into the young man who was striding up and down in the rose arbor that led into the gardens proper. His recoil from her and the roar of thunder seemed to occur in the same moment, and she jumped back, hampered by her wet skirts.

The man was very blond, his eyes so blue, they appeared to fade into gray, and his features might have been polished by a sculptor. Recognition flared into malevolence and was revealed in Julian's own face. He was George Attenwood's lover, the man of the forest, he who had whispered of women as though they were vermin. Where Attenwood went, there would his lover follow.

If this were fresh danger, Julian's battered spirit could take no more. She spoke recklessly, "Forgive me, sir. I have not intentionally walked in your path, nor would I ever do so." Her aquamarine gaze locked with his. Suddenly she felt bold and savage, the events of the day having pushed her beyond endurance and into wildness.

The young man stared, all expression leaving his face. One smooth hand went to adjust the already immaculate lace at his throat and dropped to the silver chain on his chest. "My dear madam, I fear I do not understand you. Our paths are divergent." The blue eyes drifted over her figure. "They will remain so."

He rounded the corner and was gone, his stride purposeful and rapid. Gone to report to Attenwood? What did it matter so long as they left her alone? Julian reveled in the next crack of thunder and leaned over to pick a drenched golden rose. The heady scent drifted upward and her spirits with it. Survival was what mattered, and she had won over odds that might have destroyed another.

Julian repeated that to herself as she went into the palace, the storm at her heels and the unknown before her.

CHAPTER TWENTY-TWO

"Good health to you, my lady of the sea." The elegant figure in scarlet and gold swept an impossibly low bow as he doffed the tiny mask in the last figure of the dance.

"And to you, most powerful lord whose dominions must be beyond all counting." Julian spread her skirts wide and twirled before Ortega, who now caught her nimbly and led her in the beginning measure of a new dance.

"You are fair this night, Lady Julian." The red lips and the knowing eyes laughed down at her. "If there are many more masques and mummings in honor of the peace, I vow I shall not know how to speak in ordinary language."

She smiled and uttered some inanity to which he responded in kind. It was well over a month since Charles had vanished, ostensibly to his estates, and there was no word of the treason he had declared was against his name. The watch around the queen was trebled, and she remained more with her older ladies, but there had been no move against Julian or anyone else. The court attitude toward the girl was one of cold politeness, and she had grown to expect nothing else. Ortega had been a godsend in these weeks, courteous, amusing, friendly. He sat with her at table often and danced with her in the evenings, even strolled with her in the gardens in full view of everyone. Julian knew that she must be on her guard with him, but she was still glad of his presence.

"England is still at war with France. I wonder that we celebrate so long." She spoke idly. Ortega was far too experienced to give anything away, but she enjoyed prying at him. The queen's suspected pregnancy was openly known now and caused much speculation in view of her age and health. "The king's own troops are disbanding on the Continent."

He leaned closer. "No talk of politics this night. I vow, your eyes are the waves at dawn." His sardonic smile invited her to laugh with him and she did, thankful for the camaraderie that she had not known she could share with another.

Julian's thoughts went back to part of that brief audience with the queen several days after the burning at Smithfield. Her Majesty had indeed promised all that she had told Charles, and it had been reaffirmed then. But the horror of that fearful death hung between the one who had ordered it and the one who had inadvertently brought it about. "I would leave the court, madam, and return to my home, mine by your kindness." She was sickened by all that had once enchanted her and only wanted the queen to fulfill her promise and let her go.

Mary Tudor's sandy brows had come together, and the light eyes had gone opaque as she seemed to sway. The gruff voice was surprisingly soft as she said, "You preserved us for this realm, Lady Redenter. I would that you had wed Lord Attenwood; he is my bastion of the north against France, against heretic plotters, and one I can trust, a worthy husband for one such as you." She shook her head at the girl's shudder. "I know you will not reconsider, but I ask that you remain at court for at least another month. There are matters . . ." Her words had trailed away. "For my sake?"

Julian had agreed; there was no reason not to. But now the ominous warning that Charles had given her came back to warn her. She would have sworn that the queen had affection for her, but who knew the will of the great? She wished now that she had gone; the queen would have given way if she had wept, surely.

Outwardly Julian had much. New gowns and jewels and slippers, a room to herself, a new maid who was quiet and efficient but totally reserved, special wine ordered by the

queen herself; everything and nothing. She had asked for
Nan but was told she left the queen's service. Attenwood
did not come up again in conversation, and the young
blond man had not appeared again. Her days were as
ashes, and her dreams were filled with Charles Varland.
Once she had questioned Ortega, who gracefully remarked
that Varland was a lucky man that she was even remotely
interested but that he himself knew nothing. "It is a long
way to Cornwall, my dear. My interest is in the queen and
the court." He would say no more.

The musicians began to play the zarabanda now as they
had each night since the celebrations had begun. Always
Julian and Ortega danced it together, and she threw herself into it with gay abandon. Tonight she had dressed for
the approval in his eyes and for the figure she could cut
before those who had scorned her. Her hair was braided
high and threaded with sapphires to form a coronet
around her shapely head. A collar of pearls and diamonds
encircled her long throat. Her gown was green with under-
skirts of watered blue silk, the bodice a cunning mixture
of the two colors and cut low enough to reveal the thrusting white breasts. Her sleeves were long and flowing but
fell back to show the smooth arms. She wore white satin
slippers with pearl buckles that flashed as she moved in the
dance. Excitement and Ortega's words had caused the
flush to mount to her cheeks so that she bloomed. She
knew herself fair this night, and as always in such moments, her eyes lifted in the search for the man she knew
would never walk the court of Queen Mary again.

The dance was frenzied and wild now, all the propriety
of the court momentarily laid by. The castanets made their
own rhythm, and this was lifted higher by the stamping
feet of the few dancers. Julian gave herself to it but spared
a moment to wonder at the several men standing in the
doorway to the great hall. Their faces were stern and their
clothing sober in contrast to the brilliance of the courtiers.
Messengers? But the queen retired early these nights. Then
Ortega's hand caught hers in their own special movements
and she forgot all else. Activity, she had found, was a
good panacea.

Suddenly the tramp of feet broke through the music, and it died away. Ortega's eyes glittered into Julian's as he stepped back. She stood frozen as the leader of the men she had seen at the door came up to her. Two others came to stand beside her. The courtiers backed away against the walls so that Julian stood alone in the light of the massed candles and banners overhead.

"Lady Julian Redenter, I arrest you in the name of Her Majesty the Queen. You will come with us immediately and as you are." The man seemed to be made of oak, for he had that unyielding quality.

"On what charge?" Julian heard her own voice ring clearly and wondered at her own calm. "Where do you take me?"

"The charge is treason, madam, and you go to the Tower of London, there to remain at Her Majesty's pleasure." He touched her arm and she jerked away.

"Who makes this charge? It is without basis." Julian turned to look at Ortega, who shrugged and nodded at the men. Then she knew that she had been fortunate in saying little to him about her true feelings and that Charles had been right all along. "Is this your hand, Diego?" Her lip curled and her brilliant eyes flashed.

"You are overwrought, Lady Redenter. There is nothing to fear if you are true to Her Majesty as I hope will indeed be the case." The comrade of the past days was gone, and she saw the flames of the Inquisition in his eyes.

Julian stepped forward and drew her nails down the side of his smooth face in a quick gesture that wrung a cry of pain from him. The blood gushed up and with it his fury.

"Take her! Why do you stand there? Obey!"

Julian said, "My faith is in my innocence." And then, because she knew that she had nothing to lose and possibly already stood in peril of her life, added, "It could be any one of you who stand there watching and deem yourselves safe. Beware the false friend!"

The guards encircled her then, and she walked from the palace, head high, in all her shimmering beauty, into that captivity from which few returned safely, into the very shadow of death.

That shadow sharpened all her senses, yet gave her the feeling of standing apart to watch another girl helped onto a plain barge, given a dark cloak against the autumnal chill, taken down the dark river and the perilous landing, then the walk on endless winding stairs to a cold cell. It was interesting, she thought, that in the space of a few hours one could fall so rapidly from the edges of favor to the very pits. Interesting, nay. Fascinating! She began to shake, and with that physical reaction the detachment left her and terror took over.

She sank down on the icy floor and recalled all the bloody history of this place, some so recent that the blood might still be fresh. Queens, princes of the land, commoners, all had suffered here. Why should it be less for her? The queen had believed Isabella's words and had only waited for her own reasons to act on them. "Ah, God, why did I not go with Charles while I could?" Her hands twisted together and rose to her face. She knew that she would not be able to bear torment any more than Isabella had. What would she say? Thank God she knew no names, no locations, nothing.

Nightmare walked before her and took visible form during that long night. The relief that tears could bring did not come; her eyes were dry and hot. She started at the rustling of her skirts and tried to laugh at being afraid of rats when you faced fire or the ax. She shivered and burned and tried to pray, but there was nothing to hear her. Laughter bubbled up and she fought it back. One could go mad this way. People had been left in prison for years and lived; would she be one of them?

In the end, in the long darkness that held her, in the tunnel of her own anguish, it was the face of Charles that comforted her. The memory of their brief sharing remained with her and was a small bastion against the horror of this prison and all that it meant. When exhaustion finally left her limp and unconscious, the dream that came was not of blood and the shining axes that might make up reality. She dreamed of the meadows of Redeswan, a golden mare, and a dark man who rode beside her into the mists of morning.

When Julian awoke and shifted from her cramped position on the cold stones, she saw that some faint light was filtering down from some irregularly spaced blocks in the wall high above. Her prison was a narrow space with a small trestle bed and dirty blanket and one broken stool. The door had another smaller one below it and she guessed, again from tales that she had heard, that food and water were passed in and wastes taken out through this. The prisoner never saw his captors unless they willed it. She felt that she was entombed, walled away from life. Numbly she sat down on the bed and stretched her sore muscles. Waiting was all she had left.

There was a clatter at the small door and a bucket was pushed through. She stared for a second, expecting something else to follow, but the opening was closing. Julian leaped up and threw herself at the space. One hand jerked an earring loose, and she thrust the jewel out into the unknown.

"I have others. Others, do you hear? Tell your masters I wish to talk. Summon them. I will pay."

A hard hand slapped at hers, then the door was abruptly closed. She still held the jewel in her fingers. She knew herself abysmally foolish to have offered it, but the very fact that it was not taken told her that she was to be forgotten. Rare was the Tower prisoner who was not given the opportunity to buy himself more comfort than the old prison allowed. It was stranger still that the jewels had not been taken when she entered; they were lesser ones the queen had allowed her to use and were given back each day to the lady-in-waiting who was charged with keeping them.

She went quite mad then as she threw herself on the bed and began to weep the hard tears of the desperate. Her fists slammed against stone and her fingernails broke. Her hair tumbled over her face, and she threw the glittering jewels from her so that they rattled like peas on the floor. The pain and loss of a lifetime mingled with a fear so acute that she strangled with it. When the tears ceased

she cried aloud until her voice was nearly gone and her
body shook as if with an ague. There was to be no uncon-
sciousness for Julian Redenter, only the awareness of her
long despair.

The thin light faded, the cell grew dark and cold, but
Julian lay face downward in her misery, feeling the absence of all hope. She had been told once that this was
hell itself; Lady Gwendolyn had had her own agonies, but
she at least had some freedom of movement. Julian's mind
swung over the misfortunes of her family and her preoccu-
pation with them and then her own predicament; she
pondered and reshaped events until her mind was as raw
as her eyes. Why? Why? The single word etched itself on
the walls around her, and she almost hoped that she could
go mad.

She had tried to eat the hard bread and thin gruel, but
her stomach rebelled. When the stupor came it was welcome, but even there the core of her mind and will
remained sharp. Her attempts at prayer were clumsy and
futile; her cries for death equally so. She took the food
and ate enough to live. In the end it was sufficient.

Julian was never to know when the determination to
fight was reborn in her. It might have been the time that
she wondered if she were in a true dungeon or one of the
cells aboveground and actually cared which. Or it might
have been the returning thought that death in a torpor was
not the way of the Redenters, and her proud name was all
that was truly hers in this narrowed world. It might have
been only that her healthy mind and spirit had fallen as
far as they could and must revive or flicker out. Whatever
the reason, Julian ate all that was given her one day,
drank some of the water, washed in the rest, and wondered what she looked like.

From that time on she refused to let herself think of
what the future might hold or the painful aspects of the
past. She forced herself to walk up and down until her legs
trembled. She swung her arms back and forth, practiced
the movements of fencing, performed the court dances
and those of her own invention, even ran in the short
spaces of the cell as her strength grew. In the endless time

that seemed to go on forever, Julian told herself stories and turned them back into Latin and French, created characters and spoke their lines for them, sang nonsense songs and ballads, recalled every story and poem that she had ever read or been told.

The once lovely dress was now grimy and stiff, her hair hung in dank coils, and her hands were still lacerated from the terror that overcame her in the dark reaches of the nights and she hammered again on the enclosing walls. She had no control over her dreams, and they followed her into death and the pits of hell to the return of the light that meant another endless period of waking. If Julian sometimes wondered why she did not simply give up, she pushed the thought away and struggled on, not in bravery but in refusal to submit.

It grew colder in the cell and more of her time was spent in activity to keep warm. Her sleeping time was sporadic, for chills woke her often, and her hands or feet would be numb even in that short time. The nightmares now were not of fire or the ax; they were of freezing to death and growing ill in her prison without anyone to see or care. There was no way to keep track of time, but she marked the comings and goings of the light with one of the pins that had held her hair, using it to scrape the painful litany of time on the stone beside her bed. As well as she could tell, it had been well over a month since she had come to her own decision to struggle. Estimate that she had been overcome by the terror of her plight for four or five other days, and that told her that it was now full winter. Would she survive it? She could not look ahead. This minute, this now, was all that was bearable.

She had been conscious of her beauty; now she was aware only of her long hair in terms of warmth. Clothes had mattered, but their value here was as covering for her chilled flesh. Mind and intellect at one time were supreme; here thought was held at bay. Her passion for Charles Varland had ruled in the outer world, but the cravings of the flesh melted down to the stone that enclosed her. Julian herself was being stripped down to the essentials.

One morning she sat huddled in the blanket and the old

cloak at the edge of the thin spear of light. It was very
cold, and her breath hung on the air. She dreaded the first
few minutes of activity but knew that this was the only
way to gain any warmth. Her head was bent in the crook
of her arm, and the cloth around her head muffled sounds
as she braved herself for those swift movements that began the day for her.

Suddenly there was a clatter at the door and it was
thrown back so that it rattled hard against the wall. A
harsh voice cried, "Is this the way the prisoner is
preserved? By the saints, it is freezing in here! Bring that
brazier in and hurry up about it!"

Julian jerked her head up to see a barrel-chested man in
a furred short coat berating two guards who stood in front
of him. She could not at first take in the fact that something was happening; she had been alone too long. Then
guile caught at her, and she made her face dull, her eyes
blank in the torpor of the abandoned. Behind it her brain
watched and awaited opportunity.

The guard came in with the smoking brazier that gave
off welcome warmth. He placed it near Julian, and she
had to fight not to strain toward it. The barrel-chested
man came so close that she saw the red veins in his heavy
face and the anxiety in his little eyes. He touched her
hands, and she drew them slowly away.

"Madam? Madam? Do you understand me?" His normal voice might have been a shout, but now he tried to be
soothing.

"I hear." She made her words slurring and let her lips
tremble.

"Food is being brought. Wine, also. I must talk to you."

"I hear."

He jumped up and bellowed for the guard, who came
running. He lowered his voice, but she could hear every
word. "Bring the other things in. Be quick about it! She
must be ready for the holy questioners, and you know who
will be blamed if her senses are gone!"

Julian kept her face still and her body in the huddled
pose, but the fear that she had fought back rose again.
The time of her ordeal was at last upon her.

CHAPTER TWENTY-THREE

Julian drank of the cup of soup that the serving man held to her mouth and felt its restorative warmth even as she wondered how long she could maintain this pose. The barrel-chested man stamped back and forth in the corridor outside, muttering imprecations and berating the guards, who dared not speak. She withdrew her mind to rejoice temporarily in the feel of the coarse clean cloth against her newly sponged skin, and the heavy cloak resting over her shoulders added more heat. The wine she had been given made her light-headed and shivery.

"Madam, are you able to speak now?" He came to her again, and this time she smelled the fear on him. Little beads of sweat shimmered on his forehead.

She swung the blank gaze on him and beyond as a long shadow paused in the doorway before entering. It lifted a long hand which grew skeletal in the flicker of the candles. All sound ceased so that she heard only the slap of his sandals as he approached. "He" and "it" twisted together in her mind, and she would not have been surprised to see a bony skull look out at her.

"Julian Redenter, you stand accused both of heresy and of liaison with the dark powers. There is also a charge of treason. The penalty for these is death, and the manner of it can be both hideous and horrifying. The Church can be merciful if you do cast yourself upon her, naming those implicated with you and outlining the details of the plots in which you indulged, explaining the blandishments of the demons who came to you."

Julian let her blank gaze grow more so. Father Sebastino's gaunt face drew in and his eyes dominated it. His fingers rubbed together and he licked dry lips. The guards were staring ahead; they saw many such scenes and could predict the outcome of all this.

"Cromp, come here!" The barrel-chested man rushed up to babble explanations and apologies which ceased as the priest made an impatient gesture. "Has she been ill-treated? Starved? Why is she this way?"

Cromp cried, "She has been left strictly alone, lord priest. I vow it. Nothing has been done to disturb her senses! Perhaps they were weak to begin with after the way of woman."

Julian felt a tiny trickle of triumph; it seemed that her subterfuge was gaining ground, but she had no idea what she intended. The import of the charges might not have been realized in all their fearful aspects; it was as though the priest had talked of another person whom she barely knew.

"Or too clever! Such women as this are dangerous! Think you, Cromp, that in addition to plotting against the life of the queen for riches, she has reportedly startled sleepers from their nightly repose so that they woke in fear at a time when the Devil may more easily take souls! And in her belongings there has been found a talisman of bound sticks from the hawthorn tree, that symbol of the witch by means of which she can work her evil spells! Not content there, this woman has consorted with the outlaw, Varland, who may even have plotted against the life of the king who counted him friend. Are you not horrified, Cromp?"

Father Sebastino fixed his glittering eyes on the man, who cringed and babbled agreement. Julian felt her control slipping and knew that he had penetrated her guise. Her fate was being outlined for her; the flames of Isabella's pyre rose high in the bleak cell.

Father Sebastino's gaze swung back to Julian, and the tips of his rotted teeth showed as he said, "And yet, such a merciful lady is the queen that she would have seen this wretched woman, heard her tale, listened to her lies. I was forced to speak to her with God's own voice, reminding her of her duty to Him and this realm. She wept, Cromp, can you image that? Her Majesty wept before me and told me she was grateful that I spoke so." He grinned now and rubbed his hands together.

Julian's heart warmed toward the queen, who had tried to be kind even in the face of what she thought was treason. Mary would be just, she thought, but it would be according to her own stern lights, and she was easily influenced. No doubt the priest had brought up Philip's name and wifely duty. She must keep her face calm now and not reveal herself. Father Sebastino loved cruelty for its own sake; that had been evident to her long ago. He shared the predilections of Attenwood, it seemed.

"Feed her and prepare her to answer questions," the priest ordered. "Show her some of the pleasures of this place. I daresay several of these guards could demonstrate." He turned to look straight at Julian as he spoke. Cromp followed his gaze. "This woman had the opportunity for instruction and dissembled, well nigh refused it, even ran away! She is inhabited by Satan, and he must be driven forth!" His voice rose and he spread his arms wide. "The flames will be the least of it!"

Julian could bear no more. She let her eyes widen, leaned forward on her stool, and shrieked, "The bat! He has come! Ah, the stench . . . what are you?" Her hands went before her in the sign of the cross, and she stared at the priest with all the terror of her heart and mind in her eyes.

The others stared and moved away as the priest said, "The woman has been a mummer in her time, but she cannot fool the eye of God! She must be ready for the questioners of whom I will be one. I bear the queen's own commission in this!"

"Aye, aye, all shall be as you say!" Cromp gave Julian a baleful look. "When is she required?"

"Prepare her immediately! I see to this matter personally." The fierce eyes glittered at Julian, and not for the first time, she saw the hunger there. Then he spun on his heels and was gone. She heard him calling to those who had remained outside and heard the rush of their feet as they hurried to obey.

"Out." Cromp recovered his composure now that the holy man was gone, and the guards with him drew back obediently. When the cell was clear he looked at Julian, who tried once again to maintain her air of dazed idiocy. Then in three steps he was at her side and pulled her to him. Before she could resist, his mouth ground down on hers, and his foul-smelling breath threatened to overcome her pose.

She made her body limp and let her head loll back. Her legs buckled and almost threw both off balance. He thrust her aside and put both hands on his hips as he surveyed the swell of her breasts and the gauntness of her young body. "I'm going to show what it'll be like for you, girl, when they take you. Best enjoy what you can get; the fire takes a long time." He snarled the words of deviation and cruelty at her while the little eyes never left her whitening face. At the end he said, "Flesh is nothing; spirit everything. The priest all but said so. I'll enjoy your last moments."

She sat numbly on the floor after he left. Had he gone for wine and refreshments or spectators or instruments of torture? All those days of nothingness and then her enemies returning with savage intent had drained Julian even of the ability to pretend. Her reason did flicker as she sat there and waited for whatever might come.

Again time drew long for Julian, and this time she had no defense. Tears had long since dried up in her, and anger melted before fear. Prayer was a useless thing when you could not believe. She hated the queen, who had given her up to the beast, and she loathed Father Sebastino, who was her instrument and took such pleasure in what he did. When they came to rape and pillage her body would it be for her as she imagined it must have been for Isabella?

"Would God I had let them kill the bitch queen!" She said the words into the cooling air, for they had taken the brazier away, and felt the hatred consume her. It must be enough to sustain her in the time ahead, for there was nothing else.

Light was showing faintly in the cell when the lock on the door rattled and the heavy portal slid back. A dark shape stood revealed there, a hood concealing the features. A servant stood behind, candle in hand. The first one advanced and peered toward Julian, who now lay huddled on her bed.

She watched through the tangle of her hair. There had been no sleep or rest for her as she waited, but she was not conscious of any weariness. She clenched her fingers, then forced herself to relax. Not yet.

"Madam? Madam?" The whisper was soft, but there was a familiar note in it. He was closer now, the padding quality of his movements and the dark cloak making him seem animallike in the shadows.

Now! Julian sprang from the bed, her nails sharp claws, her lips drawn back from her teeth, the still lithe body poised for battle. She hit the figure and tumbled him backward so that he fell against the wall and started to pant. Her fingers touched the softness of beard and jerked. She heard, as if from a distance, her voice repeating a savage curse over and over. The force of her anger drove her on as she slapped at him with her other hand. Let him kill her! Better to die in struggle than submit tamely.

"Osiris! Osiris! I am sent!" The man tried to shield himself from her and did not strike back. He fended her off as she tore at his cloak, but the hood fell back, and she saw the face that she knew.

"Matthew!" Julian jerked back, the red fury still licking at her. It was so good to strike back! "What are you doing here?"

He rose to his feet, a small man with tousled graying hair and a thinner face than when she had last seen him. "Madam, stay your hand. I am sent to help you!"

"No one can help me, least of all you. And why should you, anyway? A guard in this place?" Her voice went dull and flat. She wondered if those who ruled the Tower knew that this man had once served Charles Varland and helped lure her to his arms. A generation ago that had been and in a different world.

"Put on this robe and come. At this early hour several guards and a priest will attract little attention. The place is full of prisoners, and gold has been well placed." He began to unwrap some of the cloth that swathed his body.

"It is a trick to torment me! How do I know that you mean to help me? It is impossible to escape from the Tower; all know that! What do you know of Osiris?" Julian knew she must not let herself hope; she could not afford to lose the hatred that was sustaining her. She would fan the anger, let the hatred burn upward, and hope that death was swift. Her hands lifted and her aquamarine eyes glittered in the faint light. "Fiends! Fiends!"

There was a movement at the door as the servant who had been standing beside it now came closer and put down the candle. He straightened up and shook the folds of his own cloak back so that he stood revealed in the coarse cloth of a menial. Charles, Lord Varland, peer of the realm and now truly outlaw. The crest of dark hair was ruffled, and the dark face had not altered a jot. Incredibly, he was smiling, his mouth turning upward in the mocking gesture she so well remembered.

"Many might use the name of Charles Varland, lady, but few know the name of my dog. You have frightened poor Matthew far more than all the warders of the Tower, but you cannot do so to me. What say you? Would you leave this prison now?"

Julian stared at him, and her tongue could barely find speech. "You came here for me?"

"So it seems. I see no other prisoner here." He came closer, and she caught the wind-fresh scent of him. "Put on the robe. You will trust us now?"

Julian seemed to feel nothing as she took the dark robe he handed her. Matthew stood revealed now in stained garments which were in the queen's colors. He turned away as she fumbled with the ties of the sacklike garment she had been given that day or several days ago. Charles stepped close and whisked it away, then settled the robe over her and tied the cord at her waist. Her fingers rose to pull the hood over her face and were stopped by his hand which folded them over a needle-sharp dagger.

"Walk behind Matthew and myself. Your thoughts are on things not of this world. If we are stopped, remember that; it may prove the salvation of us all. If it appears that we are taken, use the dagger as seems best to you." His voice was as calm as though they stood in the London streets and planned which cookshop to visit.

"Charles, I cannot believe that you are here, that this is real." She faltered and began again to tell him of Father Sebastino's visit and what was planned for her. "They will come at any time, and you both run great risk."

"More if we stand here and chatter. You did ever talk a great deal." Charles gave her a sharp look. "Are you ready?"

"Aye." The dangerous emotion that made her voice shake was abruptly stilled as the anger returned. Anger at those who had taken her prisoner and anger at this dark man who had dared much for her sake. She knew he spoke as he did to bolster her, but Matthew's quick bark of laughter irritated her. "And have been these many minutes. Let us go if you are done."

For the first time since that night of her entry, which she could now barely remember, Julian saw the outside world. The corridor was narrow and dim, lit only by one torch that cast a guttering light. Matthew drew out a ring of keys and locked the door to her cell, then they walked in single formation down the narrowing passage that led off to the left and was dewed with droplets of water. It rapidly grew so small that there was only room enough for one person to walk comfortably and became very dim. Charles had taken one of the torches and held it high in the turning passage. The air was growing fetid and rank, the stone floor wetter by the minute. Julian's feet in the court slippers were icy and sopping. She was shaking with the cold and a rising element of elation. "No longer alone," said her brain and heart, "no longer alone."

They came to a barred door set low in a stone wall at the end of the twisting corridor. A residue of water sloshed about, and she heard the crackle of ice as it moved. The

light from the torch showed the heavy stones reaching up
to a low ceiling where beads of water were gathered. It
took little imagination to see the fugitive, panting and exhausted, arriving here and clutching at the bars, seeking to
tear them away while the guards came toward him to
carry him back into captivity. Julian caught her breath in
a little sob. It was unbearable to be so close, cruel joke
this!

"Can you find it?" Matthew turned to Charles and took
the torch from him to hold it high in his turn.

"The curved one with the broken edge near the top."
Charles reached up and began to examine the wet stones
that looked alike to the others. He probed as Matthew
held the light closer. "Nothing. They seem to change in
the wet and the shadows."

"You have wasted your gold." Matthew sank back on
his heels and spoke flatly, the words all the more terrible
for their complete lack of emotion. "We should have
known it was too easy."

"Nonsense." Charles spoke briskly and resumed his
search, the torch in his own hand this time.

Julian heard the sweep of cloth and felt the furtive
movement before she actually saw anything. By that time
it was too late, for the burly figure brushed by her, light
flashing on his drawn sword as he held it against Charles's
back.

"Thought you were out, didn't you? Well, you're going
right back to the cells, the lot of you, and there'll be a
turn of the lash for trying to escape. How did you manage
it, anyway?" He wore the queen's colors, and a leather
helmet rested squarely on his head. "Don't move or I'll
run you through!"

Charles remained still, not daring to move or shift the
torch backward. Matthew was on the floor and off balance, his own weapon set aside. Julian registered all this in
a single, stricken glance even as it dawned on her why the
guard had not glimpsed her or, if he had, taken her to be
one of the shadows of this place of fear. Her black robe
mingled with the darkness, and she stood apart in one of
the natural coverts of the wall.

She did not think or plan as the keen blade rose in her hand with a life all its own and buried itself to the hilt in the fleshy shoulder just beyond. The man fell with a muted cry, and Matthew was on him in the second, his fingers squeezing the life away while helpless feet hammered in the icy water. Charles whirled and looked at Julian.

"Get over here and hold this. You did well, but others are doubtless behind him even at this moment. Come!"

The matter-of-fact voice lifted Julian up and kept the screams back. She took the torch in one shaking hand and started to raise it, ignoring the dragging sounds Matthew made as he hauled the body back into the shadows. Something caught her eye and held it. Charles looked down, gave a quick exclamation, and pulled at the protruding edge of the stone with one hand. It gave a little and then began to move with a slow grating sound that rasped on all their nerves.

Julian's voice rose high. "A way out! Can it be true?" She watched as the gaping darkness showed more steps that seemed to lead down into the pits themselves.

"Eventually." Charles moved close beside her, and his arm was warm around her shoulders. "Matthew, bring him in here and we will leave him. Hurry."

"Aye, my lord." He stepped away, appearing suddenly years younger than he had looked moments before.

"We are all murderers." Julian spoke the words fearfully as she looked into the gray eyes so close to her own.

"You are as brave as you are beautiful, Julian. Deborah of old did as you have done and was honored by her God and her people all her days." Charles kissed her full on the lips and drew her close.

In this most dangerous moment of their lives, poised between several horrible deaths and standing in blood of their own shedding, Julian Redenter and Charles Varland were closer than when they shared the bed of passion.

CHAPTER TWENTY-FOUR

The air was fetid and thick in the passage which was so small that they had to bend slightly as they walked, feet planted carefully, the smoking torch held low. Shudders racked Julian's body as the slime oozed over her icy toes. Matthew went before her, Charles came after, and she felt a sense of relief that was out of proportion to the never ending nightmare in which she moved. It seemed impossible to her that she had ever lived in a world of sunlight or drawn a free breath; now she fought in the anger that might eventually help to save them. Julian was beginning to understand something of the force that drove Charles Varland.

The way began to level off and rise as they went along it. Rough stones jutted out on both sides of the walls, and the ceiling shone black in the faint light. Water dripped steadily in some places, but in others little rims of ice were formed. Their breaths blew out frostily ahead of them, and the sloshing noises of their shoes were the only sounds in this underground tunnel. Julian thought of the old tales of those who fled, only to turn back on themselves and return unwittingly to the same place from which they had gone forth. This might be such a thing, a refined sort of torture to lure the plotters together. She thought it funny, her senses swung, and she almost stumbled but caught herself in time. Was this how one lost one's reason?

She heard a far-off roaring sound which faded and rose again before it was joined by another. Chills ran down her back that were not due to the cold, but Matthew gave a chuckle of satisfaction, and Charles came round Julian to stare at the expanse of corridor.

"Now will tell the tale, my comrades." He spoke casually, but she heard the underlying strain.

A few swift strides and he was bending down to a section of stone and running long fingers over it. There was a rumble of iron as the lower part slid back to reveal an empty, vile-smelling room of Stygian blackness that torchlight could barely dispel. Droppings and rushes were on the floor, and the odor of angry wild animals made her gag. Strangely enough, Julian remembered, that very same smell had been at Smithfield at the time of Isabella's burning.

Charles hurried them through and pulled the panel back into place. His hand gripped Julian's hard for a brief moment, and then, single file, they went rapidly across the room and into another, smaller one containing the same compressed odors. They bent to go through a door set low in the wall and this time emerged into an ill-lit passage that curved away into murkiness.

"Ho, what do you do here at this hour, sirs?" The voice was harsh, breath rattling in the lungs, coming from directly in front of them.

Julian peered up from the depths of her cowl to see an extremely fat man swaying as he watched them, a leather bottle clutched in one hand, a wide grin on his pudding face. The roar she had previously heard came again, and this time the sound was so wild and desperate that she flinched; once again her control threatened to break.

The man cocked his head to the side. "The pets do not care for the rain, I think, but then they can't have this, can they?" He waved the bottle and began to laugh, then to wheeze. "No one comes here if they can help it. Why do you?"

Matthew's voice was wheedling, pitched low. "Nothing for it, the good father must see all in this place. He is newly come from Spain, you know, and the Tower is famous. Now he is chilled and tired; after he takes the air we will escort him to a bed and fire. He meditates even at this moment."

Julian saw that Charles balanced the torch in both hands and shifted his weight as if restless. He would thrust or throw it as might become necessary. Her own weapons must be the coiled anger within her and her sharp nails; the little dagger had been left behind with the body of the guard.

The fat one guffawed and scratched as he said, "Listen to the lions. They do not need prayers—they need food! Fresh meat!" The roaring came steadily now, and he gulped at the bottle.

Julian entered into the guise now and lifted her head so that she regarded him from the depths of the cowl much as Father Sebastino had viewed her. He caught the movement and drew back. No one in Mary's England laughed at the priests and went safely.

Fat hands patted the air and his eyes rolled back in his head as Julian took a step forward. Matthew touched her arm and shook his head. The man whispered, "I meant no offense, Father. I only keep the beasts; sometimes I forget how to speak respectfully. Your pardon."

Charles moved closer to her and spoke in rapid Spanish which was too quick for her ear, but she nodded and mumbled. Then he said in English, "He is ready for fresh air and did not really understand your amusement. Be thankful for that. Now, shall we go?"

The fat man moved as far away as his bulk would allow and made an ostentatious sign of the cross. They started down the corridor and were brought up short by the tramp of feet and animated conversation as four soldiers, helmets speckled with water, came toward them. The men paused to stare, their eyes boring into the fugitives. Julian made as if to pause, but Charles drew her on.

"Bad weather for burning today. Smithfield will be quiet." The half derisive words hung on the air along with the sour odor of cheap wine. The soldier making the remark was younger than the others, his face hard even in the drunken slackness.

The fat man's hiss split the sudden silence. "Spanish! Careful!"

The light of the torch that Charles held flickered long in the drafty passage as the three moved on without another pause. Julian felt that any minute they would be rushed upon and carried back into captivity. No walk of her life was ever longer; all her senses were acutely tuned. *Let them kill me. I will not go back.* She thought she might have spoken out loud and truly given them away, so real were the words.

The men behind them began to shuffle, and Julian heard them begin to chaffer with the fat man, who was muttering uneasily. Then they rounded the corner and turned into another passage with a partially open door at the end of it. Beyond this was a narrow, smaller corridor redolent with the scent of animals and captivity. Julian felt that she would begin to scream and beat on the stone walls if this went on much longer, but there was no time to venture a question. The faces of Charles and Matthew were set and stern, the lines deep as they walked more rapidly now. She knew that time was becoming short; the instincts of the hunted were sharpened with the expectation of pursuit.

The dimness became gray light which showed an arched wall in the distance where a lone guard sheltered under a cloak from the pouring rain. The first freshness in many weeks came to Julian's nostrils, and she breathed so deeply that she almost coughed. Charles turned his head to look at her, and their eyes met with an impact that was nearly physical.

The rain soaked them almost immediately, and the shock of the icy air made them all tremble as they walked swiftly toward the gate. The guard was cold and the night had been long. His challenge was half-hearted and faded with Charles's brisk explanation. Well he might wonder that anyone wanted to walk on Tower Wharf in such weather.

"Come, Father, it is too chill for you to remain long out here." Matthew's roughened country voice held a nice blend of deference and annoyance that made the guard's lips twitch as he stood aside to let them pass.

All boats going up to the city paused at the wharf as did most of those going out to sea. Normally it swarmed with activity, but on this freezing, rain-swept day only a few craft were visible, and in the distance several people walked slowly as they bent against the gale. Julian followed the others off to the side and around some stacked materials to a low wall. Beyond it steps led down to the turbulent water. Charles scanned the expanse and gave a low exultant laugh.

Julian followed his gaze and saw that a small dark barge waited in shadows of the nearby building. At his high, piercing whistle it began to move toward them, the oarsmen rowing with rapid strokes. It seemed to be years that they stood there, silent and waiting, watching the rescuers come. Julian would not allow herself to think of freedom, not yet. It was enough to stand in the rain, drinking of the freshness, shivering and feeling the blood rise strongly in her veins.

Then it was there, bumping and knocking against the old steps, seeming a toy in the wildness of the day. There were three oarsmen and a squat bearded man, who threw a rope to Matthew with the ease of long practice. Now pretense was ended as Charles scooped Julian into his arms and swung lithely into the little craft. Seconds later Matthew almost fell on top of them as they all retreated into the makeshift in the center, which was made of tattered cloth that rattled in the wind. They huddled down in a heap, and the oarsmen swung the barge around so that she headed downstream. An observer might have thought them giving way before the rough passage and retreating to brave the weather another day.

"We'd given you up almost, sir, but Roger said you'd be coming, that we would wait all day." One of the oarsmen, sober brown face intent, spoke to Charles. "God be praised that you made it."

The squat man, Roger, laughed. "And the bad weather and Fortune herself, plus my lord's own ingenuity, had a lot to do with it. Best stay down, everyone. We're not safe yet."

The arrogant Charles Varland, always in command of

himself, slightly contemptuous of those who were not, looked up from his place beside Julian, and his voice shook with the power of his feeling. "You have put yourselves in great peril at my wish, and I shall be forever grateful. I could not have commanded you in such an enterprise; your choosing to come did me great honor."

Roger shifted uncomfortably. "Are you not our liege lord and good friend? Come, let us drink. I vow we are all frozen and will be for yet a while!" He produced a flat bottle and handed it to Julian. "Here, sir, you have been long in Tower, I am told."

She looked up at him then, and the cowl lifted away from her face. He could not stifle the gasp as his glance swung to Charles, who began to laugh. She tilted the bottle and let the fine French brandy run down her throat, reviving and restoring her to warmth and life.

Now Charles spoke lightly. "We have rescued a fair lady from gaol, and she shall pay us with a song given in freedom. Is it not so, madam?"

"A just fee, my lords all." She was surprised that the court language remained in her memory or that she had any emotions left save that of anger, so long had she nurtured it. Now gratitude and relief swamped her, and she could only smile mistily at those who had risked much for her sake.

Julian lost all sense of time as the barge went rapidly along. The fiery liquid she had drunk moved in her body and gave her a sense of well-being. Matthew settled himself to rest, but his eyes flicked everywhere. Charles and Roger carried on a low-voiced conversation a few feet away. The rain was sweeping the brown river in icy curtains, almost obscuring the dwellings on the banks and the few other craft that were out. The few trees she could see stretched torn branches into the hanging clouds and were snapped back by the wind. Now and then snatches of sleet were tossed in her face as the barge rode on the waves, and she was vaguely conscious of loss of feeling in her extremities. It did not matter; she could go this way forever, for it was the breath and taste of freedom.

A torch flared briefly, was held up, and was as quickly

extinguished. Another answered as briefly from a small
brown ship moored with several others in a partial bend of
the river. A casual observer would have thought them all
deserted, missing the half-raised sails and the ready oars.
He would have thought, as Julian did at first glance, the
owner demented who did not tend his ships more carefully
lest they break loose into the river.

"Can you climb?" Charles was beside her, helping her
up and balancing her swaying body as the barge rocked
against the battered side of the ship, which now seemed
enormous.

Her legs buckled, but she stamped her feet in the frozen
slippers and slapped her hands together. The wind and
rain together blew back the priest's robe and iced it over
her flesh. She laughed in the face of it and answered, "Of
course! I am only a little chilled."

Charles closed his hand over hers, and the gray eyes,
the exact color of the clouds above them, slanted with an
emotion she could not identify. "Then come."

The rope ladder, already wet and growing icy, bounced
even with their weight as Julian struggled to pull her suddenly heavy body upward. Charles behind and several men
above would have helped, she knew, could have pulled her
into the ship with lowered ropes and someone could have
held her secure, but this was a thing she had to do for herself if she fell into the river. She thought wryly that pride
could kill one, but she would not ask for help. Frozen
hands grasped and clutched, all but bare feet scrabbled
on the thin lines, and her nose scraped the wooden side
as the wind flung her inward. She looked down and saw
the waves lifting as if to pluck her down; the world spun
and shifted as her grip loosened.

"Shut your eyes, Julian, and hold still for a moment."

Charles could have rescued her, but he knew that this
was a thing she had to prove for herself. The quiet voice
calmed her and she obeyed. With it she felt again the summer sun and the tenderness they had had toward each
other. Another, older voice spoke in her mind. "Peace, be
still."

The ferocity of the wind and rain seemed to slow or

else the activity had warmed her sufficiently so that she could regain her bearings. When she opened her eyes again she held their gaze straight in front of her and moved arms and legs in a stiff rhythm. She encountered a ledge and began to pull at it, but hands were on hers, and she was being lifted up even while her body continued the climbing motions.

The several faces, old and young, of the seamen blended as they set her down on the windy deck, where she swayed until Charles vaulted over and came to cup his arm under her elbow, lending his strength to her sudden bonelessness. He called to one of the hovering men, "Sail immediately!"

"Toward Cornwall, my lord?"

"Cornwall." The sudden lilt in his voice made Julian try to turn her head and look up at him, but her muscles rebelled. He felt the shudder that was pulling at her and picked her up in both arms. "Enough of this, Julian."

Moments later she was wrapped in heavy blankets and lay in a real bed with a brazier's warmth close by. Charles rubbed her feet and hands with a swift competence, then held more of the brandy to her mouth while she drank. Immediately the world began to spin, the colors of the small cabin merging with the lights that came on in her brain. The dark face that bent over her twisted a little, and one hand rose to brush the hair from her forehead.

"My fair one, you have suffered even as England does. You should have come with me when I asked. Foolish one to trust the Tudor." He spoke absently, but his eyes had an angry glitter.

Julian whispered, "What will happen now? I have a debt to repay to you, Charles." The words were clear in her brain, but her lips were still icy and they emerged in a mumble.

"You are still freezing! There is much to tell you, but we can speak when you are rested and refreshed." He swung up into the bed with her and pulled her close, adding his warmth to that she was already feeling. One hand rubbed the taut muscles of her neck. "You are safe for now. For now." He repeated the words, his face grim.

Something coalesced in Julian and she remembered, as if from a dream or prophecy, flaming ships, a cliff, and running men. Now bloody swords clashed in the red light, and a face that she knew well blazed up with triumph. "Dangerous, Charles, dangerous!" She tried to communicate her fears to him, but the body and mind that had served her so well during the long ordeal were collapsing. She was being drawn into a cave of darkness and heat, a womb of safety that she yearned for with all her heart.

"Aye, lady. You have been wondrous brave." The gentleness in Charles Varland's words was more profound than it had ever been. "Lady mine." He touched his lips to her forehead, and she carried that talisman into the cave with her.

CHAPTER TWENTY-FIVE

Julian ran before huge shadows, fell miles down into pits that opened to reveal stakes and burning women, shivered in the expanses of a snowy landscape, and climbed into a frozen sky. She started up in terror and sank back into oblivion, followed always by a low voice murmuring comforting words. Hands held hers, and she remembered pulling on them as she crept through endless passages that ended in blank walls.

She opened her eyes to gray light drifting over a low ceiling to show a small room dwarfed further by the bed in which she lay and the chair beside it. A chair occupied by Charles, whose gray eyes regarded her quizzically, his hands steepled under his chin, his sober brown garments not detracting one whit from the proud demeanor that was always his.

"Charles, have you been here all night? Surely you must rest?" She was surprised at the weakness of her voice.

He laughed, the planes of his face breaking into warmth. "One night? You have lain here three, and your rest has been much broken. Are you able to take food and drink, do you think?" He sobered at the look on her face. "Ah, no, Julian, I have seen many exhausted and worn as you were. You will recover, I promise you that."

She pulled herself up in the bed while he went to the door and called for food. The world spun, and she could see the thin shape of her hands, feel the sharp edges of her cheekbones. "Where are we?"

He turned back to her, face remote again. "In the sea just off my own country, Cornwall."

She started to speak, but the rap at the portal made her jump. The tow-headed boy gaped at her and almost fell over his feet as he deposited a board with food across the side of the bed as Charles indicated. Julian put both hands across her stomach and felt the flatness of it. Saliva rose in her mouth; she could not wait. The rough bread that came with the cheese might have been the best of Whitehall's own as she tore at it. Charles waved the boy away impatiently and opened a leather-stoppered bottle.

"Broth. It will ease the pangs. You will be able to eat little for a time."

The tepid liquid gave her new strength, but she reached again for the cheese. "I do not wish to presume, Charles— so much has been done for me already—but I long for a bath. Is it possible?" She wanted to ask so many questions, but the time of ignorance must be drawn out. For this little space she wanted to think only of herself, of this blessed release. This warm cabin, this attentive man, safely—let nothing intrude.

He smiled at her and went toward the door. "The bath will not be one of luxury, but it will clean you, and our smallest cabin boy has offered you his best clothes. We will talk when you feel ready."

The easy tears of exhaustion came into her eyes.

"Charles, how can I ever repay what you have done for me?"

"For you, Julian?" His glance was puzzled. "Not totally for you, foolish though you had been not to come when I warned you. There were other reasons; this is war, and every opportunity must be taken to harry the enemy." He shut the door behind with an emphatic click, and she heard his boots ring as he strode away.

There was no time to ponder his meaning, for the wooden tub half-filled with water was carried in by two of the crew who ducked their heads in greeting and then stared before backing out. The same boy brought clothes, a bit of cleansing substance with a dubious odor, and a furry robe almost the same shade as Julian's hair. There was even a ladies' comb and a vial of sweet ointment.

She thanked them and then asked, "I feel no movement of the ship. Are we still at sea?"

The boy's gaze was worshipful. "No, lady, only in the private cove that his lordship always uses before going out to seek the queen's shipping. Nobody knows it, you see, and . . ."

One of the seamen caught his arm and pulled him out in mid-sentence. "We must hurry, lady, forgive us."

The words were enough. Julian had known all along that Charles was truly outlaw; nay, pirate—*traitor,* if the correct word were used. Why did the word cause chills to go along her arms? Was she given in loyalty to the regime that had sought to destroy her? Had not her own father risen against tyranny? His daughter was no different, yet all the generations of Redenters who had served the rulers of England seemed to rise in protest. She pushed the thoughts back; she would serve her own cause and live.

Now Julian laved herself in the rapidly cooling water, scrubbed at the long mass of hair, and rinsed it again in the second tub that apparently had been brought earlier before she woke and was now icy. No matter; she was clean for the first time in months. With a start she realized that she did not know the day or the month of the year, only that it was now deep winter and she had entered the Tower in early autumn.

Her weakness was fading, and she folded herself into the furry robe as she finished the rest of the food and gulped the thin ale. The brazier still gave off warmth, so she settled by it and began to rub her hair with one of the shirts. The questions that seethed through her mind began to seem more answerable now; if only Charles would return and talk to her! She looked down at her ivory slenderness, the tilted breasts, the tiny waist; surely she was still fair, though ethereal. Longing began to beat in her, and she looked for something to distract her mind.

A chest sat in one corner and looked to be securely locked, but two leather-bound books lay on top of it. How long since she had read anything? She crossed to it eagerly, pausing to enjoy the new steadiness of her legs, and picked up the volumes. Her knowledge of Greek was small, she could only barely pick out that one was the *Republic* of Plato, but the other was in Latin, Homer's *Odyssey*. Never had she been so grateful for the language that had been hammered into her by the priests who fled the anger of the eighth Henry and sheltered at Redeswan. All that they had been able to give in return was the strength of their faith to Lady Gwendolyn and knowledge to Julian; that knowledge had, in part, given her the power and the will to endure the Tower of London, a place that had driven many to madness.

Julian sat beside the brazier in the light of the flickering candle and let the winter world fade as she gave herself up to the canvas of gods and men that the old Greek had wrought so many centuries before. The poetry rang in her beauty-starved soul, and the wily Ulysses wore the face of Charles Varland. The daughter of Zeus watched over him, and he honored her before all the gods. Julian's fancy drifted to the gray-eyed goddess, and she thought, as she often did, that the anger of the Christian God and his followers was never so appealing as the pantheon of the clear-minded Greeks.

The hand that touched her shoulder was a human one, but she jumped to her feet with a cry and let the book tumble to the floor. The robe hung open, her shining flesh clearly visible to Charles as he stood beside the chair, his face concerned, his eyes half-averted from the display of her nudity.

"I see that you have the means of occupying yourself. You are better, then?"

Julian felt the flush mount to her face. "Much, thank you."

They stood staring at each other, so close that they could touch, two people who had shared much and yet were now so far apart. Julian's mouth went dry, and she found her breath hard to catch. It seemed stifling in the cabin that was comfortably warm only minutes before. The gray eyes that bored into her were tangled with those of the mythology she had just read and the passionate gratitude that she felt toward him despite his disclaimer, mingled with the love that had been so strong before she came to fear it.

Charles made as if to withdraw, his brow furrowed, and he opened his mouth to speak. In another minute he would retreat and the time would be lost. Julian's blood began to move as rapidly as though she had been running. Her lips parted and she moved slightly so that the fur glistened in the light and reflected on her pale skin. One hand rose and pulled at the neckline so that one rosy breast was revealed.

"Madam, I came to ask if you wished to take the air." His voice was hard, but a flush was mounting under the dark skin, and a pulse moved rapidly in his throat.

Greatly daring, Julian said, "Not the air, Charles." Her eyes met his and they looked long before his head jerked backward. "Charles." She drew back slightly, and the robe dipped again. *Brazen creature,* she thought, but still she did not cease to lure.

Then the matter was taken from her. Charles caught her to him, and their mouths locked in an explosion of hunger that rocked them backward. Their tongues explored greedily, their bodies pressed so tightly together that they might have been one flesh. Julian felt her breasts ache, and the throbbing in her loins became physical pain. Her hands sought his bare flesh, the heated length of him that belonged in her moist corridors.

Charles released her with a push that sent her tumbling back on the bed in the folds of the soft fur. Her chestnut hair spilled around her shoulders and over the rose-pointed breasts. The light shone on her translucent skin and picked out the brilliance of her aquamarine eyes. Julian read the confirmation of her beauty in his hungry face and his own anger that he could not control the desire for her that he felt.

He jerked at his clothes, almost ripping them in his eagerness. She knew that this would be no tender taking; no gentleness would hold them this time. She had urged him on, and now he would be the master. The long fingers pulled at his boots, the gaze with which he surveyed her was almost black. She savored the moments of waiting, drawn out with anticipation, as she looked at the wide shoulders, tapering waist and long legs, the trim buttocks, the lines of his ridged muscles, and the powerful shaft, raised and moisture-tipped, that would join them and slake their longing.

"I vowed to keep from you!" He grated out the words as he poised above her, a statue in this last moment of hesitation.

"The decision was not wholly yours to make!" She came up from the position in which she had half posed, half reclined. "Did you think it so?" She balanced on her knees in a partial crouch, knowing that the globes of her breasts swung free, and the light shone on the triangle of soft hair that was just lighter in hue than her cascading curls.

Charles reached out very gently and touched her nipple. She remained very quiet as he put both hands on her shoulders and ran them over the whole length of her upper body, causing the skin to pucker in response. He came to her waist and squeezed it so tightly that she gasped and put her hands out, first toward his face and then down toward the powerful hips and shaft that seemed to rise to her hand.

"Shameless!" He gritted the words out, and a little smile of pleasure curled one side of his mouth.

"Aye. Is it shameless when you do these things?" She let

her finger drift over the tip and back toward the pulse. "Did you not teach me the delights of the body?"

He caught her in both arms and twisted so that they lay together, she his willing prisoner. The dark eyes met hers without subterfuge. "I was another man then."

Julian freed her arms and flung them around his neck, pressing the whole warmth of her body against him and moving her legs so that he was between them. With a moan he shifted and took her on top of him. His face was as set as if he went into battle, but the hunger was winning. He thrust deeply into her, lifting and lowering her as she rode, eager and triumphant on top of the piercing shaft that went deeper each time, bringing her closer to the point of ecstasy.

He balanced as she did, then held her with one hand while the other rubbed her breasts. The flush of passion blazed in him now, and the heat was growing so consuming in them both that the rest of the world faded. She rose slightly on her bent legs and came down, he pulled her forward, and they melted in a combination of pain and fiery pleasure that seemed to rend Julian asunder. The strong force of penetration was part of the hard hands that held her sides, his tongue in her mouth, and the subjection of man and woman in this glory that was beyond endurance. She sagged over him and relaxed in the blessed release.

Julian came back from the timeless void where she drifted, bodiless, mindless, wholly content, in a sleep that was less sleep than utter relaxation of all her faculties. Instinctively she reached for the hard body, the supple length, that should be beside her. Now was the time for tenderness, for exploration, for the explanation of her eagerness, as they lay close and whispered their yearnings and secrets while he touched the inner places of her body and she his, and they waited for the fire to take them both in equality. The thoughts rose easily, and she felt her lips curve upward as she smiled in the continuation of happiness.

Reality was something brutally different. The hands that could bring such delight now flipped her over on her back

and pinned her hands above her head. The seeking gray
eyes were black now with anger as he straddled her body
and brought the engorged shaft up toward her chin.
Charles was smiling, but it was a mask for the fury within
him. Julian recognized it, for was that not akin to the anger that had burned within her so long? But here and with
all that they had shared? She opened her mouth to speak
and was stilled by a burst of laughter.

"You used the wiles of a slut on me for your own
whims and not for the first time. Do as I tell you now or
you will regret it. Do you understand me?"

She tried to twist free and was held in the grip so tightly
that she could barely breathe much less continue to flail
her legs. He bent forward and kissed her mouth in a
mocking, painful gesture. Then he moved closer on her
and rested the tip of his shaft on the edge of her chin.

"Take it. Take what you have sought."

In any other circumstances she might have been willing
to experiment and explore the less plumbed depths and
ways of passion, but not this way, not in this mockery of
all that she cared for in Charles Varland.

"No. No!" She gave a wrench that nearly unseated him
and writhed against the power of his grip.

Charles let her struggle for another minute, then he
transferred his grip so that he still held her with one hand.
He pressed the other into the softness of her throat, moved
it hastily over her neck and back to her face. He stared
down at her, anger blazing in his eyes. His grip grew
harder as he fought for control. Then he released her and
swung to the side of her, watching her face intently.

"Count yourself lucky that I have not the time to master you as you need to be mastered. That will be the
unfortunate task of your husband if you attain one." His
words were slighting, but the tone was reflective, almost
gentle.

Julian wondered at the change from black fury to
musing in a matter of seconds. She put out both hands to
him. "Charles, what is it?"

He caught her in his arms and crushed her to him. She
felt him shudder and started to put her arms around him.

Instantly he drew back and looked down at her, his mouth
curling upward. The blackness was in his face again.

"This is what you need." He pushed her down, holding
her firmly though she did not try to free herself. She lay at
his side, his leg over hers, her hands held once more in his,
and this time he inserted himself more strongly in her,
driving deeply inward. Hunger enveloped Julian, and her
body began to lift in eager response though she fought it
back. He drew nearly out of her and hammered in again
and again. She felt the cries rising from her and could not
bite them back. His sardonic look faded; passion and an
odd yearning came over his clear features.

He did not release her to participate with him; she was
prisoner and captive and willing slave to his touch. His
mouth drained her of all except longing. She could not get
close enough. His body held her down and she willed it so.
She lifted her hips to go downward with his thrusts, but he
pushed her flat and came over her. Julian did not want to
give in before this demand, but the clamoring of her body
could not be denied. The storm rolled over her, lifting her
up, bearing her high, and throwing love's receptacle down
before the man who now lay beside her, one arm over his
eyes, his mouth twisted and pained.

Julian stared at the ceiling and counted herself used, her
dignity ripped away. Charles had helped her, saved her
life, taught her the ways of love, but never for her own
sake. The flag of her pride rose and with it her temper.
She turned and set her fingernails in the brown shoulder.
He looked at her and she saw that he was a stranger, not
the man of violence she had just seen nor the tender lover
nor yet the comrade she had known. This was a man who
was somehow ravaged. The angry words died in her
throat, and her mouth softened.

"Ah, Julian, you will never be tamed. Why could I not
have met you a century ago in another life?" He sat up
and reached for his clothes. "I must go."

"Charles, stay with me!" She wanted to reach out, to
hold him and comfort him.

It was the wrong thing to say to Charles Varland. He
spoke icily. "I have other matters to attend besides your

gratification, madam." He adjusted his cloak and started for the door.

"Then get out! Out!" She rose in the bed, naked body slender and gleaming, tears filming her eyes.

He slammed the door as Julian threw herself down on the bed and wept all the tears of her life.

CHAPTER TWENTY-SIX

When Julian next woke, first starting up in the unfamiliar surroundings, then settling back into the warmth of the covers, she was amazed at how well she felt and how peaceful in view of all the fearful happenings of the day before. Time had twisted round again, but she could not doubt that she had slept for many hours. She touched her eyelids; they seemed a bit swollen and why not? All the stored-up misery of the past months had come out along with the cruelty that Charles had shown. She pushed back the gleaming strands of hair and wondered what he had found so reprehensible in her stirring of the passion he knew was in them both. If there was one thing she had learned in these last months it was that the moment must be seized while you lived and with no regrets. There should be none now.

She rose and stood nude in the cabin's dimness. It looked to be a gray day from the light showing in the little high window; surely it was morning to judge by the lightness she felt and the hunger. How to face Charles after all that had passed between them? She was purged, cleansed of anger and pain. Perhaps it would return, but for now it was enough that she was no longer embittered. Her fingers touched the faint indentations on her breasts, and her blood leaped in response. Memory must be enough from now on.

She scrambled into the black breeches that fit quite well, the boots less so, the clean white shirt smelling of fresh winds, and added the coat that was far too large but would give good warmth. She plaited her hair up into great braids which were then wound around her head and left little curls springing up at her temples. It seemed to Julian as she ran her hands over her face that even in this short time the bones were less prominent.

Her eagerness to know what was happening in the world outside her own small self and all that had transpired since her imprisonment suddenly boiled up. The reluctance of yesterday was gone; Julian Redenter was herself again. Honesty forced her to admit that this, even as her life, she owed to Charles Varland. In him the strains of anguish were deep; perhaps they had comforted each other.

She opened the door and stepped out into a small corridor which gave onto the deck where rain peppered down. A blast of icy wind invigorated her as she peered out first and then walked boldly to the railing. The ship was almost entirely sheltered from the weather by the slate-dark cliffs that rose up to meet the heavy clouds. She stared at their jagged tops and heard the booming of the surf that seemed to come from behind the ship. When she walked back she saw that there was a tiny aperture far beyond and almost hidden by mist as well as two great sheets of rock that clawed out for each other. The sails were furled, and the ship seemed to be part of the rocks and the wind. Far overhead some remnants of small trees, tortured into agonized shapes by the battering winds that did not reach this low, were visible. Sea birds wheeled near, and one sank to a branch only to be torn away by a savage gust.

Julian caught her breath in excitement and pleasure. She would give much to be able to go ashore and walk those paths, to dodge the wind and feel the mystery of this land open up to her. Arthur's country, legend-haunted, a fey world, full of romance. She spread her arms and said aloud, "Perhaps the Holy Grail is here, yonder in those cliffs."

"On the contrary, lady, there is more of the present than the past in the paths and caves and inlets here." The amused voice belonged to the heavy-set man, Roger, who had been on the barge at their rescue. "Had you best not come out of the weather? I came to offer you food and found your door ajar." He caught her questioning look and spread expressive hands. "Lord Varland sleeps; he labored long over maps and plans last night."

Julian drew back into the comparative shelter of an overhanging plank. "What day is this? What is the news? Are we pursued? What news of the queen?" All the questions she felt she should have asked Charles burst out of her now as she lifted her head to the fresh winter winds.

There was a movement at Roger's elbow, and the same boy who had been in the cabin the night before now tugged at his sleeve and jerked his head backward. The man said, "The food is ready in your cabin, Lady Redenter. I will tell you all that you wish if you do not mind the company of a rough sailor. This lad shall wait at the door for your peace of mind."

There was something in the way he spoke the words that told Julian orders had been given by Charles for just this exigency. She smiled, willing all her vagrant charm to rise. "I should be honored, sir."

Over broth, ham, the inevitable bread and cheese and thin ale, Julian learned that it was early December, the French were pressing on against the English and the war was not going well, burnings of heretics continued in London, and that as far as they could tell there had been no ships in pursuit of them. "That is not surprising, lady; there are many who are with us. Fortunate we were that some of these had access to the Tower and liked the feel of gold in their palms. Later it was noised abroad that the queen's own lady, unjustly imprisoned, was taken from under the very noses of her keepers. I doubt not that the city talks of it still. What London knows the whole country will know." He leaned forward confidingly. "They say that the queen will be brought to bed in early spring. Bah! The only danger is that Spain might believe it. She is old and her health is bad." He poured out more ale and drank hungrily.

Julian felt that strange stirring of pity and fought it back. As well to feel sorry for the Lord Pope himself! "Then Charles fights with the French?"

Roger gave an outraged gasp and even the boy turned to stare. "Never so! We harry the Spaniards who come, and we take her ships that set out for Spain; English gold is for England. Sometimes we engage the French in battle, and at other times we protect those victims such as yourself. Would you call us traitors who seek to preserve the land until the old harridan lies dead and Elizabeth is queen?"

Julian said, "What is her opinion of that, this princess whom you would hurry to the throne?" She herself could not have said why she took the opposing view. Lady Gwendolyn's face, with deep-set, reproachful eyes, rose in front of her and slowly faded.

Roger stood up, his skin flushing red under the deep tan. "I will leave you to rest now, lady." He compressed his lips as if he wished to say more and dared not give vent to his feelings.

Julian sank down on the bed and tried to sort out her emotions. She had no doubt that Charles would take her to France as he had once offered; there was nothing for her in England now except death and danger. Certainly she did not want to remain with him, nor would he have her. Then her natural wit asserted itself, and she knew that she wanted Charles Varland more than ever. *I will not lie to myself, at least.*

A sudden blast of sound rang in her ears just then, and the ship bounced upward to settle back. Running feet and cries came from the direction of the deck where she had recently stood, and someone began to scream, cursing in the same breath. She rushed to the door and then outside. Nothing but the cliffs and the fog could be seen, but she smelled smoke and powder. There was another blast that shook the timbers and then an answering one. She started for the back deck, where there now came a babble of voices, and was halted as a slender sailor ran into her, knocking them both back.

"What is happening?" Several other men ran by them, and she had to shout to make herself heard. The ship shook once more and shifted to the left before righting. The dark cliffs blurred before Julian's eyes as she dreaded the answer that was too obvious.

"Get below, lady! We're attacked, betrayed more like it. They can't get in here." He was little more than a boy and continued to babble while Julian watched in horror.

"Where are the weapons? Tell me!" She lashed her words across his and saw the pale eyes bulge. "Tell me— you'll need all the fighting hands you can get!"

The ship spun half around, and this time Julian saw a smaller one at the entrance to the inlet between the cliffs. It was the one that was firing at them to such advantage. Behind it loomed another in full panoply of sail, the arms of England and Spain. There was a belch of flame and smoke, a thundering roar, and the boards at her very feet kicked up. Somewhere a man cried in agony, and Julian was thrown flat on her face.

She put both arms over her head and waited for the final blow, but nothing else happened. In the distance someone cried, "The small boats are coming in! Aim for them!" Opening one eye, she moved cautiously and saw that all her limbs were intact, but the sailor to whom she had been talking lay decapitated in his own gore.

Red rage blinded her to the danger and the ghastly sight in front of her. She slithered on her stomach up to him and drew the short sword and dagger from his belt. Then she started to rise, but the listing movement of the ship threw her back down again. A curse escaped her lips, and she reached for the sagging railing to pull herself up.

"What in hell's name are you doing, you little fool?" The familiar voice came at her from behind, and she whirled to meet it.

"Do not tell me to go below, Charles Varland. I fight with your men! We were tracked here after all, and I will not go back." Her voice rose high and keening. One foot went out automatically to steady herself as the ship tilted again.

Charles's face was expressionless, the gray eyes unmoved by the carnage around them. He wore black, the heavy folds of a long cloak swirling over his shoulders. A sword and dagger were in his belt, and a long pistol hung from one side. He spoke so calmly that she had to strain to hear. "We are leaving the ship; she cannot hold out. It is not my men they really want. Come."

Julian cried, "What kind of a commander leaves his men in such peril and abandons his ship? What sort of man are you?" She knew it was ridiculous to stand in the midst of a battle and argue ethics, but a person had to believe in something, and for all their differences, she yet thought him a man of honor.

The guns boomed again; one shot hit the far cliff and shale rained down. A man cried out in anger and then in pain that must have been unendurable, for the last gurgles of death began as someone started a prayer to the Virgin. Charles lifted his hand almost casually, and the blow, light though it was, made Julian reel to her knees. She snatched at the dagger without thinking, and he kicked it away.

"Your head is stuffed with gallant tales. Sorry that I cannot oblige you." His legs were spread wide as he stood over her. "Come if you wish, or stay here and wait for them to return you to prison. I delay no longer." He ducked a fragment of falling timber and sail, then strode away.

Julian sat in shock for several seconds. She had fought for life too long to give it up now. The ship was doomed; it did not take a sailor to know that soon she would sink. The cold wind sliced at her as she rose to look in the direction that Charles had gone. The ringing of swords on each other was very plain in her ears as were the shouts and curses. Smoke was heavy on the wet air and death was everywhere.

She dashed for the cabin where she had felt so safe such a brief time ago and caught up the long warm cloak and thick muffler that had been provided, then picked her way back out on deck and after Charles. Her decision had not been made a moment too soon, for a small boat was already being launched from the front of the ship. Roger and the tow-headed boy were in it, and Matthew was going down the rope. Another young sailor waited with Charles, who was rapping out commands to an older man at his side. She saw that another small boat was vanishing into the mists that shrouded the cliff directly ahead and gave sudden thanks that at least some of the men would escape death or surrender.

" . . . knowing nothing. Paid for this voyage only and at the beginning of it. Be dull and dumb, as determined as they are. By all the gods, I wish it were different. . . ." Charles broke off as Julian ran up. "Changed your mind, I see. Get to the rope and be quick about it."

The gray-haired man to whom he had been speaking said, "You must be preserved for the cause, sir. God be with you."

Julian did as she was bidden, but her eyes saw the emotion with which Charles clasped the other's hand, and she regretted her own outburst. Would she, in his place, have done differently?

There was no more time for thought. The young man gave the rope into her suddenly slippery fingers, and she looked at the little boat far below, felt the shifting motion of the ship, saw the waves of the comparatively quiet inlet, and could not move. The wind tore at her cloak and whipped it about her body. The men below called up at her, but it was no use.

"Hurry up! We can delay no longer!" Charles hurried over to them. "What is the matter?"

"I can't. I can't." Julian could barely force the words out of her mouth for shame, but she could not go down that tiny thread fastened to the edge of the ship. Her fingers would not bend. The enemy that was already boarding could slash it with a single sword thrust, and she would fall into the sea. She gazed at Charles in panic; he would leave her for certain.

He was on her in a single stride. Before she could draw back, he pulled her into the crook of one arm, made a half salute with the other, then took the rope in that hand,

and stepped over into space. Julian clutched at him but remained still, for she could not endanger them both with her terror. They went down, down, swinging out and back, going faster and faster. Then it was over, and Charles sank down with her in the boat. Another several minutes and the young sailor joined them, the oars were lifted, and they rowed rapidly away from the dying ship.

Julian shifted her position and looked back. She did not want to look any of the others in the eye; she had fancied herself as brave as any man, and now she had acted as a puling maiden might. The ship was rearing high in the water, and flames cast brilliant lights on the low clouds. Men in boats were drawing nearer, and others fought on the decks. Another was setting out in pursuit of them but was having difficulty getting around the dying ship. Far beyond, and barely glimpsed, she could see the hulking outline of the ones who had pursued them to such advantage. The rearing, jagged cliffs, the destruction in the dark day, and the leaping fires that mingled with the cries of men in anger and despair, their own flight, came together in her mind, and she remembered her dreams that had foretold this. Julian shuddered even in the folds of her heavy cloak—she had felt so safe for a time, and now it seemed that fear would follow her wherever she ran.

Charles bent to his own oar as they passed under an arch of stone which almost seemed to scrape their heads, and the wind from the other side appeared to be a northern hand holding them back. Julian huddled where she was, knowing that in these circumstances there was nothing she could do. She did not turn to look again, for she was thinking that past and future merged into destruction, and all slipped down to the darkness of death. What mattered?

"I have frozen in the midst of battle and, had it not been for my comrade, would have had my skull cloven in two. Only the foolish are not afraid. Take that oar and do as I do. Every hand is welcome."

Julian looked up into the glittering eyes that were all light with no expression in them. Charles thrust the smaller oar into her hand and pulled his cloak up more warmly about his neck before bending over his own task. To the big back she said, "I thank you." The words were nearly tossed away on the wind shafts and the noise that was beginning to fade behind them, but Charles heard, and one corner of his mouth lifted as he turned to her and made swifter paddling motions. Comforted, she bent to the task that was theirs.

The little boat swept under another rock thrust, down a stream so shallow that at times the bottom of it grated on stone, and around to a deeper pool from which the barren face of another cliff reared up. They heard the deep-throated boom of the surf here and the sucking noise as the sea withdrew. Julian thought fancifully that it meant to eat through the solid rock and drag them down.

Oars ground on stone, and they drew up on a ledge that appeared to stretch out for a short way and then fall off into inky water. In a moment they all stood on the jagged stones, and the two younger men were carrying the boat behind a fall of rocks. Charles gazed up at the landscape of cliffs and boulders, out to the watery passage that led to the scene of his defeat, squared his shoulders and said, "The old trail up should still be here. I remember it well." The half smile curved his lips, and Julian found herself answering it involuntarily. "Let us go."

And so they came to the misty land of Cornwall in the legendary domain of King Arthur for to seek their own version of the Holy Grail.

CHAPTER TWENTY-SEVEN

The hut loomed dark in the failing light that made it seem almost part of the hillside. Sheets of rain, driven by the icy wind, swept over Julian and Nim, the tow-headed boy, as they stood beside a large boulder and waited for Charles to return. A flash of lightning tore at the sky and vanished into the cliffs, and thunder rolled in the north. Julian beat her hands together in an effort to try to feel them and thought of every fire she had ever known.

They had walked since landing yesterday with only a brief pause for exhausted collapse in a damp cave that Charles remembered from tales of his youth as being in this vicinity. Early that morning he had ordered Matthew, Roger, and the young sailor, Thomas, to separate. They were to go to several of the rallying places in this country and see, discreetly, what was afoot. He himself would find a safe place for Julian and meet them at a prearranged place four days hence. "If I do not come, you must assume the worst and go." They had protested, none more fiercely than Julian, but Charles had commanded silence and was not to be disobeyed.

Now the red-lit door swung open, and Charles stood waving at them. They joined hands and half ran, half stumbled over the rough ground, their wet clothes and heavy limbs impeding them only slightly at the thought of shelter from the storm. The woman who rose from the hearth to greet them might have been old forever or born that way. She wore rusty black that contrasted vividly with the white hair and eyebrows. Her head was sunk into her shoulders, her fingers were twisted with the stiffening disease, but her face was round and only partially lined, her teeth sharp and white in the smile of welcome.

"Come, get by the fire. There is ale, bitter, but it will warm you. I am Clara, long of these cliffs. Welcome to my home." Her speech had the same soft lilt that Charles's had when he let his guard down, and it was far more educated than a simple woman's might be expected to be. Julian suspected the wandering priests again; they had spread their learning far and wide after the dissolution of the monasteries.

The hut was one-roomed, meanly furnished, cooking was done on the hearth, sleeping around it, and there was one stool for sitting. A small hole gave ventilation and let in some rain, but the pervading odor was somewhat musky, a staleness long present. Julian thought it as marvelous as Whitehall or Greenwich; shelter against the evil weather, warmth, one's comrades close by, that simple did life seem now. She sat beside the leaping fire, watching her clothes steam with those of the others, and drew the old woman's tattered cloak around her body. Here in the midst of the safety that had been so hard and bitterly won, listening to Charles as he spoke of ill-fortune, smuggling, the ship aground in the storm, why did she feel the prickles of a fear that was older than the fear for one's dear flesh?

She swayed with the need for sleep that was suddenly boundless, a veritable bludgeon against her. Nim had dropped forward, head on his arms, in a position that would surely render him agonized on the morrow, and his snores rang loud in the room. Clara's gaze met Julian's when Charles paused to drink from the horn cup that must have been as old as Clara herself. The girl felt the shivers increase and stretched out her shaking hands to the fire. Why fight the sleep she so hungered for? The black gaze bored deeper, and she could not move. Charles noticed nothing; he was yawning and reaching over to replenish his cup, which he had drained. In the last moments before she drifted into the void, Julian knew what she feared. It was one of the charges that was to have been brought against herself, that while one slept the soul might be stolen away, and in the moment of waking the person was vulnerable to a yet greater evil. Then the gaze pushed harder, and she faded from all thought or memory.

She woke to the embers of the dying fire, the rush of the eternal rain, and a sense of being thoroughly chilled. The sense of aloneness was overwhelming as she jerked the dried cloak around her shoulders and rose hastily, the dizziness of sound sleep still on her. Had she been abandoned by Charles as one solution to the vexing problem of what to do with her? Strangely disproportionate to her feelings of both fear and safety the night before, Julian now felt that whatever had been intended was done; she had lost a battle because the weapons and the stakes were unknown.

"How silly I am being. Too much has happened after months of nothingness." She spoke aloud to give herself heart, but her voice rang shrill in the emptiness.

She heard a step and her nerves gave way. Her hands sought the sword she had taken and kept with her, but instead of holding it as a weapon she involuntarily raised it against her breasts in the sign to ward off evil, the sign of the cross of the Christians.

"Julian?" The familiar voice spoke from the doorway, and Charles stood regarding her with disapproval as he shook the rain from his cloak. "What is the matter with you?"

Relief and delight at seeing him when she had expected she knew not what made her burst into laughter. Everything was the matter with her world and his, yet he could stand there in common irritation and ask such a thing. She opened her mouth to share the joke, and the salt tears ran into it, splashing onto her hands and the shining sword.

Charles crossed over to build up the fire and, with his back to her, said quite matter-of-factly, "Women can weep and be the freer for it. A man is thought a weakling and a coward if he yields. He must ride out wildly, seek battle, or roar in anger. I have done them all and am no less."

"And rose to survive. You will survive this, too, and one

day will be honored for it." Julian dashed the tears back
and put down the sword. How very much she seemed to
have wept lately! Her feeling of helplessness was fading at
this human contact, and he did not even seem to be angry
for all that there had been so much discord between them
lately.

He turned around to face her then, and she saw the new
resolution in the fierce eyes, the new quietness in his bearing. In some strange way he was more at peace with
himself, more remote, far removed from the man who had
abducted her those weeks ago and equally removed from
the man who had stood looking down at her naked body,
attempting to revile her for the pleasure they had
shared.

She spoke again, nervous in front of his scrutiny.
"Where did everyone go? What is going to happen? I woke
and felt an absence of everything . . . everyone." She
wanted to get dressed; she must look the very hag of the
bog standing there with her hair mussed and the stains of
the hearth still on her hands.

"I sent Nim out to scout. Clara will be back soon. But
you . . ." He hesitated with an uncertainty that was no
usual part of Charles Varland. "Julian, I will find a place
for you in one of the villages that dot these hills. You will
have to act as one of the people, but you are adaptable
and brave. You can do it. When I have another ship and
crew and have discovered what went wrong that we were
tracked down, I will set you safely in France. Then my responsibility will be ended. But do not be afraid now." He
leaned toward her, and she caught the fresh scent of wind
and male warmth.

"Why should you feel responsibility toward me? I
should have gone with you when you risked much to warn
me. It is my fault. Your ship, your men, destroyed!" She
faced him with chin up, knowing that the burden must be
borne. Was this the man she had teased and taunted only
days before, this stranger with the closed face? Did she
seem different to him as well?

"Comport yourself, lady. We all know the risks we take.
I would not have you think that I dared assault the Tower

for your sake alone as we have said. You were told of the vast rallying it gave to so beard the queen—men will speak of it in years to come. But you are young and foolish, and I have taken your body in hunger and often given you short shrift. I vowed to stay away and did so try." He watched the color mount up into her pale face and shook his head. "Let all that be ended between us, for there is much to be done otherwise and I will ask your help, knowing that you hold one ruler to be as another. Even so."

Julian had never heard him speak in this manner. Always the wildness had been between them, and she had not known the man. Perhaps it had been so for him with her. She said, "Truly, I cannot see that one ruler is better than another; they all persecute. Have I and my family not reason to know that? The god worshiped is one of cruelty, no matter that he wears their own faces. Were all your reasons so abstract, Charles?"

"No. Isabella was full willing to die as she did; she was a fanatic, and there are many in all our camps. But you were a victim, and so was my Beth. So was Geraldine in her way. So are most people." Weariness tinged the dark face, and Julian knew that he believed all he said. "I, I have only battle left. That can be surcease."

He stared down into the fire moodily, then whirled, hand on his sword as the door banged in the rising wind. Julian did not know what to say, for she perceived that he was fully as jumpy as she. Abruptly he sat down but poised, ready to leap up. Julian went across to the cups of the night before and poured out the dregs of ale, dividing them between herself and Charles.

He said, "Cornwall is one of our rallying places, strong for the princess here, fierce for the queen in a dozen others. Here my name is powerful, and here, it has been said, the salvation of England will come when Arthur rises." His eyes sought hers and held them. "We could have hidden and recuperated in these coves, been restored, but there is treachery in my own camp. Julian, Clara is no woman of the crags, but one schooled in the arts; she is an astrologer. I meant to seek her in private even before your rescue and our destruction in the ship."

Julian almost dropped her cup and her eyes went wide. "An astrologer! But that is death. Especially now!"

Charles drained his cup and set it down on the stone. "Tonight we shall cast the horoscope of Queen Mary Tudor, Philip of Spain, and the Princess Elizabeth! If the latter is favorable, my men shall know and gain heart from it."

"It is held to be sorcery, magic. Several have been banished from the kingdom, tried for their lives. And, still, men have faith in a nebulous God, why not the stars and their patterns? We can at least see those." Her face flamed with excitement. "Charles, will you let me be present? I must!"

"There is the strangeness of it all, Julian. Clara insists that you be. Our fates, she says, are inextricably interwoven with those of the great ones. That is why I have gone to such lengths to explain it all to you. I thought you would wail or demur." The sardonic grin quirked at his mouth, and he stretched lithely. "I should have known you were bolder than that."

"So you should, my lord." She gave the imitation of a curtsy, glad of the lightness between them and hoping to conceal the terror she felt. It was death to cast the horoscope of a reigning sovereign and a sin to go beyond the laws of God.

Charles sighed and folded himself in his cloak. "I must sleep. Keep watch until Clara returns." He pillowed his head on one arm and closed his eyes.

Julian watched the clear profile, the line of the straight nose, and the presently relaxed lips. One phase of their relationship was done, she thought, and felt the rigor on her once more.

The short afternoon light had given way to almost instant darkness before Clara returned, waking Charles, waving Julian aside with an impatient gesture, and settled herself in the back of the hut where she spread charts, parchments, two old books with heavy clasps, and what appeared to be a jar of stones around her. "The dates and times, to the instant if you can, and the places of their births. Tell me again. Quickly." She demanded the dates of both Charles's and Julian's births, frowned, bent over her charts, and began to mutter. "I must have absolute silence if this is to be done properly. There is not much time."

Charles went back, apparently to resume his rest, but Julian saw that he held himself tense and alert. She sat staring into the fire, wondering at what point he had revealed himself as other than a ship-wrecked commander to Clara. She had expected something far more mysterious than the process now visible. What had those scandals been about that astrologers should seem a menace to the peace of the kingdom? More persecution!

The crackling fire cast long shadows on the walls of the hut and turned Clara's hair into a red-tinged aureole as she pored over the starry maps that Julian remembered vaguely were supposed to indicate not only past but future if correctly viewed. The rain seemed to have lessened outside, but the wind still clamored for admittance, and the two smelly candles swayed thin flames in the cold air that entered despite the stuffed cracks.

"Ah!" Clara threw down the reed pen she had been using to calculate and reached for the stones in the jar. She drew out one that was cylindrical and reflected light, then another large as her fist and perfectly smooth. She lifted these and looked long into them. Charles and Julian followed her gaze, but Julian could see nothing. Slowly Clara lowered them and stared straight into the eyes of Charles Varland, a tiny smile touching her lips. Julian felt the chills lift the hair on her arms. It was as if great leathery wings beat in the little room, and she began to repeat the words of the Hail Mary in her mind in repetition that must constitute protection.

"What is it? What do you see? Have you finished? You have only just begun!" Charles came closer, the urgency in his voice making him sound angry. "Tell me, woman!"

Clara rose to her feet, the black robe seeming to billow about her in the red glow. Her shadow ran longer on the wall and over the ceiling as she held out the cylindrical stone in much the same manner that Julian had brandished the cross of the sword earlier. Her voice was deep, growling, powerful, not that of the old woman, authoritative though she had been. "You would know what the stars have shown me, Charles Varland? Would you know your own future and that of this woman?"

Charles put both hands on his hips, and the light etched his carved profile in brilliance. "That is what I have asked, though not of myself, but of the powers of England. What of the queen? The princess? Why do you hesitate?"

"There is war, many ships, terrible danger in a far time. Not now. Prepare." Clara's voice fell to a whisper and rose again. "Your star and that of this woman are of different houses. The danger is also now, now and in your joining."

Charles spoke louder. "That was not my question. My future does not matter, nor does the future of a far time. The woman I will care for. Answer me, Clara!"

She whirled on him and gave a snarling laugh that made Julian rise to her feet. "I have seen Mary Tudor lie dead in her palace and all the world depart from her. She will die, and all the world will be ranged against England just as it is now. Your own cause will fade and wither before another light."

"When will it be?" Julian forced the words out, surprised at the strength of her voice, delighted at the lifting joy she felt that the woman spoke of Charles and herself together. The brief moment died as the farseeing gaze fastened on her.

"You have seen the shape of future and ignored it. Be warned."

Then the hut faded for Julian, and she saw again the cliffs and the red lights that meant death and worse. She saw Charles and the darkness that enveloped him. She saw herself alone on a dark plain and knew that she would be that way for whatever little part of her life remained.

". . . I am sorry, but I can do no more. It is as I said. The queen will die in bitterness, and England will suffer. No more can I read. The weariness is come upon me."

Julian was standing where she had been moments before. But now Clara was half crumpled in the corner as she gathered her materials together, her hands shaking. Charles was saying angrily, "But that is mere fortune-telling. You are one of the best astrologers and highly commended. Have I not said that you will have payment? Do you doubt the word of a Varland?"

"It is not that. I have something of the sight. The woman can see a little—I felt it." Clara's voice trembled, and for once she looked her age, as old woman, shaking, pitiable. "I can calculate nothing when it comes upon me. I have endured enough; it tears me in twain, the double burden."

"You will not pursue this?" Charles retreated into ice. "You will not try?"

"I cannot."

His anger flamed even as the fire had done, and he drove one fist into another with a hammering motion that made Clara shrink away, her hands over her face. He took a step toward her, his foot trampling on the charts and toppling the jar of stones.

"Charles, you must not!" Julian ran at him and threw her arms around him, spinning him back so that he faced away from Clara. She clung to him with all the power in her slender body even as the fury racked him.

He twisted for a moment and then was still, the hard eyes staring into hers, then he relaxed. Around the wide shoulder, Julian saw Clara's smile, wide and triumphant and evil, flash out before she bent to gather her materials.

CHAPTER TWENTY-EIGHT

Julian walked several paces behind Charles, her hand near the sword at her waist, ready even as he was for the sight or sound of pursuit. The December winds roared across the craggy land and tore at all in its way. Julian's cloak was not sufficient protection against it, and she shivered steadily. The cold at least helped to take her mind off the increasing pain in her feet. She wondered if Charles knew where he was going and almost did not care—cessation of motion would be enough. Would she ever be warm again?

The events of the past night rose again in her mind, and she did not try to stop the memory or the fear that rendered her as icy as the wind. Charles had spent most of the time staring into the fire after his fury at Clara was turned aside by Julian. The old woman had not spoken then, nor had she this morning when they started to leave. She remained rigid on her pallet, black eyes gazing at something they could not see. They could not have left in the night because the weather was both pouring rain and sleety; it had held Nim up, and when he returned in the early light Charles had bidden him tend Clara. "That much we owe her. Then go to the coast and the meeting place. I will join you when this task is done." He had surveyed Julian unpleasantly, and she felt as if she were a bale of unwanted goods.

They had been walking ever since, and not a word had he addressed to her. She vowed that the first one would not be hers, but physical discomfort was becoming real

distress. Sooner or later he must stop, even Charles Varland could not know this land so well that he could
traverse it in the dark under a sleety gale. The tenderness
mingled with anger that was ever part of her caring for him
was beginning to yield to a flinty determination. He would
see no more of her heart spread open before him. She
would draw into herself and be courteous only, for she
owed him more than her life and would never forget that.

They climbed up a slippery stretch of rock, then Charles
turned off to the left and approached what seemed to be a
massive pile of boulders twined with summer's remnants
of vines and creepers. She followed numbly as he went behind them and bent down as if searching. At that her
control broke.

"Charles, what is this? Have you gone mad to scrabble
in this pile? Surely there is some sort of shelter in this
benighted area that we can look for without digging for
it?" The wind carried her words high and dumped them
down again, and the sleet slashed her lips, momentarily removed from the damp muffler.

"Come." He rose and caught her arm, pulling her
toward the hole in the ground that had been revealed by
his fingers. "It will be better soon, I promise."

The warmth in his tone threatened to bring the tears,
and she regretted her savagery. Now she followed him into
the passageway that was leading downward. Incredibly, he
produced a candle fragment and struck a rock against another to provide, after several attempts, a flame to light it.
Then the earth and rocks were pulled back so that no evidence of their entry should remain.

The space at the bottom of the stairs had obviously
been used as a lair by others, for it was wide and long at
one end, narrowing at the other into a passage much like
the one they entered by, and there were coverlets, an old
chest standing open which held clothing, more candle fragments, and a pallet in one corner from which the occupant
could survey the entrances. Wonder of wonders, there was
even a small hearth and debris piled beside it.

Charles met Julian's amazed stare and gave the quirking
grin. "There are many of us, Julian, and there are many

hiding places. When we leave we will prepare it as well as we can for the next fugitive. It is blessed shelter, and we will be safe here until the storm blows itself out."

"Blessed shelter." She spoke the words as he did and began to help with the igniting of the fire that was to restore them both. Her stiffened fingers were clumsy at first, and Charles lifted a branch for her. The touch on her skin made it burn and she drew back, well aware of her reaction to his simplest gesture.

They slept close to each other that night for warmth, since the fire must be carefully watched, and it was very cold even in this sheltered place. Weariness held them aloof from any talk, but Julian knew that it was more than that the next day when Charles, the bare gray light of dawn streaming in from the other passage, an aperture planned for rapid exit if need be, touched her shoulder, pointed out the bread and cheese, and stalked away. She tried to sleep again, but it was hopeless. Rising, she walked up and down to get warm, then inspected the chest which produced another, welcome, jacket, and a countrywoman's dress of coarse brown cloth, a man's shirt and breeches, and a short cape. She wondered what manner of people had been through here and what their fates had been.

The day was an eternity, but when she tried to venture out the one open way, sleet and wind beat her back. The other by which they had entered could not be opened from this side. Charles, finally returning iced and withdrawn, said only, "It shows no signs of abating. We must rest while we can. I watched the entire day from a covert, and nothing moved on the face of the land."

"Let me come with you tomorrow. I feel as if I were in prison again down here."

"You will remain here." His darkened eyes glittered into hers, and she was forced to turn away. He fought a battle she could not fathom, and Julian knew that they were as far apart from each other as though they were separated by miles.

Two more days with hours a hundred years long. Two more nights lying still beside the equally unmoving big body that had once given her such joy. She wanted to lean over and say, "Can we not comfort ourselves?" The rebuff was not to be imagined. She thought of the time in the Tower and how hope had restored itself then. Greedy to have life and yet want more!

When the gale continued to blow and snow drifted into the passageway, even Charles gave up and returned to sit by the meager fire they dared to make. He stared into it and did not move. Julian watched and finally spoke his name, then again. The face he turned to her bore a look that seemed to come from far away, and she knew that he walked in another time. The question that she meant to ask about the village where he was taking her faded, and words that she would once have never dared utter now came naturally.

"Charles. Is what happened to Beth the reason that you feel as you do?" She wanted to add "toward me" but had not quite the courage for that. If he resented this probing in the past, he would quickly tell her and that would halt it. Still, the uncertainty of his temper she had reason to know.

"Are you witch that you know I thought of her?" His gaze was less blind now, and she saw that it disguised, and had all along, the bareness of pain. "There has never been anyone around me that I would permit to speak that name, and yet when you speak it I think how long ago all that was."

Julian saw the soft look in the mist gray eyes, a look he had never turned on her, tender though he had been at times, and felt jealous of a dead woman. "When my mother lay in her last illness she spoke to my father as though he sat beside her bed. He was killed, as you know, before I was born, and she never saw another face but that it bore his own." She felt the anger of her childhood —she had never been compensation enough for Lady Gwendolyn. "I think that here in Cornwall, in the land that is your own, the past returns and bears upon you. Talk to me, Charles, it will ease you." She stretched out both hands to the fire and felt the warmth run up her arms under the hanging sleeves of the shirt.

"Ease your curiosity, you mean." He jibed at her, then lowered his gaze to the fire shapes. "You need not think, madam, that because we have lain together you are privy to my thoughts and privacies, nor shall be."

"You know that is not true." She spoke quietly, for she had known bitterness enough to be aware of the open wounds it left. "I only know that the past and present often are interchangeable."

He rose and began to pace up and down, causing the cold wind to swirl around them both. His hand hammered into the other palm in the gesture that was typical of him when frustrated. "I must get back to sea. The French are pushing against Calais. If England loses that foothold in France it could spell the end of Mary Tudor! This cursed storm! Curse the fate that betrayed us and destroyed my ship!"

"You would fight against the queen even when English territory is at stake?" Julian was horrified in spite of herself. Calais was the only part of the English conquest of France in the last century that remained to her country. "Even your princess would count that a traitor's scheme, whatever the motive."

"Traitor is only a word! I do what is right for myself and those who follow me. Your queen is a traitor that she tears this realm in pieces, and Spain waits to gobble it up!" He came to stand over her, the words pouring from him as from a goblet of bitter medicine. "You wonder that I can feel this way, you who have seen the hand of cruelty in the name of religion and who have been its victim yet waited blindly for the slaughter. Ah, Julian Redenter, you have been bored in this cavern, all that remains of the castle of a man I knew in my youth. Destroyed by the troops of Her Majesty and he dead on Tower Hill as I should be if I believed the mouthings of those who call themselves great." He put a hand to her chin and held it in a hard grip for a few moments. She met his eyes boldly, and he jerked away.

"You wish amusement? You shall have it. My name is old, the family wealth long departed. Listen well, for I do not speak of these things to all. My parents died in a

boating accident the year I was born. My uncle, a recluse
and a scholar, inherited and almost immediately ran afoul
of King Henry on the matter of his divorce. The king was
at that time sending about to various members to most
discreetly sound them out as to what was called 'his secret
matter.' Uncle Roger, immersed in the world of the
Greeks, minced no words. Neither did King Henry, who
was not as bold as he later came to be. The royal interest
was withdrawn, the royal privilege revoked. The place,
however small, that my father's son might have expected
at court was not there. No monies were available for Varfair, not that my uncle cared; he would not have noticed if
the encroaching sea devoured the castle so long as his
books were safe. I grew up to think all men were as he,
and he taught me something of his love for knowledge,
which I have never regretted. Our family was always remote and apart but never so in the arts. I was still very
young when Uncle Roger began to stir himself in my be-
half. One of his contacts was the matchless poet, Thomas
Wyatt, still a young man when he and my uncle wrote. He
was on a mission for the king in Italy; it was simple enough
to add an obscure lad's name to the rolls of service. When
Wyatt died in the next few months, I remained with some
of the others to represent England."

Charles went over to the pile of wood and trash,
gathered an armful, and tossed it on the fire, causing the
blaze to leap and soar as the warmth began to spread. His
face had lost the mask of caution, his eyes their hooded
glitter. Julian wondered at the flood she had unleashed and
how long it had been since he had spoken of these matters
festering in his heart.

"I traveled—Venice, Padua, Geneva and elsewhere—a
clerk living on little. My uncle died and I entered into the
title, but the king was very ill then and I knew that I
would be ill-advised to go home. I met Beth—Elizabeth
Tinta, part French, part English, maybe a little Irish—in
Rome, where she was taking in the Holy City of the Pope
with her grandmother, who was very old and wealthy.
Young as we both were, we fell fiercely in love. The old
lady opposed it and had my antecedents checked. She

thought it was for the money. Beth knew better. We ran away and were wed by a priest in a little town in northern Italy, then we moved about. We learned that King Henry had been notified and that it was demanded that I return. I think it would have been my death, for no one defied him in those last days. Religious strife was going on everywhere between Catholic and Protestant, some places less violent than others, but we never noticed. Spies had been put onto us by power of the grandmother's wealth, and they waited to close in. We were living in a border town then, a dispute arose in one of the taverns over religion, it spread, and I returned to our little house . . . you know what I found." He stood staring into space, the dark face closed up and anguished.

Julian knew. The pregnant young girl dead and raped, the perpetrators not to be found, troops coming in to quell the populace, both sides blamed. Charles hating then and that hatred growing with the long years.

"Beth. Blue eyes, black hair, always laughing and telling me I was too somber, that our child would learn laughter from her. He would have been a boy. We had ten months together. Nothing and everything. The old woman died of the shock but blamed me for all that happened and made sure that it was known. Her wealth was given to the Church; that was the greatest irony of all. I cared for nothing then, and so I returned to England. Squire Harry, God's light on earth, was dead and Varfair mine. I once loved it; now it could fall to ruin and I would only watch. The young king was most interested in what were called the injustices of his father's reign; I was honored, given sympathy, asked to travel in his concerns. All useless and too late. I grew to abhor the Protestants even more and the Catholics the same. They were all fanatics, and the boy king was one of the worst. I saw things in Geneva and the German states that tore my very soul. I went to Spain and encountered the workings of the Inquisition. I felt myself drowning in hatred and loss. Nothing mattered. It was during this time that I met Prince Philip of Spain at a minor court function. We both had too much to drink and began to talk. I spoke of Beth, and he told me of his first

wife, Maria, who died in childbirth, and of the son whom
the doctors suspected would never be normal. He had
loved her deeply, he said, and did not expect it to come
again. We shared pain and it seemed to lessen; later we
drank and sported together often. He told me that I might
wed where I would, but he must obey his father, Emperor
Charles, in all things. Further, he confided, madness ran in
his family, and he feared it above all things. Adherence to
the true Catholic faith might bring relief, and he would
bring all he could to it. He had the makings of another fanatic, but we were true friends in those days, and I began
to think life could be palatable. I owe him much, Julian.
But England and her welfare are foremost."

Julian understood. If she had been a man her story
might be very much the same as Charles's. The fire was
hot now, and she shrugged back the cloak, then lifted the
heavy hair from her neck. Charles watched her and his
mouth softened.

"I returned to take up my duties to King Edward, but
my cynicism showed and I was no longer welcome in the
councils. He decided to reward my past service with an
heiress. A man must be wed, he said. Geraldine was only
a child, and I knew the propensity of her breed, but I allowed the betrothal. It was easier than struggle. Then I left
court, traveled again, tended Varfair, relearned the
pleasures of the intellectual life, dreaded the eventual day
of marriage, even returned to see the king when those
around him felt a different voice was needed. I saw Philip
of Spain in those years and saw him growing more determined that all the world should be Catholic, yet we
remained friends, though not as we had been.

"I was on the Continent when the young king died and
through Mary's triumphal rise to the throne. I vowed to
stay away, but she knew my history and wanted to watch
me. I was commanded to return, and I knew that I wanted
to live in England despite everything. The Spanish marriage was about to become a reality; I thought I might be
some mitigating influence on Philip. It was with horror but
no surprise that I learned of the Spanish wish to officially
establish the Inquisition in England. Queen Mary was

besotted with him and would do anything he wished; moreover, her own Spanish blood and Catholicism told her this was the right thing to do. You know my views of her. It was from those days at court that I vowed to bring her down—to fight against my ruler and my friend. It was a bitter choice, but I could do no other. Many that I met were of like mind and we joined forces. I do not know why they fought, but I desired freedom of thought, not to be ruled by religion which permeated every facet of life. I want my country to go forward in rationality and not to be steeped in blood and hatred. Elizabeth, pure English born, can give us a chance. That is my cause and my belief."

They sat in silence for a few minutes, and then Julian said, "I am glad that you have spoken so freely to me, Charles. My own cause is less noble, I fear. I simply want personal freedom, to live as I choose, to believe or not as I wish, to wed or not to wed." She looked up and saw the gray eyes intent on her face. Her blood began to move more swiftly, for she knew that look and wondered if her own face mirrored it.

"Julian, dear Julian, that is what every person in this land wants. That is my cause." His voice was low and throbbing. One hand reached out to touch hers and then drew back. "I have vowed myself to it, and there is no room for anything else. I loved Beth with all the passion of a young man's first love. Geraldine and I would have had a mutual arrangement, beneficial to us both. Then there was you, Julian, with your pride and outspoken bravery and your beauty. I was lured and had to have you."

"Charles." She could only whisper his name, proud beyond the telling that he could share so much with her. Dread began to build, for she thought she knew what he would say.

"I called it the power of the flesh, and perhaps it was in the beginning. But this struggle for England's very life demands everything from those who work for it. I cannot involve another innocent. My own feelings can have no precedence. The cause is all. I will do anything for it. I suppose that I, too, am a fanatic." He laughed a little unsteadily.

Now Julian saw the reason for his reticence and coldness; he would have scorned to mention the stories about him at the court or to suggest a refutation. He would withdraw and walk his own path, a man apart. He might be suspected, but actual proof would be all the harder to come by and conspiracy not really considered by those who knew his temperament. His heart was locked away because of the past and for the achievement of the larger goal. If he could give it, Julian thought that he might truly love her, but Charles Varland would never speak those words until he was free to do so.

"Perhaps you are right to call yourself a fanatic, Charles, but I must call myself one as well. The Inquisition is a dreadful thing. You must do what you have to do." Julian Redenter had her pride also; she would not demand what he could not give. How well she understood the anger that often ruled him and the gentleness that vied with it. Understanding enabled her to give him the reassurance he sought, proud that she could do so for his sake. "Do as seems right; I understand all that you have said."

Charles sat back on his heels and looked straight at her. "Old Clara saw our linked fates. I have spoken to you as to no other person in years. This time here may be all that we have. Ever."

Julian said, "While the storm lasts there is this time of sharing." She spread her palms to the fire and his swordsman's fingers closed on them.

"This time of sharing," he repeated, "so long as it is understood that you and I have different destinies. That there are no demands." His jaw jutted slightly, and the pulse in his throat began to hammer.

Julian had learned in the events of the past months that the moment must be taken, for in very truth there might not be another. She had prayed uselessly in the Tower and yet had been delivered from madness by her own determination. The whirl of events had brought her to this time, and she would have lied with her last breath to have and prolong it. That premonition which seemed a part of her in these days rose again to tell her that never again would she be with Charles Varland in this manner.

She lifted her face to his. "There are no demands, nor will there be."

He brought her hand to his mouth as the fire blazed higher beside them.

CHAPTER TWENTY-NINE

Charles and Julian lay together on his heavy cloak in front of the fire, their bodies locked in a passionate embrace. Her shining hair spilled over his arms and her hands pulled him ever closer. His mouth took hers, held and drew from it. In this first eagerness, this first search for satiation, there was only hunger to make up for all the times that they had not taken each other. Julian felt the wetness of her loins and the pain in her breasts, the ache that had begun to permeate her body. She moved her hands up and down the firm length of Charles's back and buttocks, tugging at him, moaning for the beginning of the delight that would lift them both.

He turned her over on her back and rose slightly above her, his eyes looking down into hers, but this time there was no struggle over mastery. They were man and woman, woman and man. His mouth corners rose in a half smile which she returned, knowing that he remembered the last time and their battle. His manhood stood firm and erect, and she shuddered for the pleasure it would bring them both. She writhed on the soft surface of the cloak, her breasts moving with her hips in the gyrations that would soon grow deeper.

"Now, Charles, now!" Her hunger would not be denied.

"Yes!" He thrust into her slowly and deliberately, withdrawing a little and then going deeper. She lifted to meet the thrustings, her hands drawing him closer until at last he was atop her, and they were one in the timeless rhythm which would draw into consummation. Julian felt the fire lick at her body and thought for a second that the actual hearth flame had extended. Then Charles kissed her again, and the heated blood ran so savagely that she cared nothing for external matters, only that he pierce her more deeply, that she pull him yet more hungrily into her. The burning rose, exploded, and yet was not enough. They held each other, whispered, and lifted again in the joining that welded and did not loosen. Sweat beaded their bodies, drenched them. Charles reached for Julian's hand and clasped it. That above all else brought the tears to her eyes.

They slept and woke to passion, then returned to sleep again. Julian roused once when Charles went to check the storm, thought that the snowflakes in his dark hair and the flush on his high cheekbones from the cold added to his physical beauty, smiled at her own whimsy, and fell into the depths of satiated slumber once again.

"Julian? Julian, wake up." His hands were warm on her breasts, touching the already lifted nipples, rubbing the fullness of them and luring her up from the warm depths where she dreamed of him.

"And the dream is real." Her lips shaped the words, her eyes told the rest. There was no need to speak more, for he understood.

Now Charles led her into strange paths, into the hot thickets of desire and the glowing pits of savagery barely withheld which paused and culminated in tenderness. Now she bent to his urgings and, after the initial hesitation, took him in her mouth and moved her lips on the pulsating shaft while her fingers clasped the firm buttocks and trailed gently over the flat stomach. His carved face seemed a thousand miles above her and his pleasure a shattering thing that burst in her mouth and made her tremble with the power of it. Now she lay in her turn while his mouth explored the tiny lips of her maiden mound to send tongues of molten flame straight over her. His fingers explored the crevices that his own tongue traced out and spread out. Julian lifted to his mouth, tongue, and fingers, then fell again to find his mouth drawing on her breasts, tracing out their curves and then the spear of him taking the trembling, willing quarry which became in the next breath the Amazon huntress, bold for to seek.

Now Charles lay prone, his hands on her own smooth moons while she lifted up and down on the impaler that never rested but rose again rejuvenated. Her heels thrust side and backward, her hands stroked and touched and coaxed. He held back, almost daring the skill that had burgeoned under his teaching and her own instinct to bring him to the edges. Julian caressed, licked, and let her fingers drift in his secret places until the wide brow was tinged with red and dripping with sweat. She lowered her head to take the swollen tip of him into her mouth, working at it with instinctive lore, her two fingers reaching for his hilt, the almost green eyes shining into his, which were black with desire. From rapidity she went to such softness that each second lasted an hour. Her body shone pink and white in the firelight, and Charles was the dark man of legend and fantasy; their mingling would create a new race. Julian had the brief thought and then fought to hold back the shudderings that heralded her own collapse. She began to convulse and looked at Charles, who could wait no longer as he gushed forth. The quaking rhythm took her as well, and they went separately into the sweetest oblivion of them all.

Later they cuddled close together as he played with her satiny hair that covered his chest. "You are marvelous learned in these matters, my dear lord." "It is a talent. I am modest." "I, also. Have you no compliments?" "Ah." His lips found hers and the drowsy comments drifted into murmurs of contentment that were punctuated with laughter as he tickled the smooth contours of her sides and

back. Julian tangled her fingers in the dark hair and
nuzzled his firm chin before burying her face in the cup
between neck and shoulder. He tilted her head back and
kissed the long line of her throat with little soft movements that were curiously like those of his first taking of
her. She began to tremble and one hand went to her chest;
it was growing hard to breathe and the wings of rising
desire gave no respite. Once again the sweet tyranny began.

Once Julian had longed for freedom and security. Now
in this cellar of a burned-out castle with their only food
hard bread and stale cheese, their drink melted sleet, their
warmth each other and the blazing beams hauled in by
other long-ago fugitives, she was happier than she had ever
been or was ever likely to be again. They did not talk of
the future; for them there was none. By tacit agreement
they shared their pasts with each other, the golden moments
of laughter or poignancy, Elspeth's admonitions, Uncle Roger's absentmindedness, childhood escapades, experiences
of the great world and the knowledge of the inner world
that existed for them both in history and poetry and mythology. Julian prayed to the God in whom she barely
believed that the storm would continue; these days together would lighten all her days to come. For Julian
Redenter there could be no other man; she had always
known that. Yet unlike her mother, unlike the very queen
of England, she would live despite the immolating passion
that tore and shook her at every movement Charles made.

"My little fire-goddess, lady of light, the beautiful one."
The soft words curled in her consciousness as he touched
her lifting nipples while they lay in love's exhaustion during a time that might have been night or day.

"Flattery." She turned her head and looked into his
eyes, which were clear and warm in these unguarded moments. " 'I know that I speak truth. I look at you and am
water which pours down me, so like the very god . . .' "
She stopped and the laughter tumbled forth.

Charles rose on one elbow and assumed a horrified expression. "Is that all you can quote of Sappho, the divine
poetess? We must look to your Greek. Let me see, what is

the name for this most delectable section of your most delicious body?" He touched her quivering mound with a fingertip.

Julian moved languidly to one side, then caught him around the neck and they tossed together in mock battle, laughing in their nudity, rolling as the puppies did in spring, caught in delight in this shining time of their lives that renewed and restored them both with Aphrodite's golden blessing.

She came awake suddenly and reached out to feel the powerful body that had been beside her so often of late. In a moment he would whisper extravagant words into her ears, then gather her close as the fires mounted in them both. It seemed to Julian that she could not get enough of him nor he of her in these days that were so short. She turned on her side to see if he were playing a trick, lying just beyond the reach of her fingers. He was gone, but his cloak lay over her for warmth in the event the fire should die down.

"Charles? Where are you?" She called softly, then more urgently. A mounting sense of danger made her leap for her clothes and thrust the dagger into the band at her waist. A few steps to the passage and a glance upward told her all that she needed to know.

The blowing storm had ceased. The land was rimed with ice, and a freezing wind nipped at her exposed face. The sky was heavy and gray, a thick cap fitted down after the wildness of the past days. There was some snow but not enough to impede progress. Julian knew what that meant, and she knew the face that she must wear. Their bargain had been made, and now it was time to keep it.

She was sitting wrapped in her cloak, watching the fire die down and making no effort to replenish it when Charles came in. He wore his austere look again, and the sight of him so shook her that she was glad she had had the time to remind herself of what must be.

"You know that the weather has changed." The words were flat, grating.

"I am ready." Julian rose to face him and was thankful that her face did not give away the anguish within.

"Then we will go." He lifted his head and shook back the dark hair.

Their eyes met and neither knew which one moved first, but they were in each other's arms, their mouths locked as they strained together and still could not get close enough. Still fused, they lowered their bodies to the cloak pallet, and in the fading firelight with the chill beginning once again to permeate the hiding place, they made love in the deepest sense of the word. This time mouths and hands and bodies touched and lifted into tenderness that transmuted passion beyond itself. Short in time, forever in caring, this welded Charles and Julian together in the one flesh which was more than poetry; it was truth made manifest.

Afterward they held each other close, arms wrapped together, her face in his neck, his lips on her hair, man and woman, one for the other, in the caring that should have been for all the years and might not go beyond this day's end. Julian wanted to cry and plead with him to stay, that they not part, and from the less than firm hands on her back, she thought that he might have other ideas as well. But this time must stand inviolable for them both. Charles was as he was, and she could accept that now just as she could accept her passion and go on.

"Get your cloak and your weapons together. Go and wait for me in the crags. I will bring all to order here and come to you in a few minutes." He spoke above her head, his voice in perfect control.

Julian knew that he did not trust himself to thrust aside any pleas she might have. She might not hold to her own resolve if it came to that. She yielded to the inflexible pressure of his arms and let herself be pushed back. She did not look at him; she dared not, for she knew that she would weep and disgrace the vow she had made. She wanted to cry out that rulers were always in evidence, one little better than another, that they could live in Cornwall and times would change, or they could go to France, both of them, that what they had was rare beyond all compare. . . .

"Charles." She heard her voice quaver and turned to busy

herself with the adjustment of her skirt and cloak. "I will keep watch but do hurry." She spoke briskly, as if she were in a hurry.

"I will." Behind the commonplace words rang his gratitude, the tribute of a knight of chivalry to his lady fair who had not demanded the ultimate that he could not give. "I will, my lady."

Later Julian crouched in the crags where she could see the entrance to the passageway and gave vent to the quick harsh sobs that tore at her. She buried the sounds in the thick muffler that protected her face. It was the only relief she was likely to get and that was quite enough, for soon he would come and exposure to the wind would not account for red eyes. Fiercely she forced herself to silence and touched some of the snow remnants to her face. It took all her willpower to stand up and wave when he emerged from their place of safety, their created heaven of delight, the place where they had each truly known the other. It took more than her courage not to look backward as, without speaking, they set their faces toward the west and began, once again, the journey that would separate them perhaps forever. He would go to his cause and she to France in the long road of their differing destinies.

When they began to move steadily the cold did not seem so intense. Charles knew exactly where he was going, every move sure and precise as he led them over snow patches and to rocky trails where their feet left few or no tracks. Julian was thankful for the pace and for the cold, since she could concentrate on that and not on the past few days. She inhaled the fresh air, breathing deeply, and walked a few steps behind Charles, watchful as he.

Once when they paused on the edge of an open expanse which would be green meadow in summer but was now barren and gray-white as it gave way to slate-colored rocks, Charles looked back at Julian and said, "It will be no easy life that you go to. The village is very small, only a few families, and you must fit in so that if soldiers come they will suspect nothing."

She said, "You forget, Charles, I worked with my household at Redeswan, often at tasks they could have refused to do. I am not gently reared." There might never have been intimacy between them, so coolly did they speak, and yet it was better so in view of the inevitable parting. She had held her feelings in hard check too often in these last years; it had been a relief to experience the passion and anger she felt, to be herself with Charles, and still some core of Julian was not to be released to anyone. That she knew instinctively.

He said wryly, "Nor I when I think of some of the things that I have had to do at Varfair." His stride lengthening, he moved ahead of her and out into the cut of the wind. "If we hasten we can be there by full dark, I believe."

The brusqueness made it easier for her to ask the question she had wanted to pose. "Is the princess herself safe from these rebellions raised in her name? Do such efforts not risk her life as Wyatt's did several years ago?" Julian told herself that she did not really care about the Princess Elizabeth. All she wanted was some reassurance that Charles would have a regard for his own safekeeping.

He stopped and looked back at her, the mask coming back down over the features that only a short time ago had been suffused with caring for herself. "Julian, do not pry; I have told you that she has declared ignorance of all plots. It is for her protection and that of this realm. Now, come."

Let be! Let be! One part of her mind warned; the other pressed. "Anne Boleyn's daughter would be so, would she not? Mary Tudor rallied Englishmen to her in the very teeth of rebellion, and they gave their hearts. Who knows that it might not happen again? I fear for you and for us all!" Julian heard her voice crack and knew that her eyes swam with tears.

He did not answer but only went more rapidly. The stiffness of his back and his head held higher let Julian know his anger was rising. She cursed that she had brought up any vexing question, especially one that divided them from the amity they had just come to know. She was often perverse; now that very quality had marred the memory that he would hold of her. Why could he not have shown a little warmth outside the cocoon of their cave? Julian knew that she must be reasonable, that Charles had his cause to serve; she had thought herself reconciled to it and now knew rebellion was never really quelled within herself.

They went on in silence that lasted for hours as the short day dwindled into gray afternoon and the dark clouds hung closer to the crags and low bunched tree skeletons swayed in the lashing wind. Julian huddled deeper in the cloak and wondered if she would freeze before shelter was found. Charles did not appear to be affected; his pace did not abate.

A hill thickly crowned with trees and boulders gave way to a series of smaller ones. Charles stopped just before the top of one of them and lifted his hand. "Walk apart from me so that they may see we are harmless. They may not be expecting us if no messenger has reached them. They will know me, of course, for Varfair is not far away. A stranger is another matter." The look he gave her was no longer cold, it was one comrade to another in a common cause.

Julian was dizzied by it; this man could be friend as well as lover. The enormity of her loss shook her anew, and she could not respond to him. Instead she walked on ahead and stood staring into the little valley, hardly more than a depression in the rocky land. Both hands went to her mouth and a whimper came out. If the boulder had not been directly behind her she would have fallen.

"What is the matter?" Charles came up beside her, thrusting out an impatient hand.

She pointed to the piled debris, the few embers of a fire that had devastated, and a low tree where figures swayed back and forth in the wind. Six bodies hung there, and just beyond the gallows were others, dead and piled together in man's obscenity to his own kind.

CHAPTER THIRTY

"Stay here." In the space of a few moments Charles seemed to have aged; his eyes were deeper in their sockets, the lines around his mouth etched hard. This was the face he would wear into battle, into middle years if he lived so long. Even as he spoke, he drew the shining sword, which flashed in the gray chill.

Julian jerked out her own sword, fumbling at the handle, determined to use it if she had to. "No. I come with you."

Charles might not have seen her, so fixed were his eyes on the horror below. He said, as to another man, "Do not be a fool." Then he was running down the hill toward the ruins of the village.

Julian was behind him, and her shocked eyes recorded the horror. Beside the hanged men, there were several women who lay with their heads bashed in, shirts over their chests, privates exposed in the final degradation. A young girl, an arrow impaled in her back, had tried to shield a small boy beneath her body. Now both were dead. An old woman, assaulted from behind, lay in the remains of her earthen hut.

"Old Miles—Martha, his wife—there's Mary and her husband, Jack—yonder lies the old midwife. Tormented and murdered! I knew these people and they me, some all my life!" Charles clenched his teeth and waved the sword back and forth over his destroyed friends. "Betrayal again!

There were other closer villages to which we might have gone. Those who did this knew special knowledge."

"But who? And why? Why kill them in such a way?" Julian looked at the scene of death under the lowering sky and felt the bite of the coming snow on her cheeks. She welcomed the reviving anger that came. Only minutes ago she had felt betrayed because he had so swiftly shifted emotions; now there was passionate gratitude that she still lived, that Charles was by her side unharmed.

He spat curses to the unhearing gods of vengeance, and tears ran unashamedly down his face as he threw the sword aside and began to investigate the pitiful bodies as they lay. Julian could do no less, and her voice rose in the agonized cry of all men in every time and every place.

"What kind of God permits this from creatures who worship? I say that man is truly made in His image and that it is vile as He is vile!"

"It took you long to see that, did it not?" Charles's tone was almost conversational. "There is nothing we can do here, Julian. They have not been dead long. We will cut them down and let the snow bury them; this ground is frozen solid. Then we will make for the coast and another of the meeting places. It is all we can do."

"What difference does it make? We will die in the end." The shivering was reaching over her whole body, and she could not control it. "What difference does anything make?"

Charles rose up from the corpse he had just lowered to the stony earth and put both hands on her shoulders, turning her so that she faced him. "Probably nothing, Julian, but we must try. Try in spite of everything, thought and proof to the contrary. Do you understand me? In the face of nothingness, simply because we live and breathe and because something we, you and I, do that may change the history of this land for the better."

"I do not care! I have never cared! Why can't you understand that, Charles Varland?" She lashed out at him, grateful to have some sort of scapegoat.

He stared into her vivid face, and his own twisted again with the upsurge of pain. His hands dropped away and he whispered, "How much the greater was their agony and pain? The responsibility is mine. If I had not lingered with you, if I had left you at the ruins and come ahead through the storm, this might have been averted. I bring disaster always."

"This is not true! You must not blame yourself!"

"I can. I do. We are both to blame, Julian, for yielding to the demands of the flesh. Now we will carry this vision with us." He swung round to indicate the valley and the crags which were now almost one with the dark clouds. His face changed, and Julian drew in her breath sharply as she followed his gaze.

Two torches were carried aloft by running men, and behind them came a troop of soldiers, all marching at a rapid pace as they poured down the path from which Charles and Julian had come. Charles cursed and reached for his sword. At the same time another torch rose brilliant off to the left and more soldiers appeared. Julian took the handle of the sword in both hands and looked at Charles.

"There is no more time for visions. They will kill us if we surrender, take us to captivity and torture. I would as soon die here among these, your friends, and not be alone." Julian, the lover of life, could say these words and know that with him she could court death; alone she would go mad.

"I should kill you myself. If you survive this you cannot escape the stake." Charles lifted the sword and swung it over his head so that it gleamed like that of a hero out of legend. "But you speak truly. The choice is yours."

"We fight." Legends rang in her head, then the pure terror of Isabella's end obscured all else. Not that! "We fight."

A familiar voice rang across the distance. "Varland! Give it up, man, we know all there is to know. See, here is your servant who has informed us!" The swaggering figure of Alphonso Diego Ortega, once friend, emerged into the light. His own sword was sheathed, and one gloved hand was raised to hold his men in check. They were now so close that Julian could see the satisfied grin on the dark face and the flash of the jewels at his neck.

But it was the man behind Ortega who held her attention and riveted it even as Charles went white under the tan of his face. Matthew stood tall and straight, a ruby on his knuckle, wearing new garments of red and yellow only half-hidden under a warm dark cloak of finest weave. His head went even higher as Charles cried out.

"What is this? What is it, Matthew? You have served me long. . . ." His words could not catch up with his incredulity, and the hand that was not holding his sword fumbled under his loose shirt.

The other soldiers were close now also, and they stood well ranked, waiting for a movement from Ortega. Julian gripped the sword harder, but her palms were slippery with sweat and it shook in her fingers.

Matthew laughed. "What profit or wisdom is it to be a hungry outlaw when I can serve my country and gain by doing so? I have long spied on you and reported all that I saw. The plan to take the woman from the Tower took me by surprise and I was forced to help you, but the information I passed on has been most useful. Your men and those who helped them will pay the price for that. I like not lords or their ilk!" He spat derisively and pulled his cloak closer.

"There speaks your loyal servant." Ortega stepped nearer, his eyes glittering in the red light of the torches. "Put your sword down, Varland. Fight is useless, as you can see, and there is danger to the girl."

"More danger to your black soul!" Julian threw back her head and the long hair rippled in the wind.

"Surrender, Varland, and I promise that the girl shall live. Your fate is ordained, but think of her." He might have been Satan himself, tempting from the reaches of hell.

Charles hesitated and Julian saw it. She saw him come alive with a kind of hope, and that gave her all the courage she needed. To believe the promise of the Spaniard would destroy the little they had left; she knew he lied. In that instant she lifted the sword, swung it with all her

power high in the air, and brought it down on the cleft between neck and shoulder so that Ortega stumbled and fell
backward among his men.

Charles made one swift movement, and the dagger flew
straight from his hand to lodge in the throat of his for-
mer servant. Blood spurted out geyserlike as Matthew
strangled and fell in his own gore. The stunned soldiers
hesitated only a second before closing in on Charles. Their
swords rang against his, and Julian saw one enter his arm
and thrust through to the other side.

She swung her own sword again, the fury such that they
did not immediately encircle her. Then, incredibly, the yel-
low-clad figure at her feet rose and pulled her so hard that
she fell off balance and tumbled down with him on the
ground. The black eyes shone into hers, the full lips parting in a smile of pure amusement as he held her. Ortega
was totally unharmed despite the blow she had dealt.

"Did my pretty court garb fool you, little Julian? I often
wear a corselet and half brace for my neck under it.
Most useful in dangerous situations, would you not
agree?"

She lifted her hand and slapped his face so hard that
the blow stung her hand. Ortega sent her reeling back
among the soldiers, who caught her arms and wrenched
them back. She saw Charles then, lying on the ground
beside the body of Matthew. His head was bloody, and
one arm twisted under him. The white shirt was soaked
with more blood, and his face was very pale.

"You have killed him! Let me go!" She began to kick
and writhe as if she were a wild woman.

Ortega said, "Let her look at her lover one last time."
He began to adjust his cloak and smoothed his cap down
on his black hair.

The soldiers released Julian so quickly that she almost
fell, and she threw herself down beside Charles, lifting the
heavy head so that it rolled inertly in her lap. She stared
down at the carved lips, high forehead, and arching brows
of the man she loved, then set her lips to his in farewell.
The bitterness of it was not to be borne.

It might have been a dream that they moved under hers,

but reality was when the gray eyes looked into the aqua-marine ones. For a little longer Charles Varland lived. The rest of the world and its cruelties faded. He murmured, "Julian, you will be safe? Safe?"

"Aye, dear lord." The loss of blood had taken his sense of reality, and it was better so. Already the brief recovery was fading, that waxen look more pronounced. Say it quickly and let him go as was more merciful. "Charles, I love you. I always did and I always will."

For the space of a heartbeat his breath lingered and came sighing out in words so low that she had to strain to hear. ". . . love you. Tried not to, could not fight it. I, too." Then his head fell forward on his chest and blood dribbled from his mouth onto her supporting hands.

The man she loved loved her in return and spoke it with his dying breath. One fact outweighed the other for the instant, and all the trumpets rang there in that valley of death and despair under the heavy clouds. In the next breath she thought of all that they both had lost and of those who had triumphed. Bitterness and fury roiled together in her as she rose and flung herself upon the approaching Ortega, her fingernails raking his face and clawing for his eyes. She felt the flesh give way and the blood come. One fist hit his nose and the resulting squashing sound was delightful.

Ortega slashed at her and roared curses, other hands pulled at her, and she felt nothing. When she was jerked away she rounded on that captor and kicked, clawed, and screamed. Someone caught the flowing hair and yanked it so hard that it was nearly torn from her head. She fell heavily and spat straight up into the leering face that bent over hers.

"Can't you fools subdue one small girl?" Ortega's hated voice rang in her ears.

Julian fought to rise, but this time the combined soldiers were too much for her and she was forced to lie still. Ortega came near, too near, and one of her booted feet caught him in the groin as she kicked out with the super-human strength that had come upon her.

"All the demons of hell curse you into everlasting perdition! May you drown in the black pit that is your very soul, you spawn of the fiend. I curse you, do you hear, I curse you!"

Julian screamed the words into the ring of faces, the huddle of bodies that held her down, and at the dark figure that again bulked above her. This time Ortega's temper and gut fury had taken total possession of him. She saw the heavy hands bunch together and come down toward her face, felt the blow that sent her falling into the outer darkness and felt the pain lift in a great red wave that peaked and froze, holding her burning within its depths. Something in her rose then and went in search of Charles Varland down all the highways of the dead.

CHAPTER THIRTY-ONE

There were, it seemed, thoughts and impressions and feelings even though you were dead. There was pain, too, and such desolation as only the truly lost must know. But where were the flames of hell where the unbelievers roasted and cried out their woe for all eternity? The demons of Satan? The Evil One himself? Surely those still living needed to know that death was but a continuation of life in its more painful aspects of body and mind. Only the red haze was true.

Julian drifted sometimes in such thoughts, and then she heard voices, both male and female, talking far above what she assumed to be her bier. The sense of the words never came through, but she had sensations of drinking, of taking in warmth, even the headiness of wine. She hurt and was jolted, she was turned and tossed, even wept and remembered the Scriptures saying that this would go on forever. The feeling of loss was so great. Was it for Charles, who lay dead, or was it for the loss of God as the priests taught? She saw the flames of the stake and Isabella's contorted figure. Had this fate pursued her even in hell? What an ironic joke it all was. She wanted to laugh and did so in spite of the pain that savaged her chest.

". . . by the still waters . . . goodness and mercy . . ." The words wove themselves into the grayness of her lonely drifting. How strange that the comforting words should be spoken in the land of the dead, perhaps the anteroom to the more savage aspects of hell. "Who shall ascend to the hill of the Lord . . . clean hands and a pure heart?" A voice low and soft as that of Elspeth, who could not read but had remembered all the words she had been taught over a lifetime. "Thy word in my heart . . ." And again, "Rise, my daughter, and come . . ."

Julian opened her eyes and stared into a proliferation of roses, red and white and Tudor, surrounded by angels blowing trumpets while a unicorn waited to bound into the nearby woods. She turned her head slightly and saw faded tapestries come into shape on a far wall, their depiction of a long done battle still gleaming in threads of a vivid red for the blood that survived. Blood! Battle! Memory rushed back, and she sat up so suddenly that her head rang and the room turned around. In that spinning she saw that the surroundings were richly appointed with other tapestries and hangings, carved chairs, a fire leaping in a hearth. The covers of her ornate bed were fur-lined, and the curtains boasted a crest of fighting animals surmounted by the sun and moon and intertwined with roses.

"You will want to know where you are and who I am and what you are doing here. Well, I am not supposed to answer questions, only watch and report, so do not exhaust yourself by asking. Girl! Say that the woman is awake! Bring nourishment!"

Julian stared at the portly figure by her bed, a priest from the look of him—the tonsure and the brown robe— but the querulous brown eyes and the purple-veined nose bespoke something else. He was perhaps sixty, but as he sat there something of the mischief of extreme youth remained with him.

Because she was still alive, no longer in pain, warm and comfortable, with food and drink on the way and death a distant memory, Julian said, "This is not hell or ever was. I did dream."

The presumed priest stared in his turn, then burst into laughter that shook his whole body. Julian was forced to smile herself, because such mirth bred itself in another. Their eyes met, and the laughter rose again. She put one hand to her mouth and drew it away slightly. Still her hand, still real, but there was a healed scar across it that had not been there before. It looked as though she had grasped the bare blade of a sword and pulled. But how long ago?

The priest sobered and rescued the illuminated book that had been in danger of tumbling to the floor. "Not hell, lady. But I think that you may have been there if one may judge by your cries. You have a very healthy and piercing voice in which you called out many curses of a most illuminating nature. I must confess that I tried, in the interests of my ears, to silence you. The fate to which you consigned me was fascinating. Your mind is most perceptive. How, I wonder, did our sovereign Madam the Queen enjoy having you as a lady-in-waiting?"

"What did I say?" Julian's voice was husky from disuse in normal conversation.

"I, a priest of God, to speak so! I am shocked!" He laughed again and she with him.

The door opened softly just then, and a maidservant entered carrying refreshments. Julian felt the pangs in her stomach and wondered how long it had been since she had really eaten. She remembered most of what had happened to her including the final blow from Ortega and Charles's death, but it was much like a story or a dream, certainly not the stuff of reality. Reality was being safe and warm, eating, sharing a joke.

She raised her eyes, and the curtain was torn away. She

was back in danger and cold and terror. Reality was the bulk of George Attenwood standing just inside the door, the dispassionate eyes staring into hers.

CHAPTER THIRTY-TWO

"Your servant, Lady Julian. I trust that you are better?" Lord George Attenwood advanced slightly toward her, noticed her recoil, and paused where he was.

Julian saw the consideration, and a little of her wild animal fear receded. He still appeared as he had when she last saw him, the color of sand with penetrating eyes of the same shade, his face a little leaner and a small hunch to his shoulders. He wore green velvet, and two emeralds shimmered on his square, capable fingers.

"Better, yes. But where am I? What has happened?" The words came out her dry throat in spates that seemed choking.

"I will answer your questions, of course. But you are newly roused for the first time in many weeks. Rest and refresh yourself first." The stolidity he had shown at the time Philip of Spain introduced them was entirely gone. Now he was any gentleman, concerned about the health of his guest.

"My lord, now! I must know my fate."

"Madam, you are my honored guest."

"Prisoner! Better I had died on that field than live so." She wondered when he would have his peculiar pleasure of her.

George Attenwood smiled, and it served to soften the

harsh cut of his craggy face, making him look younger than his fifty-odd years. He flicked his fingers at the priest and the little maidservant. "Go, both of you. Emily, have the bath readied and summon the tiring woman. Have the new gowns brought out that Lady Redenter may choose the ones to be finished." They scurried away, and he turned to Julian. "Drink the good Bordeaux, and there is capon freshly roasted. I will sit here, and when you are done you shall ask what questions you choose."

The scent of the food rose up to tantalize her nostrils and she reached warily for it on the chest where the priest had propped his book. As she did so the coverlet fell away, exposing her white bosom, for she was naked under it. She snatched the warm thing higher, and the flush burned in her face. Attenwood paid no attention but began to turn the pages of the book with a casual air. He had seen, she knew it; likely he had no interest in women, but where was his lover, the one who had been jealous?

Never had food tasted so good. Never had she been so glad to be alive. Julian knew that for all her proud talk she would do anything to live. Deeply and dearly had she loved Charles Varland, but she would not lay down her life to be with him in the nebulous beyond of which the priests spoke. Shame painted her face scarlet, and she took a deep drink of wine, which made her head reel. *Charles, I will love you always.* That much was true and must be enough for the coming time of her life.

Attenwood closed the book with a thump and said, "To begin with, you are in my castle of Altyn on the coast in the North Country and far from both London and Cornwall. It is February 1558. The final putting down of the rebellion in Cornwall was accomplished in December, the executions took place after the holy days were finished. Madam the Queen still looks to bear her child, and the war continues."

Julian stared at him. Why did he not get to the gist of the matter?

"You fought Ortega and the soldiers until you were beaten into the very ground. Some of the scars you will bear all your life. The physicians thought that the fever must have been working in you already, and the injuries you suffered fanned it. You have a determination to live that surprised them. Well, you smashed the handsome Spaniard's nose, and it was growing back with a definite crook. Moreover, one of the longer scratches would not heal for a time, and that scar will remain with him. Needless to say, he was not overfond of my insistence that I would have you just as you were, broken and raving about your lover."

"Charles, was he given honorable burial?" Julian leaned forward, all her anxiety shining in her pale face. If the body were carrion only, why did it matter? She only knew that it did.

"Lady Julian, he was one of the foremost of the traitors, and an example was made of him. You must know that his head adorns London Bridge as is customary. He was a brave man who made the wrong choices. His name is honored that you loved him."

Wind, summer rot, the empty skelton head to fall apart there, that mind and body that she had so passionately loved. All to nothingness and destruction, a bare place in the world and in the ages, her heart torn out as by the Furies. She fought the tears and could not. She bent over and the sobs began to shake her.

The hard hand rested on her soft hair and Attenwood said, "It is best for you to purge the wound." Just so had Charles spoken. Not to be endured! "And if it would comfort you, I will have masses said for his soul. One priest shall speak his name before the Virgin again and yet again. She is compassionate and will understand."

Julian muttered, "I do not believe that. He is dead forever."

"Listen. Take the forms of our faith and let the age-old ritual be done. Do not use reason. Let yourself be comforted, for is not our God greater than we?" He smoothed her head again, patted her back, and slowly the hard bonds of pain began to lessen.

When Julian could sit up again, she found him ready with the restorative wine. She would weep often for Charles, she knew, but Attenwood's unexpected kindness

was blessed relief in her weakened state. She wiped her
nose and tried to make apologies which he waved away.
The words of reassurance he gave were strangely comforting, and for the time being she would cling to them. Her
health was what mattered now. She heard the quiet voice
speaking again.

"Varland's body was brought back to London as well as
the wretches who had fought with him earlier. Those of
noble blood were dealt with properly, the others as well,
but you were another matter. Ortega wanted revenge, but
one who was the queen's ward, traitor or not, could not be
summarily handled. He is, as I think you may know, one
of the foremost representatives of King Philip in England,
but this fact is not well known. He has kept his king well
informed as to the thinking of the court and people. The
king of Spain is not pleased; he means to take power here
when the queen dies or, as has seemed likely, is deposed.
Civil War is likely, and he will take advantage of it. Ortega was summoned for an accounting, and in his absence
I, being then at court, asked for you that our betrothal
might be honored. I swore to be responsible for you if you
lived." His light eyes watched her face; not a muscle
stirred in his.

"But the queen? The charges against me? That awful
priest cited all manner of fearful things. I so feared the
fire." Julian felt the trickle of sweat on her back and knew
that she had burned many times over in her dreams.

"Her Majesty has reason to trust me, for I hold much
of the north and am of the Old Catholic loyalty even as
your family. I told her of Varland's bravery, which none
ever denied—and pointed out your many difficulties, that
you had fallen in love and been led astray. She said she
understood but that an example must be made."

He paused to sip wine and Julian could see the small set
face of the queen, obdurate for what she believed to be
the right. Yet she had given Julian her life and this delivered her to the man she dreaded.

"So then I remarked that she was well known to love
and honor the king of Spain; what if he had been such a
one as Varland? Was one to be punished for love? She, the

queen, had come through great tribulation and had won her throne and love as well. Could she not be merciful? She stared at me with those strange eyes so like King Henry's and told me that she had come to drink of the cup of bitterness a thousand times over. 'Take the girl and remain from this court, but hold the north ready if I ask it. Keep her straitly.' Then she sent me away. I and my men brought you here by ship, and so the tale is done."

Because it must be asked, Julian whispered, "And what now is your will?"

The red flush came up under his skin and he looked past her, then down at his fingernails. "Forgive that I speak this way, but you are no maid. The things that you said proved that amply."

"I would have told you had you asked." Her head went up proudly, and the small chin never wavered.

Attenwood met her eyes then. "Very well, I will speak out. Until there is no chance that you might bear Varland's child, I must ask you to remain here unwed. The women have told me that no flux came, so you could be with child. If so, you will have it, and it will be sent away. If not, I will marry you and you will have my sons, my heirs. It will be a quiet life for a time, but when matters of state are settled . . ."

"You could not destroy the child!" Julian felt the glory rise in her at the thought of bearing a son to Charles Varland. Such had not even entered her mind. Of that passionate last loving something must come!

"Be sensible. He would be reared apart. There would be other sons." He watched her, and she knew that on this point he would not yield. "I will not give house to Varland's bastard!"

She would deal with that when and if it arose. Behind his kindness, she sensed a strength of purpose that could not be shaken. It was not the time to question or push. As to his lover or lovers, that did not seem to interfere with his intention to have sons. He had saved her life and he was older; with a little more luck she might rule here. Take things as they came. Julian let all these things run swiftly through her mind as she said, "My lord, I am most

grateful for all that you have done. Naturally I shall obey
you in all things."

George Attenwood laughed and reached forward to
clasp her fingers. "You are a veritable hellcat, Julian Redenter, and you fought as that warrior queen, Boadicea of
old. Our sons will be wild and brave." His gaze sharpened
on her face. "You must rest and grow strong."

It was easy to smile at him, for he was both perceptive
and kind. Had it not been for Charles Varland and what
she knew of Lord Attenwood's penchant for boys, it might
have been simple enough to rest in what could have been
caring. If he wanted the shell of Julian Redenter he was
welcome. "As my lord commands." How very much she
had changed, she thought with a shiver.

The bath water must have grown cold and the gowns
remained unaltered, for it was another week before Julian
could rise from the bed for longer than an hour or so. The
spinning dizziness would come upon her unexpectedly and
fling her into the void. The physician, an angry bantam of
a man, muttered in Latin and gave orders to her maid but
simply told Julian to rest and not think. "Your wound is of
the heart. It will heal." Brother Robert bade her call him
Rob—"far simpler, that way"—and became her close
companion as they read and talked, sparring with each
other in a wry way. Edith, the maidservant, soon lost her
awe of Julian and chatted guilelessly of her Tom and the
family they hoped to start. Julian relaxed and the war in
her ended. The day she knew that she would not have
Charles's child marked the end of her resistance to this
new way of life. She could not weep, but her mourning
would one day cease.

"I have changed, Edith." Julian surveyed herself in the
Italian mirror backed with gold, then put it down and
twirled before the longer one that would have been the
envy of any great lady in London.

"Madam is beautiful." The little maid touched the box
of glimmering jewels and jerked her hand away as if it
were burned.

Julian wore a flowing gown of creamy beige satin which
made her waist very small. The sleeves were long and full,

edged with lace of a deeper shade that was almost brown over her hands. Her bosom was full and white at the low bodice, which was also framed with pale lace. Her underskirt was palest yellow, her slippers the same color. The chestnut hair had been dressed high in coils threaded with pearls and small emeralds. One perfect diamond crowned the pure parting in the center of her head and threw back the reflections of deep color. Her hair had been washed and polished with silk, combed and polished again. But it was her face that held Julian. The white scar on her cheekbone had been powdered over but it would remain with her while she lived. That half of her face had been laid open, Rob told her, and the physician had used all his skill to restore it. "His is a talent that fled from the Inquisition." There was another on her back that went from one shoulder down to her buttocks. In time it would vanish. The one on her hand would not, for it was very deep and still pained when the weather was wet.

Her face was no longer that of a girl. It was longer, more serious; the high cheekbones had shadows under them, and the deep aquamarine eyes almost slanted in a certain light. Her neck seemed longer, her chin more stubborn; it was, she thought suddenly, Lady Gwendolyn's face in the rose miniature that Guy Edmont had shown her again so long ago. Pray that the rest of her life did not match her mother's!

"My lord will be pleased that you join him." Edith pushed the box of jewels toward her mistress.

Julian smiled and drew a long rope of pearls toward her, then put it back. "Not yet. I go as I am."

That she had made a wise choice was totally evident when she approached George in the small dining room where the table was set for them alone and curtsied with the grace of the royal court. He raised her up and kissed her fingertips. "You honor me this night, Lady Julian. I and my house shall try to be worthy."

"It is I who am honored." She bent her head, then raised it to surprise a look of contemplation in his eyes. Well, what if he did decide to take what was surely his by right? She belonged to him by royal decree and by virtue of the fact that he had saved her life. Let it happen; her body could belong only completely to one man, but perhaps it would quicken with an Attenwood heir and give her surcease.

They ate of capon and venison, strange little meat pies with differing flavors, sweet, and cheese, drank one wine that tasted of flowers and another that might have been distilled warmth on a summer night. The fire crackled in the hearth and reminded Julian of another hearth. Her fingers slipped on the golden goblet, and she fought for composure.

"Julian, I wonder, is it too soon? Do you feel ready to talk of the future?" George wore his favorite green velvet and emeralds tonight, the color flattering the set of his shoulders and his skin, pointing up the brilliance of his deep eyes.

It had come. She lifted her chin to face what she must. The gesture was not lost on the watching man and he smiled a little. "Aye. I am ready." *Forgive me, dear Charles, I must live as I can. You would be the first to wish me well.*

George leaned back in his chair and moved his own goblet back and forth without seeing it. "You hold no fondness for the present queen, I gather?"

Julian's mouth opened and shut quickly. Of all the questions he might have posed, that was perhaps the most unexpected. "Of course not." She would never tell anyone of that pity she had felt, of her gratitude for kindness shown at first, and of the queen's true concern for her welfare. There had been misery enough since. She repeated, "Of course not. How can you even ask?"

"Women change their minds." The emphasis on the word *women* so slight that she might not have noticed it if she were not aware of his habits. Her eyes widened and her mouth twisted in involuntary gestures before she caught herself. But he had seen. "You have no reason to change yours, so I will proceed."

"Please." She held the goblet to her lips and tasted the wine that suddenly might have become water.

"If the queen is with child, it will kill her. If not, then

she is mad and the English will bear no more of this persecution. We have lost Calais; it happened in January—the last bastion we held on French soil! She can lose England if this continues, and France will be waiting, not to mention Spain. Philip is hated here, and they will fight. One can discount the bastard, Elizabeth. But the young queen of Scots, betrothed to the dauphin of France, is in the rightful line of succession—and she is Catholic. I can rouse the North Country for her, peace can be made with France, and the settlement will be generous. We could be present at the true uniting of the two countries and powerful in both. The girl would be easily managed, I have reason to know."

Mad, Julian thought, *mad*. Aloud, she said, "One ruler is like another. I do not care. The present queen trusts you, but when misfortune comes to her, your power will fade, is that it?"

George Attenwood said, "Precisely. I shall not be such a fool as to wage open rebellion the way Varland and his ilk did. England will be a battleground for a time, anyway, and those on the scene will come off the better. Certainly a young girl is better than a madwoman wed to Spain, which seeks to rule the world."

"What would you have me do?" Julian sat straighter and touched one hand to her gleaming hair. She felt untouched by the revelations; if he were so occupied with such matters there would be little time to take her body. Her mind would remain her own.

"I will have messengers from London fairly regularly. You will speak with them after I have done so, a pretty woman offering wine and chatter, a relative who is visiting. You need not fear scandal that way, and afterward none will challenge my wife and sons. I will glean extra knowledge and you expertise. Is it a bargain?" He lifted his golden goblet and turned it so that the jewels shimmered on the rim. "Shall we drink to it?"

Julian pushed back her chair and stood up. "To that and to power! Is that a bargain?"

Attenwood gazed at the beautiful woman in her glowing

gown and then at the candlelight which sheathed her in soft flame. "Aye, madam, to power!"

And the shade of Charles Varland moved in the background.

CHAPTER THIRTY-THREE

"Tell me, Rob, how came you here, to this isolated country and the service of one lord? I would have thought you more interested in the livelier aspects of city life." Julian slanted a glance at the priest as they walked on the battlements of the castle one icy afternoon just before the winter dusk settled in. They had talked often of books and life and gay foolishness but never of themselves. Now she wanted to share her difficulties with another person. Weeks had passed since George Attenwood had told her of his ambitions; he had been polite and serious with her since that time, but no one had come, and she wondered.

Rob pulled his robes closer and shivered. "Why do you pick such a day to walk? It is far more comfortable by the great hearth. In answer to your question, I will say that when I was only a little younger I formed a great fascination for a lady, a habit which is frowned upon by the Lord Pope and our late worthy kings. We lived together, she died of the plague, and I think I have sought her counterpart ever since. To be crude, my dear, Lord Attenwood understands these things, and I have few duties of a spiritual nature at certain times."

Julian suppressed a smile and said, "Lord Attenwood has indeed proven to be most understanding. I have reason to be grateful for that." She thought of the entertainments that had been arranged, the books and gowns and jewels given, conversations which, after the first personal ones, dealt with the past or with government or castle matters, nothing that might cause her to be upset or hinder the recovery of mind and flesh. In part, it had been successful. She still wept for Charles in the long reaches of the night, but she schooled herself to think of other things by day. Resignation had never been a part of Julian Redenter, but she was coming to know its value.

A long howl came over the icy plain that bordered one side of the castle. They looked toward the band of scrubby trees that bent before the wind, and Julian fancied that she saw movement there. She shivered and drew the brown-furred cloak close to her chin. Edith had produced a warmer one of softest gray and white fur to frame her face. She had forced herself to speak calmly, saying that she did not have a liking for the color, and the girl had gone away, one hand stroking the silky surface. It had been like looking into the very color of Charles Varland's eyes. Thank God she was stronger now!

Altyn was a warrior castle, built near the northern coast in the days of William Rufus, a fierce gray pile made to withstand attacks of armies. Attenwood had transformed part of it into a warm and comfortable dwelling with fires and tapestries and rugs, but on days such as this, one recalled its true purpose. Julian shuddered at the thought of spending the rest of her life here or in others like it, then admonished herself sternly, knowing that but for George Attenwood she would be dead. Her strong young body rejoiced in the return to life, even the thought that soon it would be possessed by another could not diminish that joy.

She thought of what Attenwood had said to her only a few days earlier: "I am well aware that you no longer hold to the faith of your ancestors and mine, but tell no others of this. Act as if you believe and trust me in these matters, for the times are perilous. We must risk nothing." The beige and amber flecks had run together in his strange eyes and the long face was set, eager for her answer. Agreement had cost her nothing, but she wondered anew that it mattered so much. Well, he was older and thinking of the family he hoped would come. Faith was comforting if one could obtain it. Anything so long as he did not show that other side of himself.

"Julian." Rob paused and faced her with an expression quite unlike his usual amused one. "Maintain your favorable opinion of our mutual master and show it always. If you falter, make sure that he does not see."

"What do you mean?" It was not only the wind that made her tremble.

"Remember my words." He smiled roguishly. "Now, come on before we both freeze here."

For all his kindness to her, George Attenwood had kept Julian apart from the not inconsiderable household, and someone was always with her when she walked in the tilt-yard or in the battlements. He had taken her riding in the woods and along the small beach nearby. The half-blind castle minstrel sang privately to her in the company of Edith and Barbara, the maids, and the almost senile old woman, Edwarda, who tended the gowns and spoke little. Rob was the closest companion she had, and he was always careful. It had not mattered in the days when she was grateful for human closeness and thankful for any hand that was not raised against her, but now the bruises of spirit were fading as those of the body had long ago. She was ready now to question, to take part in her own destiny. Rob would not clarify what he had said; she knew him too well to think that he would. But George—she must learn to think of him that way—was remote, yet she dreaded the time he became less so.

"Mistress, there is a guest! All the way from London! My lord asks that you talk with him while he makes ready." Edith was excited, the pale little face blooming with curiosity. "All the way from London!"

"When did he arrive?" Julian smiled at the young girl. "You would think that guests were few here. I understand that my lord receives them from London quite regularly."

"This is the first in a very long time, lady. Months!" Edith was wary at the puzzlement in Julian's eyes. "Shall I fetch your jewels to you?"

"Please." She sat still while the ice began to rise in her blood. She had not been entirely easy in her mind since that conversation with Rob five days before; he was fond of the wine and sometimes tippled to excess, but his warning was not born of that. Now her instincts lifted to the tiny threat, and she regarded herself in the mirror. This night she would be fair indeed, fair and watchful.

"My dear, you do me proud." George Attenwood, tall in dull yellow velvet banded with fur, lifted her hand to his lips and surveyed her with satisfied eyes that held no hint of interest in her physical beauty.

Julian wore a gown of blue velvet with a paler satin bodice and full belling sleeves. The underskirt was of aquamarine silk, the near color of her eyes, and the material shimmered with changing lights as she walked. The pearls she loved were on thumb and forefinger and wound in her hair, which was dressed low on her neck and back from the oval purity of her face. A pearl and diamond collar circled her throat and tilted her chin higher. White slippers buckled with diamonds encased her slender feet. The cleft between her firm breasts was touched with lacy shadows from the thin satin over it, and her waist showed slim before the skirts spread out. Beautiful as the gown was, it was only one of many that had been prepared for her in the last weeks, and Julian's delight in the beautiful clothes she had never had made the dour seamstresses smile.

George Attenwood lifted her from the curtsy and, in the first gesture of physical intimacy that he had ever made toward her, kissed the red lips and let his own trail toward her neck. His mouth was firm but smooth, the hands that held hers warm. Julian could not help the recoil that pulled her back from him, not from any personal distaste—for she had long schooled herself to acceptance of the fate that he ordained—but from the knowledge that he found touching her repugnant and that he forced himself to it as a man might force himself to a bitter draft.

"You are not ready. Forgive me that I press you." The smile was not in his eyes. They were cold and bleak with distaste. "Are you finished with your toilet now?"

"George, I am sorry. I did not mean . . ." She stuttered

to a halt before the anger that blazed up in him and was
as quickly brought under control so that his face twisted
and smoothed out in a matter of seconds. "It must be as
you wish, of course."

"Then let us go to greet our guest. Precede me, please."
He did not offer her his arm as was customary, and Julian
knew with all the power of her intuition that he could not
bear to touch her. "There is yet time for you."

As they walked through the cold passages Julian believed that George Attenwood was very near to demanding
payment from her, but in what coin must it be given if he
could not endure female flesh? Still, the debt was an honorable one and must be paid. What did men of his
persuasion do with a woman, or would he require that she
act to him as a male lover? She thought of Charles and
their passion, then put the longing away. Those days were
done forever.

The great hall of Altyn Castle was far too cold and
drafty for any festivities at this time of year. They went
directly to a smaller room where a well-laid fire blazed up,
a room adorned with brilliant tapestries and the finest ornamented chairs, where soft rugs after the manner of the
East were laid and many candles lit the warm air. The
guest was studying the major tapestry, an intricately worked
thing depicting the travels and perils of Ulysses including
his triumphant return to Ithaca under the aegis of gray-
eyed Athena, daughter of Zeus. Julian had often admired
it, half longing for the days of mythology when the hands
of the gods were over their favorites. Had she not laugh-
ingly prayed to Hermes when she stole the horse that time
to get to Dover and Charles Varland? *Let me cease to
think of him!* Her mind hammered out the words as she
put a smile on her lips and waited to be introduced to the
guest who was even now turning.

The world spun and the candles merged into one as
George said in his smooth way, "I so regret that there is
an urgent bit of business I must finish before returning. If
you will forgive me, Lady Julian Redenter will keep you
company. She is a guest here for a short time. May I

present her to you?" He took Julian's hand, and she looked straight into the eyes of Sir Guy Edmont.

She heard her name again and that of Sir Guy, made a suitable response, and smiled as was seemly. It was impossible that a man as perceptive as George Attenwood did not catch the bearing down on the significant words of Sir Guy as he said, "Never, ah, never have I had such charming company. You honor me. Lady . . . Redenter? My ear is slow—I do pronounce your name properly?"

The crinkles around his eyes were deeper and his face more weathered since that day he had arrived at Redeswan to conduct her to the queen. His mouth was narrower, his body sturdier, but the appraising gaze was the same, and it conveyed a warning to her.

"That is correct, sir." She felt George stiffen at her side and wondered what game this was. Was a little silliness called for? "Come and partake of this wine. I have found it delicious. Will you tell me the latest fashions in London? I vow, we are so far north that I may be completely out of the style now." She waved her arm in the long, full sleeve and began to walk toward the table where refreshments were already placed.

"Ah, madam, I am but a soldier and know little of such things." He took the offered goblet and held it uneasily, a man uncomfortable in the presence of a fair, giddy woman.

"That I cannot believe." She began to mention this material and that while George hesitated at the door and Sir Guy lowered his eyes.

George said, "I will return very shortly, but I leave you in good hands, Sir Guy. Julian, our guest appeared interested in the tapestry. Dare I suggest that he might enjoy examining it with you rather than attempting to give an account of women's apparel?" He laughed indulgently and departed.

Julian and Guy stared at each other and he started to speak, but she made a quick gesture to silence him, then let her voice run on in a smooth patter about the beauties of the Ulysses tapestry and the perils of the hero. He nodded very slightly and interjected a question. Time hung as they both listened, waiting for the proper moment. She saw the patina of perspiration on his high forehead and felt the palm of her hand where the sword had bitten through begin to pain.

Julian let her voice rise and sigh away once more as the silence grew absolute. She spoke then in a low whisper. "Why did you not wish your host to know that you recognized me, Sir Guy?"

"Why did you fall in with it so quickly?" The countertrust was sharp. "I knew the name, but you are greatly altered. I heard of your troubles and, frankly, thought you dead or imprisoned. Lord Attenwood is known to be short of temper, and I deemed it best not to let our acquaintance be known." He sipped his wine and gave an appreciative nod. "I have come with messages from Her Majesty regarding certain fortresses to be prepared and men to be rallied for the spring. I do not wish to bore a fair lady with such things, however."

His eyes on her were bold now and faintly hungry, but his manners were impeccable. Julian knew that he thought her to be George's paramour, and the thought stung her pride. "My lord has been most kind to me. We will wed soon, and I think he will allow me to visit Redeswan. Tell me, Sir Guy, what have you heard of my estate and those on it?" She had the sensation of being watched, but the walls were of solid stone and the door securely closed. If there were a peephole in the tapestry, as so often occurred, they were speaking softly enough not to be heard.

Guy put both hands on his hips and moved away from the fire. "The court is a dangerous place now. The queen's health is everyone's concern. She has made her will but plans for the babe she will bear. The fires blaze continuously though Philip himself has suggested moderation. The life of the Princess Elizabeth is said to be in mortal danger." He swung back to her, and this time there was no mistaking the boldness in him. "Redeswan is forfeit to the queen, lady, what little there was. I asked after you and was told that your fate was an example to others. It was said in such a manner that you might as well have been dead."

Julian grew more uncomfortable. Surely George must return soon. "Will you not wish me happiness, Sir Guy?"

"I am a soldier, Lady Redenter, a soldier of Her Majesty the Queen until I die. I am not one for the subtle."

"What do you mean?"

He set the goblet down and started for the door. "I must find Lord George and give the messages, then ride on with my other commissions."

"Answer me!" Julian's voice rose to full volume as she darted in front of him.

Sir Guy was angered in his turn and discretion left him. "Lord Attenwood will not wed you, Julian. He is betrothed to the heiress whose land marches with his, Lady Augusta Nymour, recently returned from Ireland since her father died. The queen holds her as ward and has given her blessings to the marriage, which will be celebrated in London in the month of May. I carry her words to Lord Attenwood; this is one of the ways the north will be bound to our queen." He watched the blood leave Julian's face and the pale skin grow paler still. "You did not know? I thought you taunted me for my earlier caution."

"He told me he would. He told the queen when she let him take me." Julian spoke half to herself. There was no denying the fact that Guy spoke the truth. Every line of the earnest face gave proof of that. No wonder he had regarded her as he did. But why had Attenwood lied? She was certainly in no position to demand anything of him.

"He has not been to London for many months and has not had audience with Her Majesty since well before the king left. That is the reason for the message I carry. His petitions have been many and determined. Lady Nymour is a great heiress." Guy handed her a sweet cake and a fresh goblet of wine. "Drink and eat. You will feel better. Julian, I am sorry."

She thrust her hands deeply into her sleeves as a sudden wind seemed to come from the corner though nothing stirred there. Her eyes shone up into his that were now only concerned. "Do not be." In several quick sentences she told him Attenwood's tale about his supposed rescue of her. "It has all been lies and to what purpose?" She would not speak to this man about Attenwood's interest in men; that of all things could not be voiced. Impulse took her and she said, "Sir Guy, help me to leave this place. I was brought here under a false aegis and have no loyalty to its master. I am not his paramour, believe me."

He drew himself up. "I could never do that. He is the servant of Her Majesty, and all must give way to that virtue. I cannot help you."

He might as well have said that he did not believe her and who could blame him? "Would you let me ride back toward London at least part way with you so that I would not have to go alone? I can get out of here, I know I can, and meet you in the woods after your work here is done. At least help me that far!"

"I cannot." He walked rapidly toward the door, and this time she saw that he meant to go through it.

Attenwood had shown himself a liar several times over; the incredible thought took her, and she forgot herself for a moment. "Hold, Sir Guy! Answer me one other question and I will trouble you no more. What was the fate of Charles Varland? Where does he lie buried?"

"What game do you play, Lady Julian? You must have heard that he was gravely wounded and thought dead on the field of battle. He was brought back and found to be alive but only barely. They threw him in the Tower and planned a commoner's death, but his mind gave way and he was moved to a better residence—though under strict guard—at the special command of the king himself. The queen would not go against her husband's order though his death is urged daily."

Julian felt the glory blaze up through her body and permeate her whole being. She saw the shock in Guy Edmont's eyes and did not care. This lie had been worse than all the others. Charles Varland lived and inhabited the same world with her. He lived and so did she. The light on her face reflected their passion and Guy's own face grew warm.

Her fingers went up in the sign of the cross. "That I have lived to see this day."

CHAPTER THIRTY-FOUR

The long table glistened with gold and silver, napery, candles in jewel-studded holders, as dish after savory dish flowed across it and wine succeeded wine. Guy and Julian sat stiffly erect while Father Robert dedicated himself to drink and monosyllables. George Attenwood sat at his ease, keeping up a string of comments on the extreme cold mingled with hunting talk of deer, boar, and wolves. There were, it seemed, many of all in the woods near the castle. Julian could not eat; her stomach twisted together, and she longed to shriek out her accusations at him. A man far less perceptive than he could feel the tension in them all and would mark it well.

George finished a bit of marchpane and leaned back in the ornate chair. "I have often wondered at the folk tales and their logic. It is said that ever the fair maiden lures the hunter, as she lures the unicorn, into destruction." His mouth smiled at Julian. "A calumny of your sex, my dear. I believe there is a rare tapestry somewhere here which shows Diana, the maiden huntress, seeking the wild deer and being sent astray by a youth onto a path where the lion waits. I have only just thought of it. Rob, in what chamber does it hang?"

Rob poured more wine, and his hand shook as he conveyed it to his mouth. "I have no idea, I'm sure."

The words just missed insolence, and George's lips tightened. "We will find it tomorrow, then. Lady Julian and our guest will find it most interesting." His gaze roved over them all again, and Julian was not the only one to feel the menace there.

Later Julian sat in the withdrawing chamber and tried to read the French romance she had started in a happier time, but she could not concentrate. The men conferred in another room, and Father Rob had slouched away to bed. The candles burned low, but she was not sleepy. The glory that suffused her being at the news of Charles had not dimmed, but now the other aspect of it caught her up. Only the power of Philip of Spain had saved him; much as she disliked the thought of the Spaniard, her heart rose glad and warm to him for that mercy. But was it mercy or policy? Could one slay a madman? That cool intelligence, that sharp wit, and firm idealism—he but feigned, and well she knew it.

She put the book down and rose, the long trailing gown tangling around her feet as she began to pace. There was little that she could do for herself and nothing for Charles except consign him to the capricious fates. The old battle fire of the Redenters in their impossible causes came now to their daughter. Guy Edmont would not help her, and who could blame him? George Attenwood had fooled Julian herself, and she had every reason to be wary. But there was another with whom she had laughed and probed and watched. He had reason to be loyal, true enough, but he, a priest of God, had loved once and still remembered how it was. Julian would try for his memory, and for its sake, he might help her to be free. This life would be unendurable. She could not be the mistress of a man she hated all the more for his lies.

The night was long drawn when she slipped out of the room and down the icy hallway to the general section of the castle where she had heard Rob say he had a chamber large and royal enough in which to hold his own court. It might be wiser to wait until she met him normally in the routine of Altyn, but something told her that George planned to take full advantage of her soon, and beyond that, it was as if the darkness that had been hidden from view in him would emerge. She could not wait, for sometimes days went by when she did not see Rob; there was no time.

Her feet were almost frozen in the thin slippers and the lacy shawl was no protection, but she hurried on, her skirts lifted so that they would not rustle. There were no guards, for none could enter or leave this war castle except by the one gate and it was heavily patrolled. Three huge doors rose up at a turn in the corridor, and one shone bolted at the end of it. Which one? She put a hesitant hand to the second and pushed. Nothing. It was locked from the inside, and there was no way to tell if this might be the one she sought. Even if she found Rob, he might still be drunk from all the wine he had consumed. Julian put such thoughts from her mind and pushed on the third door, which was across the hall. This time it gave, and she heard snores coming from inside.

She peered through the crack and saw a tumbled area of books, guttering candles, what appeared to be several portraits in progress at one side, and a jumble of flasks, charts, and some vats close by. The smell was musky, almost heady, and reminded her of some medicines that Elspeth brewed in the basements of Redeswan. The light shone off Father Rob's tonsure as he snored heavily, his head resting on the cluttered table.

"He is this way every night and much of the day. I could have saved you a cold journey had you mentioned that you wished to consult our worthy priest. Are you in need of ghostly counsel?"

The smooth voice made Julian jump. She pivoted to see George Attenwood standing at his ease only a few feet from her. One eyebrow was quirked up, and he was smiling with genuine amusement. Julian felt the suppressed fury in him, however, and knew that this was the moment of their confrontation.

"Or can it be that you seek to persuade that less than ardent gentleman of the court to take you away from my hospitality? Interesting, is it not? I wonder how you planned to leave the castle and meet him?" He seemed so casual, the tone so deceptive that Julian found herself wondering if he were actually saying these things.

She decided to gamble. "I could not sleep and wanted to talk of the faith with Father Robert. Have you not advised me of such?" Anything to get away from those impaling eyes! She knew that he had listened to all the conversation she and Guy had had, probably from a false panel set in the stone of the chamber or a peephole somewhere. It was hopeless, yet she had to try.

The mask slipped, and Julian looked into the face of a man who had absolute power and would not be thwarted. "I have something I want you to see. I think it will interest you greatly, for I have observed that you find the classical absorbing. After you view it we will talk. I can tell you are yearning to burst forth with accusations and the like. Such things bore me, and you had best hope that you do not." He reached out a hand to touch her, and again she felt the recoil even before the emotion.

Julian tilted her head high and stared at him. Her voice was level as she said, "You are quite correct, Lord Attenwood. There are matters to be mentioned, but inasmuch as you are the host and guide here, I will be pleased to see whatever scene you wish." If she yielded to the fear that swept her, Julian knew that the anger or revulsion that he kept leashed would burst out and the consequences likely unthinkable.

The pattern of the snores altered a trifle, and the chair scraped under Rob's bulk as he shifted in his sleep. Attenwood glanced inside, and his expression grew wary. Julian laughed shrilly, letting the sound rise and float on the freezing air. He jerked around, and one hand went to his dagger. She laughed again and put both arms around herself to forestall the shaking that she hoped he would attribute to cold only. The chair creaked again, but the rhythm of the snores picked up in the same tempo. Attenwood pulled the door firmly forward and shut it, then advanced on Julian, his tread hard.

"Could we hurry and go? It is perishingly cold standing here." There was normal irritation in her voice, and she saw that her arms where the sleeves of her gown fell back were prickled with gooseflesh.

He laughed softly but with a hint of eagerness that was

almost sly. "Yes, of course. I am glad that you have a proud spirit. It always makes matters so much more amusing."

"I trust there will be a fire?" She shook out her skirts and moved ahead of him so that he was forced to follow.

"You may count on it, Lady Julian." He caught her full sleeve and guided her toward one of the smaller passages that led downward. "You may count on it."

Endless stairs and corridors later, George paused before an elaborately carved door which he unlocked with a brightly polished key taken from a chain around his neck. A torch flared dimly above them, and Julian could see that the passage ran downward as if to the sea. She was reminded of the Tower, and her shivers became more pronounced. George hesitated, then nodded his head and pushed the door open. He was so close that Julian felt his quick-drawn breath on the nape of her neck.

Her first impression was of an explosion of color and heat. The huge chamber was filled with gauzy hangings, tapestries, life-size pictures, rugs of all shapes in every shade imaginable and blendings unthought of, statues of men and women together in strange poses, screens and collections of golden vessels. It was a storehouse of treasure, artfully arranged to overwhelm at first and then to lure the eye back to new freshness and marvels. Julian looked at the hearth, where a great fire blazed, and wondered at the absence of smoke, for a fresh earthy scent permeated the air. A few strides from the hearth was a collection of several golden trees with jewels for leaves and flowers, diamonds for the centers, and rubies of the deeper color. Further on she saw a standing suit of silver armor embossed with black and plumes of gray feathers rising from the helmet to curl downward.

"You are intrigued. Good. Yours is an eye to appreciate the tapestry of which I spoke. It is in here." Attenwood might have been any proud host showing off his trove.

"Is it not time that you explained yourself, my lord?" She tried for composure but was forced to follow the pulling hand as he took her over to a screen of ivory and pulled it aside, leading her up three carpeted steps and into a smaller chamber which was hung in green velvet. There was a recessed area set deep in the wall and there hung a picture which was at once the loveliest and most repugnant thing she had ever seen.

It depicted a view of the heavenly city with kneeling saints and obedient angels before a throne where a presence was suggested by an artful mingling of purple and gold but no physical characteristics were given. Below was the earth in shades of brown and ocher, and here toiling man remained in one segment to struggle his life away. Here he wrenched and fought and repelled demons of such hideous visages that Julian could only think the artist had reproduced them as he saw them in truth. No act of ugliness was left untouched, though all was done in matchless power. Beside the throne of the grace was the Virgin and her Son, their faces twisted in bestiality. As you looked closer you saw that the city had a red haze over it. But the dominating figure that stood between heaven and earth was that of a young man in the full beauty of his youth, very fair of skin and hair. His cheeks were touched with pink, the sheen of health on his bare arms and legs. His stomach was flat, his member firm and erect. His nude body was all of beauty, and the sword he gripped in one hand seemed but to enhance it. He stood the length of the canvas, young warrior triumphant, the smile on his face proclaiming his pleasure and amusement.

"Who is the artist? It is magnificent! Matchless!" Julian stared at the canvas again, and her flesh went cold, for she knew the model. "Matchless and evil!"

Attenwood laughed beside her. "I will not dispute philosophy with you. This is my effort with which I have found some small degree of satisfaction. Would you meet the model? Behold Michael, Archangel of God, Defender of the Gates of Heaven!" His voice rose and became hating, angry. "He has fallen on worse days, and this is all the more fitting, do you not find it so?"

He gestured toward a dark hole in the floor close by the picture and picked up one of the candle holders so that she might see into the depths. The hole was shallow and no more than the length of her own body. The cover for it lay near at hand to be replaced, and she could see that the prisoner who lay there was not used to any light, for his manacled fingers reached out to cover his eyes. The body was twisted and emaciated, naked and covered with sores; the hair and beard ran together and the jaw hung loosely as though broken and not tended. Chains held him in place, and the cries of rage that rose up when he saw them were those of purest hatred. Julian remembered the young lover as she had last seen him in his handsome arrogance, and her head tilted to the loveliness above which he, too, could see when permitted.

She could not watch anymore for very pity. Julian no longer wondered at the evil of man or his gods. This man seemed to epitomize it all. She cried, "What manner of demon are you, George Attenwood? I thought you kind and merciful, now you are from the very courts of the Evil One. Are you capable of no feeling, you who have such talent, such ability?"

The face that she had once thought stolid ran together in twisting lines, and the burning eyes were those of the predator. His mouth maintained the travesty of a smile, and excitement shook his voice. "I knew that you saw us that day and so did Michael there. He was jealous and thought he had the upper hand; he persisted although he knew that my fancy is ever short. I need heirs and did mean to marry you, one child and a brother for him, then the North Sea; that was to be simple enough. We came here and he grew importunate; I taught him a lesson, and he is still learning."

"What do you want with me?" Julian's eyes caught the surge of movement in his breeches and knew sickly that he was enjoying this, that he was working himself up to a purpose. "Why did you bring me here at first? I know that you lied to me about everything."

"I watched when you talked to that messenger. It was my game, the excitement by which I live, I who am called the somber northern prop of the throne! You want the truth! You shall have it. Ortega and I have conspired at times; he thinks me a good friend to Spain, and I have used him in dealings with France. He does not know that I support the young queen of Scots or that I mean to have power through that support. If civil war comes, I stand to gain either way." His eyes glittered at her. "You were half dead and raving when I met Ortega in Dover after the battle. He wanted to let you die slowly; it seems that you insulted his pride at court, resisted his charms, and disfigured him. He thinks women should be meek and obedient. Anyway, he knows of my interests and was quite glad to give you to me with all that that implied. It was fitting, he said. I promised to tell him all that would happen—he enjoys such tales just as I do—and so our bargain was made."

Keep him talking, Julian thought, anything to postpone the moment when he laid hands on her! Julian spoke desperately. "But you are to wed! What of the heiress? Why me?" She edged back away from him and toward the pit from where the inhuman noises still emerged.

He hooked both hands in the dagger belt he wore and swayed back and forth. "She will encounter the utmost respect until she bears my heir. Then she will fade into a decline brought on by childbirth. I, meanwhile, will seek several new boys to replace young Michael here. Beautiful as he was, he was too bold. I will not make that mistake again." He looked at her from under slanted lids. "You are wondering where you enter into all this? Naturally, a woman can see no point beyond her very self. You rejected me, Julian Redenter, and therefore I have a score to settle with you. You were my betrothed, and you turned to a traitor. Can you not understand the depth of my feelings?"

"You wanted me no more than I wanted you!" She drew back a little more and wanted to kick at the hampering skirts of her gown that had seemed so lovely only a short time ago.

"True, but that is not the issue. I enjoy power, you see; that is one reason I support the machinations of France and the young queen of Scotland. The French are civilized about such matters as my preferences; I could be quite happy there with a hand in the government at times. You have amused me, my dear, I must say that. That Varland must be a veritable lion! You were quite explicit in your fevered utterances!" He walked toward her and put both hands firmly on her shoulders.

Julian willed herself not to cringe away, but the shivers started up in her body. He pulled her into his arms and his mouth ground down on hers in a mockery of everything that she and Charles had shared. She lay passive in his grip, and slowly he set her away from him. As soon as she was free, she scrubbed one hand across her mouth and eyed him icily.

"I have never understood what pleasure people find in that sort of thing." His tone was almost conversational.

"Let me go free, George! I promise that I will say nothing of all that has happened. I can make my own way, live in the villages, on the roadside, anything!" The plea was a mistake; she knew that as soon as she saw his nostrils flare and the bulge grow large again. He wanted her cringing and fearful!

"I will paint you, of course. Now, who shall you be? Jael or Judith? Deborah?" He tilted his head to one side. "No, you are more of the Greek beauty. Perhaps even the Byzantine, though your coloring is a bit off for that. Well, I can decide later. Your face won't be affected."

Julian stood there in that fantastic place, the agonized cries of the young lover rising in her ears, and looked into the face of the man who was altogether sane in his own form of madness. How could this be happening to her? No nightmare could be so savage!

"What are you going to do?" She braced herself to fight as Julian Redenter would always do no matter what the odds.

"I certainly am not going to attack you, Julian." He spoke as if in reassurance. "You have shown yourself lusty by your own admissions. The men of my guard have been long without women and will be receptive to your charms, I doubt not. I will watch, of course. I wonder what that slender body will be like after a few of my hearty northerners have subdued it. Life will be interesting for us both."

With a shudder of horror, Julian realized that he meant to kill her by degrees and paint her death throes.

CHAPTER THIRTY-FIVE

George Attenwood continued to watch Julian avidly as one hand strayed down toward his genitals and rose again. "I mentioned to several of my men only this noon that entertainment would be forthcoming. I think now is the time to summon them."

Julian tensed her muscles, and the slight movement caused his lips to curve in what seemed to be real amusement. He anticipated her resistance and was eager for it. She fought against the deadly fear that would destroy her and, with a supreme effort of will, pulled her gaze from his and lifted it to the picture above them. As she did so, a piece of casually stated information from one of the many conversations with Charles slipped into place in her mind. The wonder in her voice was not wholly simulated as she looked at the glorious canvas and then at its creator.

"The style of that! The painter that King Philip admires so—Bosch! The grotesque and the beautiful done with such perfection of detail. He was a master, and I think you are also. Why? George, you waste yourself in these savageries. You are a true artist."

"Hieronymous Bosch, the Dutchman. Strange that you know him; his work is unlikely to interest a fair woman. He had the truly seeing eye, I believe. You are wrong to

compare us. I could be far greater. I see the twisted behind the lovely and know which will triumph. Is not
Michael brought down?" George moved forward to study
the picture again, but he watched Julian out of the corner
of his eye.

She was struck once again by the resemblance to the
style that Charles had described so vividly that day when
he talked of Philip's admiration for the artist and his own
delight in his friend's pleasure. Now she said, "Of course,
you are right. But the quality of the imagination, the very
strokes of the brush, the expressions rendered, all are
matchless. All the power you could ever need or want is in
those hands." The sincerity in her words struck the man,
and she saw that for the moment he was diverted from the
velvet rope at the side which would certainly summon his
men. Diversion was her intent, for each second of life was
precious. Lure him back from the rope and into the carefully placed treasures, grasp the nearest thing and throw it,
reach for another and pray that he counted the beauty of
them more to be preserved than instant revenge. If she
could be fortunate enough to put her hands on a dagger or
sword . . .

"But I must have the inspiration to be great. You must
understand that if you can appreciate the work of that
Dutchman dead these how many years?" George's eyes
roamed downward, and he stepped a little closer to the pit
where Michael groaned and uttered those pitiable noises
that reminded Julian of an animal dying by inches. "The
act of destruction inspires me, you see. It is done for my
great talent. My wife, the poison, that canvas is truly a
masterpiece. If we had time I could show it to you. And
the boy, Gareth, a perfect Saint Sebastian."

Julian was now truly terrified at what she had unleashed
in him. Her suspicions had not gone this far. She spoke
through stiff lips. "But you are the arbiter of time. Take it
and show me. I assure you that I understand the difficulties and severities imposed by the burden of a talent such
as yours, such an incomparable talent."

"That is true, but I cannot wait." He fixed his eyes on

her face and she saw the bestiality there, the very face of her lingering death.

"Wait! Tell me what form the picture involving me will take. At least you can do that." *Foolish, foolish,* her mind raged. *Better to run openly and be done.* All her senses were alert, and she felt the gathering passion of action in him that would explode momentarily.

"George, the guest is awake and seeking you. He has to leave, he says, and would pay his respects." The low voice spoke behind Julian and to the side.

She could not see him, but she recognized the sound of Father Robert's distinctive intonation, half-accented, slightly drunken. Did he then condone this madness, or was he in league with the travesty of manhood that was George Attenwood? She whirled to make ready to run, to fight them both if she had to, and the sudden motion loosed the final bond that had restrained George. His lips rose above his long teeth into a wolf snarl, and the cry that came from him was curiously like that of the young man he was destroying. He flung himself at Julian, both hands reaching out for her.

"Now is the time! I will call them now! You have beguiled me with words after the manner of your kind, but I am wiser, better!"

The strong arm of Rob thrust Julian away and tried to catch George, but it was too late. He tumbled into the open pit, and the cry that immediately began was not human, but a demonic scream of triumph followed by the wail of a trapped thing. They heard the thrashing and flailing even over the steady screaming. Rob went forward and bent to look. Julian came up beside him, but he tried to push her away.

"Get back. It is no sight for anyone to see. There is nothing to be done."

Julian moved back, but the sight of George Attenwood choking to death on the chain wrapped around his throat, his eyes bulging, one already burst from the long finger that had been poked into it, and the bloody mass that was his head, all this writhing with the sore-ridden near skeleton that was exacting its own revenge would remain with her in nightmares. The murderer was dying a murderer's death.

One final drawn-out scream rose, and then there was a long sigh as the noise in the pit ceased. Father Rob turned a white face to Julian and said, "They are dead. The boy used the dagger in Attenwood's belt on himself. It is better so."

He had saved her life, and she would not flinch now or yearn after the Evil One. Julian said, "There was a man sent from God and his name is Robert." The paraphrase would let him know the depth of her gratitude.

He said, "I have done many things in my long life, but murder is now counted among them and yet is it not written, '. . . a life for a life . . . a burning for a burning . . .' I am no father of my church, but brother to men. Call me so."

She went to him then and put her arms around him. After a moment his went around her, and they stood together in that place of beauty and destruction, the bodies at their feet and the triumphant angel above them.

Julian pulled back suddenly, half expecting the guards to come upon them. "Rob, we have to get out of here! Those screams will have roused the castle!"

He recovered the old aplomb that had first made them friends. "This level is so deep that nothing would have been heard. No one comes here except by the express order of my lord; I doubt that more than one or two persons in the castle even know what goes on in these rooms. He was devious, that one." He turned to her, noting the pallor of her face and the red flags in her cheeks. "Sit down, my dear, and calm yourself. You have endured much and now we must plan."

"I must leave this place! Go anywhere, just away. I do not care if it is in a snowstorm!" Julian paced up and down, then abruptly pushed around the screen and went out into the treasure room, this time almost insensitive to the hoarded beauty there. "What of Sir Guy? What will we tell him?"

"Nothing. He still sleeps. I heard your laughter, and I was not nearly as drunk as I appeared. It is a habit of mine which has been useful in the past. Truly, Julian, I did not think he meant to harm you, only keep you as a mistress."

She felt a flash of scorn that vanished quickly as she looked at the earnest lined face, the serious dark eyes. "I am grateful for your help, Rob. But for you he would have worked his will on me." She would never know what the priest had intended, whether to remonstrate or divert or really attack, and she did not want to know. Life was too dear, friendship too precious, love too seldom found. Attenwood's scheme struck her in all its power then, and she leaned against the wall, chills running up and down her arms.

Rob looked discreetly away as he said, "I can only think that we must take Sir Guy into our limited confidence, saying that you have no wish to be the mistress of my lord, and I will go with you to distant relatives who will protect you for my sake. That way the men will think nothing of the three of us leaving, just two others to provide escort for the messenger of the queen who has honored us with his presence. I can seal the door and none will dare come here for a lengthy time. These are times of turmoil, and I doubt that his betrothed will have the matter pursued."

"You knew all the time!" She felt the stab of pain and knew it for foolishness. One was as one was, she no less than he.

"Not entirely, Lady Julian. I am still a priest of your Lord God, and I do not wholly condone evil."

She put her hand on the burly arm. "Forgive me, my friend."

"He seemed to be less preoccupied with that side of his nature, the cruelty and the recording of it. I dared to hope." He sighed and patted her fingers. "I will speak to this courtier if you think that would be best. I gather that he was not wholly receptive to your pleas." He shrugged at her questioning look. "George hinted at what he saw and heard. That was another reason I was on guard."

Julian's resolve had been growing with the minutes, and now it was firm. She would not be deflected. Her gaze roved over the treasures, seeing enough to ransom a

Saracen king. Many would buy and ask no questions; many would take and do as they were bidden. But the trust and help of the priest was essential. She knew that she was correct in her assessment of him as essentially weak, but in times of stress he was equal to the need.

"Sir, I would speak to you now as a priest." The formal words touched him to the very core, and he stood the straighter.

"Say on, daughter, bearing in mind all that has been done here."

She sank down on an ornate stool, and he did likewise. This would be one of the most important performances of her life, and it must be accomplished in a very few minutes. "A priest forever" went the Biblical injunction, and it was to this that she, the lapsed one, must appeal. "You will have been at my bedside and heard me speak much of Lord Varland, whom I truly love and who loves me. He and I both turned from the ways of the faith due to all that has happened in this land and what it did to us and those who cared for us. He lies now a prisoner. . . ." Swiftly Julian outlined all that had gone before, placing emphasis on the right and justice and true faith. Abstractions all when murder had been done around them. "And we have the chance to make some restitution. We can take part of this treasure, what we can carry with us, go to London, and there make bargain for the release of Varland and any others implicated with him. Then we can leave England, returning when the queen sees reason or when the young heir-to-be is settled in the succession. This gathered horde will at least do something for us and for the realm." She paused, her mouth dry, her skin flushed. The priest started to speak, but she forestalled him. "You have loved, you know what it is like. You know what Attenwood was like, and there is no accounting for the evil he must have done. Let one wipe out the other. You may say that I wish only to free my beloved and that is very true, but there is the faith to be considered, and you can be that instrument."

Brother Rob smiled at her, and the flash of idealism was obscured. "You are eloquent, Julian, and I admire the

purity of your motives, but you need not have worked so
hard to convince me. I am first and foremost greatly concerned with the safety of this my flesh for all that I serve
God. We will free Lord Varland, and I may say that I
greatly envy him. Then I will take some share of this
wealth and depart to a suitable monastery with agreeable
views. My sins will, I think, be purged in part."

Their eyes met in conspiracy, and Julian felt some of
her dragging burden lift in hope. She said briskly, "Then
go and tell Sir Guy what you must. Bring me some sort of
shabby clothes to travel in, the more disreputable and the
baggier the better. I will gather jewels and the things we
can very easily carry. If we leave by the light of dawn
there should be very little suspicion." As she spoke she advanced on the jewel-laden trees to pry loose some of the
stones.

"There is nothing so practical as a woman." Rob paused
at the door. "I will hasten. There is a special panel that
can be worked to obscure this. I will work it when I return
from speaking to the messenger."

"And what will you say to the messenger? No, don't
move, either of you. I mean to find out what is going on
here." Sir Guy Edmont, lean face shadowed and cold,
moved into the gleam of the firelight which gleamed on
the great sword in his hand. "I have had some practice
with locks. I heard screams, wild laughter, there were the
intimations that Julian gave me, then my wine was
drugged for all that I drank very little and yet was borne
down by sleep. Then this . . ." He advanced further into
the room and stared about in wonder, but the weapon was
held at the ready.

Brother Rob opened his mouth and shut it abruptly. His
shoulders slumped under the robe and he heaved a sigh.
Whatever he had intended to say to Guy was not forthcoming. Julian waited a fraction of time for him to speak,
then she took the power. She was so utterly weary of trying to persuade people to do things and of being at the
mercy of others. A heavy golden ball banded with diamonds was on the green velvet at the foot of the jeweled

trees. One blow with that would make a man's senses blur, and she would have the time she needed.

"Go and look in that room yonder, Sir Guy. Take us with you if you will. Look long upon what you see there, and then tell me what you wish us to do." She stooped slowly and picked up the ball, a casual action she could only hope he would not think too strange. "There are such lovely things here, are there not?"

Guy herded them ahead of him into the chamber they had just quit and did not speak again, but the comprehending horror on his face was enough as he glanced at the picture above the pit and then into it. His face paled, and the free hand clutched his stomach. The sword dropped to the floor, and he raised sick eyes to Julian. "What horror is this?"

"The horror to which you would have left me, Sir Guy." In one swift movement she was near to him, kicking the skirts of the gown out of her way and catching up the sword, the point of which she leveled at his throat. "Rob and I go from this place with the dawn. You can stay here in this room or join us; the choice is yours."

He stared at her set face and carefully refrained from looking at the gruesome contents of the pit. "What do you want of me? What is this coil?"

Brother Rob outlined their plan in swift sentences that showed no sign of hesitation. Julian put down the golden ball and maneuvered the sword into striking position. She spared a thought for the way she had changed since that tall man had come to Redeswan almost a year earlier. Would she see another?

"I am the servant of Mary, the rightful queen. I will take part in no plots against her." He spoke as if to trumpets that he alone could hear. "It is my oath."

Julian knew she could not use the sword if he continued recalcitrant. He had been kind to her on the long journey from Redeswan that time, and his warmth had borne her up during the fearful speculations she had had. No, she could not find it in herself to harm Sir Guy Edmont.

She said, "The queen was once kind to me, and my mother served hers. I have no wish to plot against her, and

her husband has stood good friend to Charles Varland. I
only want to free him and escape to France with him. He
will fight no more, I guarantee that." She remembered the
passion in his voice with his dying breath and truly believed that love would win him from war. Had they not
nearly died together? "You have my oath on that. But
there is no time left to bicker."

"Varland is mad. The whole city knows it. His keepers
have an easy time of it because of that." Guy was hesitating, his brow furrowed.

"Mad or sane, he is the only man I will ever have, and
I will rescue him or die in the attempt." The light shimmered on her gown and wreathed her in the glow. Her hair
had fallen loose and tumbled over her shoulders; the brilliant eyes had a fire of battles in them.

Rob remembered the long-ago woman who had set his
soul from the priesthood, and Sir Guy thought of the frail
woman who was his wife in the Suffolk manor. Had such
passion ever been theirs? The romantic in them both responded to the power that was Julian's in that moment.

Rob said, "Come with us. It is right. I vow it by the
very cross!"

"And I." All her sincerity was in her voice, but Charles
Varland's face was before her eyes.

With the courtliness born of the romances of the dead
days of chivalry and his own honor, Sir Guy Edmont
spoke to Julian alone. "As long as the right of Queen
Mary to remain on her throne is not jeopardized, I will
serve you, Lady Julian. My oath on it."

Julian answered him in the same tone. "To our quest,
then, my friends."

Thus, in the chamber of death and anguish, the three
swore fealty to each other.

CHAPTER THIRTY-SIX

Two hours later the queen's messenger, accompanied by two men to guide him through the snow and small trails, left Altyn Castle. Orders had been conveyed by the priest, Brother Robert, well known to have the ear of the master. None found it strange that Lord Attenwood should not appear; he was strange and moody, and those who questioned him would do so at their peril. Those daring to go into the depths of the castle where he often spent much time would find a dull wooden door superimposed over the ornate one. Attenwood's tomb was sealed for a week, perhaps more if they were lucky.

Julian thought she would remember that journey down England in the icy weather and feel the cold even in the heat of summer. They rode fast and lightly, barely pausing to rest at night, sometimes exchanging horses and allowing Rob to do the bargaining, for he had the skill of it, changing clothes in the same way, then riding on to the next small village. They were comrades in a venture, bound in a friendship that might have seemed ridiculous only days before. Guy would tell the queen that he had delivered her messages, then been overcome with the fever and had lain insensible in a village for days. On his recovery he had hastened back for instructions. It was not hard to persuade him to do this, and Julian knew she had reason to be thankful that he was the caliber of man she believed him to be.

To those met casually in the road, they said that they

were men summoned by their lord to Dover, there to embark as part of the maintained army of Philip of Spain.
They grumbled as such men might be expected to do in
the various ale houses where they stopped, and learned
over and over again the temper of the country which
wanted nothing to do with either French or Spanish intervention. Often they drank to the expected heir, hearing
that the queen was to deliver in March but many thought
her truly addled in her wits. It was a revelation to Sir
Guy, and the lines of his face grew deeper at the bitterness and downright hatred expressed. The name most
frequently on the lips of those in the streets and taverns
was that of the Princess Elizabeth, who was more and
more the hope of England. "Anne Boleyn's daughter!"
Julian sniffed the words to herself as she remembered
Mary Tudor's very justifiable bitterness and early
memories of Lady Gwendolyn, who had served the pa-
tient, wronged Katherine of Aragon. Still, the fires raged
at the queen's behest.

Much of the time they exchanged jokes, snatches of
songs, discussed the weather and hunting, anything but the
struggle to come, as they plodded down the roads of iced
muck. It was a time suspended for all that they listened
eagerly to gossip and for alarms. In her warm, but very
old, boy's clothes and perched on a horse that had seen
better days years ago, Julian experienced a lightness and
sense of freedom such as she had never known. Often her
voice rose high and cracked in the current war songs; the
snickers of her comrades would make her turn and utter
mock threats. They sang no better than she, and the verbal
abuse was one way of sharing.

They entered the city of London early one morning in
mid-March, just another motley collection of men drifting
about the capital, settling on the dirty, crowded streets,
pausing to gape of whatever free entertainment in the way
of processions, arrests, fights, floggings, or sport might be
presented. They appeared to be three men wandering and
looking, turning aside offers made in laughter from prostitutes, shoved aside by gentry, shunned by thieves who
counted them as poor pickings. When they paused in the

alley behind a small shop, a passer-by might have thought
that they made plans to rob it.

"Are you sure this is the place? It looks so tawdry!"
Julian looked up at Sir Guy, who was already pulling out
the richly furred cloak from the disreputable pack he carried.

"I know him of old. He will do anything for money and
jewels." He gave her the cloak and watched her pull it up
over her head. "Now the rings." When she had slipped no
less than six on her fingers and fastened a burst of diamonds to the inner collar of the cloak, he touched her
face with a warm hand. "I must go and report to Her
Majesty. God preserve us all. I shall return as soon as I
can."

Julian and Rob spoke as one to this man who was going
against much that he believed in for the sake of the right.
"God preserve you and keep you!" Then he was gone,
sauntering along the street and scratching his head as he
went, a bumpkin newly come to town.

The master of the shop was small and skinny with
watchful eyes; he was not one who had come by this
discreet place with its excellent goods, quiet rooms off to
the side, and servants who vanished at the wave of a hand.
He eyed Rob with distaste and Julian with apprehension
which changed to servile admiration as he assessed the
jewels she wore and the bag of rubies tossed so casually
before him in the little room to which he had reluctantly
taken them.

"I need gowns immediately! You have some on hand, of
course? And I want a bath, too. You were recommended
to me. I understand that you deal in many things and have
an eye for good business. Is that true?" She snapped the
words at him and watched his eyes grow wide. "I have
made a vow to the Blessed Mother and its fulfillment re-
quires the greatest discretion. Well, shall I proceed?"

He bowed so low that he bent nearly double. "I am the
soul of silence and obedience. Am I permitted to know
madam's name that I may address her more correctly?"
He peered at the tumbling hair and patrician face inside

the hood and stared again at the rings. "I am your servant; my silence shall be as the grave."

Rob fixed him with a hard look. "If you boast of the strangers who have come to you this day, blood shall be your payment instead of rubies."

Julian lifted her head regally and studied the proprietor, who by now was cringing in earnest. "I think he can do as we require. They spoke of you, you know, in my father's house. Yes, and I must not reveal his name but you shall know that he has the honor to wait daily upon the king!" She paused for effect and saw the goggling eyes flood with fear. "The king of Spain! Call me Madame Asterion."

"Tell me your wishes and they shall be obeyed instantly." His voice had sunk to a whisper.

How greatly was Philip of Spain feared! Julian waved her hand again to dazzle him with the rings and issued her commands. "I need a small house, discreetly located but central, servants who obey and do not chatter, a dressmaker who will come immediately, several guards to do my bidding, and some good horses. All this must be done within the day. If you cannot see to it, then I have wasted my time and will go to the next name on my list."

"No, no. All is in readiness for you here to make yourself prepared. Please, Madame Asterion." The unfamiliar syllables twitched off his tongue, and he smiled hesitantly as she nodded her head.

Julian ordered the gaping servant girl out of the little room set aside for her and then luxuriated in her first bath in weeks. Her hair was washed and rinsed, polished and dried by the fire, wound high in plaits and veiled in misty black gauze. She donned the gown and cloak, added more jewels to those already in evidence, and settled down to wait. The man could be counted on to gossip despite all her warnings, and this was as it must be. All her senses were sharpened; the scheme must succeed. Mad or sane, she would have Charles Varland if all the hoarded wealth of George Attenwood could deliver him to her.

Time quivered as she thought again of that frantic period when they three pried jewels out of the little trees, caught up figurines of gold, ivory, and silver, dug into an ornamented chest and found necklaces, pendants, rings, and bracelets of such quality as any lord in the kingdom might envy. She took them without compunction, wondering how Attenwood had come by such trove. It had been Guy who found the rolled canvases hidden in a corner of the chamber, and that sight had been all the convincing he needed to be with Julian and Robert heart and mind and soul. Demons, monkeys, snakes, and monsters danced and sucked at women and children; beautiful boys watched and were themselves struck down, the marks of their blood in the paintings. One felt the leering face of the human monster to be very close. And yet he had presented such a facade of gentility to the world.

There was a hammering at the door, then she heard Rob's familiar voice. "Mistress, all is done as you demanded. Will it please you to leave this noisome place?" She rose, adjusted her veil, shook out the fashionable skirts, and sailed haughtily out to meet him.

Later she sat with him over hot wine in the drawing room of the little house so swiftly obtained for her by whatever nefarious means, and they plotted in whispers. There were three maids, four guards, and a surly doorman, all probably found in the vast underworld of London and threatened with swift extinction if they did other than they were told. Rob had made the initial arrangements with the man, saying that wealth could buy anything and that he had lived in London long ago; it was all a matter of memory. Certainly the neat house with its own garden, servants' quarters, three bedrooms, and separate private sitting rooms was a jewel in an avenue that was not at least respectable. To Julian it smacked of sudden eviction, but she found that she did not care.

Now she said, "Surely Guy must return soon. He will obtain what information he can. I pray he is not suspected. We must act swiftly. Learn the location where Charles is held, his condition, and the best means of approach."

"If he is in his right mind, there is much we can do. If not, then I shall be forced to other means." Rob had regained much of his roguish approach to life, and now he clawed about in the multiplicity of goods purchased that afternoon. "If you will forgive me, Julian, I will get to my preparations."

"Madame Asterion gives you permission." She laughed and saw his face brighten.

"A mysterious lady who has made a vow and desires to see the criminal Varland, for she knew him of old. A fair tale, lady, and a bold one. They will truly believe you to be of Spain." He touched her shoulder and departed for his own special lair.

Julian sighed and leaned back. It was hard getting used to being elegant after all the days of slouching comfort. She must not let her mind linger on what was to come, or she would run screaming with terror. Instead she would think of what she and Charles would do when they were safely in France and together. Marriage would not be necessary; they would both want to be free. She dreamed for a short few minutes of a gleaming future of love, of the time alone that they had never really had except in the ruined castle.

It was very late when Sir Guy returned, walking boldly in the doorway, still dressed in his humble garb but unchallenged by the guards. Julian sprang up and took his arm. "Guy! You are safe! I feared for you. What news is there? What have you found out?"

He sank down in the carved chair that she vacated and rested his head on his hands. "I listened only to the talk around the taverns near the court. More turmoil, more talk of rebellion, more burnings. No heir. News from Spain that even King Philip tries for moderation, but she is adamant. It is as if she wanted to destroy this country."

Julian wanted to cry out, but in the face of such bewilderment she could not. After all, he risked much to help her, and now the danger of being branded a traitor was even stronger than it had been. She poured out a drink of rich wine into a simple goblet, one which had come with the house, and set it near his hand.

"Drink, it will ease you." Would God she had something to ease herself!

"Take comfort, Julian. Varland is held under heavy guard in a small separate house on what was once his estate on the Thames and now, of course, forfeit to the crown. This is by order of the king, and his own ambassador, De Feria, goes to see him regularly. The queen's physicians check him, and it is said that when the child is born and she recovered, he will be executed, mad or not. Of the madness I could learn only that it is some sort of apathy, not violence. These things are common knowledge. I represented myself as straight in from the country and curious."

She knelt at his side and put both hands on his hard ones. "Is it so painful, Guy? If so, we will willingly absolve you of your oath." How could they manage without him? Yet the offer must be made. "We will not plot against the true ruler."

"I know, Julian. We all do what we must. Now we must move with dispatch, for the child is expected daily. Let us lay our plans and be ready." His eyes searched her face. "I cannot come here again lest I be followed; there is much suspicion these days, and no one is immune. I will keep you informed, however. There are many ways of sending messages if one is discreet and can pay."

"Guy, you risk so much and have been so unfailingly kind."

His hands clenched on hers as his voice dropped. "Kind? Yes, that is one word for it, Julian." He became matter-of-fact at the question in her eyes. "I think it best that I be the one to make the arrangements for our escape from the city after the actual rescue of Varland. We must have fast horses and good disguises. It will take time. Where is Brother Rob? Fetch him and let us talk."

Julian knew then that Guy cared for her. Perhaps it was not yet love, but in time it might have flowered. He was a good and true man, a loyal friend, and she cared for him, but there was no room for anyone but Charles Varland in her heart. She looked up at him and saw the same earnest look that he always had. If only all went well for all of them! She rose to her feet and went in search of Rob, fear of the future burning in her.

* * *

Day slipped into day, and Julian chafed with the passage of each. They had done all they could, and the plans endlessly rehearsed for each contingency until she could think of them only as plays put on for amusement. She grew snappish, and the maids remarked to themselves that this was truly a mysterious great lady with all the arrogance of true royalty. This tale spread and greater deference was given to the inhabitants of the little house. Julian spoke often with the dressmaker, recommended for her discretion, and was indeed having several ravishing gowns made, but when the woman visited in all her plethora of materials and advice about the changing fashions, there were sturdy peasant clothes, ointments to stain the skin, and potions to alter the color of the hair. For the remainder of the time Julian walked in the tiny garden until it felt to her that she wore paths in the earth; each day she watched the skies grow less leaden, the air imperceptibly warmer. Any time now. Any time the world would alter, and she, Julian Redenter, would play the part of life and death.

On the gray and cool evening that Brother Rob, clad in the nondescript black gown and cap he wore on his forays around the streets, came to her and said quite calmly, "I have seen him, and he appears quite physically healthy," Julian watched him as through a dream. The reality had come at last.

Rob was going on, "The guards grew used to me; as we planned, it was simple enough to have one more learned gentleman, a bit vague but interested in strange cases, arrive in the wake of the several physicians who have examined my lord. With the queen the way she is, there is more respect given toward all those who may taste power. One of the guards took me in, and I saw that he stares at the wall and did not even turn though we made noises and spoke quite loudly. I looked into his eyes and believe that he has quite retreated, although the examination was only cursory."

"I will not think that! Such a mind as his does not fade away. It is time to act." She spun around and looked squarely at him. "He could be pretending. Have we not heard that they would put him to torture if he were at himself?"

"I do not think any man, not even the incomparable Varland, could be in such control of himself." Rob spoke wryly. The tension was telling on them all. "Still, it is a possibility. I will speak of my discoveries on the morrow and the learned dissertation I mean to present to the king of Spain, who is rumored coming to be here for the birth. Our second plan will have to be the one, Julian. We have feared that all along."

"I will be ready." Now that matters were moving along, she felt the sick anxiety leave her and the determination well up. If they failed all would die, but that was a thing they had long ago faced. Her brief thought went to Charles's rescue of her from the Tower and the manner in which he had decried it. A life for a life, a love for a love.

"The madwoman thinks she is in labor, and all the physicians have been summoned! The court is in an uproar." The network of beggars, thieves, and prostitutes whose services George Attenwood's wealth had brought into play now delivered the latest news into the attentive ears of Brother Rob in the early hours of the morning. "Plans and counterplans are being made, secret messages go to the king, the Princess Elizabeth, and to France. There is bickering and dissent, every man's hand poised against the other." As he spoke to Julian he watched her great eyes bloom to life.

"Madame Asterion and her entourage go forth this day. The old woman is fully willing and knows what is to be done?"

"Three of the choicest rubies are being held for her in addition to the pearls she has already received." Rob was as excited as she and the weight of the adventure began to bear down. "Guy has made arrangements at the inn near the gate."

The litter which swayed through the crowded, smelly streets an hour later was an undistinguished one that drew no comment. Two guards, Brother Rob, a shrouded maid-servant whose shuffle indicated age, and a sprightly younger one made up the party. Julian sat inside, wearing

her voluminous black silk gown and a coif in the old
Spanish mode which left only a few strands of midnight
hair revealed. Black gloves concealed her hands, but the
sparkle of diamonds showed at throat and wrists. Her dark
brows were drawn emphatically above her eyes, and her
normally pink mouth was painted into a narrow line that
added years to her age. A heavy veil swathed her face,
and a shining necklace of diamonds and rubies hung over
her bosom. She called out to the bearers that they must
hurry, testing the voice of middle-age and pleased to find
that it sounded both haughty and emphatic.

Be with me, god of battles. The words hammered over
and over in her brain. *Let us win the day.*

After what seemed an endless journey, the litter halted
abruptly, and she heard the sounds of whispered conversation, then an angry expostulation and a curse all the more
pithy for being in Spanish. An English voice snapped, "I
never said any such thing. You know I didn't!"

The curse came again and that was Julian's cue. She
parted the curtains and leaned forward, staring straight
into the beefy, obdurate face that turned to hers. The expression of fright on Brother Rob's face would have been
comical in any other circumstances.

"What is this? I was promised entrance with this man
who investigates the illness of one of these English crimi-
nals. Why do you delay us? I am Madame Asterion of
Madrid." She let her imperious gaze turn to Rob. "Have
you explained just who I am?"

The other guard came up to his fellow, they gaped at
her diamonds and at her autocratic face twisted with the
royal anger, and backed away. She said savagely, "The
king shall hear of this when he arrives. Take me back!"

The older of the two said, "A mistake has been made,
of course. Let them pass. Your pardon, my lady."

"About time!" Julian slapped the curtains together and
leaned back, both hands pressed to her mouth as the litter
swayed past the high walls and into the prison of Charles
Varland.

CHAPTER THIRTY-SEVEN

The litter halted before a separate area sheltered by trees now bare against the chill sky, and Julian was helped out by one of the guards who paced before this stone house that might have been the remains of a Saxon fort so old did it seem. Rob went before her, the old woman they had hired shuffled in the back, white hair hanging out of the hood, and the watching guards stared at the regal woman whose voice had been heard complaining even before she came into view. She did it now. "A fascinating experiment to tell the king, you said! In this primitive waste! I am bored already! I warn you, this had best not take long!"

"Lady, lady, I assure you . . . did I not say all England was a penance? But you had to come!" Rob half turned on her with the air of a man who has borne enough.

"Silence!" She swept on and was gratified to see some of the guards who seemed to be posted at every turn grow relaxed and even wink at each other.

One final guard stood before a bolted door. He took his time regarding them, even to the old woman, whom Rob mentioned tersely as "my talisman and necessary," then he waved them in, and the bolts slammed shut.

Julian stood in the half darkness of one room for a second before moving into a wider bedroom with iron bars set closely over the small window. It was lighter here, and she could see the river in the distance. The man on the bed lay with arms crossed over his chest in the manner of dead crusaders, his carved profile very clear, the high cheekbones perfectly modeled, his black brows still winged. His face was smooth and calm. He blinked and breathed, but his long body in the loose brown robe of a mendicant monk was quiet.

Julian stood over him and looked for what seemed an eternity before Rob came up with a tiny vial in his hand. He knelt beside Charles and lifted up one hand, which fell back flaccid. The gray eyes still watched the ceiling. He called to the old woman, "Chant something out of your youth, mutter, mumble, but keep it up."

"Aye, master." She must have been eighty, but her voice was shrill and high with an ominous note to it and enough vigor for two others.

"This will revive him no matter what gray world he wanders in. I have seen this work every time on the mad. If only there were time enough to make it such as I have had. He may not understand, but he will obey." Rob was smiling, eager to begin his work.

"Wait." Julian sat on the edge of the bed and pushed her coif back a little, thrusting the veil to one side. Then she laid her lips on Charles's and almost jerked back, for they were warm and living. The unmoving gray eyes that looked into hers were those of the man she loved, alive and aware, comprehending. The tiny pulse began to beat in his temple as it had always done in times of stress for him. She lifted her mouth and said, "It is all right. We have come to rescue you. It is not a trick. I am Julian, and these are friends who will help."

"He does not know. . . ." Rob's mouth fell open, and he stared at Charles Varland, who was pulling himself up on the bed with one hand and clasping Julian's radiant face with the other.

Charles spoke rustily. "A long pretense. How can you hope to free me? It cannot be done."

"It can and will, but you must trust us utterly." Rob recovered his wits and put away the vial a bit regretfully. "First, sir, have you been in possession of your wits all these months that you have been imprisoned? No lapses?"

Julian put her arms around Charles, and he returned the embrace with a hunger that shook them both. He said,

"No lapses, although they tried. I learned the art long ago of retreating into myself and even knew an old scholar once who said the mind could quite leave the body. It was invaluable to me here."

"I must ask you to give your mind into my keeping, Lord Varland, and yield yourself up to me so that your body will be malleable and you can walk out of here as yon old woman." Rob jerked his head at Martha, who had thrown herself into the task of chanting with great determination. One would have thought that an entire coven was practicing. "I have studied much of the hypnotic art during my travels. Trust me."

"It is impossible. You will all be caught." Charles tried to smile and could not. His face set in harsh lines. "Julian, you know what fate is set for you. Please go."

Julian put both hands on his and let the strength of her will go to battle his. "We have planned and risked all on this venture, Charles. You must do what Rob says, what I say, else all is in vain, and you will be the cause for our failure. Obey, Charles, for all our sakes."

Their eyes locked, and the old arrogance leaped up. Then Charles said, "I yield to you all. Do as you think best." Only Julian could know what that statement cost the proud man she loved.

"Watch this, my lord, and let yourself go into the red depths. Drift there and know that when you return you will be free and with Julian." Rob swung the great ruby with the tiny curved moon in it back and forth in front of Charles, who allowed his gaze to be impaled on it. Old Martha slipped into a lower key of chanting that seemed to draw the senses upward and out.

Julian took his hand again and treasured the alacrity with which it closed around hers. The movement of the ruby lured her own eyes, and she forced herself to look at the drab surroundings, the dark low ceiling, and lack of any comforts. He had had his own version of the Tower.

"Drift, drift. It is warm and summery here. Go with it and rest, the first good rest you have had in a long time. When you wake you will see her face, but now drift." Rob sounded the litany over and over, his voice low, soothing.

How long had they been here? What if the bribes given did not satisfy all those involved or were compared? Panic clawed upward in Julian, but she forced it back. At any moment they might all be arrested, but she must think of nothing but the way his hand was growing limp in her own, the gray eyes distant and closing, his features softer.

"You are very old and tired. Your name is Martha, and you have worked all your life. Borne children, many of them. You are going home to rest, and you want to get there as quickly as possible, but your feet, all your flesh, hurts. You are waiting on Madame Asterion and do her bidding."

Charles slumped over and rubbed his knee, twisted a piece of hair, and reached out for the comfort of a fire. Then he sat in the bent position of the old and worn, sighing as he did so. Julian had known he would do this, yet for all the times they had rehearsed it, she felt the shiver as if demonic power sat within the shell of Brother Rob.

He put out a hand, and Martha grew silent as she jerked out the stitched clumps of white hair that had been fastened to her scrawny neck. The draggled gray gown followed, and the deep hem of her old cloak was loosed. Julian took them and put swift fingers on the robe Charles wore, he standing obediently as she nudged him. He fell again in the pose of the weary old woman even as Martha stood. He wore only a brief shirt of torn linen under the robe that she tossed to Martha, but she was thankful that it had a hood so his face could be covered. Had he ever used it of his own volition, or had he endured the stares and thrusts of the state physicians?

Rob was speaking to Martha, his voice urgent and provocative as he swung the jewel. "Follow it and think of the riches you will have. All that you can do. When you wake you will remember nothing of us, nothing of how you came here. Rest." She seemed to grow taller and straighter as he talked. Some of the lines on her face smoothed out, and her shoulders went back. From a bent crone's cautious movements there came the motion of a vigorous person a third her age. She put on the robe Charles had discarded and lay down in his posture. "Turn on your side and pull up the hood. Stretch out. You will sleep for many hours and will remember nothing."

Julian watched her obey and went to pull the covers high. From her own cloak she took some of the silky hair that was close to Charles's color and fitted it over the still head. Already the old woman's flesh was flaccid and relaxed. It would be hard to fool a watchful gaurd, but this, too, was part of their plan.

Now they stood ready. Charles was enveloped in the cloak and hood, stooped and bent, hands hidden in the folds of his garments, white hair hanging out. Julian caught her breath and said, "I shall be even more imperious and annoyed with the explanations you feel constrained to give."

Rob smiled at her. "We physicians are a wordy lot. I thank God that I had reason to remember all those arcane studies long ago."

Julian lifted her gloved hand and hammered impatiently on the door to the first room they had entered. Fear gave its power, and she gave it a kick just as the guard swung the heavy thing outward. She connected with his shin, and her eyes glittered into his. Immediately she raised her voice in the harridan complaint.

"Take forever to come and keep me, *me*, waiting! A good dose of the lash is what these people need. In Spain we know how to deal with such matters! Furthermore, I have been bored for those hours in there. All the stupid man did was mutter. Come on, Sir Physician, this instant!"

The guard drew back, but he was alert and so was the one who joined him. He said, "The prisoner spoke to you? What did he say?"

Julian drew herself up haughtily. "Why are you questioning me? I do not care about louts who mumble. I can certainly say that I have nothing exciting to tell my king, my kinsman, who is going to be just as bored with this silly land as I am."

Rob spoke to the older guard, who had now summoned two others. Julian missed his first words as she stared hard at the waiting litter. Nothing had altered; bearers, their own men, and her young maidservant waited as they had been left. She stamped one foot, but the presumed old woman stood without moving beside Rob, just as old Martha had done on their entrance.

". . . too early to tell, of course, but he is definitely returning to this world. He seems to think he is still in a battle, calling for weapons and comrades. Now he sleeps naturally instead of that dead stare. Let him do so, and I will return on the morrow. He will regard me as a friend, and that will be useful in future."

"A miracle of God!" The older guard spoke the words devoutly. "The great ones will be pleased."

Rob rubbed his chin reflectively. They might have had all the time in the world to stand here in the damp wind and discuss treatment. Julian glared at him, a feeling manifested not only by the role she played. He ignored her and began his discourse. "Severely wounded, naturally, and roughly handled thereafter. Now, miracles are direct acts of God, but we know that he works through men as well, and I have been greatly privileged to study in the great universities of Spain. . . ." He wound on and on, sometimes in Latin and what might have been Arabic or Hebrew for all they knew.

Julian called to the young maidservant, her voice sharp, and the girl came running to assist her mistress toward the litter. "Hurry, Martha, I must sit. I do not know about you, priest, but I am leaving." She stalked to the litter, her back stiff, and hoped that Rob would follow.

She heard him say, "At seven then. Be sure to let him rest."

"But the Lord Ortega comes soon to view him." The younger guard was agitated. "Our orders were specific. He cannot be turned away."

Julian literally felt her blood freeze in her veins. She had thought him in Spain. She dared not respond to the name or show any emotion. Even the hauteur of a noble lady had been exhausted beyond the point of believability. Ortega might be on his way here now, and if one tenth of what Attenwood had told her was the truth, he would have a score to settle with Julian Redenter. They had bribed these guards within limits, but treason was another matter to the common man.

Rob said, "A thousand pardons, madam. I have subjected you to much this day. I am coming just now." Then he called to the guards, "The Lord Ortega will wish his recovery as much as we. Hint that he is better and speak of the morrow. I think he will wait."

Julian looked back at them then and saw that they hesitated. Another moment and her party would be held for the inspection of others and that would be fatal. Madame Asterion had had enough. "Raise the litter. I go. Martha, you and Alice come immediately."

The stern voice swept uncertainty away. The litter was lifted, and the small entourage moved toward the gate. Julian held the curtains back, thinking correctly that her veiled face and sharp eyes would quell any hesitancy. The guard opened it and waved them through into the street. She heard the bolts fall behind them as they went into freedom.

The street was crowded with people rushing about, and few took any notice of the litter that now sped along. Rob wore his hood and had brushed back the white hair from Charles's forehead. They were simply a party of the merchant class out to shop in the early morning. When they turned the corner away from the Thames and toward the narrower streets that could lose them in the city proper, Julian breathed a heavy sigh. It came too soon, for a blare of trumpets rang out close by, and the heavily accented words broke into her mind that tried to shut them out.

"Make way for Alphonso Diego Ortega, representative of the King's Majesty! Make way! Make way!"

She risked a look. It was true, for a small troop of horses was moving toward the area from which they had just come. The red and gold and black of their colors gave light to the gray day. People were scattering, some beginning to jeer at the foot soldiers while others stood in clumps, their faces sour. Mud spattered the brilliant coat of the herald who walked in front, and a young boy darted into the assembling crowd which now began to laugh.

"Turn into yonder street, then leave the litter and go. You know nothing." Julian gave the order and was instantly obeyed. The pushing people stood away, but some curious glances did follow them, and she knew that they would remember. Whether they answered the soldiers of Spain was something else, but the risk could not be taken.

A few minutes later Julian, Rob, and the obedient shell that was Charles Varland stood in the shadow of a small church that had once been brave with glass and color and statuary but was now a continuing victim of the English anger against the policies of the queen. There was no money and no will for restoration. Julian wondered that she had time to think this way when pursuit was only minutes away.

"The horses will be ready at the inn hard by the west gate. We can take all day to get there so long as we are out of the city by the time the gates close." Rob looked at Julian's elegance. "You need to get rid of those clothes, how I cannot think."

The city was wild enough these days so that it might very well be thought the occupants of a litter found abandoned were either killed or taken away. In spite of their plight Julian could not resist a smile at the look on Rob's face as he watched her unloosen the black dress to let sleeves and bodice fall away.

"What are you doing? Someone will see you!"

"What will they see? A woman of the streets speaking with a priest. They at least need no disguise!" She blessed the inspiration that had made her pull on the thin wool gown before the rich court apparel that Madame Asterion would have worn. The skirts followed, and she bundled them away in a pile of drifted refuse near the wall. "It is colder but safer. Now, rouse Charles, and we can go the faster."

Charles still stood as he had halted, a mindless thing that made her heart ache for the power and elegance that had been his. The wind seemed colder here, and people were beginning to hurry toward the cresting excitement that could be heard across the intervening streets. They must rush away while life still remained. The strange curtain that sometimes came across Julian's mind at times of stress blurred things for her now, and she saw the backward whirl of events. The burning ship and the cliffs of Cornwall, Attenwood's sand-colored eyes, the looming expanse of the Tower walls, the calculating look in Brother Rob's eyes, and a dark room where the world as she knew it ended.

"I cannot rouse him yet, Julian. It is one of the effects of such treatment that the person may suffer some derangement of mind. We dare not risk that until we are beyond the walls of the city."

The trumpet sounded clear and high in the air, a call to arms. It was answered by another while the crowd screamed beyond. Time was narrowing down. Julian stared at Rob. "Why did you not tell me this? Have we saved his body to risk his mind? We could have pretended; it might have worked."

He caught her arm and pulled her in the alley that ran parallel to the street. "It would not. Fear can be smelled out. And did you not say that you would have Charles Varland mad or sane?"

CHAPTER THIRTY-EIGHT

"That is the price, masters. It is yours to take or leave as you will." The innkeeper folded broad arms across his chest and rocked back and forth on his heels. A grin flicked over his pursed mouth and vanished into his beard.

"But the arrangements were made days ago! You agreed to them!" Rob's voice rose and was as quickly lowered.

"My wife, myself, and my old aunt to be well mounted and provisioned and an extra horse for our baggage. My brother came here. Do you not recall?"

The grin faded and the innkeeper glared at them. "No one came and no arrangements have been made. Do you say that I lie?"

A red flush came over Rob's face, and he started to answer but Julian stepped close to the innkeeper, letting her voice go shrill. "We will take the beasts you have though they are certainly no bargain! My husband probably drank up the money before even looking for that no-good brother of his!" She poured the collection of coins traded earlier for pearls into his eager hands. "Husband, let us go. I am exhausted and so is Aunt Mary." She gave Rob and the innkeeper a scathing glance.

The innkeeper waved a negligent hand. "The beasts are in the stable. You have seen them. Take them and go. But think twice before you accuse an honest man." He began to check the coins, losing interest in the trio.

Julian was thankful that they had concealed the remainder of the coins in their clothes. He had seen the empty pouch and knew that no more was forthcoming. She and Rob bickered for the benefit of any watchers as they guided Charles toward the stable, mounted the thin horses which the prudent stableboy had ready, and shambled away into the cold afternoon. They could only hope that their act had been convincing.

They went into the narrow street which was filled with shoppers, merchants, pickpockets, and travelers all rushing about. The city gate which led to the Salisbury road was very close, but Julian drew rein, her eyes scanning the streets and the crowds. She watched Charles for an instant, fighting all her screaming senses. He might have been the very old woman he posed as, for his movements were slow and laborious. His legs clamped around the distended barrel of the horse he sat upon and clung there. He bent forward, and his cloak concealed both face and hands. The very look of his figure was one of age and exhaustion.

"Julian, we have to go. The hunt may already have begun in earnest." Rob's strained voice pulled at her. "We cannot wait, I tell you."

"What if something has happened to him? He must have been taken. He sent word that he was making the deal with the innkeeper just as you said. It was all planned, and we were to join the party of pilgrims." Her words broke off as she stared imploringly at Rob. She knew that he was right, but tears were burning her eyes. What if Sir Guy were even now looking for them?

They had spent the time since that morning in two churches and a tavern as they sought to avoid notice. There had been no evidence of the hunt and no sign that they had been followed. Charles moved easily when they guided him, though Julian's heart ached to see him so. The city abounded with rumors: the queen had or had not been delivered of a healthy boy or a monster; she was dead or dying; she had been abducted; Philip of Spain had arrived with soldiers to take over the realm that would not crown him. Every moment they lingered was another step closer to death. It was already hours past the time they had set to meet.

"Julian?" Rob spoke sharply. "He would not want us to jeopardize what we have already won, you know that."

She did know it, and that made the fear for him all the more agonizing. Her friend who had helped them in spite of what it might mean for him, the faithful servant of the queen who yet had been kind to Julian Redenter from the first and whose eyes had told her he could be more. "They will kill him!" The words were almost a wail, and several people turned to stare. It was enough. She must make the decision and weep for it later. "Very well, Rob. Let us go."

Other people were leaving as well, and their party mingled with them, but all were conscious of the soldiers walking about, eyes alert. A drifting rain had begun, and the wind had risen as night approached. Some tumblers were showing their skills near the gates, and children begged close by. Julian hunched her shoulders and tried to appear inconspicuous, but she remembered what Rob had said about fear giving off its own scent. The pacing clop of the horses brought them nearer to the soldiers, nearer to the road outside and freedom.

Then they were outside and moving down the muddy track with all the others who, like themselves, had journeys to make as well as those who lived close by and would bring their wares to the city tomorrow and all the other days of the year. Julian wanted to look at Charles and Rob but dared not lift her face lest the luck turn. For the first time she felt the cold through the wool gown and old cloak. The hood of thin cloth did little to protect her head, but she was beyond caring. Now they entered into the state of freedom, that most precious thing of all.

"Release him from this state. We must go more swiftly." They crouched in the shelter of an old wall that protruded from a copse away from the road down which the soldiers had just ridden. Julian did not want to admit that she was growing more nervous with Rob, good friend that he was. Her instincts of danger were awakened and she knew better than to ignore them. "Rouse him, I say."

"We must have warmth and quiet to do it properly. It is late, we can find an inn, stable these old horses, and begin. Come, Julian, would you risk his mind?" Rob spoke as reasonably as ever. "How do you think those soldiers might have been after us? Riding with those flaming torches they could have been seeking anyone, including another troop. We have not been traced."

"Now! I demand it!" Her teeth clenched as she faced him, his face a blur in the darkness.

"Why?" He leaned toward her, and suddenly he was no longer her friend but an alien in this dark, wet world.

"Why do you hesitate, Sir Priest?" Charles Varland threw back the hood of the old woman's cloak and stood before them as himself, the peer of the realm and leader of those who dissented.

Julian and Rob cried out as one, and the tall figure reached past them to fumble in the bags for the breeches and shirt there. Then Julian crossed to him and put both hands on his arms. His flesh was warm, the dark hair crisp. He was himself.

"How long . . . ?" Rob stuttered and faltered into silence.

"Since just before we left London. It was the dark and the torches, those children crying out, and the sight of Julian's face in the light. Those are the last words you spoke to me, remember? I am familiar with such states from my own journeys, but have never seen that there was a danger from them. Nonetheless, I am grateful for all that you have done." Charles scrambled into the clothes under the shelter of the robe, then reversed it and threw it around his shoulders. He did not take his eyes from Rob, and Julian felt the leashed anger in him.

Brother Rob said, "We have undergone much these last weeks. Are we now to walk in fear of each other? Your life has been preserved, Lord Varland, and the wealth of a dead man bought it. I would not question too far if I were you."

Julian started to speak, but Charles reached out a hand in the darkness and caught hers, squeezing it tightly. It was a warning. She said, "For what reason do we quibble? Charles is restored and safe. Let us go on while we can find some sort of shelter."

"But first there is this." Charles pulled her to him and held her against the length of his body before touching his mouth to her forehead in a gesture of such gentleness that her eyes misted. There was no passion, but who could expect it after all that had happened? The camaraderie was sufficient for now. She leaned against him and knew peace for the first time in many weeks.

They rode without stopping again for the remainder of the night and all the next day. The main road was long since left behind, and they went into the little trails and pathways that dotted this part of the landscape. Rain buffeted them, but it had a hint of spring in its touch, and the bare branches of the trees danced against the low clouds. Exhausted and tired as they were, the promise of the warmth to come lifted them up. All knew that they must find a place to go to ground, and in these suspicious times, that would be a task nearly as difficult as the feat they had accomplished in freeing Charles. From time to time they saw small bands of soldiers even in the hamlets and dared not pause; their pursuers would be seeking a small group such as themselves, and it was entirely feasible that all could be checked. Julain thought to herself that Ortega would have demanded entrance and discovered the ploy within minutes of their departure. He could command the resources of England and Spain; they had only their wits and the wealth of George Attenwood.

Late in the afternoon of that same day Rob's horse stumbled and went lame on one of the woody trails through which they were pressing. Investigation showed that it was not a serious condition, but the animal could not be ridden further that day. The horses were tethered to a tree branch, and then they huddled together under an impromptu shelter made of matted branches, a small rock overhang, and the largest cloak.

Julian and Charles lay in each other's arms with Rob at Julian's back. She felt the hairs on the back of her neck prickle but thought it merely tiredness. She shifted position a little, and Charles whispered, "Sleep, Julian, sleep." It was softer than a lullaby, this tenderness that she had seldom known from him, and she tumbled into restful slumber with his name on her lips, his mouth on her hair.

The muttered cursing seemed at first the part of a dream that changed from warmth to chill, from human closeness to the emptiness beyond all communication. She reached out for Charles and to pull the covers up around her shoulders, then came wide awake as reality struck. He stood a few yards away, out in the gray light of early morning, and she could see the cords of his neck standing out as he kicked at an offending branch.

"What is it?" She jumped up, thrust her hair back, and looked about, half expecting to see them besieged by soldiers of the queen.

Charles strode nearer and waved a piece of paper under her nose. "It was marked for you, but I am not sorry I read it. At least the edge of my rage has cooled. How could he do this after all that we have endured?" He thrust the scrap at her.

Julian read in the fine Latin of the monasteries: *Forgive*

me, Julian. You began to know what would happen. I cannot be other than I am or as I was made long ago. Lord Varland will protect you. Forgive.

She looked up at Charles and then around blankly. The suspicions over which she had felt guilty came back, and she put a hand to her mouth. "No! But he carried the major part of the jewels and the gold. I had only a few pieces and some pearls. Oh, Rob! Culpable after all." They had been through many trials, and she did not doubt that, armed with most of the wealth, he could buy a comfortable life at any worldly monastery in France or even any of the remaining ones in England. "I counted him friend." The words came out softly, and she knew that never would she think of Brother Rob as anything but that. Some part of her drew back from commitment. Could the dark man she loved be trusted even now?

"He took the best horse, too." Charles made the sour remark as he looked at the other two, one of which was still lame. "These holy ones are devious." He swung back to Julian and took in her pale face, which harbored traces of her hurt. "Julian, come now. We are free, and I owe you my life. We surely have enough to find some sort of shelter for a month or so while I find out what is going on in the land and how to contact those left of my men."

"I hope he will be happy. I wish him well. His arcane knowledge and ability gave us what we now have." She took the hand Charles extended, and they looked at each other ruefully. It was true; both of them knew it. And knowing it, they could say farewell to a friend.

They alternately walked and rode that day, which saw the coming of the pale sun and a true lessening of the chill. Julian told Charles all that she could remember of affairs of state, while he spoke of the months of recovery and captivity, the omnipresent certainty of death, and the final protection of Philip of Spain. "He has stood my good friend, but I shall have to forswear it in the bitter times to come." She saw that Charles himself had changed, he was less arrogant of spirit, more quietly determined and settled within himself. When he thought she did not see, he reached out to touch a swaying branch, his fingers closing on the wet thickness of it as if he could feel summer's leaves. The fleeting expression on his face made her heart shake.

It was to this new Charles that she could speak of George Attenwood, the manner of his life and death, the plans he had had for her, and the way these had been foiled by those who had helped. She added, "We saw no more of Sir Guy after he went to the palace that morning to find out what he could and present himself to those of the council standing for the queen at her lying-in. Matters moved more swiftly than we intended with the coming of Ortega."

Charles dismissed Ortega with a flip of his fingers. "That lackey will get what he deserves." He took Julian's chin in one hand and put the other on her shoulder as his mouth grazed hers, then took it more fully.

She put both arms around him, and they stood together in the winding road, fused together in the passion that had ever bound them, now deepened by the adversity that had brought them into a new closeness. Once Charles would have spoken savagely of Attenwood and her own motives; now he accepted her words and went to what was important. Life itself. His breath was warm as it mingled with hers, his tongue lured and drew hers in the well-remembered fire. Her loins grew heated, and she leaned into him. His fingers tightened as he muttered in his throat.

The horses whickered behind them, and one stamped the wet ground. Instantly, Charles broke free of Julian, thrust her behind him, and reached for his nonexistent sword. The road was bare as were most of the trees beside it, but an evergreen stand a few feet away quivered although the wind was still.

"Who is there? Come out. We will not harm you. We are all travelers here who seek peace." Charles maintained his watchful stance, but his voice was curiously blurred, dropping down into muted accents unlike the sharper ones of the court.

Julian moved up to his side, her hand ready on her own dagger. The days when she awaited a man's protection were gone. Now she, too, could fight for those things precious to her.

The bush twitched once more, suddenly parted, and the would-be assailant stepped boldly out, hands on hips, black curls rioting from under a green cap the color of the leaves above. "This is my private pathway. What are you doing here?"

"Your pardon." Charles swept a bow, remembered himself, and rose clumsily from it. "Have we your leave to pass?"

The little girl, no more than five, considered him and lifted her eyes to Julian. "Do you want to pass, too?" Her skin was lightly touched with sun, the face tiny and impish. The black eyes seemed to hold a depth of knowledge far at variance with the young face.

Julian smiled at her and started to respond when two people crashed through the other evergreens which led up to the crest of a small hill. They ranged themselves beside the child, and it was as if a mirror reflected back woman and child. The man was in his early thirties, she a bit younger; both had the dark hair and eyes and slightly dark skin that made them appear exotic. Their clothes were not those of peasants, made as they were of bright cloth, flimsy and too cool for this time of the year. But it was not their appearances that drew Julian, nor yet the defensiveness with which they drew together. It was the wary caution that looked out at her, a look she had seen on her own face. These people were fugitives even as she and Charles.

The woman said, "Our child wanders away sometimes. She has not been pert to you?" She had the faintest of accents, and the way the little girl looked up at her made Julian wonder if they spoke this way when they were alone.

"Do you live near here?" Charles asked the seemingly innocent question, his gray eyes narrowed with concentration as he watched the child.

"No." The man almost spat the word, then turned to his family. "Come. There is no time. We have work to do."

"Wait!" The faint stirrings that had begun in Julian's mind now became certainty. If handled properly, and if she were correct, they might obtain information and a bed for the night, perhaps even learn of some remote area where they might go to ground for a time. "Do you go on to the next town, then?"

"No." This time the hostility was more evident as the man pushed the little girl ahead of him. Only the young woman looked at Julian with interest.

Julian took the chance that could destroy them. It had to be done. She had no illusions about what Brother Rob would do if he were taken, and who knew how close the soldiers were on their trail. Charles, shrugging, had turned away and was gathering up the reins of the horses. Nothing could disguise that bearing, that carved profile, just as the distinctive color of her eyes could not be hidden.

"The Romany are not the only ones who flee in these days. We seek only a quiet place to rest. The danger is not from us but from those who rule."

The others stood very still, the man's face growing darker as the woman moved closer to him. He fingered his knife and Julian thought, belatedly, that once again they must fight for their lives.

CHAPTER THIRTY-NINE

The small bird sounded his one-note call over and over. Julian was acutely conscious of the dog-shaped cloud merging with another one on the horizon. Her right foot was numb from the puddle of water she had inadvertently stepped in moments before. Charles came to grip her arm, his fingers closing on the very bone. A cow bawled in the distance, and a tiny green lizard flicked over a stone beside the child who knelt to touch it.

The woman spoke to Julian in a rush of strange syllables, her brows lifted in a question. Julian shook her head as the woman stared assessingly at her, then subjected Charles to the same scrutiny. Elspeth had often complained of beggars and Egyptians in the grounds of Redeswan, but Julian had never been allowed near them; later persecutions had made the household more sympathetic toward those who fled.

"Why do you tell us your secret?" The woman put her hand on the man's, and he let it fall from the knife.

"You are Romany. You know the ways of hiding." Julian was surprised that her voice did not shake. "We are all fugitive, are we not?"

"Come with us for now. You shall share our food and tell us your tale." She smiled, and the black eyes lit up. "You are bold and that is amusing."

Charles expelled his breath with an audible sound. The dark man grunted, jerked his head at them, and strode away toward the distant hill, the child at his heels. The very set of his back was one of resistance.

The woman said, "I am Armita, that is my husband, Yarno, and our daughter, Tasa."

"Alison and Ned." Julian spoke quickly before Charles could. The simple tale that had come to her would have to suffice.

"Come." Armita began to walk swiftly ahead.

Charles held Julian back for an instant and looked into her face, his gray eyes serious. "Boldly done. I hope it is wise. Those who seek us would do anything to get us back, pierce any guise, take any revenge."

Julian wondered if the old Charles Varland would have cared for the fate of others. Had she considered that, or had she thought only of the fact that they two were distinctive in appearance and known to be good at disguise? "We can give each other protection in a group." She took his hand then, and they followed Armita.

A temporary shelter was built into the side of the hill and was bordered with rocks, concealed with brush and cloth nearly the color of the ground. Unless one looked for it, the gaze would pass completely over. Now, however, a carefully tended fire burned in a niche close by, and delicious smells rose from a suspended pot. A bearded man of anywhere from forty to sixty whispered with Yarno, who indicated him as "my uncle, Sedril." Sedril glared and said nothing.

As they sat over stew and water, Julian spoke while Charles nodded encouragement. They had been betrothed since youth, loving each other always. She had gone to work in a great house in the northern part of England while he went with Philip's armies. The master took liberties with her, then dismissed her in anger with no pay. Her family was dead, there was nowhere to turn, and she was then accused of theft, a hanging offense. Luckily, Ned deserted the army and returned to help her escape. Both were sought and had had some difficult escapes. Ned, she added, had noble blood. The wrong side of the blanket, of course, but still there. Their natural pride had to be explained in some manner. They were weary and needed something of safety.

Armita was spokesman for the group, and her soft voice seemed the catalogue of Mary's reign to Julian as she said, "Once we were a proud tribe, traveling in many lands. One branch came here and settled as much as we ever do, harming no one by holding to our ancient ways. We lived apart and wandered in the summer, returning in the winter to restore ourselves. The soldiers came early one morning last fall and fell upon us in the name of their Christian God and the queen. Few escaped, and now we wander from one place to another, barely pausing and suspicious of all."

"We are grateful for this shelter," Julian told them.

"The honor is ours." Sedril spoke for the first time. "The tradition is ours and the words spoken. Welcome."

Charles said, "How can we repay your hospitality, this brief respite from fear? We are more than grateful."

Sedril laughed, and the sound was good to hear. "Take the shelter this night, you and the woman of your flesh. We will speak in the morning. I have a plan."

Julian felt her face flame in the dim light of the fire. Betrothal was counted as marriage and they had lain together many times, but this was before others and somehow different. She could not protest, nor did she really want to. The flames were reflected in the gray eyes opposite her, and her flesh longed for his.

Later she waited for Charles, her body newly sponged and anointed with aromatic herbs, her hair a gleaming coppery mass down her slender back. The one candle gave off enough light to show the arranged pallets also scattered with herbs. She lay there, a soft garment of thin yellow cloth covering her from breasts to thighs, the pink tips of the nipples thrusting up. For the first time in a long while Julian was content to live in the moment and savor it, to anticipate the coming of her lover as any maid might do.

"My love, my fair one." Charles slowly divested himself of the cloak he wore over his nudity. His body was honed hard and muscular despite the months of captivity; he had often exercised as he lay still, pressing muscle against muscle, relaxing and tensing them in a struggle to remain fit and to keep from going mad. There were scars on his back, and one ran from shoulder to hip over his chest. The tapering legs, the proud column of his neck, the thrusting shaft that was lifted erect, all joined in an eagerness that could not wait.

They caught each other, clasped, and she opened to the hunger that threatened to overcome them both. There was pain, a quick igniting, an explosion. Then they lay fused but not satisfied, arms wrapped around and mouths together, waiting for the power that had ever been between them, that which had first lured and then taken and now was a part of the growing richness of their relationship.

The fire came again and was as quickly assuaged. Neither of them could forget the times they had been torn, both by themselves and the forces of circumstance, but this was not the time for words. Their bodies spoke of loss and loneliness, the deep yearning that may go forever unsatisfied, and the ultimate departure of all flesh. In sensation, deep-locked kisses, and thrustings they pushed away the inevitable.

When the joy came Julian was ready. Her hands remembered the secret places of the beloved body, her mouth recalled the taste of his manhood and the power of it on her tongue. This time she welcomed him into her mouth, drawing on him with eager lips, her fingers on the base of his delight. He erupted and she took it, making his juices her own, then writhing in her turn as his tongue found its way to the tiny, flaming mound and reduced her to shivering splinters of light.

His mouth took one rosy nipple and pulled on it gently while one hand rose to the other. Julian touched the stalk that had penetrated and drained her, and saw that it grew strongly in her fingers. She began to tremble as she put her fist on his chest and pushed him backward. "I will have you now." The voice might not have been her own, so soft was it, and his eyes widened as she rose to stand over him, her body bare and golden in the light. His face grew eager, some of the new lines were wiped away as his flesh arched expectantly.

Julian swayed toward him, her legs spread so that she stood over his chest and face, her long hair tumbling almost to meet the darker at her womanhood, which was pulsating with banked longing. Charles lifted both hands to pull her down, but she shook her head. The time was not ripe. She began to move as though in the first part of a luring dance. Her fingers curled and slipped down her smooth sides, then rose again above her head so that her full breasts bounced, the nipples high and hard. One foot lifted, touched his chest and drifted down his stomach. She sank so low that his tongue reached out to flick at her warmth; she paused and almost yielded to the urge to remain there and let him take her. Then she pulled back and rose to sway back and forth, hands now lifting her hair, now cupping her breasts as she bent to kiss him. His manhood rose harder, and his mouth twisted but he lay still, watching her.

Julian knelt and lowered herself onto the spike, letting it go to the fullest depth as it almost split her. Impaled and impaling she rose to the very end of it and came down again and yet again. Legs, arms, and body melted over

Charles as she felt herself pulled by the storm that would take them both and over which neither had any control. Jagged flashes came before her eyes and she stiffened, then rose into brilliant light as sweat poured over her. Charles caught her to him, and his mouth locked with hers, their tongues going deep. Twined together they entered into the flames and rose as the phoenix.

Later when a brief sleep had refreshed them, Charles sat up and drew Julian onto his lap while he teased and tantalized her breasts, caressed her mouth with brief kisses, and finally let his fingers drift lower to send little chills over her stomach and lead the way for the conflagration that was to come. In her turn she teased his manhood with her soft mouth, touching the tiny lips there until Charles clutched her waist for sheer hunger and both implored her to continue and to stop. They joined themselves together in exploratory fashion, her legs beyond his hips, and began to move slowly at first as they looked into each other's eyes and tried to hold back the time of rising. It could not be done, and once again that magic that was peculiarly their own raised and tossed and burned. Julian felt that she could not get enough of him, that some part of them remained unjoined, and they clung together so tightly that neither could move. Their mouths locked, and he firmly remained in the depths of her body that refused to relinquish him—joyous prisoners of each other.

Julian woke once in what must have been the deepest reaches of the night. The candle had gone out, but she could see the aquiline nose, the patrician lines of his profile as he slept on his back, open and vulnerable to her. She reached out to touch the long scar, then put her lips to it in the shuddering realization of how close they had come to death. He did not wake, but the sound of her name sighed across the darkness, and then he was still. She slipped closer to him and drew the covers over them both. Instinctively he fit his body to hers and sighed once more. "Love, dear love." Was it her name or another's? It did not matter, for this time and this moment they were together in passion and tenderness; that was all and enough.

In the gray light of dawn Julian and Charles met again

in a union of lips, hands, and flesh so slow and heart-
breakingly tender that she thought she would remember it
all her life. Their mouths met, cherished, drew apart and
merged again as their hands touched and stroked. The final coupling was gentle and warm, a blessed thing that
made her understand the true meaning of the words that
had previously been only that, "one flesh."

When they moved apart, she said, "I love you, Charles.
I always will." Bare as her flesh was her heart before him,
her natural guard down in this time like no other.

He touched her lips with one finger and whispered, "I
should have met you long ago, Julian. Can you believe
that?" His eyes spoke of love, but he would not say the
words that might bind him.

"Aye." He had said them once in his extremity. In time
he would say them again and freely. "I believe you, dear
lord."

They curled close again; this time sleep was deep and
profound.

Julian had no idea of the time when she came languidly
awake, stretched so that all the joints of her body seemed
fluid, and rolled over to lie on her back, thinking of the
enchanting things they had done in the past hours. How
their bodies had ignited each other! Was this how it was
for those who truly loved? Her lips curved into a smile,
and she stretched again.

"You are a purring cat, a tawny lioness, a lazy wench. I
have been up these hours." Charles entered the shelter and
stood smiling down at her, his eyes alight as she had not
seen in a long time. "Well, maybe just an hour. Get up,
there is stew for breakfast."

"A delicacy I love. What have you been doing?" She
drew the coverlet over her bare body and saw his gaze
flicker with the beginning of the heat. At the same time
she realized how hungry she was. They must be on the
road as soon as possible, but the night had been a dream,
a fantasy. She smiled up at him and welcomed the brilliant
one he returned to her.

He sat down on the edge of the pallet, his expression
now grave. "I have been talking to Sedril. Soon it will be

time for their spring and summer wanderings; they have lost many of their kin in that surprise raid and do not wish to return. He invites us to join them and become part of their group. He did not say so, but I think any suspicion might be allayed by the presence of two who are so obviously of the born English." His lips quirked wryly. "I think we must do it for our safety, but I said that I must consult you."

It was one answer, Julian knew, and they would be far less recognizable in company. She could have hoped for no more, and she knew that Sedril was keeping the code of the gypsies. Charles knew it, too.

"I can imagine what Sedril thinks of a man who thinks that he must consult a woman!" They both laughed, and her hand went out to cover his. "Agree and offer them our heartfelt thanks. How bitter it must be for all who are persecuted, and the way things are today, anyone is likely to be."

He shifted uneasily and said, "He told me another thing. All the country must know for certain what has been rumored for months. There was no labor, only a great convulsion, and the queen sustained a fever which passed. She is not with child for all that her stomach is distended. One of the physicians said so and barely escaped with his life; further, he said that her days were numbered. England will at least escape the fearful danger of a Catholic heir. The queen has been said to be in ill health before and has lived on. I must find out what is going on and how stands the cause of the princess." The new peace had departed from his brow, which was furrowed with concentration.

Julian caught desperately for the happiness that was just born. "We will find out in our travels, Charles, for much information can be picked up in the towns and inns. Are not gypsies welcome in many places simply for the mirth they bring? And safe enough so long as they move quickly about?"

He slapped his hands together and rose, his expression lightening. "I am sure you are right. Dress quickly, wench, the stew awaits!" He strode from the shelter, leaving her to search for her gown.

The days that followed were those that Julian was ever afterward to call the days of the kingfisher, a halcyon time of drifting securely on the waves of a quiet sea. The first tentative spring winds opened and hardy buds of trees, and grass showed green by the roadsides. The noons were now a warm gold, the span of hours longer before the fragrant, chilly nights set in. Flowers showed in the hedges, and sometimes they saw a tree crowned in shimmering leaves as if to anticipate all that April and an English spring could bring. Julian's heart opened out to the beauty around her and to the love that grew with each passing moment.

They kept to the forest paths, venturing down into a hamlet only once. No one paid them any heed, but it was not a comfortable feeling for all that they tried to act as if they were friends or relatives traveling together. The others rolled in cloaks and slept outside at night. Charles grew adept at constructing a shelter of sorts for himself and Julian, and they remained apart from their friends, taking their pleasure of each other in the scented nights until they were exhausted.

Charles talked no more of state affairs or the princess he served. Julian thought only now and then of the queen, who was near to losing the little she had. For now they two were man and woman in the spring world that might have been created for them alone.

In this time, too, they talked as they had in the cave of poetry and philosophy and the ways of history, of themselves and their childhoods, of their delights and hurts. Charles came to speak of Beth naturally to Julian, and she, for her own part, found that much of the degradation she had felt by association with George Attenwood was leaving her. As time passed she even mourned the death of such a talent to Charles and found that he understood that, too. But of the future and what it might hold they did not speak.

They lay in their bower one night after love had had its bright sway, Julian holding Charles in her arms, his head on her breast, both shivering in anticipation of the thrustings and hunger to come, and he said so softly that she had to bend closer to hear, "I think the gods are jealous, lady mine. They are truer than the God of the present faith, for man has ever worshiped himself."

"Do not speak so!" She stopped his cynical mouth with her own and, as his hands rose to caress her breasts, knew that she feared the inevitable end of the days of the kingfisher.

CHAPTER FORTY

Julian and Charles sat side by side in the early summer sun on the outdoor benches of the tavern which had a great deal of custom even so early in the morning. Their informant had plainly been there all night and was quick to respond to Julian's remark about the scent. Now they looked sickly at each other and away. This was no place to visit later with the gypsies, mumming and juggling, singing a fine tune for coins as they had done so successfully in the past months.

The scent of burned flesh still hung over the marketplace at Edington although the tailor had gone to his death over a week ago, his neighbors standing by while the soldiers held them at bay. "Grew up here he did, had three sons and all in the armies of Philip, whom God destroy. He wouldn't have truck with the mass or the saints and said so openly. Called it heresy, talked as we all do and now . . . how did they know? Why did it happen to him?" The little man's beard almost drooped in his beer.

"After it was over and the soldiers ready to leave with the priest, that black scarecrow, they saw the pictures of the queen as a harlot and a witch that somebody put up. Tore 'em down, they did, and threatened to be back." He drank deeply, tears springing to his eyes.

The burly man who had furnished their ale was coming up now and murmuring to the little man. They caught a few words. ". . . home and sleep . . . not safe . . . quiet . . ." Moments later he staggered away, muttering to himself and wiping his beard. The host shrugged and said, "Drinks all the time and has for years. It'll kill him one day." The dark eyes sharpened. "Going far?"

Charles looked at Julian, who lowered her eyes and glanced away in the ruse they always used in these forays. He grinned and said, "Pilgrimage to Salisbury. Our priest suggested it since we want a boy. Two girls in the house already is enough, I say." Julian jerked at his sleeve. "Just one more ale, sir."

The host relaxed. "These are hard times, but a man must have a son." He moved away with only one backward glance. No business of his, of course, but why would a woman let her skin get so dark from the sun? Walking a great deal, no doubt.

Julian's flesh prickled; even the villages were dangerous, and no person was safe. They had encountered this sort of thing before, the kind of denouncing that neighbor did to neighbor under the sanction of religion. Hunger was rampant in the land and beggars multiplied despite the fair weather and warmth. Tax collectors were everywhere and pitched battles were not uncommon. Bitterness, hatred, and anger flourished; the stranger was often unsafe unless he were very careful. England was bleeding to death on the altar of Philip's wars and the queen's growing despair coupled with her determination to punish those who would not turn to the Catholic fold.

"Julian, the time is even more ripe for revolt if we are to have a country left. Those who live must take the responsibility." Charles paced beside her as they took the road out of the dangerous town, the one they had hoped would provide their supper that night. Now all that mattered was leaving as soon as possible. "I must do something or I cannot live with myself."

"What can you do? One man?" She stretched out her hand to him, sighing at the brownness of it. The berry juice Armita applied to render her a country woman worked only too well; she might never be white again. "Sedril's kinsman we met that time said that soldiers frequent Cornwall and all is quiet."

"Nonetheless, I should go. There are meeting places and crannies that no one who had not lived there could ever find." He swung her hand absently and dropped it, then turned to face her. "The thing is, Julian, I have taken pleasure in this wandering life and with you. Birds of the field with no thought for the realities of the world."

So had she. Ah, how sweet those nights and their passion. The shared laughter at her brown-tinged face atop the white body when they made love, the light dresses of red and green so easily doffed in the shade of the greenwood when they loved or swam, camaraderie with Armita and Tasa, grave friendship with Yarno and Sedril, the nights when they sat around the low fire and told tales of other times and places, the way they had put together little plays to give in the marketplaces or on the edge of the safe villages for their daily bread. So much of love and companionship in these months. Were these not the realities of the world as well? She opened her mouth to coerce him and saw again the sternness that had well nigh left his face in these seconds of memory that touched them now return.

"What will you do, Charles?" She let go because she must. For all that they shared, he still was not hers nor, she was forced to admit, could she fully commit herself to this love that was so strong. Lovers, part of her life, yes; but marriage was not for him—had he not stated it? And yet, watching Tasa and the love her parents shared, it was difficult not to dream of Redeswan or Varfair and children in his image. She had not spoken of love again to him, but their flesh hymned it in the flower-scented nights.

The gray eyes flashed against sun-bronzed skin, his teeth shone white as he smiled with no amusement. "I shall seek out the princess and tell her what goes on in this land to which she is the guardian of the future, tell her that if she will sanction an uprising with sword and token, the country will be hers before the next dawn. But if she tarries much longer there will be only destruction, and England will be a province of Spain even more than she is now. The queen has been rumored dying so often that she may live on for years while our people suffer."

Julian felt the familiar pang at the thought of the queen, who had after all been kind to her and hers in the days of bitterness. She stood very still in the dusty track with the sun beating down on her unprotected head. Two horsemen swerved around them to kick up a fine screen of dust. Several women worked in the field opposite, the sound of their chatter mingling with the cries of children at play. Her instinct for danger rose up clearly and with it anger that he would jeopardize himself again.

"They say that she is kept secluded, almost a prisoner. How could you manage it? What makes you think she would listen to you? She is cautious and careful, the rumors say. Charles, let it go, I pray you."

"I must do my duty as I see it. She cannot really know what is going on." He began walking so swiftly that she had to rush to keep up with him.

"She can lose her life if the attempt fails." She did not add that Charles Varland would surely die also.

He stopped and faced her earnestly. "How can I make you see what Elizabeth Tudor means to this country, Julian? Young King Edward was reared a fanatical Protestant, and his advisors ruled that way in his name. You suffered, you should know. Mary is just as determined to bring England back to the Catholic faith by whatever means. We are torn apart, fighting a losing war, our Calais bastion gone, the Inquisition a possibility if Philip claims this throne, persecution on every side, and people killed for the slightest wrong word. No person is safe, no life truly worth living. Elizabeth is Protestant but has been trained in the ways of reason. King Henry and Anne Boleyn were utterly English; their daughter will have no foreign ties. She is England's hope and there is no other.

She has survived much imprisonment and suspicion. I know that King Philip counts her shrewd and fair."

Julian smiled. "I did not know you to be so fervent for a woman, my lord."

"She is our last hope." Charles sighed and took Julian's hand. "You must stay with the gypsies. You will be as safe there as anywhere, and the few jewels we have saved will give you something to fall back on. Do not think me ungrateful for all that you have done, Julian, but I am a peer of this land, and I do what I must."

"You cannot go alone."

"I must." He began to walk again and she matched her stride to his.

"I go with you and I think the others will also." The decision was never in doubt as far as she was concerned, and it was the right one. Loving him as she did, she had to remain with him and fight by his side so long as fate allowed it. She would not wait meekly by, and so long as he was determined, there was a better chance of success in the company of others, especially when that company was well used to acting and ever cognizant of danger. Rulers might be the same, but love came only once to Julian Redenter.

Charles moved in front of her and looked down into her resolute face, the brilliant eyes seeming to dominate it. "But why? You have no true stake in this."

She spoke the simple truth. "The wise woman said we were bound together, Charles, and it seems to be so. I care for you and wish you well. If you are successful, the new queen will be grateful."

"I must think on it." He said no more, and now they walked apart.

Later, Julian told Armita what had happened in the village and watched the smooth face grow somber. "I think we will go into the Welsh country in the winter as others of our people have done. There is no safety in this land. Will you come with us, you and Ned?"

Julian hung the daisy chain she had been making for Tasa around the child's neck and returned the hug with full measure. It seemed a kind of betrayal of these people

to offer them to Charles as she had. Once again the anger
shook her. Alive and free in the summer sweetness, the
crags of the Welshland waiting, friendship and the warmth
of human closeness—not her world of books, inner vistas,
and the pride of Redenters, but a new life that was now
curiously beckoning.

"It may well be that I will come with you if I am truly
welcome." The hands playing with Tasa's dark curls shook
suddenly, and the little girl froze in her lap.

Armita said, "You are welcome always, dear sister.
Alone or with Ned." It was like her that she said no more,
but began to talk of the rabbits on which they would dine
and the fresh berries she and Tasa picked while they
waited.

Julian knew, as perhaps she had always known, that the
gypsies had not wholly believed their story and yet had accepted them. It was time for honesty. Her old fear of
commitment strengthened her resolve to free herself of this
drugging passion that would ruin her as it had her mother
and her queen.

That night she put on one of the long soft gowns that
Armita still carried in memory of the days when it was
safer to be a gypsy and had loaned to Julian. This one was
the pale green of the foaming sea at dawn. A belt of sil-
vered cord went with it, and there were dangling earrings
which might have contained some fragments of silver. The
chestnut hair was swept high over her temples and
tumbled down her back in a profusion of softness. The
sleeves of the gown came over her elbows and fell in
points to her fingertips. She had only the tiny mirror of
polished steel to tell her that she was fair, but all her
woman's instincts knew it.

The woman of another was sacrosanct, but the brief
flicker in the men's eyes told Julian much. Only Charles
did not react; he saw Julian Redenter, whose family had
been one of England's bulwarks in past times and who
now challenged him to speak or that she would. He himself wore the cloth of coarse weave in brown that attracted
little attention in their wanderings, but as he tilted his
head up at her from his place at the banked fire, he had

never been more the noble lord. Even his bearing was different. Her flesh trembled at the sight of him, and her mind wept that their days together were numbered.

His voice pulled her back as he said, "My friends, there is something of which we must speak. Listen, I pray you, and do not judge us too harshly. . . ."

As the tale began Armita's eyes went to Julian, and the girl nodded. The gypsy's face was otherwise expressionless and shuttered. Was this hope of sanctuary to be shut out as well because of the lies it had been necessary to tell?

The moon dipped down, an owl called from the depths of the greenwood, and the fresh scents of deep night grew as Charles spoke, telling the bare facts of his life and that of Julian's. He put no rhetoric, no golden spangles into it but told of a man and woman, their consciences and the forces of destiny over which they had no control, and finally of his belief that a person must do what he or she could, however little, to accomplish what was thought to be right. "It can be no other way for me, no other path. We want simply to live in peace and follow our lives to the end without being torn apart for beliefs of any sort. This affects us all, and I believe the Princess Elizabeth to be strong enough to do something about it."

He let his voice die away, and the only sound was the breeze rustling in the branches to stir a sleepy bird awake. Julian looked at the others, Yarno and Sedril, their faces unreadable, Armita with her eyes downcast, and thought that Charles had been most truly eloquent this night. She who loved and slept with him had not known so much of the passion that drove him, the iron determination to duty that went beyond the demands of self and was yet most firmly rooted there. *We are not so different, he and I!* The thought rang in her head, and she knew that she could not undermine his cause with her own belief in the basic uncaring quality of rulers.

"And you, Julian, how do you feel?" It was the usually silent Yarno, who used her true name in the same easy way he had used her false one.

"It is dangerous, but if the plan succeeds we can claim help from the princess when she rules, and I do not think she would forget those who alerted her to the true condition of the country. We are in flight now and can be so again. I stand with Charles in this." She would not soon forget the blaze of gratitude in the look he turned on her there in the flickering light where destiny was met. "We ask your help if you will give it, and we understand if you cannot."

"We will think on it. . . ." Sedril started to rise, then sank back as Armita spoke sharply in the Romany language.

Seconds later Armita said in English, "I speak for us all to our friends. We, too, have been persecuted in these last years for no more than being born what we are. Our kinsmen recently dead and we flying before the soldiers. We will help in this because we must do something. Something." The word hung on the air like a drawn sword.

Charles reached out his hand and clasped hers. Yarno and Sedril put theirs down as well and Julian capped them all. Sedril said, "To the princess of England!" "Whom God assoil!" Charles breathed the words fervently and so the quest was begun.

They were drained of words and emotion as they lay on the cloaks under a flowering bush an hour later. The air was so warm, it seemed almost liquid to Julian's skin, and the sweet scents wrapped her in honey. Charles held her to him, but he had not invoked their special magic and she did not seek it. For this little moment the tenderness was paramount; both were thankful for it.

His lips found her shoulder and he whispered, "Julian, lady mine, I am glad that you are with me in this." ·

Because without you my life will be dull and devoid of meaning. Such words were not for the pride of Julian Redenter. Hunger surged up in her suddenly. She wanted all that she could have, because life might not extend beyond the next breath. "Love me, Charles, take me. Let me have you." She spoke the words in such an uprush of passion that his manhood enlarged strongly against her bare legs. Her hands found it quickly and began to stroke.

Their nest under the bush was so secure that Julian felt no compunction about giving way to the urgency that infected both Charles and herself. It was as if they lay in a separate world of flowers and softness, away from the terrors of which they had spoken shortly before. Now she turned on her side in accordance with his hands, her smooth buttocks against his skin. He held her firmly while his shaft glided deep into the corridor of her womanhood. One hand touched the quivering mound and ignited it so that she seemed to melt into one great fiery glow of molten liquid. She moaned faintly as the longing that seemed part of this power wound through her heart and mind. Charles whispered her name over and over as if it were a litany as she writhed in his grip while the thrusting continued until she was filled with it, and the great sea flowed upward into a crashing wave.

When she mounted him and began to touch the collapsed spear of his flesh, Charles said, "Ah, you have drained me, lovely one. I am the prisoner of your flesh." His smile flickered white in the darkness, and he saw the white flowers of the bush behind her chestnut head. One hand rose to touch the bobbing breasts that bore the marks of his hands in the time just past. The nipples were tiny roses on the white of her skin.

"Is it so, my lord? Then as my prisoner, I command that you rise, for I see that you are drained no longer." Her mouth went forward and began to draw on the uplifted stalk, softly at first and then harder as she demanded with tongue and hands. Charles quivered all over his muscular body and felt the dew drench of sweat on her back.

Julian leaned away from him and said, "Once more, once more. Let me feel you inside me."

Inflamed, he caught at her, lifted her buttocks and poised them above him, then gently drew her down on him but holding her away so that they could look into each other's faces at the same time that the strokes progressed. They saw the stamp of passion, the eagerness beyond the body, and that ineffable something that floated out of reach for all the many ways they sought it. Julian felt him go deeper in her to penetrate crevices yet unknown and loose the rivers that flowed molten hot to the mountain whose slopes were eternal fire. He withdrew to the very tip, then pulled her to him as he hammered home one final thrust that sent them both down into the mountain's core. Their voices called together in one lost cry before everything except sensation lost meaning and they twined into one being.

Charles was gone when Julian awoke in the high heat of the summer morning to find the thin gown spread over her, a heady bouquet of field roses in pink and white placed at her head, and near them a horn cup filled with ale along with a joint of the rabbit from the night before. She smiled at the love offerings, remembering the glory of the night just past. Then she drew one of the headiest of the roses to her as she breathed in the sweetness of it. Love's own flower, said the romances. The sun caressed her smooth limbs and turned her skin to milky glory where the berry stain did not reach. Suddenly, passionately, Julian was voicing the prayer to whatever gods might be listening.

"Let me bear his child. Give me that to take into the Welsh lands!"

CHAPTER FORTY-ONE

"She walks this way nearly ever day when the weather is fine. Her attendants often are bidden to remain well behind her. We have only to watch and wait without presenting ourselves as out of the ordinary." Charles paced up and down the little trail, then pulled aside a leafy branch to reveal a wide meadow which gave onto an oak forest. He waved a hand. "Beyond is the palace of Hatfield."

Even in conversation among themselves they had come to refer to the Princess Elizabeth as "the lady." Prying ears were everywhere and matters continued to grow worse with burnings, disease, and talk of rebellion. In the month and more since their decision was taken, the party had crossed a once populous and fertile section of the kingdom to come to this retreat some few miles from London and wherever they went men prayed for the coming of the new regime.

"Tomorrow will be the first day. Let us hope that we are soon successful." Sedril spoke the words almost hesitantly. "I sense a great unhealth abroad in this land and yearn for the mountains."

Julian and Armita exchanged glances over Tasa's small head. The child was their focal point and must not be excited. Armita said now, "We must go and practice our game, sweeting. Are you ready?"

They had taken shelter in an abandoned hunting lodge which was probably part of the grounds of the old palace but never used, possibly since the early days of Great Harry himself. There were winding passages and odd corners aplenty, but mostly they kept close together in the several rooms that at one time had been the servants' quarters. Charles and Yarno spied the land out well before sanctioning the move, and now they seldom left it except to verify that all practices of the lady remained the same.

Under the urgency to implement the plan, Charles and Julian no longer made love with the passionate urgency they once had taken. Now they came together in hunger and slept wound in each other's arms, but often one or the other would rise to walk out under the trees in the summer fragrance and return unable to sleep. It seemed to Julian that she loved Charles more each day and that each minute took him farther away from her. If the rebellion did come, he would be in the forefront of it and would probably be killed, such would be the revenge of the jealous gods.

One day it rained. Another day the entourage of the

princess was surrounded by the black figures of priests. Still another she walked with a tall soldier and one serving maid. Then it rained again. Julian was never close enough to see more than a tall, thin, straight figure with flying red hair that was sometimes severely confined, but it seemed strange to think that on such fragility depended the hopes of England and, more important to Julian, those of Charles. The rain continued.

Their nerves grew taut and they slept less. The lines in Charles's face grew deeper, and Julian found herself wanting to scream at some of the antics of Tasa. Even the phlegmatic Sedril muttered Romany curses under his breath and spat out the never ending stew they dared cook only in deepest night for fear of the smoke being seen.

Then on a morning when the air was scented with the smell of flowers and the sky was new washed, birds darting high in an ecstasy of movement and breezes shaking droplets from the leaves, they saw the girl running across the meadow and heard her high spiraling laughter as she waved several well-cloaked people back. "It is now." Charles whispered the words to Julian, and she returned the pressure of his hand. Armita kissed Tasa and urged her forward a little. Sedril and Yarno sank down more deeply in the bushes.

Tasa ran out into the flower-starred meadow, her slim fingers grasping after an errant butterfly and pausing to touch a late rose vine that trailed along the ground. Armita stayed watchfully in the shadow of a small oak while Julian went forward as if intent on capturing the child before she went too far. Obedient to her instructions, Tasa pulled off one of the hedge roses and headed straight for the girl, who was very close now.

The piping child's voice lifted on the warm air. "I have a flower just picked for you. Will you take it?"

The red-haired young woman wore a simple brown gown, and her head was bare. Julian saw that her skin was milk-white, almost translucent, her nose high-bridged, the chin pointed and cleanly cut. She had the same light brows of her sister, Mary, and her eyes were a curious mixture of blue and black that seemed to bore through Julian as she approached.

"Tasa, Tasa, come here, What will the lady think?" Julian was surprised that her voice did not shake and was thankful that the child learned quickly.

"Take my rose, pretty lady." Tasa extended the flower again, and Elizabeth took it. Julian saw that her hands were truly beautiful, long-fingered and brilliantly white, bare of rings. She held the flower so that it showed to best advantage on them, then lifted those strange eyes and looked at them both.

Her voice was curiously deep for so slight a girl, and it woke strange memories in Julian. Just so had Mary Tudor sounded when she was kind.

"I like your symbolism and your compliment, my little one. Do you and your fair mother like this lovely day? I suppose you have been mewed up by the rain?"

"Where are you, Alison? Come here, you know that the park is not for the likes of us!" Charles, hat pulled low, shoulders slumped, and wearing his peasant garb of gray cloth, approached them, the very picture of a common man looking for his wife and child.

Julian and Tasa, in order to catch and hold the eyes of the princess, wore identical gowns of wild rose color with matching bodices. Julian's hair flamed over her shoulders and there was a white ribbon in it. Tasa's curls shone brilliantly black and her small curved lips were triumphant at the important part she had had to play.

They heard a call from several people advancing to attend the princess, and she lifted a hand to wave at them. The moment was upon them. Julian said, "Madam the Princess, we are harmless folk who would beg you to listen to us for the space of a very few minutes. Grant us that, I pray!"

Elizabeth looked at the girl and her lisp twisted downward. "I have no power. That is in London."

"Only listen. We mean you no harm."

Henry VIII's daughter laughed at that, and her arm went backward to halt the approach of her servants. "Hold, good people, I will chat with these country folk for a moment." She was instantly obeyed. Then she turned back to Julian. "What is it that you think I can remedy?" There was a magnetism about her that reached out and lured. Julian felt as if the sun were already blazing down on them.

Charles was at them now, kneeling in the correct court fashion, hat in his hand. Horrified, Julian remembered that she had forgotten the curtsy that was required before royalty, she a lady-in-waiting to the queen! She sank down in her turn and heard Charles begin.

"Forgive us, Lady Princess, it was the only way to approach you." His low impassioned words began, and none could have doubted him true servant of the realm. Only Charles Varland could have crowded so much into the few sentences he accomplished before Tasa started running toward the end of the meadow where the servants stood. Her discipline had been forgotten in the excitement of the moment. Julian dashed after her, caught up the wriggling little body, and made her way back to the princess and Charles.

He was saying, "But if you would let me explain further! The time is so very right. . . ."

"I will never condone treason or rebellion against the lawful ruler! What should I expect in my own time if that ever comes? I am not even considered heir to the throne, and my sister may yet bear her own. Get you from me!" The low, slicing tone did not alter the casual stance of the princess.

Julian had never seen Charles lose the icy authority that was an integral part of his bearing though at times it was eclipsed by a warm humanity or tenderness. Now he slumped as if wounded, and his face was white under the covering stains. She could not bear it. Words rushed up. "English people die daily, madam, in persecution and for chance words. The queen is known to be ill, and many fear for her reason. We speak truly to you. Hesitate and the country may be lost."

Elizabeth gave a high, quick laugh which Julian recognized to have tones of hysteria. "You speak so for love of your man. It is treason."

"It is not treason to wish to live and be happy. What kind of lives do any of us have while the flames consume all who go against the ways of your sister and her husband? You are the only one to help." Charles seemed to wring the words from his heart.

The strange eyes that could be so like Mary Tudor's blazed on them both. "I saw only peasants this day. Obey Mary the Queen as you are bound to do. You may report that I so spoke, that I have no disloyalty toward my rulers. This is not the first attempt; it will not be the last. But then you know all that. Go."

Charles seemed not to hear her. "Come, Alison, our time is wasted. She will dare nothing." He did not trouble to bend the knee but turned and walked away, his back very straight.

Horrified, Julian looked again at the princess and saw that she was paler than ever, the blue veins shining against the translucency of her skin. Understanding caught at her then, and she whispered, "Madam, we are your true servants. . . ."

Elizabeth said, "God deliver me, I have known many such." The husky voice went deeper. "I shall pray for our country as is both meet and proper." Then she went running toward her people, laughing and waving the flower in her white hand.

Back at the oak Charles was saying, ". . . a failure, nothing. I have served a chimera. What is left? Let us go from this place before the guards come in pursuit of traitors."

Julian cried, "She is a prisoner in all but name. Did you not hear? She thinks we are sent to trap her into giving away her ambition. Charles, she but dissembles as we did while held captive. It could be her death warrant, a return to the Tower, if she were proven to be seeking the throne before her time. That is why she spoke so."

"What is that to me? The princess I thought I served would dare much for this land as we have done. Now I care no longer what she is!"

Julian looked out at the meadow where the group was just vanishing into the oak park where the great trees lifted

into the early sky. The sun caught the red hair of the
princess and made it flame, then she was gone and the
morning was the dimmer. She felt emptied of all emotion.
They had planned this day for so long, and now there was
nothing. The despair that has been the bane of philoso-
pher and common folk alike took her and went with them
all as they fled from Hatfield Park.

Charles was as a man maddened in the next few days.
He was physically with them but mentally apart; he said
little, but the pace he kept was furious and anger blazed
from all his actions. When they halted for the day he
would walk on and return late to fling himself down away
from them all. Julian had tried reason, comforting, even
anger, but he merely looked through her. His pain was evident, but he was not such a one to reveal himself as he
had done before the princess.

"The wound will heal, but you must let it be." Armita
spoke the words that should have given Julian some
measure of consolation, but it was not so.

"He has always been wounded; I thought it healed, at
least in part, by the caring we have shared. Now I know
better."

"There is another thing." Armita straightened the ker-
chief she wore over her black hair and watched Julian
carefully. "Yarno and Sedril both want to go on to the
Welsh lands before the weather starts to turn. We have
tried and failed to change anything. Now life must be
lived again."

Julian knew what she was saying, but she had only intended to go with the gypsies if Charles raised the
standard of rebellion. The wanderings of the summer, the
fierce lovings in the greenwood, the laughter and camaraderie they all shared, this could not last in the blasts of the
winter that all felt would be severe. She was torn anew
and wondered what to say to Charles.

The next day he said it for her. She was wearing the
pink gown of the meadow and had gone down by the
stream where they were encamped to fetch water but
paused to stare into its swirling depths. The wind blew her
loose hair over her shoulders and added a shower of yel-

lowing leaves to the water. She sighed and turned to see Charles standing, cold and remote, just behind her.

"I have come to say farewell to you, madam. I understand that you mean to go with our friends into the Welsh country. It may be the wisest thing to do. You have the coins, the few jewels. Who knows what will happen in time? I wish you well." He spoke as to a casual friend, little better than stranger.

"Where are you going? Can you leave so coldly, Charles?" The fierce spurting anger rose in her as it always did with him, generally the precursor to passion. This icy man had no memory of warm flesh and tender words, shared laughter under a scented bush.

"I am for the Continent, madam, and whatever army will have me. In plain words, a mercenary is welcome everywhere. Let England settle its own battles. You were certainly right there. By my own foolishness I lost Varfair and destroyed the good offices of a peer of the realm. Those who hire my sword will not be squeamish, nor shall I." The smile that spread over the lower part of his face was not a pleasant one; it was the smile of the wolf ready to rend and tear.

Did he care so little for her that he would let her go without a word of caring? After all that they had endured and been to each other? By all the gods, it should not be! She knew in some obscure way that he sought his own death, that the rejection by the woman for whom he had believed himself fighting was the final push in something that had begun with the refusal of the grandmother to let him wed Beth and which had taken firmer hold with her death. He must have a cause, this man of ideals; his own wish was never enough. Now, without a pivot, he would take the foreign sword and welcome it, never knowing but flight. He had put England in Beth's place, loved her, and been rejected. What had she, Julian Redenter, stood for in his mind?

Needed a cause, did he, by the manifold wounds of Christ she would give him one! "If that is your wish, I would not dissuade you. However, I cannot go to the mountains. My mother had a difficult time, and I rather fancy that I shall as well, for I am narrow." She lifted limpid eyes to his and waited. Everything hung on his reaction now. Perhaps he did not even care enough to have one.

Not for nothing had Charles carried in his mind that image of Beth and her extremity all the years. His face went bone-white under the bronze, and the wind stirred his dark hair so that it stood up like a crest. "You are saying . . . ? What are you saying? Now you say it?"

Go carefully. "I am saying to the father of my child that I cannot winter in the mountains of Wales. That difficult births are well known in my family. That he will be born in the spring."

They were both very quiet as they looked at each other. Not far away Tasa was playing, her voice coming to them high and shrill over the lapping of the water. Another shower of leaves drifted past their faces, and the sun rested gently on Julian's shoulders. Beyond the trees a heavy cloud presaged rain.

"You are certain?" The odd, croaking voice was unlike the self-assured tones of Charles Varland. "Your flux, well, you are certain?" He stopped and the coldness, that deadly thing, was fading. Emotion other than anger and disdain was coming to the surface.

"A woman knows these things, Charles. And I will say to you that while Julian Redenter may hold no claim on you or your affection, our child has the first and deserves the second. I am strong, of course, but I remember my mother's tales in the days of her illness. She wanted a son for the line so very much!" The old resentment stirred in her voice, causing Charles to watch her closely. "Must I ask it? Will you not give?"

"We have suffered much, Julian. With things the way they are I can offer you nothing but my presence, and that I give right willingly for what it is worth. We will stay in England this winter, hide away as best we can, and after the babe is born we will go to France or the Low Countries. I may still have some friendships I can call upon there so that you and the child will be safe. Then I will go to the wars." He put both hands on her shoulders. "I wish you were not with child, but since you are, there is no more to be said."

All neatly planned in the space of a few sentences! Everything neatly arranged and prepared as if he had thought long on it! Faith, if she were but a man! But he had not flung her away in anger or cried her harlot, had he? He did not offer to wed her, but he had warned her of that long ago. All that she had hoped to accomplish was done, so why did she want to fling herself to the ground and weep?

"I am grateful for your consideration, sir." She pushed back the tumbling hair with fingers that suddenly shook. "We shall try not to delay you unduly in your haste to make war."

"You like it no more than I, I know. It is done and I am here. Now, do not weep, it is bad for you. Come along and I will find some wine for you." He was speaking normally now, and the mask of anger with which he had faced them all in the past days had faded.

"Go, I will be along in a few minutes." She waved her hands at him as if in agitation and finally he obeyed, his tall form vanishing in the leaves.

Her time was bought and won. She would not think of the form retribution would take. Later, when Charles truly did go to war, he would at least be more aware of the scars within himself and more able to deal with them. What of herself? Would her own scars, old and fresh alike, heal?

In these days she thought often of Sir Guy and wondered about his fate, but she dared not dwell on it. Not even with Charles in their closest moments could she have shared that fear; the burden was hers to bear.

CHAPTER FORTY-TWO

Rain lashed against the sides of the two-roomed house, and Julian heard the splattering which meant another leak. She sighed and resumed her pacing, the skirts of the old green gown snapping with the force of her movements. What was worse, she wondered wryly, to live at the peak of high anticipation or to perish of boredom? Once she had thought life with Charles Varland, arrogant lord of the realm, would give her all that she had ever wanted. Now she lived with him, yes, certainly that, but it was life with a stranger. A stranger who had touched her only twice in the weeks since August, and now it was late October. Then it had been out of need and he flown with cheap wine. Touch, grasp, and roll away, her own eyes blazing with tears. Julian could not regret what she had done, but she was facing the consequences of it now.

They had been lucky to find the ramshackle little house in the copse, set well back from the London road and not close to others. Charles, surprisingly handy for a lord, had mended as best he could, even found a girl to attend Julian now and again. The fact that she was an idiot made no real difference; she was handy and too foolish to ask questions that her harelip made difficult to frame. People did not ask questions these days in any event; they minded their own business and tried not to attract adverse attention. Each day Charles walked afield to earn what coins he could and listen to the other conflicting rumors: Spain had come in full force; the queen was better, worse, dead, fleeing; the princess has been executed, declared true heiress; largesse was proclaimed in the city. He would tell Julian some of the more preposterous ones in the flat tone he used to her nowadays, quaff the sour beer which was all they could afford, and collapse in the other room. And always his eyes returned to her stomach, the stomach that she tried to conceal by wearing her two gowns looser. What had he said only this morning?

"Your face is not swollen in the mornings. Have I not heard that women with child always have that sort of thing? And you are fortunate that you have not been ill, a comfort in these surroundings, of course." Then his eyes dropped again to her stomach.

"Women are affected differently. Always it has been so." Should she begin to be sick, then? Would that make any difference in his feelings toward her? He had banged away, but soon she would be unable to answer his questions. One thing comforted her, at least. Sickness was rife in the country, it rained a great deal, and the seas were rough. The political unrest grew worse daily, and it was not hard to imagine total anarchy. Anarchy, too, in the trampeled-down feelings of Julian and Charles. They had loved so fiercely and now only spoke civilly with an effort. She had tried, after the gypsies left vowing eternal friendship, to reach him again, but he retreated so far in himself that it was impossible. "Be assured that I will do my bounden duty, madam." The freezing quality of those words had left her to be churlish if she insisted. "None has yet questioned the honor of a Varland." After that there were only the most perfunctory words.

The devil fly away with this foolish brooding! She would go mad if she did not venture out into the world, see people if only from a distance, think about something other than love gone awry. The romances never prepared one for the aftermath; it would be amusing sometime to write a realistic romance with a bitter ending as a warning to maidens. She smiled a little—she and Charles had truly loved and nothing could take that away.

Impatiently she reached for her cloak and hood, then went out into the wet day that was not so much cold as dreary and chill. The lane was muddy, and water sluiced down her neck, but it was invigorating to be outside and not the prisoner of her own thoughts. She was reminded of another day such as this when the lean, dark-eyed man summoned her to London at the queen's pleasure. Dear Guy of Edmont! What had happened to him? There was no way to know. For that matter there was no way to know if they had ever been dangerously pursued by those in search of Charles. All the gossip they had heard gave no indication. No one would think of a lord of England living on the outskirts of the city of London and working with his hands to earn his daily bread and that of his pregnant mistress. If any safety were to be gained it would be here.

She stumbled and almost went down in the slush. Her attention was jerked into the present by a troop of horses passing on the far road. They rode hard, oblivious to the weather, and curiosity stirred in Julian. She walked on to the road, heedless of the muck that covered her thin shoes and skirts. Several people stood in a knot talking, their words plainly audible to any who might be near.

"Won't be long, I tell you, until there'll be another bonny lady on the throne." "Treason, watch out." "Ah, you're just an old woman." "Those men are surely going to see the princess." The babble swirled up, and Julian could not identify who said what. One comment rang over and over in her head. "Sick she is, dying she must be, and only a few left with her. Serves her right, the cruel witch." Someone else shushed him abruptly.

Julian came up to the speakers and forsook all caution. "How does Her Majesty? What does rumor say?" Their faces darkened, and she knew that she must protect herself. "My husband went into London yesterday and has not returned. He is given to drink and his opinions are for . . . another. I fear he may have voiced them and been taken." The wind blew her hood against her face, in part concealing it, and it took no acting ability to make her own voice high and shrill.

One of the men, fat and bearded, said largely, "Your husband sounds a man of sense in his opinions! The world

will soon know, why should you not? It is said that the
false queen lies dying in St. James's Palace, and the rightful successor to the throne, our Elizabeth, has been
acknowledged by her. There is no more reason to weep,
lady."

Julian put her hand up and found that the tears were
streaming down her face. For the queen? For the princess,
who would soon rule if gossip could be trusted? For Julian
Redenter, who walked in the pathways of bitterness as she
had in the summer's glory?

"I thank you, sirs." She hitched up her skirts and ran
rapidly across the muddy tracks. She knew what she had
to do. It made no sense; in fact it was the very height of
foolishness, but no other course was open to her.

She slammed into the house and came to a full stop before the tall figure that rose up to meet her. No
concealment was possible, for the wet cloak streamed over
her shoulders and down her back. The front of her gown
was mud-spattered and dripping. It clung to her body and
outlined it clearly.

The hard, weary voice said, "I should have known that
you lied for your own reasons. Fool that I was to believe
you. Did you think that I would marry you? Was that it?
Slut, why did you lie to me?" Charles lifted both hands as
if to strike her, the gray eyes burning into hers.

"It was the only way! You would have gone abroad and
been killed in the state of mind you were in! Believe me,
Charles, I did not do it to trap you but to save you!" She
put an arm across her flat stomach and faced him boldly.
She would not cower before him.

Charles stood very tall and erect, the rough dark clothes
he wore only accentuating the proud bearing and carved
profile. The stolidity of the past months had faded, and
now he was the epitome of the dark lord she had known
in the beginning.

"Where were you running to, madam? Trying to get
back before I returned and found you gone? I was prepar-
ing to seek you. I was worried about you, a rich jest, is it
not?" He laughed and slapped one palm into the other.

"Well, do as you wish. I am for Dover and the first ship out."

"Wait!" Quickly she recounted the gist of the gossip and added, "I am going to the palace to be with the queen when she dies. I owe her much, and the bitterness of her life is not to be believed. There will be no danger now. All look to the new queen even as you must."

Charles stared at her and began to adjust his outdoor cloak. "You are mad. I should have known it. Bedlam waits for such as you, Julian Redenter. The dying are more savage in their last throes, and Mary Tudor has been the cruelest of them all. Go ahead, all that is nothing to me. The new queen will be nothing to me." He went to the door but turned at her cry.

"Charles, I have to go! How can I explain it? She has had nothing!" Julian felt her conflicting feelings, the enormity of her own loss beginning to bear down, and began to tremble.

"I do not think that Julian Redenter has so much either. I bid you farewell, madam." He was gone then and the wind banged ceaselessly on the ill-hung door.

Julian put her head in her hands and began to weep. Sobs tore at her and she was whirled back to Lady Gwendolyn's agonized death, to the loss and bitterness of that time when her mother screamed for Lionel and could not see the loving face of her daughter. The face of England's queen was superimposed on Lady Gwendolyn's then, and Julian saw once again the hopeless, passionate caring in both, the same sort of love she had feared would come to her and now had been her own undoing. The queen, single-minded and determined, had tried to destroy those who loved her as well as those who hated her in her attempt to turn England back to a lost world. Julian knew that her own mother had been much the same way—both had had so little. She, Julian, had had more and yet it all came down to nothingness in the end. The tears blotted out all reality as she stared at the door through which Charles Varland would not come again.

That truth came home all the more fully to Julian as she waited the rest of the day, all night, and into the early morning. There was no wood for fire and the little house was freezing, for the weather had turned colder. It was no longer raining, but a heavy chill rose from the ground, and mist was everywhere when Julian looked out. There was no longer any reason to delay her original plan, the force of which still drove her.

She put on her only decent gown, a rather faded brown velvet trimmed with a darker ribbon on the sleeves and skirts. The neckline was low, but some of the wider ribbon taken from the sides of the skirt tended to that. Her hair she plaited high and fastened with several of the hoarded pins she had. The old cloak and hood, the wet shoes, all would have to do. There were several pearls left; she and Charles had planned to save them until a truly great need arose. She had several coins of low value; perhaps they would be enough to enable her to reach St. James's, and after that she would see.

"I would have gone to the queen even if things had been well between Charles and myself." The words were all the more true as she said them out loud. Julian knew then that in some strange way this was her own expiation.

The road was still busy with much of the traffic going away from London, but the carter whom Julian hailed down by standing practically in front of his beasts was willing enough to take her once he had bitten on the coin she offered. Blessedly, he was not inclined to conversation, and she did not have to lie. A lone woman was no stranger in these times, especially one with a strained, worried face.

The palace stood away from the city of London, near some fields of marsh, and was within walking distance from there. Julian asked the man to set her down in that general vicinity and, ungraciously, he complied. When he creaked out of sight she pulled her cloak closer against the icy winds that swept across the barren space and battered themselves against the red-brick palace fronted with stone and decorated with turrets and battlements. Then she walked what seemed an endless number of steps, the bottom of her skirt growing even wetter and her shoes so mired that they had no shape. The late afternoon was gray and dark with occasional snippets of icy rain. The trees that normally formed a frame for the palace were barren and writhed in the blasts that shook them. A small group of people stood sadly at the gates, waiting for whatever news might be permitted to come out. A guard stood just inside, another flanking him.

Julian pushed through the people and called to one of them, asking entrance.

He approached and glanced at her curiously. "No one is permitted entrance, goodwife. Her Majesty will be grateful for the concern and prayers of all her people, however."

"You do not understand." She caught her breath and gave her life away. "I am Julian, daughter of Gwendolyn and Lionel Redenter. My mother served Queen Katherine of Aragon, and I served Her Majesty. I was forced to be away for a time, but now I come to be with her in the time of need."

"You, a great lady?" He laughed, wide teeth showing in the broad face. "Go on with you."

Julian thought back to a hunt and a fair, disdainful face. If one ever loved the queen, it was Jane Dormer, and by all accounts, the love was greatly returned. It was this girl who, it was said, would marry Philip's ambassador, De Feria. There was danger in using her name, of course, but what did that matter? Only let Julian bid farewell to the queen and pay that debt that seemed to overhang her, then she could go to Wales if she lived. Armita had given instructions as to how the gypsies might be reached.

"Send to Lady Dormer. She will vouch for me."

"She is ill and has great difficulty in leaving her own bed to attend the queen." The guard was growing impatient.

"Send to her! Would you deny the Queen's Majesty her friends in this time of horror?" Julian's voice rose arrogantly and the others heard. Instantly they came flocking around to berate the guard.

"You heard her." "This is no time for lies!" "Let her in! You never know!" One large woman crossed herself and began to pray for "that sainted lady, the queen." The guard looked at the other and shrugged.

"You vow that you know Lady Dormer and are truly what you say? By the wounds of Christ?" He sounded rather bored with the whole matter.

Julian snapped, "Of course I vow it. Now open!"

Moments later she was walking down the road to the palace as though she owned it. Would she ever emerge again?

Once inside the ornate halls that now seemed curiously empty, Julian doffed the wet cloak and hood, then scraped some of the muck from her shoes. She hoped she looked the part of impoverished gentlewoman but thought, with a strange sinking of spirits, that few were likely to question her. This was plainly the last residence of the dead; the shifting of power had already begun.

She walked down corridors into beautifully equipped rooms which held ornaments, fine hangings, carved furniture and books, a chapel, past far fewer guards than she would have expected, and into a long passage where images of the saints stood in niches and candles bloomed. A gathering of men in black robes were walking toward her, talking anxiously as they came.

She flattened herself against the wall, head deferentially bent, but they took no heed of her. Phrases came to her ears and bore out all the gossip she had heard earlier. ". . . has to acknowledge the princess, only a matter of time." "King Philip's express wish, you know." "Another Spanish marriage?" "Sinking, the physician says." Then they were gone with no word from the woman herself.

Julian gathered all her courage then and went to the end of the passage, pushed at the door, oddly unguarded, and walked into a wide chamber hung all in purple and gold and lit with only one branch of candles. Two women sat on either side of the great bed which was draped with the arms of England and Spain. Both looked to be nodding off, and their faces were pale with exhaustion. But it was the woman in the bed who held her attention.

Mary Tudor had always been small; now she seemed tiny, her face wrinkled and thin on the high pillows, her hands shrunken as they held a book between them on the purple covers. The harsh lines around her mouth had deepened in the time since Julian had seen her, and the sandy hair was scantier. She sighed heavily and opened her eyes as Julian watched.

One of the women caught sight of Julian and rose slightly as she whispered, "Who are you, madam? Her Majesty is resting and cannot be disturbed."

"I came to wish her well." Any other words stuck in Julian's throat. How could you say that you had come out of pity, pity for yourself and for the dying queen?

"Let her approach." The voice was weak, but the will was there. "Let Julian Redenter approach."

The woman fell back, and Julian took her place at the bed, more afraid than when she faced George Attenwood. Fires still burned at Smithfield. Had she not caught the scent of burning flesh on her way here? Charles's words about the savagery of the dying came back to her with full force.

"Why are you here?" The flinty Tudor gaze was still in possession. "Heard you were dead in some battle. A bold girl, I thought when I first saw you."

"Madam. Madam." Julian faltered as Lady Gwendolyn and the queen of England merged into one and shifted into the image that for Julian had ever meant peace, the shimmering hawthorn tree in spring. She shook her head and saw again the drawn face, the sunken eyes of the queen. "I did not want you to be alone, not now." And because truth was upon her in this moment of extremity, she added, "Not everyone turns away, madam. Some come to wish you well even as I have done."

Mary toyed with one of the rings on her hands, then sighed in exhaustion. "But Philip, nevermore."

"I know, madam." Because she did know of love and the agony it could bring, the assurance reached the dying woman, and the wide-open eyes stared straight into Julian's.

"All desert me and go to her. All." Her head jerked on the pillow.

"Not all, Madam the Queen. I am here, and here I shall stay if you will have me."

"In God's name, I will."

So Julian Redenter returned to the service of Mary Tudor, queen of England.

CHAPTER FORTY-THREE

Julian found it surprising how easily she slipped back into the old routine. She was scarcely noticed, and only once was her return remarked on, that by Jane Dormer, whose life stretched before her. Jane, red-eyed and shaken, said, "It is good that you have found your way back, but there are no rewards here for the backsliders." Julian let it go and met the compassionate gaze of old Susan Clarence, once her detractor. Here in this gathering of the few who waited for death there was no place for old hatreds. Many of the other ladies were very young and easily frightened, fearful of their futures. Their number decreased by the day. Often the queen was visited by her ministers and members of the council, still more frequently by the physicians and priests. Jane Dormer was sent to Elizabeth at Hatfield, bearing instructions from the queen, and returned so distraught that she was put to bed immediately.

Julian sat with the queen at intervals and read from the gospels in Latin, trying to find the comforting passages and, for all the pity she felt for this woman, could not help but think that the many she had sent to bitter deaths had had no consolation. When had the queen ever been happy? Possibly the first few years of her life when she was the beloved daughter of Henry and Katherine before all the pother of the divorce, then the year when Philip of

Spain remained with her and those few months when he returned—all the rest had been pain and hardship and rejection. Out of forty-two years on this earth so little time! And now her death was a blessing to England, the land which had so eagerly welcomed her only five years before. She had persecuted unmercifully but so had her father and brother. Julian's own early life was proof of that.

The queen sighed, the breath barely lifting the thin, wasted chest. The omnipresent prayer book slipped to the floor, and Julian bent to retrieve it. She looked down at the creased pages and saw that it fell perpetually open to the prayers for women in childbirth. The marks of her tears were there. Julian put it back in the limp fingers and went blindly to the door. The other lady-in-waiting moved up to take her place.

Was it the tears coursing down her face or did the guard at the end of the corridor have the very build of Charles Varland? She saw him nightly in her fitful dreams, thought of him every time she laced herself into the borrowed dark gowns, remembered him in the demands of her hungry flesh that could not be stilled. She could not bear to fit his face on every man of his height who moved about the court. Now as she shook her head at her own foolishness, she saw that the man was being relieved and walking away with a limping gait. Ridiculous!

Julian made her way toward the chapel with the vague idea of sitting there in the profusion of stained glass, candles, and saints to hope that some measure of peace would come to her. When the hands reached out of the dark passage and caught her, clamping her mouth shut and pulling her roughly into the adjoining room, she was so startled that she barely had time to be afraid before other hands were binding hers behind her back. She was thrust into a pool of warm light and saw the devil-mask in front of her. Her mouth opened to scream and then was stopped by the horror and shock. This travesty of a face was one she knew!

"Alphonso Diego Ortega!" The name went from her dry lips as she looked at him and the silent servant who stood just behind. "What does this mean? Let me go!"

His smashed nose was a spreading blotch on the scarred face that had been split by a sword and healed haphazardly so that he seemed to be a blur of red and white scar tissue. The black beard had threads of white in it and was quite sparse. One of his eyes had the glassy stare of the blind, but hatred flamed from the other.

"I cannot believe that you have returned to my hands, Julian Redenter! God is yet good!" He lifted one hand to his face. "You are responsible for this! Sly, tricky, never revealing anything to me! Little good that passion of yours for Charles Varland did you! I hated you. Did you know that? You were so bold and determined. It was a pleasure to give you to Attenwood, for I knew what he would do. He failed, unfortunately, and now I must finish the job. You shall die very slowly, Julian. Scream, I invite you to do so. The walls are thick, and no one will hear you."

"I will be missed. The queen is still the queen." She spoke evenly, not wanting to stir his anger further.

"There are few enough to hear you. They are flocking to Hatfield, where Princess Elizabeth waits for news of her sister's death. My master will not have me around him now. He admires beauty above all things, especially in people. He will seek the hand of the princess in marriage after a short period of mourning. She will convert to Catholicism, of course. I hope she is sensible and agrees."

"She will not." Julian was suddenly very sure of that.

Ortega drew his dagger and sighted carefully along the gleaming blade. "Perhaps. Your friend, Sir Guy, babbled on about matters of state. Do you wish to do the same? He amused me for a while and then I dealt with him. Would you like to know how long it took him to die?" His mouth twisted in what might have been a smile.

Fear and horror nearly overcame Julian. She had not spoken Sir Guy's name in months, but anguish for him had been with her constantly—a burden borne alone. "What kind of man are you that you could do such a thing? Foul betrayer! I counted you friend once."

"One of my informers followed him one day. It was easy to bribe those with whom he dealt. He was taken to my private chambers and questioned. We Spanish know

how to question! He lived less than a day and told me
nothing that I did not already know. As to the kind of
man I am? All that I have done, I have done for Spain. I
came here to watch and wait, gain confidences any way
that I could, plant the idea that King Philip would be better for England than the heretic Elizabeth or the young
Stuart girl. A strong man, I said, was needed. People listened. I learned only too late that Attenwood sought
power for his own sake through the queen of Scots."

Julian felt as if she were a mass of pain. Sir Guy had
suffered and died at the hands of this beast. If only she
could return that full measure.

Ortega laughed outright. "Enough of this. I grow bored.
I saw you a few days ago and followed you, awaiting the
moment. You shall see this face as the last of your life!"

Julian jerked her arms but could not free them from the
cords. She screamed as loudly as she could, and Ortega
burst into laughter. She screamed several more times, and
then was silent, her throat raw.

"Such pleasure as you have already given me, little
Julian. Know also that I mean to pay you back in full
coin for Varland's escape. The old woman was tortured to
death, but she knew little." He smiled at her gasp of horror. "You did not think we would hurt her, did you? I
attended to it personally. The guards who took your bribes
died too, and the manner of it was not pleasant to them.
We were after you that same day but lost your trail."

"Bastard! Fiend!" Julian thought that if she were free
for one second she could gladly sink that dagger in the
other eye.

Ortega was growing angrier now as he slashed the dagger up and down in the air, his shadow long on the high
walls. "I reported all that to King Philip personally, thinking that he would order his wife to have the kingdom
pulled apart seeking for so foul a traitor. He laughed!
Laughed! Said enough was enough and that Charles Varland and you were well-matched, that he envied his old
friend and wished him well. I was to restrain myself or
find myself back on my mountain estates. I was sent to the
Low Countries but took leave and came here when the

health of the queen began to go down. I may yet be able to persuade Elizabeth that her best interests lie with my master."

Julian thought of that whippet quality, the self-control, and the direct eyes. "She is not for the likes of Philip of Spain."

Ortega's hand slashed across her face and sent her spinning to the floor. Then with a growl that was curiously animal in character, he threw himself upon her and pulled up her skirts. Julian kicked upward, but the servant caught her feet and pulled them down, his face expressionless. Ortega balanced himself on her and said, "Your left eye first, I think. Then I will taste your skill at lovemaking. Did Varland teach you good tricks? I am sure that one so lusty must have." His laughter exploded in the room.

With all the strength that remained in her, Julian heaved at the big body even as she spat directly into the fearful face. He remained astride her, picked up the dagger, and aimed the point directly at her eye.

"Now! Now!" Almost gibbering, he pushed it forward.

Julian swayed her head back and forth and screamed again. The heavy door burst back against the wall and rang on the stone. One man hurled himself at Ortega and jerked him from Julian, another tackled the servant and sent him crashing to the floor. Two others in the queen's livery stood with swords at the ready.

Julian struggled to get her feet under her and stared blankly at the man who held Ortega. It was Charles Varland.

"Are you all right?" He was crying the words at her over the curtain of mist that veiled her eyes. One of the guards loosed her wrists and supported her to a seat.

"Yes, yes. God be praised that you came."

"Give him a sword." Charles, in the livery of the queen, gestured to one of the men. It had been he that she saw then! "I will kill him in fair battle."

Ortega said, "You cannot. I am the best swordsman of Spain. My life if I best you!"

"Done." Charles raised his own blade and waited for Ortega to inspect the sword given him. "On guard, scum."

Time narrowed down to the flashing swords, the desperate cut, thrust, and parry of two master swordsmen fighting for their lives and more. Once Charles stumbled, and only by swiftly catching himself did he manage to retain his balance and forestall Ortega's rush. Weapon rang on weapon as Julian's fingers clenched and bit down. If Ortega slew Charles, she would bury his own dagger in that evil chest. She touched the blade that had been knocked aside and caught up as she moved backward. Such horror should not be allowed to walk the earth.

Ortega was bleeding from the mouth now, and one arm was slower in motion, but he did not falter. Charles had a scratch on the side of his face, and his shirt was torn. Both men were breathing heavily, the sound of their ringing swords the only noise in the room. Ortega's face was even more the personification of evil than it had been to begin with. Julian thought that now inner and outer man were truly one.

A hard voice of authority spoke from the doorway. "What is going on here? Stop that at once. Do you not know where you are?"

Charles moved to look and in that instant Ortega struck. The blow went wild and slashed his sleeve, going lightly into the flesh and causing the blood to come out in streams. Julian rose up, turned the dagger as she had long ago done at play, and sent it flashing into the very heart of Ortega. He cried out one curse and fell to the floor in the welter of his own blood. Sir Guy was avenged.

Charles threw down his sword and caught Julian in his arms, cradling her to him, his lips moving over her hair as the incoherent words burst out of him. "I thought you dead and that I had sent you to it. Julian, Julian. There is no life without you. None. I know that now."

She clung to him, barely able to absorb the sounds she heard from this arrogant, silent man she loved. "Charles, I cannot believe it. Dear Charles. Dear love."

Over their intensity, she heard the same voice saying, "This will be investigated, but later. Now is the time to mourn."

They looked up and over the scene of death to see one

of the queen's priests standing with another official, both looking as if they had been battered from the inside.

"Weep for this land. Her Majesty is dead in the peace of God. She who sought to restore Holy Mother Church now rests secure in the arms of her Lord God. Let us pray."

Obediently they slipped to their knees, and the fervent prayers rose to heaven. Charles held Julian's hand in his and both clenched the other tightly. Julian did not know if he prayed for Mary or England, but she herself did not pray for the dead for whom there was no solace in this life; she gave thanks for life restored and for the man beside her who made it worth having. Yet, even in this time, Julian knew that she was stronger than many others. For her love would be the crown of life but not its whole being. She was herself, inviolate, and Charles would know that. For the first time in her life, Julian Redenter was free of the past and its shadows.

Later they sat in one of the smaller chambers on the main floor of the palace where they had been escorted by the priest and his follower. Charles simply stated that Julian had been attacked by Ortega, who was plainly mad and who had apparently trailed her for days. They were bidden to wait for instructions.

Now Julian said, "How did you come to find me?" She was a little light-headed from the rich wine Charles poured for her and from his nearness.

His wound had been tended, and he wore another shirt of a shade of green that made his gray eyes deeper. The harshness was gone from his face, and it was lit with the tenderness that he had all too seldom shown to her.

"I was so angry that day we parted that I came to the city and drank as much as I could hold at one of the taverns. I woke on the floor of it and knew that I had lost everything that mattered to me. When I went back to find you, you were gone. But I knew your destination. On the way here I saw some horsemen ride by and barely recognized Ortega. By then I knew what had been done to those guards and the old woman. I had my own score to settle with him as well as yours. When I heard of the queen's health it was easy enough to trade clothes with one of the guards who wanted no part of the old regime. I waited for you, and while doing so I saw that Ortega trailed you as well. You left unexpectedly, and when I came to the door to await you, I found that you were gone. I dimly heard your screams and fetched those with me." He put his arms around her and hugged her close. "I was almost too late, God forgive me."

She tilted her head back to look into his face. "I am a murderess for all that he would have done the same to me. I meant to kill him, Charles. Am I then as he?"

"You know the answer to that, Julian. It was battle and you fought as a soldier. We are quits again, for I saved your life then you saved mine." His mouth brushed her hair, and she felt his palpable longing.

Julian had battled all her life in one way or another. She would not soon forget the joy she had felt as the dagger hit home in Ortega's chest, but she was a realist as well and it would not trouble her dreams. Now Charles was looking at her ardently, and she thought what a fright she must look in the dark blue gown that was too large and with her hair streaming over her shoulders in disarray.

"You are beautiful in my sight, Julian." He took her hands in his. "I have nothing but myself to offer, yet you have that unreservedly. I love you, lady mine. Will you be my wedded wife?" He spoke the phrase deliberately and with full emphasis.

Her answer was her own affirmation. "With all my heart, Charles, and with all my mind, and with all my body's love."

Their mouths met then in a fusion so complete that they shook with the power of it. This was the melding of one mind and one flesh; unity of the body would be the high-lighting and the glory, but this was their true marriage, whatever else would come.

In the hours that followed, Charles and Julian sat close to each other and spoke of things simple and complex as they opened their hearts. They spoke of Sir Guy and his friendship; and in that sharing Julian was eased. The question of the future was held in abeyance, for who knew what path the new reign would take or in what light Elizabeth would regard them? England was still at war. This was their time. Unspoken between them was that since they had nothing of material value, they would go on to Wales and there remain with the gypsies, for with these friends they had first known the joy and camaraderie that welded them together.

The door swung open again, and this time a captain of the guard stood there. A tirewoman passed him as she brought in water, cloths, and a bundle of wearing apparel. The man said, "Make yourselves presentable and hasten with it. We leave within the hour."

"Where are you taking us?" Charles spoke with his old authority.

"You will know soon enough. Hasten." He withdrew and they heard the bolts fall on the outside of the door.

Julian dressed quickly in the shimmering green-blue gown with wide sleeves and full overskirts draped over each other in varying shades of the color. There were matching slippers of blue satin and a furred white cloak with a hood. She combed her hair and fastened it loosely at her neck, then bit her lips to make them redder.

Charles had been given the misty gray he favored with a cloak of a darker shade. His hose set off his muscular legs, and his shoes were of finest leather. His shirt was made of soft white cloth that reflected against his brown skin.

"We are passing fair, we two." He smiled at her, and she returned it bravely.

They were still smiling at each other when the door opened and the same guard said, "Come. It is time."

"Tell us where." Julian did not really expect him to answer and was surprised when he did.

"To be judged in accordance with the laws of this land."

CHAPTER FORTY-FOUR

The coach was closed, the ride lengthy. Charles and Julian held hands and waited. In those hours just past they had affirmed their bond, reiterated the promise that if they could they would be married; beyond that everything seemed to pall.

"Do you think we go to prison?" Julian felt oddly calm as she voiced the unspeakable. "Or to worse and on whose authority? Do you think Philip has come or that we are invaded?"

"Who alone can judge us?" Charles nodded at her shadowy profile. "Aye, Elizabeth the Queen, who may have been offended by us. Who knows the ways of the Tudors and those who serve them?"

Julian reached out to him, and he put his arms around her. Here was surcease, here was the reward of the hard won battle. There was nothing else to say, their love had named it all.

She whispered into his neck, "Do you know, Charles, I think I first cared for you when you approached me as a wench in the garden by the river so long ago?"

She felt his spurt of laughter. "And a marvelous wench you were, too, but full arrogant and not a bit interested in my favors."

"I am interested now."

"Are you, indeed?" He set his mouth against hers, and the flames rose around them in all the richness of long denial.

The coach came to an abrupt stop just then, and they were motioned out by the same guard. The night was piercingly cold and Julian shivered as he indicated for them to follow a muffled man who stood just beyond the rim of light cast by the torch.

Charles took Julian's hand as they entered the side door of a large building, went up some stairs and along a passage to a door which stood partially open. Their guard stepped aside and pointed but spoke no word. They entered together to face their fate.

The room was spacious enough, but much of it was taken up with tables stacked high with papers and charts. Books were placed near at hand, their bindings shining golden in the light of many candles. Tapestries blocked out the cold night and braziers made the air warm. The woman behind the table threw down some papers and rose to meet them, her face very pale under the cloud of tossing hair that had escaped the confining band.

Julian and Charles went to their knees, speaking with one voice the words that were not yet even twelve hours a reality.

"Your Majesty!"

"Your Majesty the Queen!"

"Rise and face me." Elizabeth spoke sharply, the manner of power already upon her.

They obeyed, and Julian saw that the girl of the meadow was not yet the Queen's Majesty in appearance, for there were ink stains on the long fingers and still others on the crumpled golden velvet gown she wore. But the long eyes flashed with authority, and the firm mouth was set. She was only a few years older than Julian but she was the Majesty of England as Mary Tudor had never been.

"You were rebels against your anointed queen, the both of you. Charles Varland, what do you owe to Philip of Spain that he did protect you and this girl? Did you hope to gain from him if he tried to gain the throne for himself? A thing which, incidentally, the English would never have allowed. Come, man, answer. Remember that you face your queen!"

Charles said, "Madam, we were friends, and I assume we are still. My loyalty has been to England, always. I owe Philip nothing in that regard."

Elizabeth watched him narrowly before turning to Julian. "And you, Lady Redenter? You served my sister in her fortune and returned to her when others deserted. Yet you allied yourself with this traitor and are thus one yourself. What do you say in your defense?"

Julian and Charles looked at each other, mystified. Then Julian said the safe thing. "Our loyalty is to England and to you, madam."

"Are you quite certain? How can I believe that? What if you and others like you decide that they do not approve of my rule and decide to rise against me by virtue of their great names and influence? England has been torn to pieces long enough. I will have no more of it!" Her voice rose and swelled in the room, the Tudor wrath in full cry. "No more!"

"Madam . . ." Charles tried to speak, but the imperious voice rode him down and her shadow ran long on the wall.

"The sovereign cannot tolerate rebellion. The very structure of government would be undermined. I am come into the royal estate by right of blood and heritage, owing nothing to the good offices of any but my people. The lawful succession in accordance with the law of the realm has devolved peacefully upon me. Peacefully and by right. Do you understand me, Varland? Madam?" Elizabeth bent over the table toward them, and it was all they could do not to back away, so strong was the force in her.

They sank to their knees again. It seemed the safest thing to do. Julian wondered wildly if she meant to have them executed for supporting her and speaking as frankly to her as they had done that day at Hatfield. There was no doubt that she had recognized them; she was too astute for it to be otherwise.

She was repeating, "Are the both of you struck dumb? Answer me!"

"We understand, madam." Charles spoke for them in a

low voice that was quite unlike the arrogant lord Julian knew.

"And agree?"

"Of a certainty. We will swear fealty to you, take an oath before God. What more is there?"

"What more?" Elizabeth looked down into their faces, her own inscrutable. "If you cannot take such an oath wholeheartedly, you have my leave to quit this kingdom. I remember your words to me, Charles Varland, and I think I know the low opinion you held of me when you besought me to take the throne by fire and sword. Lady Redenter, too, spoke quite firmly. You might have been sent to trap me. I took no chances. But I would never have taken chances with England. Had I encouraged rebellion by taking part, then others would have risen up against me. But I remembered you both and made it my business to know what was happening with the both of you."

"What is your pleasure, madam?" Charles sought Julian's hand in his, and she returned the pressure of it.

Her tone was stern, but the strange eyes belied it. "Get up, this is no Oriental court! What is your pleasure, sir and madam?"

Julian said, "To serve Queen Elizabeth in whatever capacity she will have us."

The white hands flashed, but her face was very still. "I do not forget what has happened to you this while, that bloodshed and murder and fear have marked you. You have been torn as England has been torn for years. I have known, but what could I do? Now it is different. I am queen!" The exultant words rang in the room and hung there. "There is this land to heal, my people to succor. England, my England."

Julian thought that few people would see the new queen so unveiled in this moment of her triumph. Chills ran up her spine, and tears burned in her eyes. It was left to Charles to speak, for she could not.

"Our England, Madam the Queen. Will you accept our fealty, given unreservedly to you?" His own voice shook with the power of his feeling.

"And in return?" the odd note of something hidden was in the words, and Julian's head jerked up.

"To serve you who are England's future."

Julian's head spun and exhaustion made her shiver. It seemed that Elizabeth played with them, drawing out words and feelings for her own delectation. Why had she bothered to explain her actions and motives? It was not a thing rulers did; they simply ordered you about. She had liked and pitied and feared Queen Mary, but Queen Elizabeth was quicksilver, both dangerous and enchanting. Charles had felt the allure, she knew, for his voice had been low and caressing in the respect it carried.

"This is one country now. There is no need for factions. I care for men's hearts and do not seek to pry into their souls." The quiet voice was wholly sincere now. "I believe you, Charles Varland and Julian Redenter. I shall accept all who come to me with England's good in their hearts. Welcome to my service, my lord and lady. Will you invite your queen to the wedding?"

The manner of her address thrust understanding upon Charles and Julian. They tried to speak at once and could not. The vanity of the queen was well pleased as she gave them the haunting smile that had won her friends and loyalty even among her sister's minions when they took her to the Tower of London by way of Traitor's Gate.

"It was necessary that I assess you both. I know loyalty when I see it. Your estates shall be returned to you, and in the days to come, the favor that I bestow upon you must be earned."

Julian gave a long, shaking sigh. "We are grateful, madam."

"It is a long service that we all embark on, my friends." She put the serious manner aside and let the delight shine forth again. "I would ask one thing of you."

"Anything." They found it impossible to resist the smile that curved her mouth, though Julian found it hauntingly remindful of Mary Tudor in her moments of kindness. Did her sister remember also in this her time of glory? No one would ever really know what Elizabeth thought unless she willed it.

"In time to come send your sons to my court even as you both grace it. England has need of all who love her."

Charles turned to Julian, and in the clear light of his eyes she saw the pattern of their love's future. They were open to each other as they had never been before, and the present held no shadows. They had overcome and lived to see this day.

Because she was newly come to the throne of her fathers after mighty trials and vicissitudes, and her dignity was never in question, Queen Elizabeth lifted the costly decanter beside her and poured out the rich wine with her own hands into golden goblets.

"I am well answered. Take and drink in honor of this moment."

She lifted her own goblet in the toast that was always closest to her heart. "To England!"

Julian and Charles held theirs toward her and said with one voice that was somehow all voices, "To Elizabeth of England!"

Their eyes met and once again they plighted their troth, this time in the dawn of a new age.

She was a prima ballerina—torn between two men and her passion to dance

Encore

BY MONIQUE RAPHEL HIGH
author of the bestselling *The Four Winds of Heaven*

"A huge, colorful novel. A strong blend of passion, tragedy and art set against the exotic and exciting world of dance."—*Publishers Weekly*

A Dell Book $3.95   12363-1

Danielle Steel

AMERICA'S LEADING LADY OF ROMANCE REIGNS OVER ANOTHER BESTSELLER

A Perfect Stranger

A flawless mix of glamour and love by Danielle Steel, the bestselling author of *The Ring, Palomino* and *Loving*.

A DELL BOOK $3.50   #17221-7